"A MASTER STORYTELLER."*

PRAISE FOR
Deborah Simmons and her novels…

"Deborah Simmons never fails to please her fans."
—*Romance Reviews Today*

"Simmons is rapidly climbing to the top peak of the historical romance genre."
—*Affaire de Coeur*

"Humor, sensuous love, and tremendous characters."
—*Literary Times*

"Deborah Simmons is an author I read automatically. Why? Because she gets it right. I can always count on her for a good tale, a wonderful hero, a feisty heroine, and a love story where it truly is *love* that makes a difference."
—*All About Romance*

"Excellent, enchanting, and exciting … I couldn't put it down."
—*Rendezvous*

"Filled with wonderful sensuality and a basic joy of living."
—*Under the Covers

"Wonderful . . . funny and sexy."
—*The Romance Reader*

"Simmons . . . delivers characters that steal your heart."
—*Bookaholics*

A LADY
OF DISTINCTION

Deborah Simmons

BERKLEY SENSATION, NEW YORK

This is a work of fiction. Names, characters, places, and incidents either are the product of the author's imagination or are used fictitiously, and any resemblance to actual persons, living or dead, business establishments, events, or locales is entirely coincidental.

A LADY OF DISTINCTION

A Berkley Sensation Book / published by arrangement with the author

PRINTING HISTORY
Berkley Sensation edition / May 2004

Copyright © 2004 by Deborah Siegenthal.
Cover illustration by Dan O'Leary.
Cover design by George Long.

For information address: The Berkley Publishing Group, a division of Penguin Group (USA) Inc., 375 Hudson Street, New York, New York 10014.

ISBN: 0-425-19656-9

BERKLEY SENSATION™
Berkley Sensation Books are published by The Berkley Publishing Group, a division of Penguin Group (USA) Inc., 375 Hudson Street, New York, New York 10014. BERKLEY SENSATION and the "B" design are trademarks belonging to Penguin Group (USA) Inc.

PRINTED IN THE UNITED STATES OF AMERICA

10 9 8 7 6 5 4 3 2 1

*This book is dedicated, with love,
to my brother Bob Smith,
who died not long after its completion.
I am still looking up to you, big bro.*

Chapter 1

LONDON, 1820

THERE was a severed hand in the ballroom.

Lady Juliet Cavendish, pausing at the entrance, gaped in horror, for the blackened flesh was perched precariously atop a canopic jar, hardly the proper place for such a specimen. Indeed, one glance told Juliet that the entire ballroom was piled high in disarray, and she loosed a sigh of disgust.

Had she been present to oversee the arrival of her father's latest acquisitions, this clutter could have been prevented. But, apparently, the shipment had been unloaded during the night, and no one had thought to wake her. Although unsurprised by the lapse, Juliet was annoyed by it, for she might have put some order to the objects as they were brought into the house. Now, her task of sorting and cataloguing would be doubly difficult.

Carefully snatching up the severed hand before it could topple and become damaged, Juliet stepped into the room, weaving her way around heavy crates and statuary toward a massive dining table that had been set over the parquet floor for her use. Unfortunately, she discovered that its surface was heaped high as well. Muttering under her breath about the general carelessness of those responsible, Juliet finally managed to clear a small space on the gleaming mahogany. It took her a few more minutes to locate the pencil and notebooks that had been moved aside, but at last she was prepared to work.

Pushing the spectacles up on her nose, she glanced about. Now, where to start? Usually, she would catalogue the heaviest objects first, but one look told her they were scattered, so she decided to reverse the order of her study, beginning with the small pieces on the table. Her gaze immediately traveled to the nearby papyri with certain longing, but she forced her attention away. She needed to follow a routine, to put order to her disorganized thoughts. Or so she had been told.

Giving the area a quick survey, Juliet spied a piece of jewelry that would need to be properly arranged for display, so she considered beginning with it before moving on to the small pottery pieces. She reached out a hand toward the gold necklace only to hesitate. Certainly, such a valuable item must be secured, but . . . On the other hand, if she chose the papyri first, she would have a chance to see the ancient writings before anyone else.

Juliet's heart picked up its pace at the thought of viewing the hieroglyphs alone, without the distraction of others, but her fierce desire was soon followed by guilt at her selfishness. Besides, the handling of the old papyri was a delicate procedure. Yet there were other examples of the ancient texts to be seen here, papyrus being only one surface used by the ancient Egyptians, who decorated everything from artwork and statuary to buildings with the mysterious pictures. Certainly no one would know if she took a look at some of those treasures far beyond price that were sitting here, waiting for someone to unlock their secrets.

Juliet drew in a deep breath, glanced at the golden rope dangling with delicately fashioned fish that would surely enchant any other woman, then back at a particularly interesting looking stela not far away, and she could not help herself. Discipline, she was often reminded, was not one of her strong suits and was to be cultivated. And she would cultivate it, Juliet vowed . . . just not today.

Stepping away from the table, she made her way carefully to the tall piece of limestone. In awe, she reached out a hand to touch the painted surface and felt an immediate connection to a past, long gone, when some scribe had created these images. They spoke to her, trying to convey his message, if only she could understand, and soon her cursory examination turned into serious study. As was her wont, she began copying the inscription as exactly as possible, the color to be added later.

So absorbed was she in her task that at first Juliet heard nothing beyond the scratching of her pencil in the stillness of the vast room. But gradually she became aware of another sound, a low rumble, like the drone of a bee, and Juliet glanced about her in puzzlement, for surely no insect could flourish in the dismal chill of a London autumn.

Juliet told herself it must be the wind rushing through the cracks and crevices that even the tightest window could not fail to admit, though the early morning sun gleaming through the glass gave no hint of a blustery day. Shaking her head, she attempted to ignore the humming, but as though determined to gain her attention, it grew louder, forcing her to halt her work.

Kneeling on the floor, she stilled, listening intently, only to again be reminded of a bee, although a single insect could hardly be held responsible for this din. *Mayhap an entire hive,* Juliet amended, momentarily alarmed at the thought. She could not imagine how such a nest could have been imported into the house and was trying to think of a logical explanation when the sound became louder and more distinctive. No longer a simple buzz, it more resembled a moan, and Juliet felt the hairs on the back of her neck rise.

Suddenly, her quiet morning of study turned eerie, the ancient objects surrounding her transforming the ballroom of her father's town house into an alien landscape of ominous portents. Holding her body rigid, Juliet slowly turned her head to the left, in the direction of the sound. Although antiquities of various sizes and shapes littered the floor, her gaze settled unerringly upon that which occupied most of the area within her line of sight, the largest and most valuable of her father's acquisitions, an alabaster mummy case.

A vast reliquary with a majesty above and beyond the more ordinary discoveries, it stood alone, as if even the loutish workmen dared not mar its gleaming surface, carved with a multitude of figures, precise and elegant. Indeed, the heavy piece was illuminated by a shaft of sunlight falling through the tall windows as though directed by some unseen hand, making it seem to glow from within.

Juliet stared for a moment, transfixed, before reason asserted itself. Obviously, the unusual effect was caused by a trick of light, coupled with the fact that the case was uncluttered and lay separate from the other items, except for a wooden crate that leaned against one side. Juliet frowned at the sight, and when a particularly odd noise assaulted her senses, she wondered if she ought to upright the container or remove it altogether. It appeared, for one wild moment, as though the mummy was making known its displeasure at the encroachment.

Juliet smiled shakily, for that flight of fancy was wholly unlike her usual clear thinking. Despite the elaborate mummifying process, the ancient Egyptians were gone, and their remains, though well preserved, had no sensate ability to observe or complain about their surroundings. Indeed, everything in the ballroom had been dead or discarded for centuries, Juliet noted. Unwittingly, her gaze stole back toward the table, where the severed hand, quite naturally, remained in its place.

Drawing a deep breath, Juliet took firm control of herself. Obviously, there was a reason for the continuing, if sporadic, sounds that were emanating from the mummy case, or rather, from that general direction. And, just as obviously, she would have to determine the source herself by gaining a closer look. She stood at once, for it never occurred to her to summon help or disturb her father. She was accustomed to taking care of herself and, more importantly, of her father's collection.

Straightening to her full height, Juliet stepped away from the stela and turned toward the ancient resting place of the dead. As she inched closer, the droning became louder, and her heart hammered with a sense of dread. Moving as quietly as possible, she realized she was holding her breath and released it slowly. Even though she tried firmly to restore order to her wayward thoughts, several highly illogical possibilities coursed through her brain—at least until she heard a new diversion, something that resembled a snort.

It was more bizarre than eerie, and sparked by curiosity, Juliet stopped beside the crate and looked down. Although unsure what she would discover, she certainly was not expecting a pair of boots. Modern in origin, dirty, and worn, they did not qualify as antiquities. Blinking, she followed the faded leather from scuffed toes up to where they ended in an equally disreputable pair of breeches sticking out of the straw that filled the crate.

For a moment, Juliet feared that a dead body, or at least one that was not mummified, had somehow been transported into the ballroom. But that outlandish supposition did not explain the noise that had interrupted her work. A corpse, whether preserved or not, could make no sounds, Juliet told herself. Sidestepping the footwear, she moved before the crate and peered into it, only to gasp aloud at the sight that met her gaze.

The owner of the boots was reclining inside as though in his own boudoir, and he was definitely not dead, for a hideous cacophony issued from him, which Juliet recognized as the mysterious sounds that had so disturbed her. No bees or errant winds or ghostly chants were at work here. Her precious labors had been cut short by the rude, nasal eruptions from this fellow, a behavior commonly known as snoring, but with which Juliet was not very familiar. Although once in awhile a footman might fall asleep at his post after a long night, she could hardly compare that gentle wheezing to this alarming din.

Hands upon her hips, Juliet leaned over to glare at the man with distaste. A thick lock of dark hair obscured his forehead, while the rest of his face sported a day's growth of unshaven stubble in keeping with the dirty state of his garments. He was probably some denizen of the docks hired to help unload the shipment, but who could not be trusted even to provide that menial service.

Undoubtedly, he had found this niche early on and slept off a drunk instead. With workmen such as this one, it was no wonder the collection was in such disarray. Only such an ignorant ruffian would dare make a bed in something used to transport antiquities, then tilt it against a priceless artifact. The thought of that perfidy moved Juliet to action, and without pausing to summon a footman or even consider her course, she loosed her temper on the miscreant.

"You there! Come out at once!" she demanded to no avail. The wretched creature slept on, snores punctuating his every breath. Juliet looked about for an object with which to poke him, but everything in the room was too precious for such a purpose, so she nudged him with her toe, encased in an elegant silk slipper.

"You, sir! Off with you!" she cried. When the fellow still didn't stir, Juliet moved to the rear of the crate and pushed, trying to dislodge it, as well as its occupant. However, he must have been heavier than he looked because the sturdy wood beneath him wouldn't budge. With a grunt, Juliet tried again, throwing all of her weight against the edge, and she felt a surge of triumph as the box tipped and fell forward, spilling its contents onto the parquet floor.

Or at least that's what was *supposed* to happen. But as soon as the crate began to tilt, the slumbering figure erupted from the interior so swiftly that before Juliet could blink, he was crouching before her in a threatening stance, a knife in one outstretched hand. Startled by this sudden transformation from layabout to menace, she could only gape as dark eyes bored into her in a bold fashion more unsettling than the weapon he was holding.

"Who the devil are you?" he demanded.

Juliet could well have asked the same, for his deep voice and well-modulated tones were hardly those of the slum dweller she had deemed him. Most likely, it was his speech that made her continue staring at him, instead of calling for a footman. Or maybe it was his brown eyes, the color of the dark, mysterious paints of the ancients, and rife with far more intelligence than she would have imagined. Obviously, this was no common sot. Yet he was dangerous, perhaps too dangerous to unleash upon the unsuspecting household help, Juliet thought, deciding to handle the man herself rather than cause the sort of furor her father despised.

Taking a deep breath, she asserted herself. "See here, you cannot sleep off your drunk in this house. Now, be off with you," she said, waving in the general direction of the door.

Instead of obeying, the fellow looked as though her attempts to shoo him away were lunatic. Glancing quickly about, as if to assess his surroundings, he slipped the blade into the top of his boot, of all places. Then, with one smooth motion, he straightened to a height that made it plain to see why he had been so difficult to budge. He stood taller than six feet, towering above Juliet even though she was not particularly dainty. He was lean but wide-shouldered and long-legged, and tossing his head back, he looked down at her out of a sun-bronzed face cut from the classic lines of an aristocrat, not a dockside drunkard.

Juliet's lips parted in surprise, and her heart, which had remained steady throughout the brief encounter, suddenly started pounding again as though threatened by some unseen force. Although his knife was sheathed, the man seemed more dangerous now than before, and she realized that she was in the ballroom, bereft of servants, alone with a stranger—an incredible, tall, rather muscular and unsavory stranger. She opened her mouth to speak, but nothing came out. Instead, she studied him as she would a fine piece of sculpture, noticing things like the creases at the corners of his eyes, the thickness of his dark lashes, and the unruliness of his dark hair. *All of it extremely unsavory, of course.*

It was only when Juliet realized that she, too, was the subject of excessive scrutiny that she found her voice once more. The man's glare had turned into a gleam of assessment as he looked her up and down in a way that proclaimed him devoid of manners or morals. Flushing at her own lapse of breeding, Juliet cleared her throat.

"Be off with you, now, or I shall be forced to call the staff," she said, though her voice lacked its usual crispness.

The rogue not only ignored her demand but seemed to lose all interest in her. Lifting a tanned and long-fingered hand, he ran it through his dark hair as he glanced around the ballroom. "Where's Carlisle?" he asked.

"The earl of Carlisle? I hardly think that's any of your concern," Juliet snapped. Although she had disdained his brazen inspection of her, the sudden loss of his attention was equally frustrating. She might be accustomed to the subtle dismissals of the men in her life, but she refused to be ignored by this interloper.

"Now, see, here—" Juliet began, only to be cut off as the fellow turned away from her.

"Is there a place where I can wash up?" he asked, tossing the question over his shoulder.

"Certainly not!" Juliet said, hurrying after him as best she could while trying not to brush her long skirts against the artifacts. Luckily, he paused at the ballroom entrance, and there she caught him, reaching out to grasp an arm encased in worn, stained linen.

Though not particularly large, the arm was shockingly hard with muscle, and heat seeped through the cloth, warming her fingers. But neither observation startled Juliet as much as a tingling sensation in her own hand, something vaguely akin to that excitement she felt when touching an artifact of great interest. Suddenly, the past and the future seemed to converge in one dizzying moment, and Juliet stared up into the stranger's face.

"*Who are you?*" she whispered.

He gave her an odd glance through narrowed eyes, whether annoyed by her presumption at seizing him or for some other reason, Juliet didn't know. But he finally answered. "I'm Morgan Beauchamp, and I'm in charge of this collection."

Juliet's fingers fell away as though burned, so shocked was she by his reply. She knew the name, having heard her father speak it often enough. Indeed, it sometimes seemed as though her father could speak of little else but the man he had engaged to procure his antiquities. Obviously, her father's faith had not been misplaced, for Mr. Beauchamp had proven quite successful. He had returned from Egypt with an impressive array of objects, which he had duly delivered to her father's town house, apparently in the dead of night. But now his job was over. He was not in charge of the collection, not now, not ever.

Recovering from her initial dismay, Juliet lifted her chin. "I fear you are mistaken, Mr. Beauchamp," she said as firmly as possible.

His response was an annoying smirk, reminiscent of so

many male dismissals of her and her abilities. And although she had spent a lifetime submitting to such condescension, Juliet was determined to hold her ground. Something about this tall, arrogant male had roused her dormant temper. Perhaps it was his snoring.

"You were hired to acquire these items, and your task is finished," Juliet said.

"Look, miss—" he began.

But Juliet stopped him. *"Lady.* Lady Juliet Cavendish. The earl of Carlisle is my father," she said, expecting the deference due her position, at least.

"Look, *lady,* I don't care *who* you are," Beauchamp said, lifting a hand to point at his wide chest. *"I'm* the one responsible for these artifacts."

Juliet caught her breath, for never had anyone spoken to her in such a way. She might have accepted the subtle snubs of her male colleagues, but she wasn't going to swallow this outrageous insult. "You may have found these pieces and overseen their shipment, but that hardly qualifies you to catalogue or preserve them," she said, standing toe to toe with the man.

Beauchamp shrugged, as though he didn't have time for her. "Look, *Lady Juliet*, if you want to go inspect the merchandise, I don't care, but you'd better be careful."

He was advising her? Juliet trembled with rage. "Just as careful as you have been unloading them in a haphazard jumble, to be placed one atop another? I'll be surprised if the papyri aren't crushed by your negligence," she said, sweeping an arm toward the disarray in the ballroom.

He scowled at her. "Your father was in a hurry. He told me to hire a few men at the docks to unload as soon as possible."

"So you let them toss priceless artifacts, that you have been well paid to transport, just anywhere while you . . . slept?" Juliet asked.

His dark eyes glittered, and Juliet took a step backward,

but she refused to let the man intimidate her. Indeed, should Mr. Beauchamp press her, she would happily tell him that she found him far worse than a common laborer sleeping off a drunk, for such men were to be excused for their carelessness, while he knew better.

Or did he? Despite the impressive results of his efforts, Mr. Beauchamp could hardly be deemed a scholar, or even a gentleman. He was one of those opportunists who trafficked in collectibles solely for the sake of his own profit, and as far as Juliet was concerned, he was one step above the grave robbers of yore.

Oh, he provided a service, as did others of his ilk, for the vast, mysterious country of Egypt and its fascinating history had been lost in shadow for centuries. It had been a lawless land in which travelers were unwelcome and imperiled, until Napoleon, in what might be construed as his only good deed, had opened up the country with his invasion of 1798. Thankfully, the Frenchman took with him not only soldiers but a group of savants, experts in every field of study, who were to observe and document the country.

When Napoleon's army later surrendered to the British, the savants ceded some spectacular finds, including the famous stone found at Rosetta, which many thought held the key to deciphering the hieroglyphs. And the reports of the returning scholars were breathtaking, especially Vivant Denon's gorgeous volume of notes and drawings, published in 1802.

Suddenly, Europe was seized by a mania for all things Egyptian. Museums sprang up, and men like Juliet's father were building illustrious private collections. Although some decried the removal of artifacts from their native land, at least these intellectuals were preserving history. Men like Morgan Beauchamp, on the other hand, were only lining their pockets and, obviously, cared little about their finds once payment was received.

As though to ward off the scorn that must have shown on her face, Beauchamp held up his hands. "I beg your pardon, *my lady,* but I've been up all night, and I dozed off after the men were finished. I won't be faulted for sleeping when I get the chance, because there have been plenty of times when I've gone without. And I've had worse berths than a crate."

Juliet flushed at the intimate turn of the conversation. How had they moved from the care of his cargo to his sleeping arrangements? Unbidden, the image of Mr. Beauchamp reclining upon some foreign couch, attended by harem women, flashed through her mind, and Juliet firmly dismissed it.

She drew herself up and looked him in the eye. "You, Mr. Beauchamp, are clearly not a gentleman, for a gentleman would concede his fault and be gone."

"Well, there you are right," Beauchamp answered. He smiled slowly, revealing a set of straight white teeth that would be the envy of anyone, and Juliet found herself staring, her heart somehow racing again as one corner of his mouth kicked upward. Although she had never found lips particularly appealing, his were somehow interesting—at least as long as their owner didn't speak.

"Because I'm no gentleman," he added, grinning wickedly.

Juliet's good sense, momentarily suspended, reasserted itself with a vengeance. "Out!" she shouted, gesturing in the general direction of the town house's exit. "Get out of here immediately, or I shall call a footman to toss you out!" Indeed, one was probably responding to the sound of her raised voice, an unheard-of occurrence in the household.

But her outburst, however atypical and astonishing, had no effect on Mr. Beauchamp. Instead of being intimidated by her threat, he simply laughed, making Juliet wonder if there were enough men in the entire town house to get rid of him. If there weren't, she would be happy to lend a hand—or foot—to the cause.

"Look, *Lady Juliet,* I'm not going anywhere," he said. "And since I don't plan to have anything to do with you, you can go back to your pianoforte and your tea things and stay out of my way. I'm strictly here to put the collection in order for the earl and his Egypt expert."

At this declaration, Juliet stilled. Then she slowly crossed her arms over her chest. "Egypt expert?" she asked.

"Yes," Beauchamp said, looking impatient.

"Ah," Juliet murmured. She paused for the maximum effect before donning the same sort of smug expression that he wore. "That expert would be . . . me."

Juliet had the fleeting pleasure of watching surprise flash across his face before he threw back his head and laughed. His response, unusual though it might be, was just as infuriating as the more polite expression of disbelief with which others greeted her expertise.

Over the years, Juliet had hardened herself to such treatment, so his outrageous response did little more than prick her already loosed temper. What hurt was her father's apparent lack of faith. He knew her to be more knowledge-able than most scholars, so why would he put this rogue in charge instead of his own daughter?

"Look, miss, uh, *Lady Juliet,*" Beauchamp said, when he managed to stop laughing. "I realize that every member of the ton, worth his or her misplaced title, feels they must dabble in the mania of the moment, but can't you find an-other hobby, like needlework?"

Even the elegant lines of his face couldn't soften his smirk, and Juliet itched to slap his tanned cheek. Instead, she asked him a simple question . . . in Coptic, the old lan-guage of the Christians of Egypt.

Beauchamp's eyes narrowed, and she realized that he

recognized something familiar in the speech that was nonetheless foreign to him. His suspicion was almost laughable, and Juliet allowed herself another small smile, albeit *not* a smirk.

"So you don't speak Coptic? What about Arabic? Or do you communicate with the natives through a series of grunts and hand signals?" Juliet asked, her contempt obvious.

When Beauchamp didn't reply, she continued. "I have a grasp of Syriac, Chaldean, Sanskrit, and Persian, among other languages, which are most helpful in my studies of the hieroglyphs. Are you even familiar with the writings found on the stone at Rosetta? Did you know that ground-breaking work is being undertaken to decipher the hieroglyphs, based upon the three languages written on the stone?"

It was now his turn to gape at her, and Juliet enjoyed every moment. "Can you tell me the names of the rulers of ancient Egypt as they are now known? Where—" she began, but Beauchamp held up a hand to halt her questioning. Although Juliet suspected he was rarely at a loss, he recovered himself quickly and shrugged, as if such knowledge was useless.

But Juliet knew it was not. "Then perhaps you can tell me what possible contribution, beyond obtaining it, that you can make to the organization and study of this collection?"

His dark eyes narrowed, and his even darker brows lowered. "Well, I can tell you where everything was found and when and how," he said. *"Since I was there."*

"Which should all be detailed in your accompanying materials," Juliet said scornfully. She would give no quarter to the man simply for traveling to Egypt, while she could not.

Beauchamp's lips quirked, an ominous sign. "Well, I promised your father that I'd stay around to help sort out my, uh, notes. There really wasn't time to document the pieces thoroughly since we left Egypt in a hurry. You see, there was a slight misunderstanding over permits," he said, with an unapologetic grin.

Juliet stared in shock, for she knew that the Egyptian government issued permits to allow any excavation or transportation of antiquities. "You *stole* all this?" she asked, her voice rising once more.

"Of course not," Beauchamp answered, though he didn't look appalled or even offended by the accusation. "As I said, there was a little misunderstanding over the permits. Don't worry. I'll take care of it."

Juliet could think of nothing less assuring, and she was just about to say so, in no uncertain terms, when she heard the sound of heavy footsteps approaching the ballroom. Unless Beauchamp had some cronies stashed about the town house, it was her father. She stepped back.

"Aha! Beauchamp!" The earl of Carlisle greeted this perpetrator of fraud, if not outright theft, with a hearty slap on the back. Only then did he notice Juliet.

"Ah, I see you've met my daughter. Splendid!" her father said, rubbing his hands together. "You'll find her to be an excellent little worker. I'm sure you two will have this collection catalogued and ready for display in no time at all."

Juliet smiled weakly. Fluent in several languages and more learned than most scholars on the subject of Egypt, she found the accolade "excellent little worker" faint praise, especially when recommending her to Mr. Beauchamp. She did not dispute it, however, focusing instead on her concerns about the antiquities themselves. "But, Father, there appears to be some question of the legality of the new arrivals."

"Nonsense, Juliet!" her father said, with a snort and a scowl. He did not like objections or arguments, as Juliet well knew, but he quickly resumed his jovial manner, presumably for Beauchamp's sake.

"Now, don't worry your pretty head about such things. You can leave that business to Beauchamp. Just give him a hand with ordering the finds, and make sure you get all the information down neatly," he said with a firm air of dismissal.

Although she could do nothing except defer to her father, when he looked away, Juliet glared daggers at Beauchamp, who was oddly reticent for a man who ought to be gloating. Well, let him gloat and let him posture, Juliet vowed, for she knew that no matter what any of them said or did, she was the one who would catalogue this collection, not her father or this arrogant ruffian.

When her father drew the rogue away for some private conference outside the ballroom, Juliet loosed a sigh of relief, the unusual tension that gripped her body easing slightly. Eager to begin her task without the interference of the less knowledgeable, she picked up her pencil once more.

She might be forced to work with Morgan Beauchamp, but that did not mean she had to like it.

Chapter 2

✠

MORGAN leaned back his head and groaned in pure bliss. Who would have thought the old earl would have a bathing room with piped-in water, hot enough to drive away the chill of this wretched climate? It was a blessed relief after the long sea voyage and the less than rigorous personal hygiene practiced in Egypt. Yes, as much as Morgan disdained his homeland, there were some advantages, such as running water, soft beds, clean linen . . . and an expert unlike any he had ever seen.

Morgan frowned as the vision of the earl's daughter sprang too quickly to mind. Of course, she didn't look anything like her father, a rather swarthy, fat fellow with more money than scruples. He was one of those outwardly genial fellows whom people often underestimated, but Morgan had not made that mistake, and so far he had no cause for complaint.

The earl's daughter was another matter entirely. Lady Juliet wasn't the least bit swarthy or fat, but slender and taller than most women with a thick mane of golden hair that seemed to oppose strict confinement. And although a pair of spectacles perched upon her nose, they couldn't hide the elegant lines of her face. Suffused with a heat that didn't come from the pipes, Morgan sank beneath the water to give himself a good dunking.

Upon surfacing, he reminded himself that no matter how beautiful she might appear, like most women of her ilk, Lady Juliet was a spoiled, selfish creature whose goal in life was to marry well—meaning into even more power and wealth. Indeed, Morgan wondered why she wasn't wed already, for she was hardly a schoolgirl. He grunted. No doubt, she and her greedy father were holding out for the highest bidder.

And if that wasn't enough to disgust him, the lady had made her contempt for Morgan, positioned as he was at the opposite end of her tidy world, quite clear. So what if she had eyes the color of sun-drenched dunes to go with that downy hair? She also had a tart tongue and a penchant for interference.

That thought made Morgan reach for the soap, for he wondered just what she was doing with his collection while he was enjoying his leisurely soak. Well, maybe it wasn't exactly *his* collection, at least not anymore. But it remained his responsibility for now, even if the earl held title to it all. And so what if he did? Morgan preferred the cold, hard cash he had received.

What would he do with all those artifacts, anyway? He didn't believe in too many possessions, and he wasn't some rich dilettante with nothing better to do than buy the spoils of someone else's toil. He could not fathom spending his time sitting around admiring his treasures or, worse yet, showing them off to the other fat idiots who clamored for Egyptian antiquities because it was fashionable to do so.

With a snort, Morgan rose dripping from the marble bath and grabbed a clean set of clothes. Maybe he wouldn't be keeping his finds, but the earl had put him in charge of documenting them, and he'd be damned if he would let some haughty aristocrat take over what he had fought to obtain. So what if that aristocrat had a disconcerting amount of knowledge to go with her flawless skin? He would just take advantage of the former, while ignoring the latter.

It certainly wasn't the memory of that golden skin that sent Morgan downstairs in such a hurry, but concern for the collection for which he was accountable. The earl had made that responsibility quite clear, at least to Morgan, and if his daughter gave any arguments . . . well, Morgan would be happy to put her in her place.

The notion made Morgan's lips quirk in anticipation of another confrontation, but when he reached the ballroom, he discovered that the lady wasn't alone. Not that he wanted her alone, particularly, but he sure didn't want another buffoon rummaging amongst his finds. Morgan swore under his breath. Next time he was going to make sure he took better notes, so he wouldn't have to stay and see what a mess these morons made of his hard-won treasures.

"Hey! Watch what you're about," Morgan called as the other occupant of the room, an overdressed coxcomb, tried to move a heavy stela.

At the sound, the fellow straightened and turned, confirming Morgan's opinion of his type. Slender and pale with nearly colorless hair, he looked at Morgan with an arrogance born of centuries of inbreeding among the upper classes. Undoubtedly rich, stupid, and useless, he was just the sort of character Morgan most despised.

"I beg your pardon?" the fellow asked in offended accents.

Morgan bared his teeth. "Be careful with that. I didn't drag it all the way to England just to watch you break it."

"Now, see here—" the coxcomb began with a huff, only to be cut off by Lady Juliet. Although she now looked to be a proper English noblewoman, cool, calm and remote,

Morgan wasn't fooled. That flyaway hair and a pulse throbbing in her throat gave away her volatile character—at least to anyone who had been a victim of it.

"Sir Cyril, this is Mr. Beauchamp, the *procurer* of these items," she said without even glancing his way.

Morgan's eyes narrowed. Although her perfectly composed expression revealed nothing of her intent, she made him sound like someone who provided a certain type of woman for another's usage. And Morgan didn't like it.

"Mr. Beauchamp, may I present Sir Cyril Lyndhurst, a noted scholar and expert on Egypt," she said with a smooth gesture of one slender hand.

Morgan tore his gaze away from her fingers to flick a glance at the coxcomb. "Lyndhurst, you say? I've never heard of him," he said with a shrug of dismissal. While the coxcomb huffed his outrage, Morgan returned his attention to the lady. Was her lip twitching in amusement, or did she have a tic?

"Mr. Beauchamp is here to assist in organizing and cataloguing the collection," she explained.

Morgan lifted his brows at her choice of words, which made it seem that he would be taking orders from her, a ludicrous possibility, especially since she was a woman. But he let the statement go for now. Soon enough he would make quite clear to the lady just who was in charge, and he would enjoy it, too. Morgan grinned.

"But, I thought . . . I . . . How is that possible?" the coxcomb stammered. "Surely this, this . . . treasure hunter cannot provide any valuable input to serious scholars!"

"Nonetheless, Father wants him to stay on to assist—" Lady Juliet began.

"*Oversee,*" Morgan put in with a smirk.

"—the collection," the lady added, giving him a look.

Morgan gave her one right back, but, to his disappointment, she didn't respond. Apparently, she maintained the genteel lady demeanor for the benefit of those such as the coxcomb here, while Morgan was treated to the less politic version, at least in private. After a moment's consideration, Morgan realized that he had the better half. After all, had she ever shouted at the coxcomb or grabbed him by the arm?

"Why that's preposterous!" Lyndhurst said, fuming. Morgan thought so, too, until he realized the coxcomb was objecting to him managing the cataloguing or assisting. Or both.

Morgan frowned and braced himself for Lady Juliet's next words. No doubt, she would enlighten Lyndhurst as to the state of Morgan's notes, so that the two dilettantes could chortle in superior fashion over his inadequacies.

Well, let them. That little dustup over permits wasn't his fault. Egypt under Ali was a complicated morass of politics, bribery, and treachery that neither one of these two knew a thing about. Why, they wouldn't last a day in the country, Morgan thought, though the feisty Lady Juliet might fare better than the coxcomb. Eyeing her sharply, Morgan waited, but to his surprise, she gave no further explanation for his presence.

The coxcomb hardly gave her time. "Preposterous, Juliet, utterly preposterous!" he repeated. Either he was not used to accommodating anyone else, or his vocabulary was limited.

"Be that as it may—" the lady began, in apparent agreement with the coxcomb.

"Now, just wait a minute—" Morgan cut in.

Lady Juliet appeared not to have heard him, even though he was standing only a few feet away. "Father is determined that Mr. Beauchamp be given every consideration," she noted before turning to give Morgan a faint smile.

Morgan didn't smile back. If she thought to make up for her insinuations with some false cordiality, she was mistaken. And if she intended to ignore him, she was in for a surprise. Capturing her gaze with his own, Morgan glared at her, but the lady didn't flinch. Indeed, she stared, as if unable to look away, and Morgan felt a swift surge of triumph.

Unfortunately, his brief sense of victory was soon replaced by a certain fascination with the color of her eyes. Morgan was seized by an urge to get closer, to see them better, and, indeed, had nearly stepped forward when a nasal sound stopped him.

Lyndhurst was choking or snorting, but Morgan was grateful for the annoying noise that brought him to his senses. He moved back, away from the earl's daughter, feeling disoriented and more than a bit wary.

"Well, I suppose if the earl has made up his mind in this regard . . ." the coxcomb began.

"He has," Lady Juliet said a bit breathlessly. She had ducked her head, and Morgan found that he missed seeing those eyes, even though they were so often obscured by the spectacles. He shook his head. He really needed to get home more often, if he was swooning over a lady like this one.

"I see," Lyndhurst said with a frown of distaste. Although he appeared to be extremely unhappy with the situation, he made no move to seek out the earl for argument, which made Morgan wonder if he really was an important scholar or simply a dabbler. Leaning against the table, Morgan crossed his arms over his chest, weary of the fellow's posturing.

However, Lyndhurst wasn't about to give in gracefully. "And just what assistance is Mr. Beauchamp to provide?" he asked.

How about if I help you out of the room? Morgan thought. Instead, he let his lips curve into a smirk. "The kind of assistance that comes from being the only one who knows just where these objects were found. The kind of experience that comes from being the only person here to ever step foot in Egypt."

Lyndhurst looked like he was going to choke again, presumably on his overweening self-importance, but before he could erupt, Lady Juliet stepped in. "Mr. Beauchamp wants to . . . go over his notes and make sure that all of his . . . pertinent observations are recorded when the items are catalogued," she explained.

"I see," the coxcomb said stiffly. "Well, if you will excuse me then, I shall return to my work. I was going to make a wax impression of this stela. I assume no one has thought to do so?"

Although the coxcomb still wore an expression of superiority, Morgan shrugged, dismissing the question. He had brought back the stela itself, so what need would he have for a copy?

Lyndhurst then turned to Lady Juliet. "You didn't begin without me, did you, Juliet?" he asked in an accusing tone.

Juliet? Why was the coxcomb addressing the lady so familiarly? And why was he using that tone with her? Morgan's eyes narrowed.

"No, Cyril. I have only just begun myself. It seems that the shipment was unloaded during the night, and no one thought to wake me," she said, obviously displeased with that turn of events.

The coxcomb either didn't notice her distress—or didn't care—for he assumed an even more priggish expression. "And that is as it should be. You should hardly be up and about at all hours, let alone amongst rough workmen," he scolded, glancing sharply toward Morgan.

Morgan's fingers twitched with the urge to show the idiot just how rough he was, but he figured it was only polite to let the lady give him a good poke first. He turned to Lady Juliet, but to his surprise, she only stiffened and glanced away. What had happened to the woman who had matched him toe to toe only a short while ago? She had obviously turned into a stiff-lipped English noble, on her best behavior for another of her ilk. Morgan snorted.

"Mr. Beauchamp?" she said, no doubt offended by his snort. He gave her a questioning look, which she promptly returned. "I'm waiting."

Morgan stared at her. Did she think he would apologize for any rude noises? If so, she would be waiting a good long time. And, of course, now that he knew how much they annoyed her, Morgan would have to make even more rude noises.

She eyed him expectantly. "For your notes?" she prompted.

Oh, those. In the heat of the moment, Morgan had nearly forgotten about them. With a shrug, he turned toward the stack of materials he had brought back with him. They had to be somewhere around here, didn't they? He rooted around the table, ignoring his companion's sounds of dismay and pushing aside some pottery until he found the precious volumes.

"Let's see . . . where shall we begin?" he asked. He reached for the topmost book, but the drawings and notes that were stuffed inside spilled forth, scattering onto the surface of the table. Morgan frowned. Perhaps he could have organized things a bit better, but he had been forced to pack in a hurry.

The sound of a loud gasp made him glance up. Lady Juliet's eyes were glazed with a look of such horror that Morgan glanced around to make sure there were no crocodiles or knife-wielding natives sneaking up on them. All he saw was Lyndhurst glaring. Was the coxcomb worried that he was abusing the lady? Morgan thought not. The fellow looked more likely to accuse her of disturbing him.

"What?" Morgan demanded loudly. He was tempted to go over there and give Lyndhurst the poke he well deserved, but the man's attitude had an unexpected side effect. In an apparent effort to maintain the decorous atmosphere she now cultivated, Lady Juliet leaned close to Morgan.

"We must try to conduct our work as quietly as possible," she whispered, and Morgan decided he might have to thank the coxcomb for his boorish behavior, especially when he caught a whiff of womanly scent. Delicate and clean, it certainly wasn't the sort of perfume liberally applied by ladies of the ton. Most likely, Lady Juliet used a subtly fragrant soap, but after the often overwhelming odors of Egypt, Morgan found it delightful. He bent nearer.

Unfortunately, she straightened, and a deep inhalation only filled his nostrils with musty air from the nearby antiquities. Frowning, Morgan watched as she gathered up the fallen papers, pausing suddenly to point at a sheet containing one of his better pieces of description.

"What is this?" she demanded. Although she spoke softly, her words held a hard edge that she hadn't used in her conversations with Lyndhurst. Morgan didn't know whether to feel annoyed or privileged.

He leaned forward, squinted at the paper, and smiled, pleased that she had chosen that particular passage. "Well—" he began.

But she cut him off in an outraged whisper. "I can't read that! What kind of writing is that? I've read centuries-old scribbling that was more legible." She practically hissed in his ear.

So the termagant was back? Morgan found he wasn't as eager to welcome her as he thought. He reared back, ready to argue, but she was too quick. Already, the lady had pulled one of his, well, less accurate drawings from the stack.

"And just what is this? How am I supposed to correctly decipher hieroglyphs from this?" she demanded. Without waiting for his answer, she went on in a rush. "Think of all the magnificent depictions undertaken by Denon and those who, at the risk of their lives, preserved the original renderings as closely as possible for posterity, for scholarly study. And I am served with this?" she asked, letting the paper drop back onto the pile. "Why on earth did you travel to Egypt?"

"Not for posterity or scholarly study," Morgan snapped back, angry now.

"I can see that!" she said, her voice rising.

"Oh, can you? I didn't think you could see beyond the nose on your face!" Morgan shot back. They stood facing each other now, and he noticed a faint flush in her cheeks, framed by wisps of blond hair that had come loose from their mooring. His gaze dipped lower to delicate lips, slightly parted, and lower still to shapely breasts that were rising and falling with each rapid breath. Sadly, those breasts were well covered by a modest garment that defied the fashion for low-cut gowns. Morgan nearly sighed in disappointment.

"I see very well, thank you, but you . . . Wh-what are you looking at?" she asked.

Although the query forced him to abandon his scrutiny of the area in question, Morgan only shrugged. "All right, so maybe I'm not the greatest artist around—" he began.

"Then you hire someone else who is!" she said, glaring up at him.

"Look, *my lady,* you may be able to recite a lot of facts, but you have no idea what the real Egypt is like, so don't try to tell me my business!" Morgan said, pointing an out-stretched finger at her in emphasis.

"Don't you dare raise a hand to me!" she said. Reaching out, she grasped hold of his fist, pointing finger and all.

And that's when everything changed.

She wore no gloves and neither did he, so their skin met unfettered, hers warm and soft, yet firm and strong. The contact sent such a jolt through Morgan that he felt it down to his toes. It was like the exhilaration of discovering a long-hidden treasure, only with something else added, something that made him want to sweep every valuable artifact off the mahogany table and take Lady Juliet right there on the gleaming surface. Struck dumb by the sudden surge of desire, Morgan simply stared wide-eyed at her, and she looked just as dazed as he felt. Luckily for them— or perhaps not—they weren't alone.

"I say, can't you two speak in measured tones over there?" The coxcomb's voice rang out loudly above the sound of their own rapid breaths. "Every time I begin my work, my concentration is broken by your shouting," he complained.

Morgan swung his head toward the coxcomb in alarm, but Lyndhurst seemed oblivious to the fact that he and the lady were standing far closer than proper decorum allowed, their hands entwined. Unfortunately, Juliet was not quite as dull-witted, and she jerked her fingers away as though she had been burned.

"I tell you that I simply cannot work under these conditions," Lyndhurst continued. "I am certain that this fellow is accustomed to less civilized environments, but I'm surprised at you, Juliet, for allowing yourself to sink to his level of manners. I cannot think this is what your father had in mind when he asked you to assist in the cataloguing."

Morgan's eyes narrowed. Who was this idiot, and why did he talk to the lady that way? *And call her Juliet?* Perhaps he was a relative, though the two looked nothing alike. Of course, in ton society, that meant little, for relations by name were not always by blood. And some men felt any connection gave them license to ill-treat women.

Morgan's own sense of honor was buried deep and hadn't been heard from in so long that he barely recognized it when it stirred. Still, he opened his mouth to defend the lady's arguments as being perfectly reasonable, although he hadn't thought so at the time. But when he glanced at Juliet, he was shocked to see her transform before his eyes, stiffening and then disappearing into herself until nothing was left except a beautiful shell, distant and rote in its movements.

"I beg your pardon, Mr. Beauchamp. I'm sure you did your best," she murmured, as cold and lifeless as a doll.

Morgan frowned. He didn't know whether to shake the coxcomb or Juliet herself. "No, you're right," he said. "I didn't copy the hieroglyphs very well, but the artist who was traveling with me died before he could complete much work. And although more people are visiting the country, competent artists willing to brave the conditions there aren't exactly lying about pining for work."

"Yes, you are right, of course," Lady Juliet said.

Morgan found he preferred being wrong. He almost told her to ignore the coxcomb and argue with him all she wanted. Hell, he *liked* a good fight. But then he shrugged. Her fire, or lack of it, wasn't his problem. He had spent many years doing his best to avoid personal entanglements, so the last thing he needed was to waste his time with these dilettantes. His only concern was that the lady take good care of his treasures and put some order to them, and the sooner she did so, the sooner he could return to Egypt.

"Where do you want to start?" Morgan asked.

Lady Juliet glanced about. "Well, I usually begin with the largest of the acquisitions, but since they seem to be strewn all over . . ."

"Good God, can't we just grab the closest thing and go from there?" Morgan said, snatching up a small piece of pottery that stood on the table close to him. And he thought dealing with the Egyptians had been difficult . . .

"Now, see here, Mr. Beauchamp!" Lyndhurst poked his head up once more.

"What the devil do you want?" Morgan asked, his temper frayed beyond repair.

"I won't have you talking to Juliet that way!"

Morgan stared at him. The lady and Morgan had practically come to blows earlier and *now* he was complaining?

"There is no need for foul language," Lyndhurst said, stiffly. "And a gentleman would not argue with a lady, but would cede to her wishes."

"He's not a gentleman," Lady Juliet said from behind him in a suspiciously amused tone. Morgan slanted a glance toward her, but her face revealed nothing.

"I fear I'm beginning to agree with you, Juliet," Lyndhurst said, frowning. "And rest assured, I shall speak to your father about it."

Morgan shrugged. He was the one with the goods—and the notes—not this idiot, whom the earl had never even bothered to mention.

"And as for the ordering of this collection, some prefer a more logical approach to the cataloguing of objects," the coxcomb said.

Logical? How could beginning with something big be called logical? Morgan could only gape in bafflement.

"And, I might add, Lady Juliet hardly needs the influence of another erratic mind encouraging her own lack of discipline," Lyndhurst said.

Morgan narrowed his eyes. Was the coxcomb insulting Lady Juliet? Again? He put down the pot and turned to face the fellow. "And just who the devil are you to say what the lady does or does not need?"

For once, Lyndhurst smiled. His wide lips curled upward as he assumed an even more superior air, and Morgan braced himself for what could only be ill news.

"I am her fiancé," the coxcomb announced in a smug tone.

Morgan stared in astonishment. He had thought these two related, but engaged? He had an odd sensation in the pit of his stomach, as if he had just ingested some bad native food that would later return to haunt him. Could it be true? Morgan nearly glanced at the lady for confirmation before recovering himself.

"Good for you," he said instead, effecting a casual shrug. "But if you can't keep from interfering with her work—and mine—I'm going to throw you out of here."

It was the coxcomb's turn to look astounded, and Morgan enjoyed watching his expression of self importance fade to be replaced by a rather florid mottling of his pale skin.

"Now, see here—" Lyndhurst began.

But Morgan had reached the end of his tether. He took a step forward.

The coxcomb took a step back. "Barbarian! Uncivilized, uncouth . . . Why, I've never—"

Morgan cut through what promised to be a lengthy diatribe. "Do you want to make your wax impression or not?"

Although the coxcomb looked as though he might have an apoplexy at any moment, he said nothing further, just drew himself up with overwrought dignity and turned back to his work. Good. Morgan had had quite enough of the prig.

As for Lady Juliet, she was suspiciously silent, but Morgan wasn't about to ask her about the wedding plans. He told himself he wasn't surprised by the arrangement. After all, it certainly wasn't unusual that the beautiful earl's daughter was betrothed to a pompous ass, presumably for money and position.

What surprised him was that he cared.

Chapter 3

✥

WHEN Morgan reached his bedroom, he found his manservant waiting, a towel carefully folded over one arm and a supercilious grin on his face. The unusual pose was so startling that, for a moment, Morgan thought the fellow had lost his senses entirely. Then he realized the smile, as well as the attempt at decorum, could only mean one thing: the earl's housemaids must be friendly.

"Good evening, sir," Chauncey said.

"You look like a halfwit," Morgan observed.

"Hey, now! I'm just trying to be a proper valet," Chauncey protested.

"Well, if you intend on aping the idiots in this house, I'll feed you to the nearest crocodile."

"Ha! You'll never find one around here," Chauncey answered.

Morgan stalked past him into the heavily appointed room, suddenly annoyed by the ostentation. He had gone from sleeping in an open tomb or tent to this oppressive place, with its dark drapes and massive furniture. It was large, to be sure, but the carved ceilings and silk-covered walls closed in on him so that he could hardly breathe.

Chauncey trailed after him. "Hey, I'm only trying to do me job!"

Morgan threw himself down in a gilt armchair. "Well, then take off my boots," he grumbled.

Tossing aside the useless towel, Chauncey bent to tug on one foot. "You'll be changing for dinner, then?" he asked, still perpetrating the fraud that he was a gentleman's gentleman. Perhaps the housemaids were impressed. Morgan certainly wasn't.

"And what do you expect me to change into?" he asked. He had no dinner clothes and wasn't planning on buying any with his hard-earned money. He had far better things to do with it than play dress-up, like book passage back to Egypt and away from the stifling society here. Already, the climate, the expectations, and the pretenses were all grating on him.

"But I thought you were to join the family for dinner," Chauncey protested.

"If the earl wants my company, he can take me as I am," Morgan said.

Chauncey shook his head. "Well, I just hope he doesn't send you off to the servant's hall to eat."

Morgan snorted. "It would probably be a more interesting gathering."

Chauncey grinned. "Except for the lady, of course."

Morgan's eyes narrowed. Chauncey had an eye for the female gender, so Morgan didn't have to ask to whom his servant was referring. It was the fact he was referring to her at all that bothered Morgan. "And what would you know about her?"

Chauncey shrugged, a little too casually for Morgan's taste. "I caught a glimpse of her, and I have to admit she's not the usual sort you work with."

Morgan snorted. "A fact for which I'm immensely

grateful. I never met a more interfering, dictatorial, arrogant creature in my life."

Chauncey laughed. "Like her, do you?"

Morgan sank back into silence.

"Well, if you have to work with someone, I'd take the lady any day. Even with those spectacles, she's a sight for sore eyes," Chauncey said.

Morgan lifted his head long enough to glare at his companion. "Well, your favorite sight is engaged to the most imbecilic coxcomb I've ever had the misfortune to encounter."

"So?" Chauncey said, backing away with the boots in hand.

"What? Do you think I care? Well, I don't," Morgan said. If he raised his voice a bit, it was only to make his point. Having had a long day in which to reassess his initial reaction, he had come to the conclusion that he had vastly overrated Lady Juliet's charms.

"Believe me, Chauncey, if we hadn't spent the last two years amid sand and rocks, she wouldn't even look good to us. It's just been so long since we've been around a true Englishwoman that we've forgotten how alluring they could be," Morgan said.

"*Alluring?*" Chauncey said, with a bark of laughter. "You used to say you'd never met a more boring passel of whey-faced twits than the ladies of the ton!"

Morgan glared at him. "Maybe it's been so long since I've seen *any* woman that even one of that ilk manages to seem appealing. In fact, I have no doubt that's what I need. A woman. And one a bit more accommodating than Lady Juliet."

Chauncey grinned. "Well, I don't mind saying there are a couple lovely little fillies right here in the earl's household."

Morgan grunted. "I'll not prey upon these poor working women, and neither should you."

"Hey, I'm giving 'em a bit of enjoyment!" Chauncey protested.

"Well, just make sure you don't get any of them—or us—run out of the place," Morgan said. "At least before I avail myself of the bathing room."

Chauncey's jaw dropped. "I thought you had a bath this morning!"

"Well, I crave another, longer, more luxurious soak," Morgan said. "Especially since my earlier one was cut short prematurely."

Chauncey eyed him sharply, as though he thought there might be some hidden meaning to Morgan's words. But unable to fathom what those might be, the servant shook his head. "You better watch out. Too much water isn't good for a man."

It was Morgan's turn to laugh. After the deprivations of Egypt, he was going to take full advantage of the amenities offered by civilization. Gathering up the forgotten towel and the clothes that had been thoughtfully cleaned in his absence, he headed out the door.

"Hey, now!" Chauncey called, forgetting his attempt at exemplary employment. "Mr. Beauchamp! *Morgan!* You can't run around this house in your bare feet!"

"Why not? It's one of the few pleasures to be had here!" Morgan answered over his shoulder. Ignoring a startled footman, he strode down the hall and grinned at the delightful sensation of the earl's expensive Aubusson carpet beneath his toes. As far as he was concerned, the pleasures of the nobleman's elaborate household came down to this: clean linen, hot water, and one beautiful blonde.

Too bad so much detritus had to accompany them.

FOR once, Juliet was glad to escape the dinner company. Usually, her father's habit of dismissing her while he had brandy or port with Cyril annoyed her, for she deemed it another male device to exclude her from conversation to which she might make a valuable contribution. Although her father had allowed her an education, which was far more than most other women could claim, he so rarely considered her opinion that sometimes Juliet wondered if he had done so only to avoid hiring outside experts to attend his collection.

But tonight Juliet did not argue or resent her dismissal. Indeed, she welcomed it, for now she would have the opportunity to view the artifacts in blessed quiet, without the interference of . . . anyone else. Moving through the still house with certain purpose, she slipped into the darkened ballroom unobserved and caught her breath in admiration of the silent splendors there.

She made her way among the treasures slowly, guided only by moonlight from the tall windows, a bit entranced by the difference nightfall had made. What had been objects of study earlier in the day were cast into an otherworldly realm of looming shadow and mystery, and Juliet could almost feel as though she were moving among shifting shapes of sand, discovering each artifact in its native berth.

Again, the mummy case seemed perfectly situated, the alabaster gleaming white in the gloom as though a beacon that beckoned all comers. Although not usually her area of interest, it drew her, and Juliet moved forward, sidestepping the stela to stand before the heavy reliquary. Lifting a hand, she traced a finger over the surface and drew a deep breath. She could almost smell the history in the air, reaching out to her over the centuries. And if she closed her eyes, she could imagine herself there, among the ancient Egyptians themselves. . . .

"A little late to be working, isn't it?"

The voice, a deep drawl, made Juliet start, and only the fact that it was decidedly English convinced her that the Egyptian dead were not rising up to speak. Whirling round, she peered into the dimness, only to find herself facing Mr. Beauchamp. Much to her dismay, he appeared even more handsome in the moonlight, as if it were his natural venue, and the heart that Juliet had thought subdued after an evening's stern lecture, now began to hammer uncontrollably.

His attire was astonishing. He wore the same sort of worn linen shirt, breeches, and boots that he had during the day, his only concession to dinner being the addition of a plain waistcoat and jacket that he had since discarded. He resembled a workman, for he was dressed more simply than her father's footmen, and yet, somehow he looked *right,* better than the footmen, better than her father, and certainly better than Cyril had in his elaborately embroidered waistcoat and carefully tied neckcloth, his collar so high that it was a wonder he could turn his head.

To appear without a jacket was unheard of, and yet this rogue's simple linen shirt stood in stark contrast to other men's attire during the day, making them look fussy and almost feminine. Juliet had spent a lifetime disgusted with the accouterments of her gender, but she had never realized that the dictates of male fashion were just as absurd.

Obviously, Mr. Beauchamp paid them no heed. With a kind of giddy awe, she wondered whether he paid anyone heed, if any person ever had managed to control this reckless adventurer with his uncivilized behavior and unguarded tongue. The thought made Juliet shiver as she stared silently across the room at the only man who had ever roused her curiosity.

Why wasn't he with her father and Cyril, two of the most uninspiring and predictable of males? Why was he here in the dark? How had he entered the room without her hearing? Obviously, she had been concentrating far too much on the past and too little on the here and now, a lapse that suddenly seemed dangerous.

"I don't think you can see much in this light, either," he said, stepping forward smoothly, despite the objects littering the floor. He was like a cat, silent and deadly, and Juliet had the fleeting, rather alarming notion that he was stalking her.

"I just wanted to check on things before I went to . . . before I retired for the evening," Juliet said.

He was close enough now for her to see his face, and a trick of the light cast his eyes into relief, while letting his hard jaw and wide shoulders sink into shadow.

"Is there someone in this house you don't trust?" he asked, his voice deep, his words resonating somewhere inside her.

Juliet tried to gather her composure, but it was difficult when she looked up into eyes as dark and mysterious as the past itself. "Certainly not. I just wanted to take a look . . . by myself."

"Oh, so you want to be rid of me?" he asked, his lips curving in a way that made her breath catch.

"I didn't say that," Juliet said, though she had to admit his departure would certainly make her work easier. Better that she piece together his illegible notes as best she could than to be put in this sort of situation, a most improper one, to be sure.

"But I would prefer that you not come here again, at night, I mean," Juliet said. She dropped her gaze from his eyes to focus on his shirtfront, but even that relatively mundane surface was cast by the moonlight with a pale glow that delineated the flesh beneath. Since the only chests she had ever examined at such close quarters were those of mummies, Juliet very naturally felt a certain admiration for this one, being wide and strong and alive. And surprisingly interesting.

Indeed, she might have remained staring at it indefinitely, if the decision had not been taken from her. One minute she was absorbed in her study, the next she felt the touch of fingers underneath her chin, nudging it upward so that she was forced to look her companion full in the face.

As if that weren't startling enough, those same fingers then brushed her cheek lightly, sending shivers of awareness through her entire being. Since Juliet had never felt such a sensation, she wasn't sure what to make of it, and she searched his face for an explanation, her gaze finally settling on his hard mouth. So often set in a smirk, his lips were softened by shadow, sweetened by moonlight, and suddenly Juliet forgot why she had ever wanted him to leave.

The thud of a door closing, although far away, sounded loud in the silence, and a bell tinkled somewhere deep in the house. No doubt, her father was calling for more port, and that knowledge brought Juliet to her senses. She stepped back, away from the man before her, and knocked into the mummy case. It banged loudly, and she whirled, mentally scolding herself for such carelessness, but she had caused no harm to the heavy alabaster.

Her fingers splayed over the surface for support, and Juliet paused to regain control of her wits, as well as her pounding heart and erratic insides. Belatedly, she realized that she should never have come here in the dark, endangering her work and the antiquities themselves with what could only be deemed inexplicable behavior.

Mr. Beauchamp was a . . . colleague and one with whom she rarely agreed, so why had she been standing here gaping at him? Any conversation he wished to have could well be deferred until tomorrow, and Juliet would simply tell him as much. Drawing a deep breath, she turned, determined to send him on his way, at least for this evening, only to find him already gone.

She blinked in surprise. How had he slipped away so quickly? And why? His abrupt departure without a word made him no gentleman, but he had proven that lack already. Loosing a sigh, Juliet leaned back against the cold alabaster, baffled by both his actions and her own response.

Her relief at his exit warred with pique and something

else, as well, a vague yearning that she had only known when searching the past, a thirst for knowledge and experience beyond her sheltered life, and the curious question of what might have been, had he remained.

ALTHOUGH it was quite early the next morning when Juliet headed down to work, she did not even pause for breakfast. The house was quiet, with only a few servants about, and yet she made her way cautiously, leery of meeting anyone. And by the time she reached the ballroom, she was tense in mind and body, relaxing only when she found it empty.

Juliet's relief was followed by resentment at having to sneak about her own house. She was a scholar, a student of Egypt, its history, its artifacts, and its hieroglyphs. That she should be forced to engage in such stealthy activity was galling, but how else was she to snatch some precious moments alone with the collection, without the interference of anyone and, most especially, Mr. Beauchamp? Of course, she really couldn't avoid him, not when her father dictated that she work with him, but she could do her best to avoid certain situations, such as the one last evening.

Lifting her chin and smoothing her skirts, Juliet proceeded toward the heavy table with a low sound of disgust. Moonlight! Lips! What nonsense! She had spent the night trying to determine what had come over her, with no success. All she knew was that her encounter with Mr. Beauchamp during the late hours had been most peculiar in every aspect, including her own behavior. Indeed, she could recall no precedent to the apparent lapse in good sense that she had suffered.

She was no henwit, after all, but a woman who had spent her entire life devoted to study and research. From her earliest efforts to read, she had been fascinated with the written word, with languages and ancient cultures, and, finally, with Egypt itself. While other young girls were learning to play the pianoforte and watercolor, she had been immersed in grammar and history. While other young ladies of the ton were dancing at Almack's and contracting marriages, she had been poring over whatever copies of ancient texts she could find.

Juliet had only one passion: the decipherment of the hieroglyphs. She certainly could not remember ever taking an interest in men. In truth, from her earliest years, she had thought them inferior, both emotionally and mentally, a fact that no doubt contributed to their efforts to keep women in a subordinate role.

Those few times when she had visited with other girls her own age, she had been baffled by their giggling and swoons over some pimply faced youth. When she grew older, one of her tutors, a gangly, skinny fellow whose expertise she questioned, had suddenly clasped her to him and declared his undying love. She had been forced to use her copy of *The Divine Legation of Moses* as a cudgel in order to free herself. That was the end of that, as well as the conclusion of her tutoring, her education being furthered by consultations with experts who were usually elderly and far more intelligent.

That incident had marked the first, and last, of her admirers. Oh, gentlemen came to visit her father and view his acquisitions, but few gave her a second glance, and those who did pronounced her a frightful bluestocking, which was just as well, since she thought them all useless twits. Only Cyril hadn't dismissed her out of turn. He had come to see some of her father's pieces and had stayed on to study the objects. His area of expertise being hieroglyphs, their shared interest had made them companionable associates.

Juliet frowned. But she was not particularly pleased with Cyril, either, since his sudden announcement yesterday that they were affianced. The proclamation had so startled her that she had said nothing at the time, and, indeed, she did not find the topic suitable for discussion among company. Nor did she have the time later to speak with him alone, a situation which would have to be remedied, no doubt, though it was an annoying distraction from her work.

Juliet sighed. She supposed Cyril might have assumed that an understanding of sorts existed between them. But he had never proposed, nor, as far as she knew, discussed a betrothal with her father. And the idea, which she might have greeted with equanimity only a few days ago, now seemed rather unappetizing. Perhaps it was because he had spoken so abruptly, without consulting her, as both he and her father had a tendency to do, much to her irritation.

If he had consulted her, Juliet was not sure what she would have said. There was certainly nothing wrong with two people who shared the same concerns joining together in matrimony. Indeed, Juliet suspected such persons would enjoy a more amiable coexistence than the usual ton alliances. And there was nothing really wrong with Cyril that precluded such an arrangement. It was just that she never had been particularly interested in him or any other man. *Until Mr. Beauchamp.*

Juliet flushed. Why that rogue should arouse her curiosity was a mystery. Perhaps it was because he was so different from the typical gentlemen of her father's social sphere or the experts with whom she corresponded. Yes, that must be it. Naturally, when confronted with an entirely new specimen, whether plant, animal, or man, one would want to study it, catalogue it, and put it neatly in its proper place. But Mr. Beauchamp wouldn't fit neatly anywhere, of that Juliet was reasonably certain.

When she realized her heart was picking up its pace at the very thought of the adventurer, Juliet turned to her work. All the time spent arguing yesterday and suffering the posturing of the two males had taken her precious attention away from where it belonged, upon the hieroglyphs. Why, she had never even had a chance to view any of those gracing the new arrivals, not even the stela that had occupied Cyril.

Normally, Juliet would have seized whatever chance she could to study the new finds, even coming down in the middle of the night, if necessary. But now that was out of the question. She would have to snatch what time she could away from the cataloguing, and it would be longer still before she had a moment to return to her efforts at deciphering. As if unleashed by the thought of that delay, a fierce longing rose up in her to closet herself with the new papyri, and only supreme strength of will—and duty—kept her from doing so.

Patience and moderation in all things, Juliet vowed, as she took up her sketchbook and moved toward the stela. Still, curiosity filled her. At dinner, Cyril had been coyly quiet about what he had seen, claiming he had not had time to make any great discoveries. Was he being circumspect or simply unwilling to share his observations? What if he should find a clue to the hidden meaning of the symbols that had eluded all others?

Juliet caught her breath, then loosed it in a low sigh, ashamed at her selfishness. As Cyril said often enough, it didn't matter who deciphered the hieroglyphs, only that someone do so. Still, the eagerness to be that person had consumed her for years, despite her attempts to quell it, which was a sad commentary on her efforts at self-discipline, she supposed.

Well, who could blame her with so many new texts to be viewed and studied, some of them right here at her fingertips? And perhaps just one of them held the key she had been missing, Juliet thought, her heart pounding with excitement as she bent to copy the ancient pictures.

So absorbed was she in her task that Juliet did not hear the arrival of her colleagues at first. Luckily, the sound of

Mr. Beauchamp's voice broke through her concentration, and she managed to close her book and rise hastily before Cyril could see what she had been doing. Although she had unlimited access to the collection, previous experience had taught her that he would accuse her of stealing the march on him should he find her examining the hieroglyphs before he had done so.

"Juliet! You are at your task early this morning," he said, but his voice held no indictment. Juliet suspected she had their guest to thank for that.

Mr. Beauchamp.

It took Juliet a moment to look at him, wary as she was of his effect upon her. But at his greeting, she flicked a glance his way. In the plain light of day, he looked more real and less a figure conjured by moonlight. However, his solid physicality was no less appealing, and she was dismayed to find him still tall and handsome, perhaps even more so. Could nothing make this man unappealing? Juliet could only hope his boorish behavior would accomplish what her own good sense could not.

"Mr. Beauchamp," she said with a nod. Wasting no time on pleasantries, she moved toward the table, ready to resume the work they had begun yesterday, only to stop and stare in confusion at the objects arrayed there.

"Is something wrong?" Mr. Beauchamp's voice came to her from a position far too close, but Juliet was so occupied with other concerns that she did not object.

"The artifacts have been moved," she said.

Cyril stepped nearer as well, presumably to view the table's cluttered surface. "Are you sure?"

"Perhaps you are mistaken," Mr. Beauchamp said.

"I most certainly am not," Juliet said. "I had stacked the papyri over there in the corner, for later study, and—"

"Maybe Lyndhurst here moved them after having a look," Mr. Beauchamp said. "That's his favorite thing, isn't it?"

"I beg your pardon, but I was working with the stela all day, as you well know," Cyril said, huffing in outrage.

"And last night?" Mr. Beauchamp asked.

"I was with the earl the whole time," Cyril said. "But I might ask the same of you."

Mr. Beauchamp swung his gaze toward Juliet, as if in question, and she flushed unaccountably. Although she had done nothing wrong during her evening encounter here, somehow she was reluctant to share the details with Cyril.

"They must have been moved during the night or early this morning," Juliet said, for she knew the objects had been where she left them during that moonlit meeting.

"Maybe a servant did it," Mr. Beauchamp said with a shrug. Apparently, he did not share her concern over the disorder.

"The servants know they are not to touch any of the antiquities, or even come into this room without good cause," Juliet said more firmly than intended.

"You were in here last night. Maybe you moved them," Mr. Beauchamp said.

Juliet glared up at him, annoyed that he would bring up their encounter again, after she had dismissed it. "Or maybe you did."

"What do you mean, she was in here last night?" Cyril demanded. "How would you know?"

Morgan shrugged. "I saw her."

"Juliet, I see no reason for you to be wandering about here at all hours," Cyril scolded. He cast a dubious glance at Beauchamp. "Especially when there are strangers in the house."

"I just wanted to check on things, but obviously it did no good, for sometime later, during the night hours, these items were moved," Juliet said.

Cyril looked at her with such a dubious expression that Juliet felt her cheeks flame. "Perhaps you simply mislaid the items. Everything is there, is it not?"

Juliet nodded, not daring herself to speak.

"Concentrate on discipline, and order will follow," Cyril advised. Then, with an air of dismissal, he turned away to resume his own study.

"Perhaps some curious servant tempted the fates, and his employment, by having a look," Mr. Beauchamp suggested.

But why would a servant, trained never to disturb anything, not put each item back where it was? The less valuable pieces of pottery had been placed in a line, while the mummified hand rested upon the papyrus, as though in protection. It was certainly an odd arrangement.

"Perhaps," Juliet said with a sigh.

"Why don't you just put it all back the way you had it, and we'll move on?" Mr. Beauchamp said. He was obviously eager to drop the subject, so Juliet could hardly waste any more time on the mystifying grouping.

Nodding, she began replacing the artifacts, but long after they had been set right once more, the incident lingered in her mind. And she was struck by the knowledge that while Cyril had not believed her, Mr. Beauchamp had. Did that mean that he had moved the objects? But why?

And if not Mr. Beauchamp, then who?

Chapter 4

❈

ONCE Juliet returned the items to their proper order, she tried to concentrate upon the task at hand. But it was a struggle to make sense out of Mr. Beauchamp's notes, even with his input. Indeed, he contributed so little that she was becoming convinced she could do better without him. Certainly, she would prefer to puzzle through the pages herself than have him standing so close that she could sense his presence without even looking.

To Juliet's dismay, she felt as though her body, a heretofore serviceable figure that had obeyed the dictates of her brain, was attuned to his. It tingled with awareness whenever he was about, whether she wished it or not. Even when she deliberately turned her head away from his imposing form, Juliet gained no respite, for she could actually *smell* him. And since she was accustomed to the odors of dust and ancient preservatives and the heavy perfume that clung to Cyril, this new scent of clean, strapping man proved intriguing.

Juliet tried not to breathe, at least through her nose, but

the effort was distracting, and she found herself growing irritable as she waited for Mr. Beauchamp to comment upon his notes. They were written in a large, sprawling hand that was hard to read, and he seemed to have just as much trouble as she did, stretching out his arm to study the scrawl as though he didn't recognize it as his own. Finally, Juliet blew out a breath of exasperation.

"Well?" she prompted.

"Don't rush me. Do you want accuracy or not?" he asked.

Since the object was not particularly valuable, a piece of pottery with little in the way of decoration, Juliet's patience was wearing thin. At this rate, she would be working with the man for months. Juliet found that possibility so alarming that she considered what would have been unthinkable just a few days ago, perhaps even hours ago. *Did it really matter precisely where the piece was found as long as its general location was known?*

Her duty to precise records warred with her desire to move on to the more interesting artifacts, especially those with hieroglyphs. She swallowed hard. "It is hardly of earth-shattering importance."

Mr. Beauchamp dropped his paper and glared at her. "Pardon me? I thought *everything* was of earth-shattering importance to you. Or didn't you spend hours badgering me yesterday about the exact square mile where that urn was unearthed?"

Juliet glared back at him. "It certainly was not hours. And I do value accuracy. However, it has never taken me this long to document only a few items," she said, her voice rising. Before she knew it, they were facing each other. And again, the tension was thick between them, but this time the air pulsed not so much with animosity as with something else. Juliet felt a wild urge to lash out at him, to goad him into some sort of action. And for a moment, she thought he would react, his mouth curling in a threatening manner, but then he shrugged.

"I need some fresh air," he said, turning to stalk off.

"Wait! You can't just leave now! What am I to put into the log?" Juliet protested.

"Whatever you please!" he answered over his shoulder, and she was left fuming in his wake.

For a minute, all Juliet could hear were the sounds of his retreating footsteps and her own rapid breathing, signaling a frustration that went beyond her work, but which she was reluctant to investigate. Then, just as she turned back to her books, the unmistakable sound of Cyril's disapproval drifted across the room. The noise startled her at first, for she had nearly forgotten the man's presence, a lapse that was not unusual when she was concentrating, but which took on new connotations in her current situation. Juliet blinked in his direction and tried to focus on what he was saying.

"I don't understand why you can't simply get on with the man," he said.

Juliet drew in a breath. Hadn't Cyril been just as outraged by Mr. Beauchamp yesterday? Or had he changed his mind after an evening of watching her father cater to the adventurer? "You, of all people, should realize how difficult it is working with him."

"Yes, but you can gain nothing from your constant bickering. It reflects ill upon you," Cyril replied.

"He upsets me," Juliet said over her shoulder.

"Obviously. But you cannot allow yourself to sink to his level, to raise your voice, no matter the provocation. Discipline, Juliet. Discipline," he intoned.

Juliet turned her head to stare at her colleague, who did not even deign to look at her, and suddenly, she felt like tossing the pottery right in his face. She drew back, genuinely shocked by such an urge. Even if the piece wasn't that valuable, it was part of history and should not be mishandled. Eyeing her shaking fingers with some surprise, Juliet deliberately set it down.

Oblivious to her reaction, Cyril continued speaking from across the room. "This querulousness is the product of a disordered mind, and nothing can be accomplished when the mind is not ordered," he said. Or rather, he *lectured*.

Juliet stared at him, startled by that discovery. Although she had never noticed it before, she realized that Cyril was always lecturing her. How long had he been doing so? she wondered in genuine bafflement.

Originally, she had welcomed Cyril's company because of their shared interests. Having spent so much time working alone, she was eager for a stimulating exchange of ideas. But at some point, the exchange had stopped, and Cyril had expounded upon his theories while dismissing her own. He told her how she ought to behave, what to think, and what to study. And she had allowed it.

Admittedly, she was usually distracted by her research and rarely paid heed to the opinions of Cyril or her father. Indeed, before Mr. Beauchamp's arrival, Juliet had settled into her male-dominated world with a degree of fatalistic acceptance, if not equanimity. But now, her long dormant resentments stirred. It was as though the adventurer had woken her from a stupor, unleashing her pent feelings as well as her tongue.

"I might ask you something, Cyril," Juliet said, emboldened by her new awareness. "Just why did you tell Mr. Beauchamp that we are engaged?"

Cyril turned to her in surprise, his face growing even paler, if that were possible. Obviously, he was stunned by her plain speech, or else he had no proper explanation for his actions.

"I simply said that to, why, to protect you, of course," he sputtered. "Men such as Beauchamp are known to prey on unsuspecting young women."

"I believe I am safe here in my father's house," Juliet said, though she felt her heart pick up its pace at the thought of the dangerous Mr. Beauchamp.

Cyril's eyes narrowed as he looked at her. "You don't want his attentions, do you?"

"Certainly not," Juliet answered. She turned back to her work, effectively dismissing the subject. But her thoughts strayed from her task, back to a moment in the moonlight, until she caught herself. She had always been a quiet sort, nearly invisible to all except the community of Egyptian scholars. She did her father's bidding and conducted her own studies in near solitude, glad of the lack of interruptions, eager for the opportunity granted her. Now, she could barely concentrate, plagued as she was by unseemly emotions, wild notions about moonlight and manly smells and erratic urges to throw things.

It was all Mr. Beauchamp's fault.

Juliet frowned. Suppressing a wave of giddiness that rushed over her at the very thought of the man, she bit her lip. This wretched state of affairs could not continue. No matter how tempting it might be to behave in an unconventional manner, she was no adventurer. She would not be flitting off to Egypt once her task was complete. Her life was here, and she had to exist in her world as best she could.

So whatever resentments Mr. Beauchamp had loosed would just have to go back where they came from, for giving vent to them would not change a thing. She would simply have to behave herself, ignoring the man's attempts at provocation and stifling her own tendencies to provoke him in turn.

Juliet heaved a sigh. She felt better already. She was determined to face Mr. Beauchamp, when he returned, with renewed patience. She even managed to glance at Cyril without wanting to toss something at his head. He was right about a disorderly mind, for it was difficult to concentrate when one wasn't completely focused on the business at hand. But he was mistaken on one point, at least.

She would never marry him.

* * *

MORGAN studied his companion carefully and made his move. If he leaned in just a bit, like so . . . Ah! He caught a whiff of the lady's subtle perfume and tried not to appear too obvious about it. His was a delicate balance between a pose of interest in whatever she was doing and his ulterior motive of disturbing her with his presence. It might be petty, but it was the only way he had found to entertain himself.

After a frustrating morning in which he had walked away rather than start another argument with the lady, Morgan had finally found the perfect working method. Not that he didn't like fighting with her. Morgan's lips quirked as he decided there was something invigorating about their exchanges. But the coxcomb complained, and Juliet stiffened, and then it wasn't much fun anymore.

Frowning, Morgan shrugged off thoughts of Lyndhurst and focused on his new technique. He had perfected it during the long afternoon hours and was quite pleased with himself. It was all too easy, really. He would edge closer, and Juliet would become flustered like some schoolgirl at her first dance, flush pink, and try to inch away. How she had managed to grow into a woman without acquiring stronger social skills was beyond Morgan, but he had to admit he found her naiveté rather appealing, especially since she seemed to know far too much about everything else.

Not that he had plans to educate her in that regard. Morgan knew better than to dally with the daughter of his employer, no matter how tempting it was to teach *her* a thing or two. But he didn't mind jolting her from her cool demeanor just to enliven the tedium of the day and to put her squarely in her place.

The woman was so maddening, with her exacting questions and her belittling looks, that Morgan had to do something, or he might just wring her neck. No. It was better not to think about touching her, even in violence, or he might remember just how soft her cheek had felt beneath his fingers last night. Too soft. So soft he couldn't help wondering just how the rest of her might feel.

Luckily, she was so exasperating that such things didn't cross his mind very often . . . except perhaps now when he noticed the gracefulness of her hands, how her slender fingers handled everything with such delicacy, and imagined them handling him. . . .

Morgan blew out a breath and reminded himself of how often she pointed accusingly with those same fingers, wagging them in a scold, or how she attempted to tell him his business, or, worst of all, order him about. Morgan's mouth tightened. He didn't take direction from anyone, especially a woman.

Morgan shifted his feet, seized by a sudden restlessness. This cataloguing reminded him too much of studies, of being tortured by some tutor or another, feeling stupid and hating it and wanting to escape to the out of doors. There was entirely too much standing around and waiting on *her ladyship*. Morgan glanced at one of the windows, eager for respite, but dismissed the notion. He had already stepped out once today, and each delay only cost him more time, postponing his eventual return to Egypt.

He was beginning to rue this assignment, which had been part of the bargain with Carlisle. It was only too bad that he hadn't found some other buyer who didn't care about accurate records, but the earl had the money to pay for what he wanted, and, caught up in the heady euphoria of a successful sale, Morgan had agreed. Now he frowned. He disliked being obligated to anyone, especially a lord— and his lady.

Morgan shifted again. Although drafty, the ballroom suddenly seemed stifling, an overdecorated hothouse that was caging him in. He opened his mouth to complain about the pace only to shut it again, wary of an argument that might set off Lyndhurst. Not that he didn't like setting off Lyndhurst . . .

Morgan grinned at the thought, then surveyed the table until he spied a nearby papyrus. He had been preoccupied with Juliet most of the day. Perhaps it was time to find his entertainment elsewhere.

"Here, record this next, as I remember exactly where it was purchased," he said, handing the piece to Juliet.

His intention was to annoy the coxcomb, who was abnormally possessive about the hieroglyphs, so he wasn't prepared for Juliet's reaction. Although Morgan knew that she liked such things, he was not expecting the sudden change his suggestion wrought. Her fingers trembled as they reached for the papyrus, and when she glanced up at him, her eyes were bright behind her spectacles, her cheeks pink, and her lovely features suffused with a glow of expectancy. It was as though his simple words had brought her to life.

Morgan found himself stirring as well.

"Do you think we should?" she whispered, and Morgan jerked in response. He probably would have agreed to anything just then. In fact, he had a hard time remembering what they were discussing. He stared down at her face, desire coursing through him, while she turned her adoring gaze to . . . the papyrus.

"What? What's that you have there?" The sound of Lyndhurst's shrill voice broke through Morgan's daze. Here, after all, was the reaction Morgan had been looking for, but now it wasn't so welcome. Had he originally sought to upset the coxcomb? Now, he only wanted the fellow to leave so he could investigate the changeable Lady Juliet more thoroughly than any artifact. He'd start by seizing her about the waist and setting her on the table, so that those glorious golden eyes, suddenly alight with warmth, looked only upon him, at the living, not the dead, the future, not the past. . . .

"Here, now, what are you doing?" Lyndhurst asked, rushing forward, his pale face even whiter than usual. "I thought we had agreed that the papyri take too long to study and should be saved until all else is completed."

Morgan barely spared him a glance. "You're the one who likes arranging things by size," he said, with a smirk.

Lyndhurst didn't answer but attached himself to Juliet's side. Like some rat snatching at his last meal, he was practically frothing at the mouth. Morgan shook his head at the frenzy, which, though expected, was not as amusing as he had anticipated. Of course, Morgan only had himself to blame for his frustration. He hadn't realized that Juliet was quite that enamored of old drawings. If so, he would have trotted out his own papyrus. Hell, he would have brought home a cartload and laid them at her feet.

Unfortunately, the object of his interest had forgotten his existence, and now that her attention was focused elsewhere, Morgan felt a bit, well, neglected. He stepped close, even going so far as to brush against her, but she remained intent on the hieroglyphs.

Indeed, she stared at the old pictures with a kind of awe that made Morgan pause, an odd sensation skittering up his spine. His eyes narrowed as he studied her, a sense of familiarity nagging him until he realized that he recognized the expression she wore. Hell, he knew what she was feeling. It was the same thing he felt when he came upon a long-hidden tomb or treasure: triumph, wonder, and reverence, all wrapped up in an exhilaration like no other.

Suddenly, Morgan was struck with a sense of kinship for this woman, a soul-deep connection that he had never even known with Chauncey, who had dug in the sand by his side. Oh, Chauncey liked a good find. He enjoyed the hunt, admired the craftsmanship of the Egyptians, and looked forward to the rewards. But it wasn't the same. Morgan knew that his friend didn't share the heart-pounding ex-

citement that he did, the wild mixture of elation and curiosity that showed right now on Lady Juliet's face.

The knowledge made Morgan back away warily even as
he tried to deny it. He told himself that he didn't have anything in common with a pampered earl's daughter, that
they couldn't be more different in every way, and yet
somehow that thought pained him. So did the realization
that she was looking at a papyrus in a way she had never
looked at him. And most likely never would.

"I can't see, Beauchamp, and I believe I can provide
more insight into the ancient symbols than you," the coxcomb said, and for once Morgan gave way, stepping aside
with a grunt.

"Ah, the bird!" Lyndhurst said, practically preening at
the chance to appear intelligent. "It is a symbol of rebirth,
of a change to come." Although the coxcomb's interest was
obvious, it was not the same as Juliet's, for he wore more
of a hungry, greedy look. "With such new additions to my
accumulated knowledge, I will soon have the entire system
deciphered."

It was a bold claim and one in which Morgan wouldn't
put much credence in the best of times. Standing here
watching the coxcomb brag as he hovered over Juliet made
it even more unpalatable. "Really?" Morgan asked, not
bothering to hide his skepticism. "There are an awful lot of
hieroglyphs. It's not like a real language."

"Of course not! The pictures contain symbolic messages, not literal translations," Lyndhurst said, making his
contempt obvious.

Morgan's fingers itched to choke the contempt out of
him. Surely, Lady Juliet wasn't impressed by the coxcomb's ramblings? She was quiet, as though oblivious to
both men, her attention firmly focused on the drawings,
and Morgan couldn't help but wonder: "And what do you
think, *my lady?*"

"What? Oh, I definitely believe it is a language, a language that existed during the times of the pharaohs, when various tongues were spoken and *this* was written," she said, reaching out to trace a finger slowly over one faded symbol. The simple gesture, tender, full of wonder, and at the same time subtly erotic, made Morgan's mouth dry. He followed her movements and found himself staring down at the pictures.

Hieroglyphs were certainly not his specialty. He knew that the Englishman Thomas Young had made some headway deciphering them, and other scholars were working on the secrets as well, but the theories varied. So far no one was sure what they meant.

"Nonsense!" Lyndhurst said, dismissing Juliet's words out of hand. "You are too enamored of Zoega!"

For once, the lady ignored the coxcomb's blustering, her finger gliding over a symbol with such delicacy that Morgan shuddered. "See that?" she whispered. "The oval ring with a bar at one end contains names of royalty or deities."

"You're not still spouting Barthelemy, are you?" Lyndhurst asked. With a sniff of disapproval, he launched into a lecture on what he deemed to be the true meaning of the drawings, but even Morgan could tell that the man was mired in old notions about symbolic messages and arcane religious ritual.

Lady Juliet, with her extraordinary knowledge of Egypt and languages, with her quiet assertions and attention to detail, seemed by far the more intelligent of the two and much closer to the ultimate goal of decipherment. It was something that Morgan had never even considered, but now, standing here, watching Juliet bend over the papyrus rapt and eager, it seemed a very real possibility. Of course, Morgan had always known the lady was intelligent, but now that he realized how devoted she was to the subject, he began to wonder about the extent of her studies—and if he could put her cleverness to good use.

And just as suddenly, her excitement became his own.

MORGAN leaned back in his chair and listened to the earl drone on. It was part of the price he had to pay for his hefty fee and the elegant accommodations. But having just eaten his fill of a variety of excellent French and English dishes, he was willing to ignore the cost for awhile, as long as he wasn't trapped all evening with the earl and the coxcomb. In fact, he was just wondering how best to escape when Lady Juliet rose from her seat.

"Adjourning already, Juliet?" her father asked. "We haven't begun to think about our brandy yet. Have we, gentlemen?"

Morgan refrained from comment. He was already thinking about how to *skip* the brandy.

"I'm sorry, Father, but I have a headache. If you don't mind, I think I'll excuse myself a bit early," she said.

"Certainly," the earl replied with a nod of dismissal. Juliet hadn't even made it to the door before her father resumed his monologue upon the difficulties of mounting a proper exhibition for his collections.

Morgan frowned at the lack of parental concern. It was not the first time he had noticed the earl's treatment of his only child. Surely, any good father would inquire about her illness? But the lapse did not surprise Morgan. The luxurious houses of the rich and pampered were often far chillier than the coldest cottage.

Morgan's own concern was felled by the suspicion that the lovely lady didn't have a headache at all but was returning, as she had last evening, to the ballroom to check on her treasures. If so, she would soon find herself with company again. Stifling a surge of expectation, Morgan turned toward his host and pretended attention, while his thoughts wandered ahead to that meeting.

So when the time came for brandy, Morgan refused the offer, professing plans to take a walk out of doors. Since the weather was hardly inviting, his suggestion did not meet with enthusiasm from his companions, and he was able to slip from the room with ease. But he did not head for the grounds or the streets. Instead, he made his way through the interior of the house. His steps were light, for he had learned to walk with some degree of stealth, and he avoided any servants who might report his destination. Although he only had vague notions of catching the lady in a lie, Morgan felt his blood heat with anticipation. It was almost as though he were heading toward a preordained tryst.

The notion drew him up short, forcing him to rein in his enthusiasm. He reminded himself that Juliet was a *lady*, a spoiled earl's daughter, even if she did have a talent for hieroglyphs. It was the latter that interested him, Morgan told himself, and he would do well to remember that. This evening rendezvous simply provided him with an opportunity to improve relations with the lady. And if she owed him for not spilling her secrets, so much the better. Morgan grinned.

At the entrance to the ballroom, he paused. Inside, he could see the glow of a candelabra that told him she had learned not to trust to moonlight. But she was here. And alone. Well, after last night, she had fair warning, Morgan thought. He felt his pulse kick and told himself it was the prospect of disturbing her that excited him. After all, he had to amuse himself somehow during this dismal assignment, didn't he?

Walking over the threshold, Morgan began his slow, silent pursuit. But this time, his quarry turned to face him well before he reached her, making him wonder if he was losing his touch. Or perhaps she was a step ahead of him. Morgan faltered as the disconcerting thought crossed his mind, then he forged ahead with new determination. Although he would have preferred to come upon her unobserved, the lady's reaction did not disappoint him.

"Mr. Beauchamp. I should have guessed you would appear here even after I expressly asked you not to," she said, all stiff and serious. But Morgan knew better. He knew *her* better.

"Did you?" he asked, stepping closer. "I'm afraid my memory of last night is a bit hazy."

Her delicate brows furrowed in a delightful manner. "Why? Were you drinking?" she asked, ever curious, ever studying. Even him. The thought gave Morgan pause. He didn't like anyone looking too closely, even himself. For a moment, he had the odd sensation that he was taking on more than he could handle, getting himself in too deep, and that this time, there was more than permits at stake. But before him, he saw only a woman, and he donned a careless smile.

"No. I wasn't drunk. Just intoxicated," Morgan said, cornering her by the mummy case.

She frowned but held her ground. "Really, I must ask you to return to the others, for you can have no business being here at this hour," she said. Despite her bold speech, Morgan noticed that she clutched at the reliquary behind her, as if seeking purchase.

"But I'm not the one with the headache," Morgan said, halting in front of her. As expected, his accusation flustered her, and he nearly shook his head in amazement. She argued the finer points of hieroglyph theories without blinking, but caught in a white lie, she lost all poise. Surely she couldn't be that rarity of rarities, an honest woman?

"I, uh, did have a touch of the megrims, but once away from the table, I began to feel better," she said.

Morgan cut her off with a lift of his hand. "Save the bouncers for the others," he said. He stretched out his fingers, but she slipped from his grasp to inch around the mummy case.

He began to wonder if the dreamy look he had seen in her exacting eyes the night before had been a product of his own hopes and the moonlight. They had stood closer to the table then. She had shivered when he touched her, her eyes huge as she stared up at him. And he had nearly kissed her, desire overcoming his better judgment, but a full day of annoyances at her tyrannical hands had brought him back to his senses. Hadn't it?

He wasn't here to woo her, Morgan reminded himself, and he hesitated, unsure for a moment exactly what he was doing. Then, something about the rather panicked look in her eyes brought a predatory smile to his face. Obviously, the lady was not unaffected by him, but just how affected was she?

Morgan stepped easily around the artifact and stopped in front of her. She had nowhere to go, having backed up against the wall, and once again, he was struck by her lack of sophistication in certain situations. She reminded him of a cornered rabbit, beautiful, vulnerable, and his for the taking. Lifting his arms, he rested his hands against the carved plaster behind her, neatly caging her.

Slowly, carefully, he looked down at her face, his gaze tracing her gilded features, delicate and lovely, yet hiding an inner strength and passion that he sensed she was unaware of, a combination that he found rather enticing. His pulse kicked up its pace, and without a thought to the consequences, he bent his head.

"Juliet!"

Morgan winced as the grating sound of Lyndhurst's voice reached his ears. He swore under his breath, his first inclination being to roust the intruder and continue where he had left off. However, he belatedly recalled that the lady trapped before him was this man's fiancée, and that he needed to keep up appearances, for her sake, if nothing else.

Although this wasn't the first time he had been caught in a difficult situation, Morgan realized that his breathing was labored and his body hard. Thankfully, the near darkness hid a multitude of sins, and Lyndhurst had barely entered the room. Casually dropping his arms, Morgan turned to face the coxcomb. He could only hope the fellow was stupid enough to believe they were working at this hour. Well, they hadn't been doing anything else. *Yet.*

"Juliet! You are not examining another papyrus, are you?" the coxcomb called out in a shrill scold.

"No, Cyril," Juliet answered, her voice a breathy whisper that sent desire skittering along Morgan's flesh. *If only she were saying, "Yes, Morgan," instead.*

Huffing, the coxcomb reached them, but rather than question their intimacy, he looked round, as though searching for evidence. "You think I don't know what you're doing?" Lyndhurst asked, his voice rising.

Morgan certainly hoped not. He tried to look appropriately innocent.

"Well, you won't steal the march on me," he said, rounding on Juliet. "Any *man* of science would never try to sneak looks at the specimens before a measured study can be conducted. I should have known when you left the dining room so precipitously that you were up to something."

Was the man raving about hieroglyphs? Morgan opened his mouth to ask, but the coxcomb cut him off.

"And you! When did you develop this sudden interest in hieroglyphs? You know nothing of them, and you should be concerned only with deciphering your own notes!" Lyndhurst said.

Morgan could only stare, dumbfounded, as he realized that the coxcomb didn't seem the slightest bit upset about finding his betrothed alone in the near darkness with another man. Rather, he was afraid she was looking at the objects in her own father's collection. Morgan shook his head. If he found his fiancée in this position, he would punch first and ask questions later. Not that he would ever have a fiancée, Morgan thought with a frown.

"We were not looking at any hieroglyphs, Cyril," Juliet said. "I just came in here to check on things, after the odd incident this morning, and Mr. Beauchamp, uh, followed me in."

The coxcomb looked from Juliet to Morgan and back again, then swallowed convulsively. "Well, I should hope that your professional ethics would hold you in good stead," he said. He drew a deep breath. "All seems to be in order then?" he asked, glancing about again.

All except you, Morgan thought, but Juliet nodded.

"Well, then, I suggest we all retire for the evening, Mr. Beauchamp obviously having thought better of his walk," Lyndhurst said, shooting Morgan an accusing glance.

"Yes, the weather did seem a bit . . . intimidating," Morgan said smoothly. He lifted his brows in invitation of any further comment, but the coxcomb wisely kept his mouth shut.

"Well, then, shall we go?" Lyndhurst asked briskly. Without waiting for assent, he turned on his heel and headed toward the doors, assuming that they would follow. Obviously, he was in a hurry to get everyone out of the ballroom.

Morgan's eyes narrowed, but he could find no real reason to linger, at least not any reason that he could offer to Lyndhurst. Reaching for the candelabra Juliet had set upon the table, Morgan held it high so that she could find her way out from behind the mummy case, while the coxcomb drifted away.

"Your fiancé seems a bit . . . agitated tonight," Morgan observed.

The lady did not even look at him but answered as she

brushed past. "We are not engaged," she said. Although tossed over her shoulder, her reply was firm and unmistakable, causing Morgan to halt in his tracks, his brows inching upward.

Interesting. Whatever the coxcomb's plans, apparently Juliet hadn't fallen in with them, a small fact that delighted him beyond all reason. But then, when had he ever been reasonable? With a grin, Morgan stepped forward, his eyes on the swaying skirts ahead.

Chapter 5

✠

JULIET anxiously scanned the table with its orderly display of artifacts and breathed a sigh of relief. Those items already catalogued were in their proper places, just where she had left them yesterday. Although concern for the collection had driven her here early again, she had been dismayed to meet Mr. Beauchamp strolling in from breakfast, with an even cockier grin than usual. Juliet had hurried past him with as little greeting as possible only to become sharply aware of him coming to stand behind her, far too close for comfort.

"Is everything in order?" he asked.

Juliet stilled, certain she could feel his breath upon her neck. But when she lifted a hand to the high collar of her gown, she found it securely in place. Obviously, she was letting the rogue distract her again, despite all her vows to the contrary. She lifted her chin, determined to keep to her purpose.

"I think all is where it should be," Juliet answered. Then

she walked the length of the table, just to make sure. It was a perfunctory inspection, conducted more to escape Mr. Beauchamp's nearness than to verify the position of the antiquities, but she paused near the end of the polished mahogany, her attention caught.

"Wait. No," she said, eyeing the neat rows of items in puzzlement.

"What? Is something out of place?" Mr. Beauchamp asked.

Juliet's heart leapt into her throat as she realized just what was wrong, a far worse mishap than any rearrangement. "Something is missing," she said, her gaze flying to his in alarm.

"Missing? What?" Mr. Beauchamp asked, beside her in an instant. And, for once, Juliet was too disturbed to step away. In fact, she was oddly glad of his presence, tall and strong, in the face of this calamity.

"There," she said, pointing to the spot where she had put the papyri. Gradually, she had been organizing the clutter, and she remembered the positioning exactly. "There were three, and now there are only two."

"It must be here somewhere," Beauchamp said, turning to look more thoroughly, but Juliet could have told him he was wasting his time. She knew he would not find it here. "Someone has taken it," she said with a certainty she couldn't explain.

"A papyrus?" Beauchamp scoffed as he searched the room. "There are other small objects far more valuable to the average thief and easier to pocket."

"No. It's gone," Juliet said. Something in her voice must have caught his attention, for he lifted his head to slant her a questioning look. "But why that particular papyrus? Why not all of them?"

"I don't know," Juliet answered, gazing at him helplessly. At least he wasn't dismissing her claims as her father or Cyril surely would have done. "It was the one with the torn corner, smaller than the others."

"And perhaps easier to hide?" Beauchamp asked. "I remember it now. I bought it off a man in Gizeh. The natives are becoming aware of the market for these things. But I still don't understand what kind of fool would take a papyrus and leave gold behind."

Juliet was about to protest that his values were far different from her own, when he swung round once more, his dark eyes meeting hers with heart-stopping intensity. "Lyndhurst," he muttered.

Juliet blinked, shocked by the suggestion. "I'm sure Cyril would never do such a thing. Why would he, when he has access to everything here?"

"Because he's afraid you will see something before he does," Mr. Beauchamp answered. "Let's face it, the fellow's as queer as Dick's hatband, especially when it comes to hieroglyphs."

Juliet drew herself up stiffly. "If Cyril is devoted to his work, that hardly makes him insane."

Mr. Beauchamp simply raised his brows, irritating her further. Perhaps Cyril wasn't the most congenial of colleagues, but he was no worse than the cadre of male scholars who made up the community of Egyptian study. Juliet opened her mouth to defend the man she had worked with these past few years when a noise made her turn toward the doorway.

As though he had been conjured by their conversation, there Cyril stood, looking no different than any other day. Juliet examined him closely, noticing the clothing that now seemed far too fussy and elaborate, the paleness of his face and hair, and the aloof expression upon his features. His was the demeanor of a man of science, a bit stuffy compared to Mr. Beauchamp's casual behavior, but certainly not that of a burglar—or a lunatic.

Apparently, Mr. Beauchamp did not share her view.

"Where's the papyrus, Lyndhurst?" he asked, his voice low and decidedly dangerous.

Swinging back toward the adventurer, Juliet recognized his threatening stance and hurried to put herself between the two men, lest they brawl in the ballroom, where the slightest misstep could wreak havoc on centuries-old artifacts. With a frantic glance toward the antiquities, she tried to slow the thundering of her heart, which was reacting to the possibility of violence and certainly *not* to Mr. Beauchamp's masculine strength.

"A papyrus is missing," she explained.

Cyril looked genuinely startled. "What? How?"

"That's what we would like to know," Mr. Beauchamp said.

"And why should I know anything about it?" Cyril demanded in his high-pitched voice.

"You were the one obsessed with hieroglyphs yesterday. I believe you even accused the lady, who owns them all, of daring to take a look before you, a simple guest in her home," Mr. Beauchamp said.

Cyril sniffed, his expression one of utter contempt. No doubt he was offended, and yet he seemed excessively arrogant, a prig looking down on the man who had provided the very items he coveted.

"First of all, this collection does not belong to Juliet but to her father," he said, and Juliet felt herself flush. She knew her place in the household without Cyril pointing it out so rudely. He took no notice of her, however, and continued to rail against Mr. Beauchamp. "And my interest in hieroglyphs hardly makes me a robber! I suppose I'm the one who rearranged the objects yesterday, as well? What is your explanation for that?" he taunted.

Juliet glanced toward Mr. Beauchamp, hoping that this would be the end of the discussion. She really didn't think Cyril capable of such perfidy, especially considering that he worked under the good graces of her father, a temperamental man, at best. So, when Mr. Beauchamp shrugged, Juliet loosed a breath of relief, only to draw it in again sharply at the hard set of his jaw.

"The earl will be notified," he said. His dark gaze held a menacing glint that Juliet recognized, but if she shivered, it was solely on Cyril's account. It certainly had nothing to do with Mr. Beauchamp's dangerous demeanor, of which no sensible woman could approve.

"And well he should be notified," Cyril said. "Though I don't see how it is any of *your* concern. You no longer own anything in this room," he added with a smirk.

Mr. Beauchamp lifted his dark brows slightly, as if turning Cyril's mocking words back upon him. "Perhaps, but once something has been marked as mine, I look after it."

His declaration hung heavy in the air, a subtle threat to Cyril, but Juliet heard a very different sort of promise in his deep voice, and her heart stepped up its beat accordingly.

ALTHOUGH Morgan wasted no time making good on his threat, he was forced to kick his heels waiting upon the earl. By the time he finally was called into the man's study, the papyrus could have been sold to one of England's other collectors . . . if it wasn't tucked away in Lyndhurst's apartments. Morgan had been tempted to have a look or to send Chauncey to investigate, but the coxcomb's valet had been sticking close to his room, perhaps on his master's orders.

Of course, it really wasn't Morgan's problem. He had delivered the merchandise agreed upon, and he couldn't be blamed for what happened afterwards, especially in the earl's own home. Still, if the coxcomb or anyone else were stealing artifacts beneath his nose, someone ought to let the old man know about it.

Or so Morgan thought. But when he stepped into the study, the earl already seemed to know why he was there.

Enthroned like Ali himself in an expansive gilt chair that was some English designer's idea of Egyptian style, Carlisle motioned for Morgan to take a far less prepossessing seat.

"I assume you're here about the missing papyrus," he said. Then, as though undisturbed by the matter, he proceeded to inspect a tray of elaborately decorated pastries presented by the burly butler himself.

After choosing a delicate cake, the earl glanced up with a smug expression of superiority. But Morgan wasn't impressed. He knew that news traveled fast, even in a household the size of this one. It would have been more startling if the earl weren't aware of every happening under his roof. What was surprising was the man's casual attitude about the disappearance.

"You aren't concerned?" Morgan asked.

"I'm sure it will turn up here somewhere," the earl said as he popped an entire confection into his mouth.

"I doubt that it has been misplaced, my lord," Morgan said. "In fact, there is some concern that it has been stolen."

Swallowing heavily, the earl dusted the crumbs from his fingers. "I can assure you that everyone in my household is utterly trustworthy. And as for those outside of it . . . No one would dare steal from me," he said, his confident gaze daring Morgan to dispute him.

But Morgan was not intimidated. He certainly had no designs on the earl's property, so he met the man's stare evenly. However, he was tempted to argue. Being rich and powerful protected the earl to some degree, but his ostentatious living invited the less fortunate members of the city's teeming populace to rob him. And all it took was one daring fellow.

"Perhaps someone should question the servants, just to see if they noticed anything unusual," Morgan suggested.

The earl's hand hovered over the tray as he considered

another sweet. "The servants are normally occupied elsewhere, for obvious reasons, but a footman who was in the general area reported hearing strange noises coming from the ballroom. Both my edict to stay out of the room and his own superstitious nature prevented him from investigating, which is just as well. I do not want any laymen rattling around amongst my treasures, and I hardly think a burglar would cause a discernable racket. Nor would he slip away with nothing except a scrap of hieroglyphs."

Morgan couldn't dispute that bit of logic. "I admit I don't see the significance of that particular papyrus," he said.

The earl finally selected a piece of marzipan. "Personally, I have little interest in writings that no one can understand, although I realize that one must preserve history where one can," he said before popping the sweet into his mouth.

Morgan nearly flinched at the earl's bald rejection of one of the most breathtaking sights in Egypt, or, indeed, the world itself. Perhaps if Carlisle had stood in the Temple of Isis and seen for himself the huge images rising on the walls to glorious heights, he might change his mind. Or perhaps not. Rich dilettantes like the earl were often more interested in gold, jewelry, and showy pieces like the alabaster mummy case—whatever might be lorded over others as the finest treasures.

On the other hand, his daughter reserved her passion for the pictures, a fact that Morgan acknowledged with grudging respect. A rush of heat at the memory of that passion caught him by surprise, and he shifted in his seat, unwilling to think about Juliet in her father's presence. However, she wasn't the only one in the household interested in the symbols. Morgan studied the older man with narrowed eyes.

"But there are others here who prefer hieroglyphs, including one who seems quite put out when your daughter and I catalogue something he hasn't inspected first," he said.

"Lyndhurst? Oh, he's harmless," the earl said, dismissing the coxcomb with a wave of one pudgy hand. "The fellow doesn't have the daring required for thievery, and besides, I put no restrictions on his studies. Why would he steal something to which he already has access?"

Why, indeed? Morgan wondered. But could Lyndhurst really see anything in the collection at any time? He was bound by a certain decorum to work during the daylight hours and to attend his host, the earl. Although he could study whatever he wished while Lady Juliet was busy cataloguing, he obviously feared she would see something he had not, no matter how briefly she looked at the writings. The coxcomb probably suspected she would progress further in her decipherment, a realistic concern, since his own theories were highly unlikely.

Of course, Morgan might be letting his opinion of the coxcomb color his thinking. Was that what the earl was doing, as well? Morgan slanted the older man a glance. Despite Juliet's denial, there was always the possibility that the earl saw the coxcomb as his heir and was grooming him as such, with or without his daughter's consent. Morgan's hand tightened into a fist.

"Perhaps Sir Lyndhurst's possessiveness is understandable, considering his expectations," he suggested.

"What's that?" the earl asked, his brows knitting in one of the few gestures that resembled his daughter. Somehow, on the earl, the sight was not endearing.

"Sir Lyndhurst claims that he is affianced to your daughter," Morgan said.

The earl's small eyes widened as though they might pop from his head, and he snorted in derision. At the sound, Morgan felt a sudden tension in his shoulders ease, and his fingers uncurled.

"I don't know where you got that idea," the earl said, chuckling.

From Lyndhurst himself, Morgan thought, but he refrained from repeating himself.

The earl leaned back in his chair. "He's a good enough fellow, to be sure, but he only has the lesser title and little property, which hardly makes him a suitable match for my daughter. As it stands now, the bulk of my estate and my titles will go to my nephew George Cavendish, not exactly the man I would have chosen, but obviously of better lineage than a mere baronet," he said, with another snort.

"Of course, all that may change if Juliet marries, which she is free to do, as long as the fellow is more suitable, someone from the ranks of the country's finest families. I have no intention of handing over my wealth to a fortune hunter," the earl said, his expression hardening. "Certainly nothing less than an earldom would be acceptable for alliance with the Carlisle title."

Morgan felt a measure of relief, a reaction he could only put down to the fact that he wouldn't wish the coxcomb on any woman. But tension crept back into his shoulders as the earl expounded upon the kind of man who would qualify as a son-in-law. Morgan couldn't claim to be surprised at the man's standards, for he had already pegged the earl as a greedy bastard, a fine example of England's most arrogant breed. What was surprising was the fact that he hadn't sold Juliet to the highest bidder already.

Most daughters of the nobility were married not long out of the schoolroom. And despite the earl's inflated opinion of himself and his family, Morgan knew that in the exacting world of the ton, beautiful young women who remained unwed were quickly labeled as ape leaders. Perhaps the earl wanted to keep his unpaid expert as long as possible, a selfish desire in keeping with his character, but one which boded ill for Juliet's future as anything other than a spinster. Morgan felt an odd, unsettling sensation in his gut at the thought.

"Don't worry about Lyndhurst, or the papyrus, for that matter," the earl said. "It has simply been misplaced. My daughter, for all her skills, is not infallible. She concentrates on one thing to the detriment of others that require her attention. No doubt, she will soon come across her missing piece," he said, carefully wiping his fingers on a linen cloth.

Morgan's head came up at the comment, and he had to bite back an argument. The earl was the fallible member of the family, he thought, disliking the man all the more. However, he paid well. So, with a shrug, Morgan rose to leave. He had done his duty and would leave it at that.

But the instincts Morgan had honed in the alleys of Cairo and Thebes remained alert. He didn't like the situation at Carlisle's town house, the strained atmosphere, the odd happenings, and most especially the theft of a papyrus, of all things. It made him wonder at the wisdom of staying, despite the money, the baths, the excellent food, and . . . other considerations.

However, there was still the possibility he could leave here even farther ahead than he had imagined, and that possibility kept him in place. For now. He would simply have to tear Chauncey away from the housemaids and put him on the lookout for anything unusual. And Morgan fully intended to keep his own eye out, as well.

Especially on the coxcomb.

JULIET tried to keep her mind on what she was doing, but she felt strangely bereft without the stolid presence of Mr. Beauchamp by her side—the stolid, annoying, and thoroughly distracting presence, she reminded herself. He had left without a word, presumably to talk to her father, and she knew she ought to be thankful he was gone. She certainly had difficulty focusing her attention on her work when he was near. But now she found it equally hard to do so without him. With no little alarm, she wondered if she would ever be able to concentrate again.

Apparently, Cyril was doing no better than she was, because Juliet kept hearing him mutter to himself. She had learned long ago not to interrupt him when he was studying hieroglyphs, so she had not commented thus far. But the noise was beginning to grate on her already strained nerves. "Did you say something?" she asked.

Cyril stopped muttering and poked his head up to glare at her. "I can't believe you stood by and allowed that . . . that adventurer to malign my good name!"

Juliet sighed. She should have expected as much. Now, more than ever, she rued Beauchamp's departure, for a lecture on what she should or should not have done during the recent contretemps was surely forthcoming.

"I cannot believe a rogue like that practically accused me of outright theft!" Cyril said, fuming.

Normally, Juliet would have listened, vaguely, to the harangue, but her patience was worn thin. "If I recall, you told me to ignore the man."

At this unusual parry, Cyril's face turned red, or rather a mixture of deathly white and crimson patches. Spotty, really. Juliet realized she had never noticed how unattractive the combination was, especially on Cyril's already bland features.

"How you can compare the minor irritations of working with the man to outright slander is beyond my comprehension!" Cyril said. "I was forced to listen to vile insinuations. . . . Why, it's preposterous, especially when he's nothing more than a robber himself, though highly paid for his thievery."

Juliet was surprised at the hot flush that rose to her cheeks at Cyril's arrogant dismissal of Mr. Beauchamp's work, which provided them both with the means to continue their studies. And even though she often found Mr. Beauchamp exasperating, Juliet decided that she did not want to hear Cyril abuse him.

Indeed, the more Cyril complained, the more Juliet felt she ought to defend the absent adventurer. After all, he was her father's liaison in Egypt and had well repaid the earl's faith in him by returning with a fantastic collection of antiquities anyone would be thrilled to see. He had not stumbled across them but had dug for them himself or bargained with volatile and dangerous natives.

Unlike some ignorant traveler, he had a solid knowledge of his subject, as evidenced by the items he had chosen. And his notes and drawings, though poorly executed, showed that he made an attempt to document his finds, along with other sites he had viewed, including tombs and temples, for which he received no reimbursement. That he had taken the time to laboriously sketch these sites for posterity said much for the man.

Setting aside her personal feelings, Juliet realized that they both owed Mr. Beauchamp their respect and gratitude. Certainly, he was annoying at times, but other than that, what was his crime? Poor organization? Bad notes? Arguing with both Cyril and herself? It all seemed so petty in the face of the man's accomplishments.

Turning toward her colleague, Juliet said as much. "I think that in light of Mr. Beauchamp's success, we should give him the thanks he is due."

"Thanks? Thanks for robbery!" Cyril said, scoffing.

Juliet frowned. "I'm sure he is no worse than the other men employed to recover artifacts from Egypt."

"Just so!" Cyril said. "They are all a pack of thieving dogs!"

Juliet blinked, taken aback by Cyril's vehemence. Had he always felt this strongly? Perhaps she had never listened closely to his ranting. But this time, she could not turn a deaf ear to such blatant nonsense. Drawing a deep breath, Juliet prepared to argue with him.

"I hardly think Drovetti, Salt, and the other men who procured vast collections for the world's museums should be lumped together with the cutpurses of London," she said.

Although Cyril looked both astounded and enraged by

her response, Juliet went on. "And what of those who purchase their finds? What exactly does that make my father?"

Cyril must have realized the error in his logic, for he appeared to regain control of himself. He stood there for a moment, mouth working, and then bowed his head. "I beg your pardon, Juliet, but you know how I feel about removing antiquities from their native soil. As much as we admire the treasures and relish the chance to examine them, they belong to the land, to history. Men such as Beauchamp, and yes, even Salt and Drovetti, are robbing Egypt of its heritage."

Now, at least, he sounded more reasonable. But if Cyril felt so strongly about the subject, why didn't he campaign to end these practices, instead of availing himself of the opportunities provided by men like her father? Indeed, Juliet realized that she had never heard Cyril express these views to the earl, who would likely withdraw his generous invitation to study at the suggestion he was little better than a grave robber.

But then, men were always talking out of both sides of their mouths, Juliet acknowledged. *Except perhaps Mr. Beauchamp.* The thought came to her unbidden, but true. He seemed to spit out his opinion without prevarication, not caring whether it would be well received or not. Reluctantly, Juliet had to admire him for that. She couldn't imagine him lying or toadying or behaving in any other manner than his own blunt way, obnoxious as that might be at times.

She smiled slightly, surprised that the thought of Mr. Beauchamp could amuse her, but it did. More surprising was the realization that it had been a long time since she had been amused. Juliet frowned. She had been working too hard lately between her father's demands and her studies of hieroglyphs. But then, that was her life. That had always been her life. So why did she suddenly feel a wistful regret for something more?

"Well?" Cyril asked.

Juliet blinked at him, having lost track of what he was saying. She assumed he was still decrying the removal of antiquities from Egypt, but if so, he knew her own opinion, which was not quite as rigid as his.

Cyril frowned at her, tight-lipped. "Focus, Juliet! Focus! Can't you at least pay attention to me when I am speaking?"

Juliet once more knew the urge to toss something, but she restrained herself. "You know how I feel, Cyril," she said. "Although I agree that the objects belong in their country of origin, it is too late to stop the wholesale trade in history. And until it is stopped, perhaps by a stronger Egyptian government, it is better that these items be purchased by museums and collectors who will take care of them."

Cyril took a deep breath, obviously preparing to dispute her words and deliver another lecture, but Juliet was spared by the return of Mr. Beauchamp. *Her rescuer.* If her heart gave a jolt at the sight of him, it was only because, well, she was so relieved by his interruption.

"Ah, Beauchamp," Cyril said, turning toward his new target. "We were just discussing your own penchant for thievery."

Juliet's brow furrowed, for Cyril's words made it sound as though she shared his views, which, she suddenly realized, she rarely did. That discovery was so startling, it kept her from protesting. However, from the looks of him, Mr. Beauchamp was perfectly capable of defending himself.

"And just what am I to have stolen?" he asked. No splotches marred his face, no anger flashed in his eyes, and no lectures lay poised upon his lips. He simply strolled forward with a graceful, self-assured gait and an expression to match. Indeed, he possessed a masculine confidence that Juliet found rather, well, affecting. His was not the arrogance that came from wealth or power or position or even scholarly achievements, but from the man himself.

Cyril sniffed. "And just what haven't you stolen?" he asked. "Everything in this room has been ripped from its proper berth, taken out of context, and bartered upon the open market."

To Juliet's surprise, Mr. Beauchamp took no offense but only gave Cyril a lazy glance, as though the man was hardly worth the effort of speech. "And you would rather these items be destroyed?"

"Destroyed?" Cyril echoed.

"Yes," Beauchamp said. "As does any other modern nation, Egypt craves so-called progress. The natives have no use for their own history, except as building blocks for a better future. Already, they are dismantling some of the ancient structures to build new ones. Would you have the temples and monuments be lost forever, and the smaller artifacts tossed aside or destroyed?" He swung toward Juliet and lifted his dark brows. "Better that we save what we can now than lose it all."

Juliet stood staring at him stupidly, for her heart appeared to have stopped abruptly, only to resume its rhythms at a redoubled pace. Cyril and the ballroom seemed to fall away, leaving nothing but Mr. Beauchamp, to be viewed in a new light. Her opinion of the man, altered already over the past few days, now underwent a change of such enormous proportions that she could only gape at him. Idly, she wondered if he was a bit of a thief, after all, for he had definitely stolen her breath.

She just hoped that was all he was taking.

Cyril did not share her changed opinion, for his expression remained one of contempt. With a stiff nod toward her, he muttered something about the "impossible working climate" and stalked from the room. Watching his retreating figure, Juliet realized she was not sorry to see him go.

Nor did she view Mr. Beauchamp's approach with her usual misgivings. Indeed, she suppressed a small shiver of pleasure, probably due to her eagerness to return to work or some semblance of it. At least, that's what Juliet told herself.

Yet her heart seemed to have settled into an unnaturally rapid rhythm as she watched him walk toward her. There was something about his very being that affected Juliet in ways she didn't understand, but suddenly, she was awfully glad he was here. She smiled tentatively in greeting, only to be met with a scowl.

"Why do you listen to that pompous ass?" Mr. Beauchamp demanded.

Startled by both the question and his ferocity, Juliet lifted her gaze to his to find it already settled upon her, so dark and intense that she blinked.

"You know he has no idea what he's talking about, and yet, when he spouts his theories, you remain silent, deferring to him," Mr. Beauchamp said. "What right does he have to rebuke you when you are so much above him in every way? He isn't fit to dust your papyri, and you know it."

Taken aback by his vehemence, Juliet didn't know what to say. Was he faulting Cyril or herself? Or both? Juliet felt a rush of color to her cheeks, along with a certain indignation. What would he have her do? If she had spent her life arguing with every man in it, she would have accomplished precious little. She had chosen her battles, and though she had not picked many in the past, now she seemed to be making up for it, thanks to this man right here.

"And you are supposed to be so much different?" she asked. "If I recall, you threw a tantrum at the notion that you might be here to assist me and not vice versa."

Now it was Beauchamp's turn to appear confounded, but he quickly recovered, as always. "That was a perfectly natural reaction, since I don't take orders from anyone, male or female," he said, flashing her a grin that was enough to make any woman weak in the knees.

Juliet bolstered her own wavering limbs.

"But we both know that no matter what your father said, you are the one in charge," he added.

Where his smile had failed, this simple admission nearly succeeded in knocking Juliet off her feet. To hear the truth spoken aloud after all the years of pretense and condescension, of hiding her resentment and even her own abilities while catering to the men in her world, brought on a rush of emotion. She felt as if someone had broken through a hole in her prison, and she could see a glimpse of daylight.

Something of what Juliet felt must have shown on her face, for her potential savior eyed her quizzically. "And since you know more than I do about most of the artifacts, I'm willing to . . . surrender to your expertise. It's as simple as that," he said with a shrug. But Juliet had to disagree.

She knew that nothing would ever be simple again.

Chapter 6

❈

WILL Timmons sat down on the fancy, curved sofa in the music room, leaned back against the wall, and grinned. He had himself some fine duty tonight. While the other lads would be running to and fro, doing errands for the butler, waiting on the earl and any guests, making sure everything was just so, Will would be snoozing.

He stretched his arms behind his head and made himself comfortable, the entrance to the ballroom still technically within his view. But not for long, he thought, as he let his lashes drift shut. Some of the other fellows made out that they wouldn't want his assignment to watch over the room that housed the earl's latest oddities, but they were fools.

A couple of them even had hinted that he wouldn't be keeping an eye on the place so much as the things inside would be keeping an eye on him. Will snorted. He wasn't one of those superstitious country lads. Born and bred right here in London, he had seen plenty in his time, and he wasn't afraid of a bunch of musty old things someone had dug up in foreign climes. No, sir. There was plenty to fear right outside a person's door, and he was glad to be safe inside one of the fanciest homes in Town.

Of course, some of the others weren't so savvy. They'd been jumpy ever since the earl filled the ballroom with his fancy bits, and now that Tyson claimed to hear strange noises coming from the place, they were more skittish than ever. Will snorted again. Everyone knew the old man was deaf as a post, so how could he hear anything? He probably was having delusions, the old coot.

As for claims that someone had been in the ballroom, rearranging stuff, Will didn't believe it for a minute. Most of the staff were leery of the place, and not one of them would risk their jobs by disobeying the butler, that nasty old Cheevy, anyway. No, Will had a mind that it was Lady Juliet herself who moved things about and then forgot. Everyone knew she was a bit, well, different . . . burying her head in books and such. Why, it was abnormal! Enough to turn anyone dotty, that's for certain.

She wasn't a bad sort, just a bit addled, and that was fine with him, Will thought, settling into his berth with a grin. Thanks to her, he had a cozy bit of duty here—just as long as Mr. Cheevy didn't catch him napping.

WILL woke with a start, bolt upright in an instant. He was a light sleeper, of necessity, and sank back in relief not to find the stocky form of the butler looming over him. He glanced around, wondering what had disturbed his slumber. The music room was pitch black, the only light the dim glow of wall sconces at the entrance to the ballroom. Stretching, Will rose to his feet and stepped forward, just to have a look, only to stop suddenly.

What was that? Cocking his head to one side, he listened, and now he heard it distinctly. It was a shuffling sound, as though something was being dragged across the floor. Here, now, someone wasn't actually stealing something from the earl's collection, were they? Will slipped forward quietly, then halted dead in his tracks as an eerie moan pierced the darkness.

It was coming straight out of the ballroom.

For a moment, Will's blood froze; then he cracked a smile. Some of the lads must be having a lark on him. He hitched up his pants and marched forward.

"All right, fellows, you've had your fun. Now you better get back to work before Mr. Cheevy finds you're not where you're supposed to be," he said.

He stopped in the doorway, expecting to see Tim and Bill coming out clutching their sides with laughter, but the ballroom was dark and empty of life. And silent as a tomb. The fear that Will had wrestled down now rose up again, making him angry.

"Hey, now, this isn't one bit funny. Do you want me to call Cheevy on you? You might get sacked or worse," he warned. But there were no sighs of resignation from the stillness nor any signs of movement.

Will stepped inside and glanced about. It looked a jumble to him, full of great black shapes and deep shadows, like some kind of graveyard. He drew a sharp breath, dismissing such thoughts, and peered around. If something had been moved, he sure wouldn't know, though he could see no marks on the floor of anything heavy being dragged. Then what had made the odd shuffling noise? And the moan?

Will lifted a hand to his hair and smoothed it back nervously. Perhaps he had dreamed the whole thing. He had been asleep, that much he was sure of, and though he could have sworn he heard something after he woke . . . Well, he might have been groggy still. Hitching up his pants, he turned to leave the room, rejecting the incident with a logic born of experience.

But, just in case, he thought he might stay awake. And if

anyone were in there, intending to lift something of the earl's, they would have Will to contend with. He would just wait the fellow out, that's all. Positioning himself right outside the entrance doors, he leaned up against the wall with grim determination and tried not to think about what was inside.

JULIET hurried through her brief toilette, waving away her sleepy maid. She was anxious to get a start on the day, having spent a restless night. Her altered perceptions of Mr. Beauchamp seemed to have made their way into all states of her awareness, for she had been plagued by dreams of sand and sky and towering monuments she had only read about . . . and Mr. Beauchamp. Juliet knew the tall, handsome adventurer had figured prominently in her visions, though his actual role remained rather vague and mysterious with the coming of the dawn.

Still, the hazy images remained on her mind, for she rarely recalled such vivid dreams. She was a practical woman, a scholar, and not one to dwell upon such nonsense, and yet they nagged at her, calling to her as clearly as her hieroglyphs, drawing her into another world, one far away and more thrilling than her own.

As she made her way downstairs, Juliet nearly bumped into one of the footmen. Avoiding his startled gaze, she realized that she must regain possession of herself. The dreams were naught but phantoms, and she had no business dwelling upon them. She had work to do and must check on the collection, especially since she had not done so before retiring.

Juliet flushed. Perhaps that was what had set off her night dramas, her failure to her duty. But she suspected that neglect of her responsibilities had nothing to do with the flights of fancy, unless the fact that she had avoided Mr. Beauchamp's inevitable evening appearance had forced

him into her bedroom. Or, rather, her sleep. Or, rather . . .
Juliet sighed, at a loss for the proper appellation until she
caught herself standing there upon the stairs, practically
dreaming again.

Daydreaming.

Juliet drew in a sharp breath, appalled by her own behavior. Never in her life had she engaged in such a useless
waste of time. Oh, when she was younger, she might have
envisioned herself traveling one day to Egypt, but she had
given up those fantasies long ago. Whatever had aroused
these dormant yearnings, whether Mr. Beauchamp or simply the arrival of the new shipment, Juliet firmly squelched
them. Then she squared her shoulders and lifted her chin
and set herself to the task at hand.

If her heart pounded a bit erratically at her approach to
the ballroom, it was only because of her concern over the
artifacts and not in anticipation of meeting Mr. Beauchamp
at this early hour. When she did not see him, Juliet told
herself she was glad for the chance to wander undisturbed
among her father's treasures. She reached out a hand to
trail across a stela, wondering at its original berth, only to
draw herself up sharply.

She was not a visitor, with time to gawk at each piece.
She was the caretaker, and she needed to make sure all was
as it should be. With new determination, she surveyed the
room, mentally calculating each object and its placement,
and breathed a sigh of relief when she could find nothing
missing.

Turning toward the table, Juliet surveyed the items there
most carefully, but all were as she had left them. Perhaps
whoever had been in the ballroom had learned his lesson
and feared to return. Mr. Beauchamp might be right about
some bold servant trespassing only to regret it. Her father
ran a tight household, and those who strayed from the rules
were quickly dismissed. She only hoped that the culprit
would return the missing papyrus.

As she reached the end of the table, Juliet spared a glance toward the mummy case, though there was little chance of its disappearance. The heavy reliquary stood, as always, in a pool of light, and Juliet gazed up at the windows, wondering at that happenstance. She shook her head, then paused, her attention caught by something below the gleaming alabaster. Curious, she knelt to inspect the parquet floor and was surprised to find a smear of dirt, rather large, almost in the shape of a human foot. Reaching out a finger to touch it, she found that it wasn't mud but a dry dust, like ash.

Of course, the servants hadn't been in to clean since the arrival of this shipment, so it was hardly unusual to find some grime had come in with the crates. What was odd was the size and shape and singularity of the mark, for when Juliet looked around, she could see no other spots marring the parquet. Nor did she remember seeing this particular one before this morning.

With a sigh of annoyance, Juliet rose to her feet and searched the room for one of the cloths used to polish the antiquities, then bent to the task of wiping up the mess herself. Sitting back on her heels, she surveyed her work, well satisfied when no sign of the soil remained.

"Now what are you up to?"

The sound of Mr. Beauchamp's low drawl made Juliet start, followed by a sort of shivery sensation that she dismissed as definitely not one of pleasure. Opening her mouth to answer, Juliet abruptly thought better of the tart reply she intended and wondered whether she ought to speak at all. If Mr. Beauchamp were responsible for the filth, another argument would ensue, or he might blame Cyril, which would only lead to more ill feelings.

Of course, someone else might have left the dirt, but she was well aware that Cyril and her father had dismissed her claims that anyone had been in the ballroom, rearranging and taking things. And she had no wish to further draw their scorn with tales of an errant footprint.

"Nothing," she finally said, rising to her feet.

"You're down on the floor doing *nothing?*" Mr. Beauchamp asked as Juliet straightened. She turned to find him studying her through narrowed eyes, and she quickly stepped aside. "All the antiquities remained undisturbed," she said, moving back toward the table and her work.

Juliet could feel his gaze upon her, too intent, and she suppressed a shiver. Nervously, she reached for a distraction. One of his poor drawings ought to do the trick, she thought, and she seized the topmost off the pile.

"I was going through some of these and thought I ought to get some further notes on them, perhaps for a wall display," Juliet said, thrusting the paper toward him.

For a moment, she thought he wasn't going to respond, but then he leaned close. Too close. Juliet caught her breath.

"The temple at Edfu," he said, looking at the sketch, and something in his whisper made her pause. Usually, she would complain about his vague renderings of the hieroglyphs and carvings, but now, faced with the echoes of her dreams or perhaps the special nuance in his tone, Juliet kept silent.

She slanted a glance at his face and was surprised to see him absorbed, for once, in his own work, his casual attitude gone. It was as though the mask of indifference had slipped, and in its place was an expression of rapt intensity, of deep feelings. Juliet stared, rapt herself.

"It is dedicated to the falcon god Horus. Originally, we thought it nothing but a few remains, but like so much else in Egypt, the first look is deceiving. We approached to find much of it still standing but nearly buried in sand. The first courtyard and portico were awash in it—the sand that eventually claims all of man's works there," he said in a reverent hush. He lifted a long, lean hand to point, and Juliet tore her gaze away from his handsome features to follow his fingers.

"See the columns?" he asked. "Who knows how tall they really are, for all we saw was the topmost portion. Look at those carvings. You can't tell from my efforts, but the delicacy of the leaves, the evenness of each curve and line, considering the massive proportions . . . It's breathtaking," he whispered.

Juliet's own breath caught, and she examined his drawing with new eyes. It reflected little of his wonder, but as she listened to him describe what he had seen, so much more eloquently than any of his writings, she watched the pencil marks transform and felt herself carried away until she was standing beside him in the sun, gazing up at the ancient symbols crafted out of the stone that rose up from the desert. She could see the march of the heavy columns and the shadowy interiors behind them. She could recognize the sounds, the smells, the colors, and the heat of the man next to her. Her heart pounding, Juliet stared so intently at the image that her eyes began to water.

But when she blinked, reality came rushing back. And along with it came disappointment, a soul-wrenching dismay that she wasn't in Egypt, that she wasn't able to see firsthand all the wonders of the country, and that she never would share what Mr. Beauchamp had experienced. That last thought made her pause as she came to a shocking realization.

Mr. Beauchamp was not whom he pretended.

The adventurer, the rogue, the explorer for hire who displayed a flippant disregard for his notes, his drawings, and even his permits, was a fraud. Beneath that careless exterior beat a heartfelt love for Egypt that had nothing to do with money and a passion for its glories that might very well equal her own.

* * *

JEM Gibbs, footman to the earl, balanced a tray and descended the dim servant stairs with a frown. As far as he was concerned, the household had been topsy-turvy ever since the arrival of this latest shipment, large enough to fill a ballroom! First the earl had insisted the lads stay up all night so the stuff could be ferried inside in the middle of the night like some sneak thief's work. Then he had forbidden anyone to go round and have a look at the lot. Why, the servants weren't even supposed to clean about the place! Mrs. Squires, the housekeeper, was having a hemorrhage.

Then some scrap of rotten old paper comes up missing, and the whole staff is turned out. Now, instead of staying away from the room, they were supposed to keep an eye on it! Jem shook his head. He was a man of routine, he was, and he liked to know what was expected of him. These conflicting orders were giving him a bellyache.

And all of it over a bunch of moldy, old, foreign rubbish. Things like bones and coffins and dead people wrapped up in linens. Why, it made a normal Englishman shudder! He knew the ladies didn't like it one bit. Mabel swore she wouldn't spend a night in the house after hearing about the mummy. Said she would go stay at her sister's, but everyone knew her sister wouldn't take her in. Jem didn't mind admitting that he'd rather be elsewhere, too, but what was a fellow to do?

As Mabel said, it just wasn't natural, collecting other people's parts. And it was said those Egyptians took a man to pieces and pickled him. Why, he heard tell they had jars with innards in them. Right here in the earl's ballroom!

It just wasn't natural. And then with Will saying he heard some strange noises from the place last night . . . well, that didn't make Jem look forward to his duty one bit. "What kind of noises?" Jem had asked. "A shuffling and a moaning," Will said. "As if the mummy itself was getting up and going for a walk."

Some of the others had laughed and said Will probably heard someone getting up all right—and going at it where they wouldn't be disturbed. But Jem couldn't imagine anyone having a go amongst all those musty old relics, dead parts and all. Will was about the only one in the house who wasn't bothered by such things, so if he was wary now, what were the rest of them to do?

Jem shuddered. Why he should be stuck in the most eccentric household in London was a mystery. His dear old mum would have been horrified at the goings-on, good God-fearing woman that she was. The thought of his dear old mum, a sainted female who had met her maker just last year, made Jem pause and swallow hard.

With a sniff, he adjusted his grip on the tray and sought his proper footing on the narrow stairs. It was late, and he couldn't see very well, but when he glanced down to the bottom, he noticed something outlined by the faint light beyond. It appeared to hover in midair right in the doorway. At first he thought the thing might be a bat or a bird, but he'd never seen one stay in place like this. Leaning forward, Jem took a few more steps, warily seeking a better look, only to recoil in horror.

The thing before him was no bird or bat, nor any living thing, at least not alive now, for Jem recognized the stiff fingers of a hand—with no body attached to it. He swallowed hard, his brain slow to process the news that a severed hand, black and horrible, was flying through the air, coming right toward him, *reaching for him*.

Screaming like a woman, Jem lost his footing and tumbled down the wooden planks, his burden loudly banging after him upon each step. He landed at the bottom in a heap, finally still and thankfully oblivious.

* * *

THANKS to Chauncey's established network within the household, Morgan knew immediately when one of the footmen was found at the bottom of the servants' stairs with a broken leg, raving that a mummy had chased him to his doom. And though the hour was late, Morgan ignored the startled looks of the servants as he entered their domain to question the fellow. There he had chanced upon the doctor, who had set the patient's leg and administered some laudanum.

The footman, a fellow named Jem, was reclining upon his bed and being questioned by the earl's butler.

"I know what I saw," he was saying. "It was a hand, all wrapped up and rotting, and it came up the stairs toward me!"

"Nonsense!" the butler growled in a harsh manner wholly unlike his usual measured tones. He glanced up at Morgan's entrance, and something crossed his face. In the dim light, Morgan wasn't sure what, but it was obvious the man was not pleased to see him.

"Mr. Beauchamp!" he said. "I'm afraid you have taken a wrong turn. This is the servants' quarters."

"Yes," Morgan said casually. "I heard that there was a mishap, and since I'm in charge of the collection, I was hoping to get some information from our patient here," he said, walking right past the butler to stand by the bed. Without waiting for an invitation, he leaned against a nearby set of drawers and addressed the footman.

"You saw something at the bottom of the stairs?" he asked.

Jem looked rather frantically between Morgan and the butler, as though he wasn't sure whether to answer or not.

"I'm afraid the earl does not sanction visits in the servants' quarters," the butler said. "May I escort you back to the public areas?" Although his manner remained polite, unlike most gentlemen's gentlemen, his eyes held a hard edge, his voice a trace of threat.

But Morgan wasn't about to be intimidated by any butler. "No, that will be all, Cheevy," he said with practiced ease.

"Now, Jem, you were heading down the servant's stair when you saw something at the bottom?" Morgan prompted.

With one last fearful glance at the butler, Jem nodded. "It was at the bottom of the steps, yet, but floating in the air, coming toward me, it was."

"And could you describe it?"

Jem shuddered. "It was a black hand, sir, all moldy and horrible. I knew right off it was one of them body parts from his lordship's collection."

"And how did you know that?" Morgan asked.

"It was all bony and falling apart, like something that's been dead for hundreds of years," Jem said, shuddering again.

"Then how do you suppose it came to be floating through the air?" Morgan asked.

"I don't know, sir. That I don't know," the fellow said, shaking his head a bit dazedly. No doubt, the laudanum was taking effect.

"I really must insist that you leave, Mr. Beauchamp," the butler said, and to prove his point, he reached out to grasp Morgan by the arm.

Morgan lifted his brows, looked pointedly down at the servant's fingers, and waited for their removal. The man was certainly not acting like a butler, and Morgan had to wonder just how far he would go. Although no taller than Morgan, he was beefier. It would be a contest, to be sure. Morgan wondered how the earl would feel about a brawl in his servants' quarters. But, after one long, tense moment, the man released his hold.

Morgan shook out his sleeve. "Don't bother to *escort* me, Cheevy. I'll find my way back," he said, giving the butler a slow, steady look that suggested he keep his hands to himself.

Then he turned and made his exit, unsure what was more startling: a butler who used force on his master's guests or a flying mummy's hand that attacked the servants.

WARY now, Morgan slipped into his own room carefully, only to encounter Chauncey brandishing a poker from the fireplace. He swore softly, then drew in a deep breath. "Gad, man, are you looking for new employment?"

Chauncey lowered the makeshift weapon with a grunt. "The way things stand around here, I like to be prepared for anything, including a hand that doesn't bother to knock," he said. "And you're awfully quick with the blade, yourself," he noted, with a wry glance toward the knife that Morgan had drawn automatically from his boot.

Morgan slipped the weapon back in place with a sigh. "Well, I'm a bit chary myself, though I'm more concerned about a whole human being waylaying me than any parts," he said.

"Why? What happened?" Chauncey asked, his eyes narrowing.

Morgan sank into a chair and proffered a booted foot. "The footman broke his leg, all right," he said. "He claims that a mummified hand, or at least that's what he described, came after him."

Chauncey snorted as he tugged at the boot. "More likely it was a purloined bit of the earl's brandy that chased him down the steps."

Morgan shook his head. "I don't know, Chauncey. He seemed pretty shaken up for a man who's making up explanations in order to keep his job."

Chauncey scoffed. "Some of these fellows are such good actors they should take to the stage," he said. He flashed a quick grin. "I ought to know."

Morgan laughed, then sobered. "Yet why concoct something so outlandish?"

Chauncey shrugged. "Perhaps he's used up all the simple excuses, and this one does have the added advantage of being timely, with the earl's new arrivals and all."

"The whole thing is stranger than anything we saw in Egypt," Morgan said, shaking his head. "And here's another odd bit of business: the earl's butler tried to prevent me from questioning the fellow."

"What?" Chauncey said, all attention now.

"Yes," Morgan said. "He began politely enough, but eventually went so far as to lay his hands on me."

Chauncey gaped at Morgan, his outrage plain. "I knew I should have gone down there with you!"

Morgan smiled. "I think I can handle one butler, thank you."

Chauncey shook his head. "But that's no ordinary butler."

"He certainly doesn't look the part, does he?" Morgan asked.

"Oh, maybe on the surface, but you don't have to scratch the man hard to find out what he's made of," Chauncey said.

Morgan nodded. "He reminds me of an old prizefighter, a bruiser who's managed to clean up his language and his manners."

"Do you think so?" Chauncey asked, his voice a low growl, heavy with suspicion. "I still have some contacts here in the city. I'll ask around."

"But why would the earl employ a butler who isn't all that he should be?" Morgan asked.

Chauncey shrugged. "This Carlisle's a cagey sort. He could have his hand in a lot of things besides Egyptian trinkets."

"Indeed," Morgan muttered.

"I hate to say so, considering our cozy berth here, but perhaps it's time we moved on," Chauncey said.

Morgan felt a denial rush to his lips, even though he had considered the same thing. He was certainly not known for his tendency to linger, especially in difficult situations, but Chauncey's suggestion struck him the wrong way. It was an unusual reaction, to be sure, and one he didn't want to examine too closely. All Morgan knew was that he wasn't ready to leave the earl's household. Not yet, anyway.

"My work isn't done here," he said.

Chauncey eyed him askance. "And what work might that be?"

Morgan frowned. "The cataloguing."

"Ah, I see," Chauncey said in a tone that said he didn't. "Your decision wouldn't have anything to do with a certain blonde with an eye for old relics from Egypt, would it?"

Morgan didn't deign to comment.

Chauncey gave him an assessing look. "Well, since you fit that description yourself, just make sure she doesn't add you to her collection."

Morgan could think of a worse feat than being delicately handled by the lady, but he said nothing.

Chauncey loosed a sigh. "Well, I'll keep watch on the household, and you keep watch on the lot from Egypt. Make sure the mummy doesn't up and attack anyone else," he added with a chuckle.

Morgan sighed. "Oh, it's all a load of nonsense." But he couldn't shake the look on Jem Gibbs's face. Although Morgan didn't believe in floating hands, there was no doubt that something had scared the man.

And he intended to find out what.

Chapter 7

❧

THE next morning, Morgan groaned as Chauncey woke him bright and early, but the thought of catching Juliet alone made him rise. He wanted to talk to her about last night's mishap without the interference of the coxcomb, who listened in on their conversations with the avidity of an overzealous chaperone. Since finding out that Lyndhurst had no claim on Lady Juliet, Morgan was even more annoyed by the fellow's attitude—and his constant presence. It was only too bad that the mummy's hand hadn't attacked him instead of the footman, Morgan thought with a smirk.

In his efforts to avoid the fellow, Morgan even considered going to the lady's bedchamber, but since he already might have strained his host's hospitality with his visit to the servants' quarters, he decided against it. Although his original intention was innocent enough, the leap of his pulse and the hot surge of blood that accompanied the thought only confirmed his decision. Perhaps it wasn't wise to seek out Juliet in such an intimate venue. With a grunt of regret, Morgan quickly dressed, hoping that the lady would be at her post before anyone else.

He wasn't disappointed. As usual, she was already in the ballroom, and he paused in the doorway to study her. She wore a simple dark blue gown, shorn of any ribbons or frills. It was hardly the sort one would expect from an earl's daughter but obviously practical for her needs. Morgan only wished her wardrobe included something a little more revealing.

The color wasn't his choice, either. With her hazel eyes, she needed deep greens and creams or a rich burgundy. Drawing a sharp breath, Morgan shook his head at the train of his thoughts. The adverse climate here must be affecting his brain. He was starting to act like some empty-headed Town fop just when he needed to keep his wits about him.

Something was going on in the earl's household, and it had nothing to do with women's fashions, Morgan reminded himself. With a grimace, he stepped forward, and Juliet turned at once. Either he was losing his touch, or else she was developing her own, another unsettling notion.

"Mr. Beauchamp. You seem determined to begin earlier each morning," she said. Although she held herself a bit stiffly, gone was the rigid condemnation that usually greeted him. Yesterday, they had reached a truce of sorts, which Morgan didn't know whether to rue or not. He had actually found himself telling her about Egypt, an act that had come naturally at the time but now left him feeling uncomfortable.

She had certainly listened. Hell, he had finally managed to shut her up, and without brushing up against her or using any of his tricks. He had even imagined a glow of admiration in her wide-eyed gaze. No doubt, it was limited to the places he had described and not to any efforts of his own.

So why did he feel so . . . awkward, as if he had laid a part of himself bare yesterday? Maybe it was because he didn't share his feelings about Egypt with anyone. They were deeply personal. So why had he suddenly begun yammering to an earl's daughter about what he had experienced?

It was all part of his plan, Morgan told himself, stifling a twinge of panic. He needed her to be receptive, and if he had to speechify to get her there, then so be it. It didn't mean a thing, except that when he had her right where he wanted her, he'd make good use of her.

She was watching him warily, and Morgan realized that he had never answered her question about his early arrival. He was also scowling. He donned a neutral expression.

"I wanted to talk to you. Alone," he said. Her wariness increased, and Morgan would have spared a smile for her skittishness, but he had no time to waste. Who knew when the coxcomb would come barging in?

"Are you aware of what happened last night?" he asked.

Juliet eyed him blankly, and Morgan could only marvel at her ignorance. Apparently, she knew everything there was to know about languages and books and antiquities but nothing of what went on around her. Didn't she talk to her maid? Maybe she didn't have one, he mused. No. Someone had to dress her hair in that hideous fashion, for ladies of the ton, no matter how bookish, did not attend themselves.

Most likely, the girl had chatted on at length about Jem's calamity, but Juliet's thoughts had been elsewhere, presumably in Egypt. Or at least upon hieroglyphs. Morgan had the sense to know she hadn't been thinking about him. More's the pity.

At least he had her attention now, and he had better make use of it. "One of the footmen, a fellow by the name of Jem Gibbs, fell down the stairs and broke his leg. He claims that something came after him, something Egyptian," Morgan said.

"What?" Juliet appeared adorably befuddled. Since she was so intelligent, the look was especially endearing, and

Morgan had to fight an urge to press his lips to her furrowed brow.

"Supposedly, the footman was chased by a . . . hand. Actually, what he described was a mummified hand, disembodied, which floated through the air at the bottom of the servants' stairs and flew toward him."

"A flying hand," Juliet repeated dully, and Morgan had to harden his heart against her. Either that or kiss her outright.

Turning, she appeared to search for something amongst the objects on the table. Apparently finding what she sought, she swung round and held up a mummified hand, part of the shipment he had brought from Egypt himself. "This one?" she asked.

Morgan shrugged, so suddenly taken by her that he couldn't do much more. What kind of woman plucked up a severed hand without blinking? *Only Juliet.*

She glanced at Morgan and then the artifact, as if unsure what to believe. Finally, she squared her shoulders. "Well, let us find out, shall we?" she said and proceeded to march toward the door. Still clutching the mummified part, she rang for a servant, and a footman soon appeared at the ballroom entrance.

"Yes, my lady?" he asked. Luckily, he did not appear to see what she had clutched near her skirts.

"Bring the injured footman here, please," she said.

The servant gaped. "Jem? I mean, Mr. Gibbs, my lady?"

"Yes," Juliet answered with the carelessness of the rich and pampered. Morgan wondered if she stopped to consider exactly how Jem was supposed to attend her with his broken leg—or if she even considered the servant at all. Sadly, he remembered just who she was and thought not.

The footman appeared uncomfortable. "I, uh, don't know what Mr. Cheevy would say to that," he hedged.

"The butler? What on earth does the butler have to do with it?" Juliet asked.

The footman reddened. "Well, he's making sure no one

sees Jem—er, Mr. Gibbs—or talks to him," he said. Then, apparently realizing just what he had said, he rephrased his words. "I mean that he's making sure Mr. Gibbs isn't disturbed, my lady."

"How odd," Juliet observed aloud. Morgan could only agree. He wondered if she realized that her butler resembled a prizefighter. Then again, Juliet probably didn't know what a prizefighter was. He was tempted to ask her about boxing, but thought better of confusing the issue.

"Well, summon Mr. Cheevy then, and I shall speak to him myself," she said.

"Very well, my lady," the footman answered, his expression dubious. Perhaps Cheevy kept the other servants in line with his fists. Morgan wouldn't put it past him.

While they waited, Morgan recited the details of the mishap, as best he knew them, though he could tell that Juliet thought he was perpetrating a hoax. Presumably, the last vestige of her good manners prevented her from calling him a liar to his face . . . although Morgan had to admit he liked it when she shouted at him. He was struggling against the urge to pick a quarrel when Cheevy appeared.

The burly servant flicked a glance at Morgan, then nodded to his mistress. "You wanted to see me, my lady?"

"Yes, I understand there was a mishap with one of the servants," she said.

"Nothing to concern you, my lady," Cheevy said.

His dismissal seemed to stiffen Juliet's spine, and Morgan applauded her privately. At least she wasn't cowering before the man as she did with that idiot Lyndhurst.

"If it happened in my household, I consider it my business. What's more, I have heard that there was mention of one of the antiquities, which definitely makes the incident my concern," she said.

Cheevy flicked another glance toward Morgan that laid the blame squarely at his feet and stopped just short of promising later retribution.

Lifting his brows slightly, Morgan effected a casual pose, but his fingers itched to respond quite differently. He didn't care if the butler had gone rounds with Gentleman Jackson himself, Morgan was ready and willing to have a go at him.

"Mr. Cheevy, I wish to see Mr., uh, Gibbs now," Juliet said, commanding the butler's attention once more.

"I'm afraid Mr. Gibbs is not well, my lady, and has taken to his bed," the butler said.

"Are you refusing to summon this man?" Juliet asked, and Morgan had to admire her tenacity. He liked her when she held her ground, when she was feisty and determined—as long as it wasn't him she was ordering about.

"No, my lady, it is simply that I am unable to do so," the butler replied.

"Well, then, I shall find him myself," Juliet said, exhibiting that penchant for stubbornness she usually reserved for Morgan. His lips curved in appreciation.

The butler, however, did not share Morgan's enthusiasm for his newly resolute mistress. For a moment, Morgan thought the man might actually try to stop her, and he stepped forward, ready to intervene. But after a moment's hesitation, Cheevy bowed slightly.

"I shall see if I can manage to convey him here," the butler said before making his exit.

"Is he usually so . . . uncooperative?" Morgan asked.

Juliet turned to him in surprise. "Cheevy? Oh, I don't think so." She again wore that befuddled expression that Morgan found so enchanting, but this time he had to admit to being just as puzzled about the servant's behavior.

In fact, he wondered if the butler was going to summon the footman or the earl in his efforts to prevent anyone from talking with the injured man. Morgan certainly didn't understand this bizarre demand for secrecy. Did the earl or his butler think the other servants would panic if they spoke with Jem? Or did they want to discredit the poor footman?

Morgan opened his mouth to ask Juliet her opinion, only to realize that she was already turning away from him and heading back to her work. Didn't the woman ever quit? Apparently, the thought of flying hands didn't disturb her one bit, and though he admired her aplomb, Morgan found her single-minded devotion to duty a bit tiresome.

"Mr. Beauchamp?" she asked, eyeing him expectantly.

Morgan stifled a groan. He felt like a recalcitrant boy called back to his studies by some tyrant of a tutor. He was far more interested in pursuing a mummified attacker than in squinting at notebooks and sorting out memories that were rather vague at this point—all for a female taskmaster who never seemed to be satisfied. The thought, innocent though it was, turned Morgan's mind toward other means of satisfying the lady, and his lips quirked. He wondered if Juliet's attention to detail would continue into the bedroom, and he felt a sudden, sharp, hunger that startled him.

Slanting a glance toward the source of his discomfort, Morgan watched her study a small statue, her whole being focused on the artifact, and something clenched inside him. It was the same sort of sensation he felt when he saw her with her hieroglyphs, a funny sort of need that bubbled up in him, struggling to be fed. Morgan frowned. It was probably the way she examined the pieces, with an intensity that shook him. He couldn't take his eyes off her. *He wanted her to look at him that way.*

Dismissing the notion, Morgan told himself the only reason Juliet held such an unusual fascination for him was because she was so damned . . . unusual. He'd certainly never met anyone like her, and he'd encountered all manner of women in his lifetime, from noblewomen to Egyptian peasants. But he had never met a bluestocking, the rather derogatory name given to educated women. Morgan always supposed they would be boring, ugly spinsters with their heads stuck in books, their avocation chosen because they lacked the necessary looks to marry. He never imagined a woman would voluntarily seek out knowledge with a passion normally reserved for more earthy pursuits.

Morgan felt his pulse kick at the thought. He had always been able to think on his feet, born with good instincts and a certain cleverness, but a poor scholar, not book smart. He grudgingly admired those who were, though he had never pictured a woman with such attributes. Yet here she was, beautiful *and* intellectual, a combination that somehow managed to arouse Morgan in a manner he never expected. There was just, something, well, *stimulating* about her mind.

Morgan shook his head. He must be really desperate for sex if he was excited by an aloof, exacting creature like the earl's daughter. He scowled in her direction, and as luck would have it, she glanced up just at that moment. Her eyes, all liquid sand and sunrise behind her spectacles, were unfocused at first, but when they met his, they clung and held as fiercely as the desert winds.

There was no contempt there, not even a subtle impatience, and Morgan was so startled, he stared, drawn into a gaze that hinted at secret depths and hidden treasures, mysteries he could spend a lifetime delving into. He was caught and held, yet he felt the opposite, as though unseen bonds that had tethered him had loosened. Indeed, his wits seemed to have scattered as well, for he found himself reaching out.

Morgan had no idea what he would have done right there in broad daylight, though he could make a good guess, but, thankfully, whatever spell that had overcome them both was broken by a sudden clatter at the entrance of the ballroom.

Jem Gibbs had arrived. Turning abruptly away from Juliet, Morgan hurried forward, suddenly eager to greet the injured footman. For his part, Jem looked none too pleased to be there. Balancing on a pair of crutches, he hovered outside the doorway and glanced nervously at the array of artifacts inside the room as though he didn't trust any one of them.

"Mr. Gibbs, is it?" Juliet prompted, and Morgan realized he was all too aware of her presence beside him, lovely and competent and far too intelligent. He released a breath and focused on Jem.

"Yes, my lady," the footman answered, his gaze centering not on his mistress but on the objects beyond her.

"Last night you were descending the servants' stair, and you fell after seeing something below?" Juliet prompted.

"It was a hand," Jem answered, apparently unmoved in his conviction, despite the skepticism of others. "I know what I saw, and I saw a hand." Whether his fellow servants had tormented him over his tale, or he chafed at being continually questioned, Morgan couldn't guess. But no one was going to shake the man's story at this point.

"I see," Juliet said. Then she lifted her arm to proffer the mummified appendage. "Was it this hand?"

Shrieking in terror at the sight, Jem backed away on his crutches, with no little difficulty, only to slip and fall. "I resign!" he cried from his position on the parquet floor. "I don't care if I starve to death. I won't stay here another minute! No man should have to serve in a household full of dead parts and the sort who keep them!"

To his credit, Cheevy stepped forward to help the man to his feet. But once upright, Jem shook off the butler's hold and stared, stricken, at the severed hand that Juliet still held in her own. "It'll come after you, too!" he warned. "You'll see! You'll all see!" Then he turned and hurried away as fast as he could, with the butler following in his wake.

Would Cheevy try to change Jem's mind or simply pay him off so he wouldn't spread the tale, once he left the house? Either way, Morgan wanted to make sure he would be able to find Jem Gibbs, should the need arise in the future. So, without a word to Juliet, he slipped away to alert Chauncey.

If Jem left the earl's house, he would do so with a bit of money and a new allegiance. To Morgan.

ALTHOUGH Morgan returned to the ballroom as quickly as possible, to his disappointment, Juliet was no longer alone. The coxcomb was there beside her. *Close beside her*. Swallowing a growl of a primitive emotion that he labeled as annoyance, Morgan stepped into the room, although no one appeared to notice his approach. They were far too engrossed in . . . whatever it was they were doing.

Something flared inside Morgan, urging him forward, though he had no idea exactly what he was going to do—step between them? At least they weren't touching, he noted as he approached. And they weren't engrossed in each other, either. They were standing at the table staring down at the mummified hand as though expecting it to levitate at any moment, he realized, and the tenseness between his shoulders eased.

"I don't think it's going anywhere," Morgan observed dryly, causing both of them to start.

"Oh, Mr. Beauchamp," Juliet said. "I was just relating the, uh, incident to Cyril."

Morgan grinned. He wished he could have heard that explanation. He crossed his arms and leaned back against the edge of the table. "And what did you conclude?"

Juliet drew a deep breath. "Well, I suspect that Mr. Gibbs saw the antiquity, perhaps on some illicit visit to the room, and in his subsequent guilt and ignorance, had a nightmare about it."

"While walking down the stairs?" Morgan asked.

Juliet's brows knit together in the most appealing fashion as she considered that small detail. Despite her vast knowledge and intelligence, common sense did not seem to be her forte. "Perhaps he was stealing it but fell and made up some excuse to be caught with it," she suggested.

"Except that he wasn't caught with it, was he? It was right here all the time," Morgan said with a glance toward the artifact. Or was it? If Gibbs were telling the truth, then perhaps the hand had taken a little trip, though not of its own accord. Most likely, the mummified appendage had some help getting around. But who would rig up a hand to fly through the air? And why? Someone with a vendetta against the *footman*? Morgan shook his head.

"Perhaps it was just a prank gone bad," he said, pushing away from the table. "One of the servants, knowing some of the others are leery of the Egyptian items, snatches up the hand and thrusts it into the stairwell. But when his victim causes a racket and breaks his leg, the perpetrator takes himself off, fearing for his job, and rightfully so. He returns the hand to its proper resting place, and everyone thinks poor Jem is a loon."

Morgan glanced up to find that for once, Juliet was eyeing him with what looked like approval. He felt a curious clutch in his chest. That wasn't admiration for his *intelligence* shining out of those glorious orbs, was it?

"No." The sound of Lyndhurst's voice answering his unspoken question jolted Morgan from his reverie.

"What?" he asked, glaring at the coxcomb.

"No. It was no prank," Lyndhurst murmured. He wore a distant expression, as though caught up in his own thoughts, then swung round to face them, so suddenly seized by excitement that Morgan wondered if he were possessed. "Can't you see? This was no isolated incident! It is all of a piece."

Morgan blinked. He had no idea what the coxcomb was talking about, and one glance at Juliet told him she didn't, either. He had always thought the fellow dicked in the nob, but now he wondered if the baronet had gone totally round the bend.

The coxcomb swept an arm to encompass the entire

room. "What has happened here? Objects being moved. Items disappearing. And now the attack upon the servant!"

Attack? "Attack?" Morgan said aloud. "Isn't that a bit strong for a joke that went awry?"

Lyndhurst's face grew mottled, his pale complexion flushing irregularly. "It wasn't a joke! And it wasn't the work of any servant."

Morgan lifted his brows. "All right. Who, then?" He couldn't wait to hear the coxcomb's theory, an exercise in idiocy on a par with his work on hieroglyphs, no doubt. Morgan crossed his arms over his chest, leaned back again, and waited. "Well?"

"It is no laughing matter, Beauchamp, but something very serious, perhaps beyond your comprehension," Lyndhurst said.

Now *that* hurt. "Try me," Morgan said.

Lyndhurst assumed his most superior air. "Such knowledge requires an understanding of hieroglyphs well above that of the so-called experts."

When Juliet began to speak, he cut her off. "Yes, I have found something, something I have been loath to share with you, Juliet, because of the nature of its meaning," he said. He was in his element now, pontificating, and Morgan had to swallow a groan. Juliet simply appeared befuddled, bless her.

"Look here," Lyndhurst said, hurrying toward the mummy case. "See this?" he pointed to a set of hieroglyphs. "The mummy. The dagger. *Death,*" he intoned.

"Death? But how do you know—" Juliet began to protest, but the coxcomb cut her off with a fierce glare.

"It is a clear warning that whoever desecrates the tomb will be punished," Lyndhurst said.

Morgan shook his head. It sure wasn't clear to him or, it seemed, to Juliet. She was wrinkling her brow in that way of hers that meant she was thinking really hard, the sight of which was starting to make him really hard. He shifted and tried to concentrate.

"How can you tell that man is dead? He hardly looks any different from all the other figures," Morgan said.

Lyndhurst made a caustic face, not even deigning to answer.

"I still don't think the hieroglyphs are symbolic of esoteric knowledge, and I don't believe one picture stands for one idea," Juliet said. She pointed to a drawing inside an oval. "That is probably the name of the mummified person, presumably of royal blood. So I imagine these hieroglyphs are a description of that person or his deeds, not a cryptic threat."

Morgan nodded. It certainly made sense to him, but Lyndhurst's expression turned ugly. "Think what you will, but I am telling you, this is a warning to any who would desecrate the mummy's tomb, a portent of evil to come, of revenge wreaked upon all those responsible."

Morgan would have laughed but for the coxcomb's seriousness. He was practically frothing at the mouth with enthusiasm for his bizarre theory. "Everything started after the arrival of this last shipment, the earl's most extensive and most expensive, and perhaps the only time an intact mummy case has been ripped from its home," Lyndhurst said, as if that explained everything.

Morgan simply lifted his brows. Hadn't every tomb in Egypt been looted many times over, beginning centuries ago? If so, why weren't mummified hands wreaking havoc all over the world?

Juliet, though sometimes lacking in common sense, appeared to be right there with Morgan on this one. "Why would a mummy rearrange things or steal a papyrus?" she asked.

Lyndhurst grimaced, as if both Juliet and Morgan were the fools. "It's all mischief, all ill will, a threat that begins with small instances of upheaval and grows in menace. A man broke his leg here last night. He could have broken his neck. And mark my words, this is only the beginning."

Morgan didn't know whether to laugh or summon a doctor to sedate the coxcomb. Knowing there was no reasoning with a lunatic, he lifted his brows. "So what do you suggest we do? Return the mummy case?"

Lyndhurst seemed to be at a loss for a reply, as well he should be. Morgan knew the earl would never agree to such a plan. Evil portent or not, the sarcophagus was worth a fortune. Hell, he doubted if Cleopatra herself, rising up in her funeral wrap, would convince the earl to give up his most expensive treasure. And, apparently, even Lyndhurst wasn't so deranged as to expect him to do so.

"No," the coxcomb said, shaking his head. "That would do no good. The tomb has already been defiled, the body moved from its sacred place to a foreign land."

Morgan nearly rolled his eyes in disbelief. Lyndhurst obviously was glorying in all the attention, concocting more outrageous claims as he went along. With a snort, Morgan pushed away from the table. "I've never heard anything more ridiculous in my life," he said. And he'd heard a lot.

The coxcomb eyed him sourly. "And what do you suggest is the cause, Mr. Beauchamp?" he asked, his voice heavy with contempt.

Morgan shrugged. "There is no cause. I think the incidents are just that, random occurrences. Some servant, probably someone interested in Egypt, sneaks in here and moves things around, lifts a few trinkets, maybe even tries to make off with the hand but thinks better of it. The events aren't even related, let alone caused by the displacement of a piece of alabaster," he said with a firm glance at both Lyndhurst and Juliet.

"Now, can we please get back to work?" he asked. It was a measure of Morgan's exasperation that he would suggest as much, but anything was better than listening to Lyndhurst's nonsense.

With a sniff of contempt, the coxcomb turned away, returning to his own studies without a qualm. Obviously, he didn't think the threat serious enough to flee the room. Too bad, Morgan thought. The man belonged in Bedlam, not in the earl's ballroom.

As for his theories, Morgan dismissed them outright. But even as he looked through his notes, rotely answering Juliet's queries, he wondered. Although he didn't believe in walking mummies or the threats of those long dead, there were those alive who could cause plenty of mischief.

Were the incidents indeed related? And, if so, what the devil was going on?

Chapter 8

AT the first opportunity, Morgan excused himself from the strained atmosphere of the ballroom and sought out Chauncey. He found the wily fellow skulking near the servants' hall, listening in on conversations. With a low hiss, Morgan sought his attention while standing back far enough to avoid a knife in the gullet.

Chauncey swung round immediately, his eyes wide. "What the devil is it now?"

"You won't believe it," Morgan answered, motioning toward a nearby room where the two could speak in private.

"I don't know. You haven't heard some of the rumors that are flying about," Chauncey said, inclining his head toward the servants' hall. Slipping into the vacant room, he stepped away from the door, then turned to face Morgan.

"By the way, I caught up with Gibbs and gave him some money and advice. I'll be able to put my finger on him, if we want him," Chauncey said. He paused to scratch his chin. "But why would we want him?"

Morgan shrugged. "I don't know. But since he's the

only one who saw . . . whatever it was, I'd like to be able to reach him, just in case something else bizarre happens."

"Sounds like it already has," Chauncey said.

"No, nothing else has happened, unless you count Lyndhurst losing his wits entirely," Morgan said. "He's claiming that the mummy is behind it all, having objected to us wresting its remains from Egypt."

Chauncey, who had been keeping one eye on the doorway, jerked his head toward Morgan, his mouth gaping open. In fact, he wore such a stupefied expression on his sharp features that Morgan cracked a grin. They had been together for a long time, Chauncey having stepped in to aid him during a particularly nasty argument with a gentleman who had not seen eye-to-eye with Morgan. After that, Chauncey had deemed it his mission in life to watch Morgan's back, though he hadn't minded escaping from the streets of London in the bargain.

They had seen a lot together, and what they hadn't, Chauncey had experienced during his checkered past, which made it extremely difficult to surprise or shock him. Leaning back against an elegantly carved gilt table, Morgan crossed his arms over his chest and enjoyed his friend's flabbergasted look with something akin to glee. After all, he had to have some fun, didn't he?

"Now, let me make sure I understand you correctly," Chauncey said, speaking slowly as though either he or Morgan—or both—were beetle-headed. "A grown man, a baronet, mind you, a fellow who calls himself an expert on artifacts from Egypt, is claiming that the mummy down there in the ballroom came to life, opened up his coffin, despite the weight of the lid, climbed out, and strolled through the corridors of the town house, where he chased poor Gibbs down until the man broke his leg?"

Morgan's smile widened. "Well, I'm not sure if the mummy itself walked or if it simply directed someone else's hand, which was conveniently nearby, to do its bidding."

Chauncey's eyes narrowed. "If you're trying to have one on me because of what I said earlier about you looking after the mummy . . ." He trailed off in a threatening tone.

Morgan lifted his brows. "Would I do that?"

"Yes. In a heartbeat," Chauncey answered. "In fact, this might be some plan of yours to get the coxcomb locked up in Bedlam, so you can take your turn with his fiancée."

"They are not engaged!" Morgan said with perhaps more vehemence than necessary.

"Yes, of course. You did tell me that, didn't you?" Chauncey asked.

Morgan glared at his companion. "And I do not intend to take my turn, as you so outrageously put it, with the earl's daughter! Hell," he muttered, horrified at the thought of the nobleman's reaction.

"Whatever you say," Chauncey said, grinning, and Morgan was tempted to wipe the smile from his friend's face. But he had bigger problems than Chauncey's efforts to goad him.

Morgan fixed his companion with a direct look, intended to silence all taunts. "That engagement is as much a fantasy as Lyndhurst's plans to decipher the hieroglyphs or his latest tale, that the mummy is responsible for every mishap that occurs in this household."

Chauncey's jaw dropped. "You're serious."

Morgan nodded. "The coxcomb is, or at least he puts on a good show of it."

"And it's all because the poor old dead fellow doesn't like his case being moved?" Chauncey asked.

Morgan nodded.

Chauncey shook his head in wonder. "Does the fool realize that in Egypt you live day to day with the dead? That we slept in open tombs? That every grave in the country has been looted countless times?"

Morgan shrugged.

"Did you remind him that Englishmen have been buying bits of mummies for years? Why, I could probably go out and get some right now," Chauncey said.

Morgan grimaced at the mention of the bizarre, age-old cure all. Arab doctors had first prescribed it, and during earlier centuries, there had been a brisk trade in the powdered remains throughout Europe. Morgan shuddered. Prescribing leeches to bleed a person was bad enough, but did the patients realize just what they were doing by ingesting mummy? Apparently, cannibalism was all right as long as the victim was dead and buried, his body preserved by the ancient Egyptian methods and a dry climate.

Chauncey grinned. "Then perhaps this mummy *is* warning them—not to eat him."

Morgan grinned.

"And, just what, exactly, are we to do to placate the fellow, besides not grind him up for medicinal use?" Chauncey asked.

Morgan shook his head. "I'm afraid the baronet had no answer for that one."

Chauncey snorted.

Unfortunately, Morgan had no answers, either, and he frowned in contemplation of that fact. "Apparently, we are to stand by while fate deals its hand, and await our doom."

DOOM certainly hung over the luncheon table, or least over Lyndhurst, Morgan observed with amusement. And Juliet didn't look too happy, either. She kept trying to steer the conversation away from recent events, apparently in an effort to prevent the coxcomb from presenting his theory to her father. Of course, no man with any sense would blame the earl's most prized possession for anything, but Morgan wasn't laying bets on the coxcomb's sense.

No, indeed. In fact, Morgan was looking forward to some fireworks. Between the excellent food, the prospect of Lyndhurst's self-destruction, and Juliet's uncharacteristic chattering, he was thoroughly enjoying himself. Of course, if the earl was as well informed as he intimated, then he might already be aware of Lyndhurst's theory, private conversation or not. But Morgan was betting the earl hadn't heard the latest, or he might not be eating with his usual enthusiasm, apparently unperturbed. Or was he? The nobleman wore his pose of gruff geniality too well to tell.

As if sensing Morgan's study, the earl spoke. "Cheevy tells me that one of the footmen ran off today without even giving notice! Some nonsense about the collection frightening him. I tell you, it is becoming more and more difficult to find reliable staff," he said, shaking his head.

Morgan said nothing, knowing full well the hapless footman would have a hard time finding work with a broken leg and no references. But the earl, like all of his ilk, wouldn't spare a thought for the man. Morgan would do well to remember the nature of the beast, he concluded, watching both Carlisle and his daughter through narrowed eyes.

"I fear that is only the beginning," Lyndhurst muttered. Until now, the coxcomb had remained silent and grim, presumably lost in contemplation of impending disaster. Or perhaps he was simply savoring his last meal at the earl's table? Morgan stifled a satisfied smile at the thought and waited for the coxcomb to hang himself.

Unfortunately, Juliet did not seem to share his eagerness, for she rushed into speech without allowing Lyndhurst to elaborate. "What excellent fish this is! I daresay, there isn't another chef in all of London who can create as many interesting sauces. Don't you think so, Father?" she asked, donning a vacuous smile.

It looked ridiculous on her. Indeed, she appeared and sounded so unlike herself that Morgan abruptly noticed just how much he appreciated her usual conversation. The inane comments she made now were the province of typical ton females, most of whom were either idiots or schemers. But Juliet was different, a simple observation that filled Morgan with unaccountable warmth. It was a sensation perilously close to pride, akin to possession even, and he found himself frowning at the realization.

"Yes, Armand does have a way with food. Nothing like a French chef," the earl said. His daughter visibly relaxed at his words, perhaps thinking that she had avoided the inevitable. But Morgan wasn't so sure. The earl was no fool, and as if to prove it, the man swung his head toward Lyndhurst, his brows furrowed. "What's that you were saying, Cyril?"

Looking grim but self-important, Lyndhurst paused dramatically before delivering the bad news. "I fear, my lord, that the fell incidents that have stricken your household will only continue—and escalate," he said. He sounded like a doctor on a death watch or some Covent Garden fortune-teller. And a bad one, at that.

"Why is that?" the earl asked, his usual affable tone sharp.

"As you know, I have made some progress in the deciphering of hieroglyphs," the coxcomb said, and Morgan was hard-pressed not to snort. "In my examination of your latest arrivals, I was especially interested in the mummy case, being a most unusual acquisition, perhaps the first intact burial chamber to find its way to these shores."

Pausing once more, Lyndhurst glanced around the table, as though to make sure all eyes were on him, and Morgan purposely became engrossed in his plate. "I found a warning on the mummy case, my lord, promising revenge against any who disturb the rest of the dead," Lyndhurst proclaimed.

"The dead?" the earl asked.

"I'm referring to the mummy, my lord," Lyndhurst said.

"Oh! Doesn't like to be moved, does he?" the earl asked, chuckling. Juliet joined him in weak amusement. Morgan grinned, all right, but in anticipation of the coxcomb's fall from grace.

Unfortunately, it wasn't forthcoming.

"I wouldn't put much faith in that primitive scribbling,"

the earl said. "A lot of gibberish and pretty pictures hardly make for coherent messages of any sort."

Perhaps Lyndhurst liked his cozy berth too much to argue with his host, but he certainly didn't exhibit the kind of fiery-eyed zealotry that he had earlier with Juliet and Morgan. Indeed, he accepted the earl's curt dismissal with a kind of stoic calm that, in a way, was more unsettling than his previous feverishness.

"Mark my words, evil is abroad in this house, and woe betide all who dwell here," he said, the theatrical threat resounding loud enough for the servants standing nearby to hear. The coxcomb liked his drama.

"I suppose that means you'll be leaving us?" Morgan asked, his brows inching upward.

But before Lyndhurst could answer, the earl broke in. "Oh, come now, Cyril! You're an enlightened man. Surely, you won't let some odd bits of drawings put you off your work."

"I? No, not I," the coxcomb said. He met Morgan's gaze with his own arrogant one. "I have every intention of remaining here to study the phenomenon and all that occurs, even if in peril of my life."

Morgan snorted.

"You're not in any danger here, Cyril," the earl said. "Nor are any of us. I run a tight household, and if anything's amiss, Cheevy will get to the bottom of it." He grunted in obvious dismissal of the subject, a warning to all at the table that the discussion was over.

And although the coxcomb said no more, Morgan wondered if they had heard the last of his wild theory. Personally, he thought the threat of the earl's burly butler far more intimidating than any dead Egyptian.

RARELY did Juliet feel a need to escape her household. She was not one of those young ladies who made frequent trips to the stores for fripperies. She didn't stroll along the avenues or ride in the park at the appropriate hour in order to see or be seen. Her few female acquaintances were all married, and their interests had always diverged.

But she corresponded with several colleagues, and sometimes when stuck with a particularly difficult conundrum, she found visiting one most helpful. Some refused to speak with a woman, and others would not discuss their work, but Herr Brueger, her former tutor and a renowned scholar who also lived in London, was always accommodating.

After Cyril's bold announcement at luncheon, Juliet thought of Herr Brueger with longing, for who else could she turn to? She trusted the professor's judgment, and his sound advice upon the recent happenings would be appreciated. Yearning quickly turned to resolve, so instead of returning to the ballroom, Juliet called for a carriage to be brought around, and a maid to accompany her.

Of course, her father wouldn't approve of her leaving her cataloguing or of her visit to Herr Brueger, but Juliet had always argued that the professor's opinions were invaluable to her research. She wouldn't have admitted, even to herself, that his warm and generous nature played any part in her choice. If Herr Brueger's cozy rooms were a refuge from Cyril, her father, and now perhaps even Mr. Beauchamp, that was not a consideration. She only hoped that her colleague would offer some insights that might make her think more clearly. Or at least concentrate.

Of course, there was no guarantee that Herr Brueger would be at home, Juliet realized, as she stepped into one of her father's elegant conveyances, but because of his age and his health, he rarely ventured from his apartments. Juliet smiled at the memory of the small set of rooms, far more welcoming than her father's vast and elegant town house. It seemed a haven to her now as never before, for this time she wasn't troubled by a bit of Coptic grammar.

Her current problem was far more difficult yet less esoteric. Or was it?

Juliet felt real confusion, a rather alarming sensation.
She had always been a determined person, certain of her
studies, cautious and exacting, but ever since the arrival
of the new shipment, she had felt less assured of herself,
of all her assumptions, and even her store of knowledge.
Her brows furrowing, she wondered if she would ever be
able to return to normalcy again. It was a most disturbing
possibility.

But the sight of Herr Brueger himself answering the
door cheered her, his delight at the unexpected visit echoing her own, as he ushered her inside.

"I thought not to see you for months as you catalogue
the new collection. So exciting!" he said as he motioned
her to a worn, overstuffed chair. His wrinkled face,
wreathed in smiles, grew suddenly pensive. "Everything
arrived safely?"

Juliet nodded as she settled into the comfortable seat.
"Yes, everything arrived, but . . ." She paused, uncertain
how to describe what had happened.

"But, what? Is it not all you had hoped for? Not a disappointment, surely?" he asked as he took a nearby chair, his
expression one of concern.

Juliet shook her head. "No, the antiquities are beautiful
specimens, far and above my expectations."

"But?" Herr Brueger prodded, leaning forward.

"But there have been various . . . aggravations," Juliet
said.

Herr Brueger leaned back and chuckled. "Always with
the new artifacts come the difficulties, but they are well
worth it, are they not? Who else has a chance to study such
fine pieces?"

Juliet smiled. "I know. I should be grateful, and I am.
Usually, I would be thoroughly engrossed in my work, but
there have been distractions and, well, odd occurrences."

She paused to draw a deep breath. "Of course, Father doesn't think anything strange is happening at all, and you can just imagine what Mr. Beauchamp has to say about it."

"Mr. Beauchamp?" Herr Brueger asked.

Juliet felt herself coloring for no apparent reason. "He's the, uh, procurer of the collection."

"Oh, yes. Your father's contact in Egypt. He is here, also, in London?" Herr Brueger asked.

Juliet realized her face was flaming now and ducked her head. "Yes. He is staying at the house. Father wanted him to assist me with the cataloguing."

"Ah! So that is a difficulty, to work with this man who is not an expert," the professor said.

Yes, that is a problem, Juliet thought, but aloud she found herself disagreeing. "Oh, it's not so difficult. It's just that I have trouble reading his writing, and it is hard to concentrate with the company . . ." Her words trailed off, for she didn't know how to explain that Mr. Beauchamp had somehow changed from an unprincipled rogue into a knowledgeable man who loved his work, someone she could admire, someone who intrigued her, someone who had made his way into her dreams, seeming to haunt her both night and day.

"Concentrate? But I have never known anyone to disturb you," Herr Brueger said.

Mr. Beauchamp disturbed her, all right, Juliet thought, shivering in spite of herself. She remembered all too well those evenings in the darkened ballroom and the times he stood too close to her, making her feel flushed and strange and full of yearning.

"This rogue is not importuning you?" Herr Brueger asked, his voice sharp.

"No, of course not," Juliet said. Mr. Beauchamp importuning her? Why, nothing could be farther from the truth—unless one counted the way he had touched her cheek and stood too near and brushed against her with his hard body. . . .

The professor was silent for such a long moment that Juliet stole a glance at him, only to find him considering her so carefully that she looked away.

"This Beauchamp. He is an ugly fellow?" the professor finally asked.

"Oh, no! He is quite handsome," Juliet answered without hesitation. "And tall." *And muscular. And hard. And delicious smelling.*

"I see," Herr Brueger said, rubbing his thick mustache, his fingers hiding his mouth. "Well, this is interesting, indeed."

"But Mr. Beauchamp is not the problem, or at least not the one I came to you about," Juliet said, trying to direct her mind back to the matter at hand. She shook her head. "See how scattered I am? I feel like a henwit!"

"That is understandable," the professor muttered, still stroking his mustache. Surely, he wasn't laughing at her?

"Well, it is understandable, considering what has been happening," Juliet said. "Things have been rearranged and even stolen. A lovely papyrus that I had yet to examine has disappeared. And one of the servants said the severed hand attacked him. His leg was broken, and now Sir Lyndhurst is claiming it is all part of some ancient retribution for removing the mummy case from its home," Juliet said, pausing to eye her companion balefully. "You know how Sir Lyndhurst feels about the acquisition of Egyptian artifacts."

Herr Brueger simply stared at her. Finally, he leaned back in his chair, his thick brows lowered. "Retribution? What is this? In all my years, I have never heard of such a thing. Where did he come up with such a notion?"

"He thinks the hieroglyphs on the mummy case give some kind of warning, but he is misreading the signs, of course," Juliet said.

"Of course," Herr Brueger said with a nod. He shared Juliet's opinions on the translation of the symbols and had little faith in Cyril's theories. "But these claims of a malevolent force at work . . ." He shook his head. "I hope they do not find an audience. Such stories can do nothing except set back the work of those who are dedicated to the task of deciphering the hieroglyphs properly, as well as the study of Egypt itself."

The professor shot Juliet a look from under his bushy brows. "Even you are anxious. Yes?" Juliet frowned. Of course, she didn't believe there was any warning on the case, but still, she had to admit that the whole business was unsettling.

"This is not good," Herr Brueger said, shaking his head. "Who will want to preserve the country's history, if they fear doing so?"

"Oh, I'm not afraid," Juliet hastened to add.

"Still, I am concerned about these incidents," the professor said, turning at the entrance of his manservant. "Ah, some tea. Thank you, Karl. Just the thing on a dreary day. Will you pour, my dear?"

Juliet nodded, and talk of Cyril's bizarre theory was set aside, for the time being at least, though she could tell from the professor's worried expression that he had not forgotten about it. And despite the warm fire and the good company, Juliet was unable to dismiss her own unease.

For once, Herr Brueger's home did not provide the haven she sought. But if she could find no peace here, then where?

Although Juliet settled down to enjoy her visit, she could not rid herself of an odd feeling of restlessness, as though those things that had once kept her contented were no longer enough. She told herself that she had all the comforts her father provided, plus satisfying work and interesting colleagues like Herr Brueger. What more could she possibly want?

When a vision rose in her mind of Mr. Beauchamp, his worn linen shirt clinging to his hard chest, Juliet nearly choked on her tea. Was there no escape from the man?

"Excuse me, sir?" Herr Brueger's manservant cleared his throat, presumably in order to be heard above Juliet's sudden coughing.

"Yes, Karl?"

"I beg your pardon, sir, but something has come to my attention," the servant said, glancing discreetly at Juliet as though loath to speak in her presence.

"Yes? Go on," Herr Brueger said, ignoring the servant's discomfiture.

"Well, sir, there seems to be someone outside asking questions," Karl answered.

The professor smiled. "And what is so bad about that? We should all be asking questions of life, shouldn't we, my lady?" he asked, turning to Juliet.

"Yes, sir," the servant said. "But he's asking about, well, *you*, sir. Mrs. Hudson says he's been loitering about outside for some time, watching the house and questioning those in the neighborhood concerning who lives here, and most specifically *you*."

Herr Brueger's brow furrowed. "Perhaps he is a student, come looking for help but reluctant to do so," he said, his face again creasing with a smile. He stood and began making his way toward one of the tall windows that looked out over the street, seemingly without worry.

Of course, the professor only thought good of people, Juliet realized, while lately, her own opinions of others had taken a turn for the worse. Indeed, she felt a queasy sensation of suspicion that made her rise and follow Herr Brueger.

"Ah! I see him," the professor said, pointing at the glass. "There! A tall, strapping fellow across the way."

Although Herr Brueger's words seemed to confirm her uneasiness, Juliet told herself there were innumerable tall, strapping fellows throughout London, many of whom might have some sort of interest in the professor. There was really no reason to believe the attention to his home had anything to do with her visit here. Smiling at her own follies, Juliet looked outside, only to gasp aloud as she recognized the figure lounging against a nearby residence.

What on earth? Without pausing to consider her actions, Juliet opened the window and leaned out, shouting into the street like some fishwife. "Mr. Beauchamp! Come here at once!"

Of course, the object of her outburst didn't even appear startled, let alone guilty. Glancing casually her way, he strode toward the house with his usual confident manner. At the sight of his easy expression, Juliet knew a sudden urge to shake him, to stir him to life, or at least to truth. But the thought of touching him made her heart pound erratically. It had already increased its pace alarmingly, a reaction that she put down to annoyance and definitely *not* excitement at his unexpected appearance.

"Mr. Beauchamp! What are you doing here?" Juliet asked even as her mind whirled, searching for possibilities. "Surely, you weren't . . . Were you following me?" she wondered aloud, both incredulous and somehow . . . hurt.

"I've come to escort you home," he replied without apology or explanation, and Juliet's heart hammered anew, for entirely different reasons.

"Why? Has something happened?" she asked, her hand drifting to her throat. Had someone else been hurt? Perhaps her father?

"No, nothing's occurred that I know about. I would simply like to get back to work," Mr. Beauchamp said in that maddening drawl of his.

Juliet blinked at him, stunned at his outrageous behavior. The temper he seemed so effortlessly to rouse roared to life, and she drew a deep breath, about to deliver a scathing scold, when Herr Brueger, momentarily forgotten, stepped between them.

"So, you are the famous Morgan Beauchamp?" he asked. "Come in, come in. It is a pleasure to meet you."

Juliet wanted to protest this greeting, but she realized that even Mr. Beauchamp could hardly be left standing on the doorstep. Unfortunately, the moment's respite gave her a chance to notice how well he looked in a greatcoat, his wide shoulders filling out the heavy fabric, his tall form carrying the long garment with ease. When she realized how her gaze was roving over the man, Juliet snapped her attention away and returned to her chair, sitting down abruptly.

"So, tell us about Egypt, Mr. Beauchamp," Herr Brueger said, moving back into the parlor. "You have been there! You have walked the ancient routes and the shifting sands."

"Well, yes, but I'm afraid I cannot give you a good accounting right now," Mr. Beauchamp said. "I'm in a bit of a hurry to return to the cataloguing. You see, Juliet went missing at a most inopportune time."

"Missing?" Juliet asked. "I did not go missing! I told Cyril that I was leaving after luncheon."

"Yes, well, you didn't tell me," Mr. Beauchamp said. The gaze he turned upon her was by no means casual but so dark and dangerous that she shivered. *"Once something has been marked as mine, I look after it."* Juliet had no idea why the phrase Mr. Beauchamp had once uttered suddenly sprang to mind. Certainly, the man had no hold over her nor any say in her whereabouts.

He swung his attention back to his host. "I'm sorry, but we've already lost quite a bit of time this afternoon. Perhaps another day?" he suggested.

"Yes, yes, indeed! Of course, I understand," Herr Brueger said, smiling. In the face of Mr. Beauchamp's rudeness, the professor was being quite magnanimous. Indeed, his eyes seemed to twinkle as he rose to his feet once more.

"Yes, yes, well, I hope that everything works out to the satisfaction of both of you," he said. He patted Juliet's hand as he escorted them to the door, grinning happily. Juliet didn't know what he had to be so pleased about, unless he was eager to be rid of her.

The thought was depressing. Had she overstayed her visit? She would have remained longer, if Mr. Beauchamp had not arrived to drag her unceremoniously from her haven, a place that had been blessedly free of him. Did the man intend to invade every aspect of her existence? Juliet felt a bit overwhelmed, neatly trapped by his larger-than-life presence, by his sudden, unwelcome influence upon her senses—and her wits. And as soon as the door closed behind them, she waved her maid to the coach and rounded upon him.

"Why are you really here?" she asked, knowing full well that he was never eager to work.

"As I already explained, you disappeared and—" he began.

Juliet cut him off with a scowl.

He shrugged, though his body appeared tense. Was he simply standing against the wind that whipped at her cloak, or was he hiding something? "After all the suspicious incidents that have occurred, I thought it wise to keep an eye on you, to see what you were doing. You might have told me you were consulting with some colleague," he said, neatly laying the blame upon her.

But Juliet heard only one thing in his pious speech, and she halted her steps to stare up at him in astonishment. "To see what I was doing?" she repeated. "And just what did you think I was doing?"

If Juliet hoped to garner a clue from his expression, she was sadly disappointed, for his face remained carefully blank, and she felt her temper loose once more. "You suspected *me?* Of what? Of stealing my own antiquities? Of chasing after a footman with a severed hand?"

The rogue shrugged again, an unconvincing gesture, considering the severity of his insinuations. "I was just trying to look into everything."

Juliet sputtered, unable to contain herself, but unsure what, exactly, to do. As always, when they quarreled, something unknown flashed between them, making her warm despite the cool weather, and she was tempted to reach out and push him. Or pull him. Alarmed by these urges, Juliet glanced at the waiting Carlisle carriage.

"I don't know how you came here, but you are not riding home with me," she said. Hurrying toward the open door, she told the coachman to leave as soon as she was inside.

Although he could have forced his way in or caused some sort of trouble, for once Mr. Beauchamp did not argue. When Juliet glanced over her shoulder, she saw him standing in the street, seemingly unaffected by her dismissal, even as a cold drizzle began. The flash of guilt that came at that sight was swiftly denied. Juliet sensed that there was something else at work here besides his stated reasoning, but she was too angry and confused to try to grasp his motives.

Indeed, she was beginning to think that, like the most complex of hieroglyphs, Mr. Beauchamp's convoluted thinking was far beyond her ability to decipher.

Chapter 9

CHAUNCEY took one look at him and burst out laughing.

Standing in his bedroom, dripping from head to toe, Morgan did not share in the amusement. Indeed, the only thing that kept him from responding with a fist was the thought of a long, hot soak in the earl's bathing room—and reaching that goal as soon as possible. A scuffle with his companion would no doubt delay that simple pleasure.

"Where the devil have you been?" Chauncey asked.

Morgan stripped his shirt over his head and dropped it in front of the fireplace. "Investigating," he mumbled.

"Investigating what? A duck pond?" Chauncey asked, tossing him a towel.

Morgan ran it over his hair, then let it fall about his shoulders as he sank into a nearby chair. He proffered his foot, while considering the placement of a nice, healthy kick to his alleged valet. Chauncey, sensing his intent, approached warily. But he didn't stop chuckling.

"What kind of fool would go out in this downpour?" he asked.

Morgan glared daggers at him. Wet daggers. "It wasn't raining when she set out."

"She?" Chauncey asked. Then, comprehension dawning on his pinched features, he grinned from ear to ear and reached for the boot. "Ah, I see."

"Do you?" Morgan muttered under his breath. Because he certainly didn't. No matter what he had told Juliet or the old man, Morgan wasn't sure what he'd been about when he had gone haring off to Herr Brueger's.

All he knew was that when he couldn't find Juliet, something had clenched in his chest, and he couldn't rest until he knew she was safe. It didn't matter that she had survived to her adult years without harm or that he didn't perceive any real threat in the coxcomb's tales of doom. Morgan had prowled through the town house, ready to battle everyone, including the mummy itself, in pursuit of her. Lyndhurst must have sensed his mood, for the coxcomb was persuaded to share all the information he possessed without prevarication.

But even the truth had been no comfort, for the news that Juliet had departed in a carriage bound for the apartments of a Herr Brueger had left Morgan feeling distinctly peculiar, as if someone had made off with one of his prized artifacts right from under his nose. Or, worse, that said artifact had risen from its berth, like the coxcomb's mummy, to chase off after another collector.

Morgan hadn't liked his odd reaction, the hot pulsing of his blood, the tension between his shoulders, and the low thrumming of various ill-defined emotions. He had wanted to strike something, and since he could hardly pummel Lyndhurst for telling him the truth, he had taken off after Juliet, looking for another target . . . like this Brueger fellow.

Getting his direction from one of the grooms, Morgan had justified his actions with his concern for the collection. After all, Juliet was not behaving in her usual manner. Why would she sneak off in the middle of her precious work, in the middle of a veritable crisis, to visit anyone? Especially a man? With no chaperone except a maid?

Morgan had even wondered if this Brueger were Juliet's lover and using his influence over her to wreak havoc among a colleague's artifacts. Although outraged over the thievery, Morgan was even more incensed at the thought of Juliet's liaison.

He had told himself that such a possibility was unlikely, considering Juliet's total lack of feminine awareness . . . even though he had glimpsed a certain passion buried deep. More likely, Brueger was trying to gather information from Juliet about the antiquities, their worth, and how best to steal them. Perhaps he had already taken the papyrus! As the one in charge, Morgan had felt duty bound to investigate.

Something grabbed at his leg, and Morgan looked down to realize that Chauncey was trying to reach his other boot while he was sitting with one stocking-clad foot still suspended in the air. He set it down.

"So where'd she go?" Chauncey asked.

"She was just visiting some old scholar," Morgan muttered.

"Perhaps he's giving her lessons in more than history," Chauncey said with a sly smile. "Sometimes these ladies prefer the older gents, and someone with a string of degrees from some foreign university might just suit our resident expert."

Morgan's jaw tightened, the suggestion that Juliet would prefer such a man striking home. His own education had been a bit, well, sporadic. "They are simply colleagues," he said through gritted teeth.

"Ah, well, that's good," Chauncey said.

It *was* good. Morgan should have been relieved that Juliet wasn't engaging in any secret rendezvous, but he still felt wound tightly, his emotions in a turmoil.

"What was she doing running off by herself to this fellow's house alone, anyway?" he asked aloud as he stripped off his stockings. "What happened to chaperones? Don't they have rules in ton households? Hell, in any household?"

Chauncey sat back on his haunches, arrested, and gave Morgan a jaundiced look. "When did you start talking like an aged governess?"

Morgan blew out a breath, ignoring the barb, while Chauncey watched him warily. "I'm thinking you're headed for trouble, my friend, and that we ought to leave before you end up in the thick of it."

Rising to his feet, Morgan shook his head. "We're staying."

Chauncey groaned. "What for?"

"Perhaps I like having a soft bed, excellent meals, a companion who is more attractive than you . . . and regular baths," Morgan said.

"What? You just got dry!" Chauncey said, and the sound of his protests followed Morgan out of the room.

JULIET had arrived home with mixed feelings, annoyed that her visit had been cut short, but with an odd sense of anticipation overriding her resentment. Something lent an urgency to her steps, an eagerness to her return home that she had never known before. But it wasn't her work that called her or the familiarity of her household or a reunion with those who resided there.

Stopping abruptly, Juliet realized it was the possibility of another sort of encounter entirely that stimulated her, a handsome face with a roguish expression that roused her interest, perhaps the chance for an invigorating argument . . . or more. Even though she had just dismissed the man, it was Mr. Beauchamp and the thought of another reckoning with him that had her hurrying to her room.

Juliet shook her head at such perversity, so at odds with

her usual logical thinking. Unfortunately, her peaceful interlude with Herr Brueger had provided no solutions to either her own confusion or the bizarre incidents that had occurred.

And Juliet found the tension in the house had only increased in her absence. It wasn't too obvious, for her father would never stand for that. But the servants were white-faced and anxious, making it plain that Cyril's wild theory of animated corpses had already spread through the staff. No doubt, there would be more resignations to follow the footman's.

Even her maid, Millie, was uncharacteristically silent as she helped Juliet change from damp clothes. Although she had escaped a soaking, Juliet found herself yearning for a bath, an odd desire in the middle of the day. But she had wasted enough time this afternoon, and Mr. Beauchamp would only complain about more delays when he arrived. The thought made Juliet's heart beat a bit faster, and she quickly exited her room.

Still, she cast a longing glance at the elegant bathing chamber her father had installed a few years ago as she hurried past it. And that glance, along with her own preoccupation, proved to be her undoing. It seemed that one moment she was rushing forward, and the next she had stopped, halted abruptly by something solid. *Something warm, smooth, and solid.*

With a gasp, Juliet looked up to find herself facing Mr. Beauchamp, but one far different than she was accustomed to seeing. His dark hair was tousled, the ends still damp, and the sight made Juliet's stomach dip. She felt an unruly urge to run her fingers among the thick locks, and her hands spread only to still as she realized they were already touching the man before her.

Her gaze dropping, she noted the towel loosely draped about his elegant neck and his wide shoulders, gleaming and golden. *And bare.* Eyes widening, Juliet glanced downward where her palms were pressed against his chest, a smooth expanse dusted with dark hair and carved from hard muscle, with intriguing slopes and dips. Her heart leapt, and beneath her fingers she could feel the echo of another's beat.

Shock, fascination, and an unaccountable delight surged through her, and Juliet, who had never known a moment's curiosity about men, suddenly experienced a palpable hunger, a need to discover all, at least about this particular man. Her gaze dropped once more, and she didn't know whether to be relieved or disappointed to discover that he wasn't entirely naked. He wore breeches, low-slung upon his hips, though below them his calves and feet were bare.

Juliet looked up from those elegant feet to where her hands still rested, and she was tempted to run her fingers along the solid wall of that chest to those glistening shoulders. Unable to act upon such a mad notion, and yet unable to pull away, she glanced up over that strong jaw to Mr. Beauchamp's lips, and finally to his eyes, so dark and intent that they took her breath away.

He said nothing, and the power of his gaze kept her silent, as well. Indeed, Juliet would have been hard-pressed to form words. Her mouth suddenly felt dry, and she wet her lips with her tongue only to feel his heightened attention, his grip upon her tighten.

When she had stumbled into him, he had put his hands upon her arms to right her, and there they remained, heating her skin through the muslin of her sleeves. Although Juliet knew he would release her should she step away, somehow she could not summon the will. Instead, she stared at his mouth, his lips, absorbed as if by some newly discovered treasure.

"Morgan!" The sound of another's voice finally forced Juliet to move, and she shifted backward just as a man came into view behind Mr. Beauchamp. "I told you, you can't run around the place half-naked," the fellow said, a bit breathlessly as he slid to a halt, brandishing some sort of robe.

Then he caught sight of Juliet. "Oh, I beg your pardon, uh, my lady." Obviously some body servant, he hung back, the robe dangling from one hand, as if uncertain what to do.

Without a word, Mr. Beauchamp took the heavy garment and slipped one arm, then another, into it. Juliet, still gaping, caught a glimpse of dark hair under one arm and felt oddly dizzy, as though she might swoon. But not from shock. Only when he had covered that glorious chest with the robe did Juliet pause to blink, disappointment uppermost amongst a host of emotions.

His expression unreadable, Mr. Beauchamp inclined his head toward her, but in the depths of his eyes, Juliet saw the glint of something. A dark promise perhaps? Juliet was too naive to know. Then he smoothly moved past her, and she heard the servant shuffle off as well, muttering something about "trouble" beneath his breath.

Juliet could only agree. Rousing herself at last, she concentrated on putting one foot in front of the other so as to reach the ballroom, but as she passed through the earl's elegantly appointed rooms, a vision of Mr. Beauchamp's naked chest was all she saw.

By the time she approached the doorway, Juliet had regained some semblance of her composure. She knew her face was flushed and her breath was still coming fast, but her wits seemed to be working again, her thoughts churning wildly. Why had Mr. Beauchamp been walking about nearly nude in the town house? The gall of the man was astounding. Had he no shame? No modesty? Was he strutting about for the maids, as well?

The thought made Juliet frown, and she paused at the entrance to the ballroom to peer inside. At this point, she wouldn't have been surprised to see Mr. Beauchamp stretched out upon the mahogany table wearing nothing at all, a possibility that she decided was best not to consider. Besides, she knew he was in the bath. Juliet frowned. She had better not think of that, either.

She loosed a small sigh of relief when she did not see Mr. Beauchamp, naked or clothed. The only occupant of the room was Cyril, copying more hieroglyphs in his usual methodical fashion, and thankfully, fully dressed. He seemed at ease alone there amongst the ancient relics, apparently unaffected by his own tales of doom.

For a moment, Juliet stood watching him, considering him as she never had before. Suspicions that she would never have entertained in the past now sprang all too quickly to mind. Mr. Beauchamp had claimed that Cyril would do anything to best her in the quest for decipherment. At the time, she had defended Cyril, unable to believe that he was capable of theft, a most illogical act for a serious scholar. But now she wasn't so sure. Had Cyril stolen the papyrus? Had he concocted his story of ancient revenge out of whole cloth? But, if so, why? Juliet could not understand such irrational behavior.

Taking a deep breath, she told herself she was reacting too strongly, as she had been often enough lately. After all, her father didn't seem concerned. Indeed, he had appeared amused by the whole business, calling Cyril's theory "fanciful" and a product of "too much study into hieroglyphs." Perhaps he was right. And yet, Juliet couldn't help wondering just what her father would have said had *she* tendered such an outrageous explanation for the recent happenings.

"Ah, there you are." The sound of Cyril's voice brought Juliet out of her musings. He had lifted his head and was eyeing her with a censorious expression that did little to welcome her. Like her father, Cyril did not care for her consulting with other colleagues, nor would he approve of her abandoning her current task, even for an afternoon. However, he did not voice his opinion, so that she might dispute it, but let his condemnation hang in the air, like a thick, dark cloud. Lifting her chin, Juliet ignored it and moved toward her table.

"Your *assistant* was here, behaving in his usual boorish, ill-mannered fashion," Cyril said. "He demanded to know where you had gone, and when I refused to tell him, he became so belligerent I feared that he might resort to violence. I was tempted to summon a servant, but he finally gave way."

Observing his expression, Juliet wondered why Cyril's smirk looked so sickly, while Mr. Beauchamp's was so much more attractive. *And annoying*, she told herself. However, Cyril was rapidly beginning to match Mr. Beauchamp's efforts at irritation, without displaying any of the adventurer's more interesting qualities, such as his ability to conjure Egypt with his words, his tall, magnificent form, his dark, mysterious gaze, his supreme confidence . . . and, of course, the glorious expanse of his naked chest.

Juliet flushed and hurried to her worktable, hardly noticing when Cyril launched into a new harangue against Mr. Beauchamp. Indeed, she hardly noticed anything, although she picked up several items for study only to return them to their place. Her nerves felt strung tight as a bow, waiting for Mr. Beauchamp's appearance. What would he say? What would he do? How could she ever look upon him again without blushing?

"Mark my words, Beauchamp will be the death of all of us," Cyril said.

Jerked from her thoughts by Cyril's vehemence, Juliet turned to face him. Unless someone could die of embarrassment, she didn't see Mr. Beauchamp effecting such a fate. "What do you mean?" she asked.

"I mean just what I said. Make no mistake, he has put us all in danger. He's the one who took the mummy case, so he's the one who draws the revenge of the ancients," Cyril said.

Juliet blinked, unable to think of a suitable reply to something so ludicrous. Yet, illogical though his claim might be, she shivered, as if the chill of the tomb had reached out to touch her. A noise from the doorway actually made her start, and when she saw Mr. Beauchamp standing there, Juliet felt a wild urge to run to him, to throw herself into his arms, whether for his protection or her own, she wasn't sure.

The look on her face must have startled him, for he stepped forward, his own expression guarded. "What is it?" he asked.

Juliet gazed at him helplessly, unable to explain herself, and yet, still longing to run to him, just as though this tall, handsome adventurer, who wore a smirk so well—and the absence of a shirt even better—would somehow ease her fears and protect them both from all ills, real or imagined. It was a notion just as farfetched as Cyril's theories, she realized.

"Perhaps she fears the perils to come," Cyril said.

Ignoring that remark, Mr. Beauchamp stalked to the table, his jaw rigid. Was he angry with Cyril or with her? Juliet suspected he hadn't been too happy about being left in the rain, though he had little showed it at the time. She held her ground as he approached, though she grasped the edge of the table behind her, as if for support.

"I can't believe you left him here alone," he said, flicking a contemptuous glance toward Cyril.

Juliet wasn't sure what she had been expecting, but this was not it. "He's not responsible—" she began automatically, but Mr. Beauchamp cut her off.

"I agree," he said.

For a moment, Juliet simply looked at him, at his hard face, his lips cut into a curve, his dark eyes full of scorn for Cyril. And then she laughed. She actually laughed, her heart suddenly light at his cleverness, at the underlying truth in his words, at the fact that he was here jesting with her after what had gone before. All the nameless terrors and even the lesser irritations of overbearing, sometimes even inscrutable males were forgotten in that moment.

The reminder returned all too quickly. "And what, might I ask, do you find so amusing?" Cyril asked from his position across the room.

"Nothing, Cyril," Juliet said.

He huffed. "How can I be expected to conduct my own serious research amidst this sort of atmosphere?"

"You can't," Mr. Beauchamp said. He was looking at Juliet but spoke over his shoulder to Cyril. "So why don't you leave?"

Juliet felt Mr. Beauchamp's gaze upon her, and she flushed with a new awareness, all too easily remembering their last encounter. She cleared her throat. "You really mustn't wander the house in a state of . . . undress," she murmured.

"You didn't seem to mind," he drawled.

Juliet's eyes widened as heat flooded her. "Well, my father might. And the staff. It's just not . . . decent," she protested.

The rogue shrugged. "If I needed a bath, it was because you left me in the rain."

Juliet frowned at such reasoning. "You shouldn't have been spying on me."

Instead of answering, he studied her with narrowed eyes. "Just what were you doing traipsing over there anyway?" he demanded.

Juliet blinked at his questioning, her temper roused once more. "That is none of your concern!"

"It is when I'm kicking my heels waiting on you!"

As usual, they faced off, toe to toe, the heat rising between them, along with their voices, as they argued. And Juliet remembered all too well why she had left him in the rain. "How could you suspect *me?*" she asked.

At her question, Mr. Beauchamp's expression changed.

Juliet had no idea what he might have said, however, for the ensuing silence was broken by the sound of Cyril's high-pitched voice. "Would you please stop?" he asked.

As one, both Juliet and her adversary turned toward him and shouted, "No!"

For a moment, Cyril simply stared at them. Then, throwing down his pencil and paper, he stalked from the room.

Juliet felt a wave of guilt as she glanced toward Cyril's retreating figure, but before she could tender an apology, Mr. Beauchamp grasped her shoulders.

"No! Don't look at him. Look at me. You're not going to disappear this time," he said.

Juliet's brow furrowed with puzzlement. "I don't know what you mean," she said. "I'm not going anywhere."

"Good," he said. "Because this isn't over yet."

And before Juliet knew what he was about, Mr. Beauchamp bent his head and kissed her. The touch of his mouth to her own was a shock, one she had never known before, but surprise soon gave way to curiosity. And delight.

His lips were firm yet soft, strong yet gentle, as they moved over hers, and Juliet loosed a sigh. He drew back only to return, again and again, each kiss more powerful than the last. Her pulse racing, her heart thundering, she followed his lead, seeking him out, leaning into him to support her quavering limbs.

He groaned, and Juliet felt the brush of his tongue, insistent, demanding, and then sweeping into her mouth. She gasped, startled, then sank against him as a riot of emotions rushed through her. Curiosity. Excitement. Bliss. And above all else, Juliet felt a yearning so deep, she wondered how she could ever fulfill it—even as she knew that she could not. For what she wanted was to become a part of this man, to fuse with him, to have him take her away to a place of freedom, of heat and desire, of mystery and pleasure far beyond the bounds of her shuttered existence.

Giving in to temptation, Juliet lifted her hands and

placed them upon his chest. The worn linen was an unwelcome barrier, but she touched him anyway, seeking the warmth beneath, running her fingers over the hard muscle in glorious exploration. He whispered an oath beneath his breath, then his arms closed around her, drawing her against him tightly.

His breath was a hot shudder against her lips, his hands brands upon her back, stroking, caressing, and molding her to him. Juliet sighed and slid her fingers upward, over his chest and wide shoulders to sift through his dark hair, still damp. Dizzy, deliriously so, she clung to him for dear life. If this man was to be the death of her, she would willingly surrender to her fate.

"Mr. Beauchamp," she whispered, and felt the soft brush of a laugh against her cheek.

"Morgan," he said, as he kissed her throat. "Morgan, Juliet." Then he lifted her, effortlessly, to the table, and she was seated on the edge, hard mahogany beneath her, hard man in front of her. He nudged her knees apart, stepping between them, pulling her skirts taut, and Juliet shamefully ignored the hiking hem. Seized by reckless abandon, she wanted to see his chest again, and she tugged at his shirt, pulling it free of his breeches and sliding her hands beneath to the glorious, hot skin that she coveted.

Muttering another curse, he closed his hands over her derriere and pulled her to him, her belly against his, her legs spread wide by his hard torso. Then he took her mouth in a hot, pulsing, union that made her weak, strong, *exhilarated.*

Something was happening inside of her. As he so easily unleashed her dormant temper, he now loosed something else, something buried deep that blossomed forth, growing and spreading through every part of her, a throbbing ache that only he could assuage. Juliet slid her hands around him to the smooth muscles of his back, seeking his heat, needing his strength.

"Juliet," he murmured, his breath brushing her ear before he buried his face against her neck, his mouth moist and feverish upon her skin. Vaguely, she heard him whisper another oath. Then he bent her backwards over one arm, the other flung wide, and Juliet heard a thud as it struck something apart from them both.

They froze, and above their labored breathing, Juliet listened as what sounded like a piece of pottery spun round and round and then . . . stopped. Whatever she had been feeling was swiftly replaced by alarm as she realized that she was sitting atop the mahogany table, surrounded by notes and ledgers and antiquities, delicate treasures worth a fortune.

Juliet dropped her arms even as she felt Mr. Beauchamp's—Morgan's—fall away. She dared a glance at him to find him stepping back, his chest heaving, his jaw tight. The heat that had engulfed her before dissolved into the musty air, and Juliet shivered, suddenly cool, as she slipped from the table.

Her feet now firmly on the floor, she turned to make sure all was well and quickly righted the piece of pottery. The orderly rows of her work were outwardly reassuring, and she mentally catalogued each item, along with its placement. But even that familiar exercise gave her little comfort, for what use was her methodical arrangement of objects when her thoughts, her emotions, her very world, had just been upended?

And somehow Juliet doubted they could be so easily righted.

Chapter 10

JULIET ventured forth the next morning with a new wariness. She had spent the evening closeted in her room, having sent her regrets for dinner, although she knew Mr. Beauchamp—*Morgan*—wouldn't be fooled. Indeed, she had worried that he might come pounding on her bedroom door, demanding she appear. When he had failed to do so, Juliet told herself she was relieved, not disappointed.

Perhaps he had avoided the meal, as well. After the . . . kiss, Juliet had turned to find him gone, and for a long time she had stood there, stupidly staring after him, swamped by a host of conflicting emotions. She still had not sorted them all out, even after a night of tossing and turning in a bed that suddenly seemed cold and empty.

That dissatisfaction with all that was familiar fed Juliet's growing resentment of a certain adventurer. Oh, she did not regret the kiss. How could she? It had been beyond anything in her limited experience. And there lay the problem. It had opened her eyes to a whole new world. And yet what was she to do? Her natural curiosity, along with an uncertain yearning, urged her to investigate further, just as she would any topic of interest to her eager mind. But that course was not possible, given her circumstances.

Just as she tried to suppress the other emotions the man had roused in her, now she must ignore these new feelings. But it would not be easy to return to her ordered world of musty artifacts, however dearly beloved, when she had glimpsed something else. How could she go about her normal routine while aware of the soaring pleasure that could be found right here, in the arms of Morgan Beauchamp?

Morgan. Even his name had become dear, and Juliet tried not to savor it. With firm resolve, she steeled herself against any fleeting thoughts of a romantic nature, especially those connected with the man's incredible heat. Or his lips. Or his bare, muscled chest. Instead, she visualized hieroglyphs and their patterns while she marched toward the ballroom.

Thankfully, the vast space was empty, except for the artifacts, silent remnants of a world long past in which Juliet had once taken her greatest delight. Now, she wasn't so sure . . . of anything.

Juliet had barely reached the long table when he arrived. She didn't have to see him or hear him or even smell him. She just *knew,* a most disconcerting sensation. Although she attempted to focus on her work, it was useless. She could do nothing except turn to face him.

He stood just inside the room, looking so good that Juliet stared at him, momentarily overcome. And in that moment, all sense of shame and blame dissolved in a rush of pure pleasure at the very sight of him. He nodded, a bit uncertainly, and since he never was uncertain, Juliet felt even more overcome. She savored the look of him, taking in his every feature, from the shine of his dark hair to the tip of those worn boots, drinking him in just as though she were a thirsty desert nomad, parched and needy.

He approached her with his usual grace, and Juliet had

to suppress a shiver of longing, of wishing for things better ignored. With a swift gesture of greeting, she turned back to her work, but she remained aware of him coming closer and closer . . . and stopping. He was by her side, easily accessible for any questions or consultations, and yet he was not as close as he usually stood. Was he keeping his distance because of the . . . kiss?

Paradoxically, Juliet found that she now missed what once had irritated her, and she frowned at her own caprice. She was *not* capricious. She was a logical, serious scholar. And she told herself that she definitely did not want Morgan to come too close, to brush against her, to *breathe* upon her. But she lied.

Loosing a sigh, Juliet admitted that she wanted all those things. And more. She wanted the man beside her to take her in his arms and kiss her until she was soaring above the mundane into a new realm, exploring what happened between them more thoroughly than she explored any ancient text. *Oh, how on earth was she to do her work now?*

"Where's the peacock?"

"What?" Juliet turned to look up at her companion in confusion. Was he asking about one of the artifacts?

He tilted his head toward the other side of the room. "The coxcomb. Lyndhurst," he said.

Juliet blinked. "Cyril?" She glanced about, having forgotten that he had not yet arrived.

"Oh, I don't know," she murmured, suddenly realizing that she and Morgan were the only occupants of the ballroom. Her nerves pricked with awareness, and her heart picked up its pace. They had been alone many times before. So why did she feel it so sharply now? Juliet reached out for the nearest artifact—lest she reach for Morgan.

"Maybe he packed up and left, for fear of the mummy," Morgan muttered.

Juliet recalled Cyril's claim that it was Morgan who drew the ire of the dead, and she felt a chill. It was all nonsense, of course, and yet . . . She glanced back down at the small statue in her hands, unsure how to respond. "I'm positive Cyril is too conscientious to abandon his work here."

Morgan snorted. "I can't believe you defend him after the way he talks to you," he said, his tone harsh. Before Juliet could open her mouth to argue, he spoke again. "I used to know a boy like you."

Juliet stiffened. She rarely considered her gender except to rue it in relation to her work. She certainly had never primped and preened like other girls, and yet the notion that she resembled a boy, especially to the man who had kissed her, was dismaying. Had she done something wrong? Her lack of expertise must have been glaringly obvious.

"Well, not *exactly* like you," Morgan said, as though reading her thoughts. "But I once knew a young man who allowed others to stifle his spirit with duty and responsibility, who let them smother him with their expectations and rules. They tried to turn him into someone else, something other than himself."

Juliet frowned. Was he criticizing her again? If she were bound by rules, it was because she was a woman, and a man's lot, at any age, was different.

"Well, don't you want to know what happened to him?" Morgan asked, eyebrow arched.

"All right," Juliet answered with little enthusiasm. "What happened to the boy?"

He paused, his gaze snagging hers, his dark eyes direct and intense. "He escaped," he said, and then he flashed that white-toothed grin that made her knees weak.

He said no more, leaving Juliet to wonder about the anecdote. Was Morgan the boy who was stifled by others? But what duties and responsibilities could he have faced? Juliet bit her lip. Probably those of gainful employment. If so, just how had he escaped such onerous obligations? Had he stooped to thievery, or had he simply begun adventuring? But how had he raised the money for passage to Egypt?

Juliet was musing over the possibilities when she was struck by an even more alarming thought. What if his duties and responsibilities had involved a family? A wife? And children? The notion struck Juliet numb, but she could not discount it, for what did she really know of this man?

Nothing at all.

The knowledge made her breath catch, and a sound of dismay must have escaped her, for he glanced her way, but Juliet turned so he would not see her stark expression. And when she did, she saw Cyril in the doorway.

She had never been so glad to see him.

"Oh, Cyril, there you are. Mr. Beauchamp was concerned about you," she said, rushing into speech.

Although technically true, the statement was hardly accurate. Yet Cyril did not appear skeptical. "If I am later than usual, it is because I slept poorly last night," he said. Then he paused dramatically. "I was kept awake by disturbances, strange noises that occurred during the late hours."

Beside her, Morgan scowled. "No doubt, it was your own snoring that woke you."

Cyril flushed. "You will see. It has begun," he intoned. He looked around as though expecting something to happen, and Juliet felt the gooseflesh rise on her arms. Then he fixed her with his pale gaze. "Is everything in order?"

Juliet felt a momentary sense of disorientation as she realized that for the first time in her long experience with her father's collecting, she had not checked all the artifacts. Her mouth worked, but nothing came out as she stood there, stunned to silence by her neglect of duty.

"We only just arrived ourselves," Morgan said, and Juliet turned to him in grateful surprise. He had come to her rescue again, she thought. Her heart thrumming, she conveniently ignored the fact that Morgan, with all his distractions, was the cause of her lapse.

"I'll see right now," Juliet said. Pushing aside all thoughts of either man, she proceeded to make mental note of each object and its position, moving about the room, pausing here and there, then stopping before a heavy cabinet where she had placed some of the smaller items. Opening the doors, she peered inside, swiftly eying each piece until she came to a thick swath of velvet that displayed the fish necklace. Beside it there was only an indentation in the cloth.

Juliet blinked, unable to believe her eyes. She stood there staring at the empty space, her lips moving, but no sounds issuing forth. Indeed, she stood utterly still, as if frozen in place, until she felt the presence of Morgan at her side. As if he had sensed her dismay, he moved closer.

"What is it?" he asked.

At the sound of his voice, low and heavy with concern, Juliet found her own. "Something else is missing," she said, reaching for him with her gaze, if not her hands. He was her anchor, her solace, her touchstone in a careening world, and she didn't even question when he had become all these things to her.

"What do you mean, something else is missing?" he asked.

Juliet took a deep breath. "The golden dagger is gone."

Morgan did not bother to hide his surprise but swore under his breath. Stepping in front of the cabinet, he looked inside.

"If you recall, I placed it there after cataloguing it," Juliet said, pointing to the vacant spot on the velvet.

Morgan's eyes met her own. "Perhaps it has simply been moved?" he suggested, but even as he spoke, she realized he knew the truth as well as she did. The dagger had been stolen.

"It is the work of the curse."

At the sound of Cyril's voice, Juliet started. She was so wrapped up with Morgan in the loss of the dagger that she had forgotten they were not alone. Perhaps Morgan had, as well, for he swung toward Cyril with sudden ferocity.

"What did you say?" he snapped.

Cyril, seemingly unperturbed by the theft, stood facing them with a stoic expression. "Now do you believe in the curse?" he asked.

"The *curse?* Is that what you're calling it?" Morgan said. He lunged forward, and Juliet realized with horror that he might tackle Cyril in his rage. She reached out and grasped his arm to stay him, the feel of the worn linen beneath her fingers more familiar now but no less thrilling. Pausing, Morgan looked down at her hand and then up at her face, and something flared in his dark eyes. Awareness? The memory of what had gone before? Juliet felt a hot rush of longing before his expression was masked once more, and he turned back to Cyril.

"We'll see what the earl is calling it," Morgan said.

THE earl called it "missing."

Juliet rarely saw her father upset; that was not his way. But his lips were set in a hard line as he stalked through the ballroom full of treasures purchased with his wealth. He dismissed Cyril's theory with a gesture, yet was unwilling to declare the dagger stolen. And he proceeded to ask Juliet so many times about the placement of the artifact that she saw Morgan step forward, as if to intervene.

The possibility so alarmed her that Juliet raised her voice. "I have not mislaid it, Father. Nor did I mislay the papyrus," she said quite firmly. "But if you think it is about somewhere, perhaps a search is in order."

Her father frowned. Obviously, he wanted an easy answer for the problems plaguing the household, but Juliet could not give it to him. He did not like it when things did not go as he planned, and she braced herself for his displeasure. Instead, with a glance at Cyril and Morgan, he nodded.

"Very well. We shall search the house," he said. "I'll have Cheevy organize some of the footmen. You three might as well stay here. I don't want them tripping over you."

Accustomed to her father's occasional curtness, Juliet did not blink, but she could see Morgan was not pleased with his orders. No doubt, he wanted to be out and about, joining the hunt instead of waiting here with her.

Swallowing a sigh, Juliet turned back to her work and wished she could recall her suggestion. How could a footman be expected to search the ballroom? The very thought of an ignorant party disturbing the artifacts made her shudder, and as she heard them troop past through the rest of the town house, she couldn't help but wonder what they expected to find.

Surely, her father didn't think she had misplaced the papyrus and the dagger upstairs? Juliet never took items elsewhere to study, having learned long ago of her tendency to allow her mind to wander. Weeks would go by before she would remember a certain book or project she had put aside, but that was in her younger days. She had adopted the practice of discipline now, and if she became lax, Cyril was there to reprimand her.

Obviously, her father did not appreciate the years she had spent cultivating a system of orderliness and still thought her a careless child. The knowledge hurt, and she turned, as always, to her work, concentrating upon that which was in front of her instead of the missing items.

She had just finished cleaning a small statuette when a shout went up, startling her so that she nearly dropped it. Turning, she found that Morgan and Cyril were already heading from the room, and she hurried to follow. The shouts led them upstairs to where one of the footman was facing her father.

"No sign of the knife, my lord, but I found one of those foreign papers . . . in there," the footman said, cocking his head.

Juliet glanced over his shoulder only to stare, wideeyed, at the guest room behind him, for there, standing beside the door and eyeing them all with a mutinous expression, stood Morgan's manservant. Surely, Morgan's valet wasn't stealing, was he? Juliet wondered. But the alternative did not bear contemplating.

"It was in a trunk in this room," the footman said.

"Now, just a moment! That was my private trunk!" The voice that rang out was Morgan's, and as he shouldered his way past Cyril, Juliet fell back. Again, and far more forcefully than before, she was reminded that she knew nothing about this man. He could have a wife and children, a dark past, or a criminal present. Hadn't he seemed to know the moment she looked in the cabinet that something was wrong? Hadn't he hurried to her side with an eerie sensibility?

Juliet had taken his concern for granted at the time, but now she wasn't so sure. Had Morgan stolen the papyrus and the dagger, hoping that his thefts would go undiscovered in the rush to complete the cataloguing? The idea was not that farfetched, for just this morning, Juliet had been so preoccupied that she had not checked the artifacts. And she might never have done so, if not for Cyril's prompting.

Drawing in a shaky breath, Juliet was struck by an even more insidious suspicion. Had Morgan deliberately distracted her with his attention? With his *kisses?* Loosing a strangled gasp, Juliet sank against the nearby wall for support. She fought against the wave of doubts, but even as she struggled, she felt a new fear. Was the man who had held her and kissed her even Morgan Beauchamp?

Juliet well remembered his trouble deciphering his notes. Was it because they were not written in his own hand? By all accounts, Egypt was a lawless country. The man who had presented himself at the town house could have murdered the real Morgan Beauchamp, taken his collection, and fled the country. That would certainly explain his difficulty with the permits.

Horrified, Juliet must have made some sound, an instinctive protest, because he glanced at her, and his expression hardened. She could almost see him shuttering his thoughts, shutting her out. Turning back toward the footman, he held out his hand. "I believe that is mine," he said.

"I'll be the judge of that." The earl's voice rose over the assemblage, and the footman quickly responded. Ignoring Morgan's outstretched palm, he gave the paper to the earl.

Unable to watch, Juliet stifled an urge to bury her face in her hands and simply looked way, at anything except the papyrus and the man who demanded its return. Her heart thundered in her chest, as it did so often in his presence, but uncomfortably so this time, as though it might burst.

"Why, it looks like some kind of map," the earl said. His observation, delivered in a tone of excitement, made Juliet lift her head. A map . . . with hieroglyphs? She leaned forward, peering at what her father held in his hands and knew such a rush of relief that she felt dizzy.

"That's not the missing papyrus," she said.

"Are you sure?" the earl asked, glancing up at her sharply.

"Yes," Juliet said. "The missing papyrus had a rough corner, as though torn." Regaining her composure, she stepped forward to examine the item. It was a map, perhaps Greek in origin, though there were hieroglyphs on it, as well. "A most interesting combination," Juliet said, her attention caught.

"Let me see," Lyndhurst said, crowding beside her. "Perhaps it records the site of a forgotten temple."

"Or a hidden tomb," the earl said, his enthusiasm for that prospect obvious. "Where does it lead, Beauchamp?"

"I don't know," Morgan said, reaching out again. "Now, if you please, I would like my property returned to me."

But Juliet's father held on. "Where did you get it? And how do I know this isn't part of the collection I purchased?"

Morgan's mouth tightened. "All you need do is look at the purchase list or the ship manifest."

"Nonetheless, it would make a splendid addition. Perhaps we can discuss a price?" her father said.

"No," Morgan answered, his expression rigid.

"There's something about a great king," Cyril said, reading the demotic inscription. "But this could be an astonishing find! Didn't you go looking for it?"

"No," Morgan answered sharply. "The directions are indecipherable, just like your hieroglyphs." Fingers closing over the papyrus, he met her father's gaze, and Juliet could almost see the contest of wills that raged between the two men before the earl finally relaxed his grip.

"All the same, it might be wise to have my daughter take a look at it," her father said, assuming a more genial tone. "She has been known to make sense of old foreign tongues and the like. This map could lead to a valuable discovery. A lost temple or tomb would be a prestigious and perhaps priceless find, a worthy addition to any collection."

Juliet saw the gleam in her father's eye and knew that his interest had been roused. No doubt, he would continue to press Morgan about the issue, using all his powers of persuasion, both monetary and otherwise. But Juliet was not so single-minded. For once, the prospect of new hieroglyphs to study was not uppermost in her mind. She was too overwhelmed with relief at the knowledge that Morgan had not stolen anything. She looked at him, eager to see him once more, but he didn't even glance her way before turning on his heel and striding into his room, his manservant not far behind.

Juliet's sharp stab of disappointment was swiftly followed by guilt. She remembered how angry she'd been when Morgan had spied on her, distrusting her. Yet, hadn't she just suspected him of thievery, and worse, even murder? Although her doubts were hardly unreasonable, considering how little she knew of the man, Juliet decided that reason probably wasn't the best tool when dealing with Morgan Beauchamp.

As startling as the thought might be, she wondered whether she should abandon logic and rely on something else entirely, like instinct or . . . feelings. For long years, she had maintained that hieroglyphs represented the written language of Egypt, though she had no real proof. And now she knew, with the same sort of certainty, that Morgan Beauchamp was no thief or murderer.

She simply was going to have to trust him.

MORGAN stalked into his room, his shoulders tense, his whole body taut. He felt like turning around and slamming his fist into the door, or preferably, into the earl's fat face. Or perhaps the coxcomb's eager mug. Or Juliet's . . . Better not to consider the look on her features, he thought, his jaw tight.

"I'm sorry. I didn't think to—" Chauncey began, his expression grim. But Morgan cut him off with a gesture.

"You aren't responsible for them finding the map. How could you know they'd search my room?" he asked.

Chauncey shook his head. "I could have hidden it better," he muttered.

Morgan shrugged. Although covetous of his own property, he had not seen a need to secret it away. But, then, who could have anticipated the recent events? Obviously, someone was lifting items from the ballroom, one at a time, things easily pocketed that could be sold to another collector. Although Morgan had suggested the earl inform those within his circle not to buy the missing artifacts, there would always be some who would never hear of the thefts and others who didn't mind acquiring stolen goods.

Morgan gritted his teeth, surprised at his own reaction to the robberies. He shouldn't care. After all, he had managed to get all the pieces here undamaged. It wasn't his problem if the earl didn't keep them safe once they arrived. And yet, he felt a possessive fury at their disappearance. He hadn't gone through hell in Egypt for the benefit of some sneak thief. And what of his reputation? No one dared take what was his without fear of repercussions, and right now, Morgan was itching to cause some.

But the earl had tied his hands, dismissing the stolen items as simply "missing." At least the greedy bastard seemed to be a bit more concerned about the pricey dagger than the papyrus that had disappeared, for today he was not as sanguine. He had even instituted a search, which Morgan had welcomed—at first.

Leaning against the mantelpiece, Morgan grunted in frustration. "When I heard the shouts, I was sure they'd found everything in the coxcomb's rooms," he muttered. Instead, he had hurried upstairs only to find the earl manhandling his private property.

And that wasn't the worst of it. He could still hear the sound of Juliet's gasp, a kind of gurgling noise that was more alarming than the earl's accusations. One look at her, and he knew just what she was thinking. The woman certainly didn't know how to hide her feelings. But how could she believe he would steal back his own antiquities? Morgan's fingers curled into a fist.

He blew out a breath and told himself it didn't matter what she thought, now or then, but the knowledge left a bitter taste in his mouth. That's what he got for touching a pampered daughter of the ton, he thought, though he had never intended for things to go that far. He had been trying to gain her favor, for his own ends, but his intended methods had not included seducing her, especially right there among her precious artifacts.

The memory, even now, made his body stir, and Morgan wondered abruptly if he ought to abandon this game of his. A sort of panic settled in his chest, sending his heart thundering. Although he was known as a man unafraid of risks, what had happened with Juliet turned out to be more like balancing on the edge of a blade, perhaps a little too daring even for his blood. The last thing he needed was to involve himself with the daughter of a man who looked down on a baronet as beneath him—and who employed a bruiser of a butler. Of course, after today, his little diversion might well be over.

"I was surprised as you when they didn't find anything in his nibs' rooms," Chauncey said, dragging Morgan from his thoughts.

"What?" he muttered, looking across the room at his friend.

"The baronet. The coxcomb. I thought for certain he was responsible, him and his walking mummy," Chauncey said scornfully.

Morgan frowned. "Yes, I did, too," he said. Obviously, the recent incidents were no longer a matter of coincidence. But neither did he think them a product of some long-dead pharaoh. Morgan sensed the fine hand of a human, especially in the thefts, and he wondered if that hand was the pale, uncallused one belonging to Sir Lyndhurst.

"Just because they didn't find anything in his rooms doesn't mean he's not responsible," Morgan said. "But what's the point of blaming the mummy? To divert attention from himself? To get himself put in charge of the collection or try to remove it?"

Chauncey shook his head. "Blame me if I can figure the fellow out."

Morgan grunted. He was just as confused, and he didn't like the sensation. He slanted Chauncey a glance. "Perhaps you can have one of the housemaids distract his valet, so that you can give his rooms a more thorough look."

His companion, who had been sunk in the dismals, visibly perked up at the suggestion. "You think I'll find something?"

Morgan shrugged. "Let's just say I believe you are a much better searcher than some doltish footman."

Cheered by the praise, Chauncey nodded. "If there's something there, I'll find it," he said. "But what if he's not our man?"

Morgan shrugged again. "Then we'll just have to look elsewhere," he said grimly. "I'm not going to let anyone, not even a dead pharaoh, destroy my collection."

Chapter 11

✠

MORGAN was in a foul mood.

It was this dismal weather, he told himself as he dressed. And the endless, wretched bookwork. And the coxcomb with his dire tales of vengeful mummies. And a certain Egypt expert who thought him no better than a thief. . . . When Chauncey stepped forward brandishing a linen strip, Morgan turned on him.

"Don't you dare hand me a new neckcloth!" he snapped, having already managed to knot his current one into a hopeless tangle.

Chauncey scowled at him. "It wouldn't hurt you to start looking like an Englishman," he muttered.

"Yes, it would. That's why I left the country in the first place," Morgan said.

"Over a neckcloth," Chauncey said, obviously skeptical.

"Among other things."

"My, aren't we in lovely spirits this morning?" Chauncey said. "Have a bad night, did we?"

"You know very well I was right here all night," Morgan said.

"Well, there's the problem," Chauncey said.

"I have no business being anywhere else, and neither do you," Morgan said, a warning in his voice. But was it for Chauncey or himself?

"Can I help it if the maids here take a liking to me?" Chauncey asked.

"Yes. And you better hope that neither the earl nor his butler find out what you're doing," Morgan said, sitting down to tug on his boots. "I don't care to get tossed out of here, not just yet, anyway."

"Well, I shouldn't mind leaving. The whole house is in an uproar over the baronet's wild tales," Chauncey said, shaking his head.

"I don't suppose you found anything interesting in his room?" Morgan asked.

"Not a thing," Chauncey answered. "And let me tell you, it took some doing to lure that valet of his away. I never saw such a queer card. I can't imagine the coxcomb paying him enough to merit such devotion to duty."

"More likely, it's the opposite, and the poor sod's wages are garnished for any infraction," Morgan said.

"Maybe," Chauncey said. "Whatever it is, he sure does a job. The place is neat as a new pin. Either the valet keeps it all in perfect order, or the coxcomb's the cleanest fellow I ever met."

Morgan snorted.

"And he sure doesn't seem like much of a scholar," Chauncey said, shaking his head. "There wasn't a book or even a stack of notes lying about."

"Odd," Morgan said. "From the way he carries on, I'd expect every inch of the premises to be covered with hieroglyphs."

Of course, Juliet was orderly, as well, though he'd never seen her bedroom. The thought made Morgan clench his teeth. There was certainly slim chance of that happening since he had barely even seen her yesterday. After the rest of the town house had been searched, the earl had set his secretary, a pinch-nosed fellow with beady eyes, to check the contents of the ballroom against the purchase list. With both the secretary and the coxcomb hovering about, private speech was impossible.

During dinner, Juliet had said little, and later in the evening Morgan had made his obligatory visit to the ballroom only to find it empty, except for a footman who eyed him suspiciously. Disappointed at her absence, he had stood there wondering if she still suspected him or whether she was angry that he had kissed her. Or had she simply learned her lesson about meeting him there in the darkness?

Morgan shook his head, suddenly uncomfortable. He felt a nagging urge to talk to her, to explain, but what exactly? That he wasn't a thief? He shouldn't have to defend himself, he thought sourly. And as for that other business, well, it wasn't as though he had forced himself on her. She had kissed him back, with an eager passion unlike anything he had ever known, a small fact that he preferred not to dwell on.

Morgan swore under his breath.

"Exactly," Chauncey said. "There's not a thing in his room that would tell you the coxcomb had ever even heard of Egypt."

"What?" Morgan swung toward his companion.

"Lyndhurst," Chauncey said, his eyes narrowing. "If he's got the artifacts, they sure aren't in his rooms."

Morgan shrugged off Chauncey's suspicious gaze. "Did you find out anything else?"

"Just that everyone's scared—of the mummy *and* the butler, who's been an intimidating presence for years. He just seems to be a bit more touchy lately, as is everyone, from what I gather, including you," Chauncey said.

He slanted Morgan a glance. "I tell you, we ought to just

cut and run. This whole business is getting murkier and murkier. And I don't like the earl searching the room and snatching up your personal property. Perhaps he's of a mind to toss you in gaol and take back his money."

The comment gave Morgan pause, and he turned a questioning gaze toward Chauncey. Had the canny fellow sensed something Morgan had missed?

"I can't put my finger on it, but there's something funny about the earl," Chauncey said. "I don't trust the man. And that butler of his. He's a right cagey sort."

Morgan frowned. He had learned to listen to Chauncey's instincts and his own, but there was always the possibility his friend was tired of playing at valet and ready to return to Egypt.

"Why would the earl steal his own artifacts and scheme to blame me?" Morgan asked. "He seems more than pleased with his purchases. I assumed he would be willing to buy anything else we find. Why would he want to put us out of business?"

Chauncey shrugged. "How would I know? Everyone in this house is a bloody lunatic, which is why we ought to be getting out while we can."

Morgan turned away. "I'm not leaving until I find out who's behind all this."

Chauncey snorted. "All of a sudden, you're a veritable Bow Streeter," he said. "What does it matter to us if the lot is stolen? We've done our part. Now, let's be off before the whole house falls down around us—unless you have another reason for kicking your heels here, such as the same reason you're in such a foul mood this morning? A certain beautiful, blonde reason?" Chauncey prompted.

Morgan eyed his friend askance. "For God's sake, Chauncey, she is not remotely like any woman I have ever wanted."

"That's the problem!"

Morgan shook his head. "She's a member of the ton, the

daughter of an earl. I believe you are well aware of my contempt for that species."

Chauncey snorted again. "She's not like any of them."

Morgan opened his mouth to argue, but he could not, for, in truth, Juliet didn't resemble those pampered, spoiled henwits in the slightest. Such women were obsessed with their appearance, while Juliet obviously couldn't care less. She was too busy with more important things.

Young marriage-minded ladies always giggled inanely and chattered incessantly. But Juliet only spoke when she had something important to convey, and she never giggled. When she was amused, a lovely, bewildered look came over her face, followed by a breathy laugh that was positively seductive. Then she appeared startled that the sound had come from her. In fact, her laughter was such a rarity that Morgan had made it his mission to summon it more often.

He frowned. She was too rigid, too wrapped up in books and study and dry old objects. Although he admired her devotion to her work, she needed other stimulation. She ought to be out and about, especially where the artifacts were found, in their native land. Morgan pictured her standing at Gizeh looking over the sunset and felt heat wash over him.

"You were saying?" Chauncey taunted.

Yanked abruptly from his vision, Morgan grimaced. And, ignoring his friend's hoots of derision, he turned on his heel and left.

MORGAN'S mood was not improved by a morning spent working beside a subdued Juliet while the earl's secretary hovered about. The man was wasting his time, for Juliet already knew where everything was, while he didn't know a scarab from a sarcophagus. He was always interrupting for some sort of clarification, and Morgan resented the intrusion as well as the diverting of Juliet's attention.

With the secretary and Cyril milling about, and a foot-man stationed at the entrance, the vast ballroom now seemed uncomfortably crowded. Morgan found it impossi-ble to talk privately with Juliet, let alone do anything else. Not that he had anything else in mind particularly, but he realized he missed the scent of her, the warmth when he stepped too close, the subtle shift in her awareness of him.

Morgan told himself he could not carry on his old tricks in front of so many interested onlookers, but, in truth, the game that he had so enjoyed had become too dangerous. Having overstepped certain boundaries once, could he trust himself to stay within them? And what was the point in trying to irritate his orderly companion when instead of scooting away, she might surrender herself to him? Blow-ing out a breath, Morgan admitted that, tempting as such tactics were, he might just reach for her. *Or she just might reach for him.*

Chancing a glance at her, Morgan couldn't help but no-tice the way her golden complexion glowed in the light from the tall windows. Her concentration was focused on her work, and the sight of her rapt in study set his body humming to life. Stifling a curse, Morgan looked away to-ward the pinched face of the secretary and wondered, not for the first time, if the man was watching him. Had the earl set the fellow to spy upon Morgan or the coxcomb? Or both?

His fingers curling into a fist, Morgan stalked to the window. Maybe Chauncey was right, and they ought to leave while they could, but the idea of turning tail made his jaw tighten, as did the thought of abandoning Juliet. One person had already been hurt. What if whoever was behind the thefts became more aggressive? Morgan envisioned Juliet alone in the ballroom, too lost in thought to suspect a threat, and his jaw tightened. He certainly didn't trust her safety to the sort of doltish footmen who saw flying sev-ered hands and couldn't tell a map from a papyrus.

The sound of someone approaching made Morgan swing round automatically. At the sight of the coxcomb, he relaxed slightly, but his eyes narrowed at the self-satisfied expression the baronet wore. Morgan frowned as the fellow strutted forward eagerly, tossing a newspaper onto the end of Juliet's long worktable.

"See! Now do you believe it?" he asked, a triumphant smile on his face.

Morgan frowned. He had no idea what the coxcomb was blathering about, but it couldn't be anything good. A few casual strides took him nearer, and he glanced down at the *Morning Post*, only to stiffen in surprise at the sight of a reference to a certain well-known collector. Snatching up the page, he read further.

According to the *Post*, the family was plagued by an ancient Egyptian curse that sent a mummified corpse walking the household at will, seeking revenge upon the Englishmen who had wrested it from its native land. The servants were reported to live in mortal dread as, one by one, they were struck down by the terrifying creature.

Morgan's fingers curled into a fist as he glanced up at the smug face of the coxcomb. "You did this," he said. His voice, low and threatening, must have caught Juliet's attention, for she turned away from her notebooks to eye the two men uneasily.

Morgan thrust the page toward her. "Take a look at that."

Juliet's brows furrowed, but even that tantalizing sight wasn't enough to distract Morgan from the coxcomb's latest antic.

"Oh, dear," Juliet said.

"Now, do you believe in the curse?" the coxcomb demanded.

Morgan gazed at him in astonishment. "Do you really think this utter nonsense somehow verifies your lunatic tales? All it proves is that the idiots at the *Morning Post* are so eager to sell papers that they printed whatever rubbish you told them."

"I? I had nothing to do with it," the coxcomb said, seemingly outraged. "The earl knows that I am discreet and have never repeated a thing that I have witnessed in his household. Why, what could I hope to gain by doing such a thing?"

"That's the question, now isn't it?" Morgan said, glaring.

"I refuse to stand here and listen to these baseless accusations, especially when you are the one responsible for our doom," the coxcomb said, his voice rising.

"And how is that?"

"You wrested the mummy from its ancestral home, from its burial place and its native country. You stole it, and you will pay with your life."

Was that a threat? Morgan took a step forward, but he felt the touch of Juliet's hand, gently staying him again. Lyndhurst, seeing his chance, took the opportunity to hurry toward the footman—and the exit. Apparently, the coxcomb was more concerned at the moment with an angry Morgan than with an angry dead Egyptian.

His jaw tight, Morgan was still tempted to go after the fool, footman or no, but he did not want to shake off Juliet's fingers. In fact, he found himself looking down at them as though he'd never seen them before. Slender, but competent, not as smooth as some, they nevertheless held an appeal beyond any others. As Morgan watched, they dropped away, and he had to stop himself from snatching them back.

"Why would Cyril want to spread such a story?" Juliet asked, redirecting his attention.

Why, indeed? Did the coxcomb want to raise a hue and cry in the city in order to force the earl to move the collection? Morgan didn't understand any of it. He shook his head.

"And, if he is so determined to prove his theory, why would he deny talking with the newspaper?" Juliet asked.

Morgan leaned a hip against the table and crossed his arms over his chest. "Perhaps because your father might not appreciate the spreading of such lies about his household," he said. "Then again, such stories would certainly deter the average criminal. And it might make other collectors think twice before buying more antiquities."

Juliet's eyes widened. "You can't think my father has reason to promote this fabrication!"

With a glance toward where the earl's secretary skulked, Morgan shook his head once more. "I'm just trying to consider all the possibilities."

"Well, no other collectors have reported problems," Juliet said, pointing to the article.

Morgan's brows inched upward. "Maybe one of them is responsible. Maybe they are hoping to scare your father into selling to them."

Juliet glanced up at him in surprise. "Makepeace!" she said.

"What?"

"William Makepeace. He's been after the alabaster mummy case ever since he heard of it, before it even arrived here," she said, her voice rising with her agitation. "He's constantly offering to buy it, raising his price each time, but Father won't sell."

Morgan frowned. "Perhaps I ought to pay a call on this Makepeace."

"Of course, there are the museums, too, though I cannot imagine any of them condoning theft or even the repetition of lurid gossip," Juliet mused.

"The museums, perhaps not, but what about those who supply them?" Morgan muttered. Salt and Drovetti, consuls for Britain and France in Eygpt, liked to divvy up the country's artifacts between the two of them and were notorious for their tactics. Even a man with a permit to dig might suddenly be surrounded by their henchmen, with his find or even his very life threatened.

Morgan's eyes narrowed. He knew that both men were livid over his discovery of the alabaster mummy case, and he had long suspected that their reactions accounted for his abrupt permit difficulties. But he had escaped with his finds, despite their machinations. Did their long arms reach to England, into the earl's very home?

Morgan hesitated, uncertain. And what would be the point of such elaborate persecution? Simple revenge? Or did they hope that the earl could be pressured to sell the mummy case to one of them or their representatives? Perhaps they hoped to discredit Morgan himself and prevent anyone from buying from him in the future, so as to protect their territory. Morgan swore under his breath at that possibility.

"So you think the person responsible is another . . . adventurer?" Juliet asked.

Morgan effected a shrug, unwilling to share his suspicions. There was no point in alarming Juliet any more than necessary, and he could well be grasping at straws.

"It could simply be that one of the servants spoke out of turn," he said. More likely, the footman who left had aired his grievances to all and sundry, and nothing more was to be gained from speculation about suspects and motives.

Deliberately, Morgan curved his lips. "And what can the newspaper stories do other than to bring more publicity to your father's collection?"

Juliet looked skeptical. "I doubt that father will appreciate that kind of interest."

"Well, people will have to admire his bravery, to say nothing of that of his daughter," Morgan said.

Juliet smiled, and Morgan felt as if the sun had just risen over the desert. His body heated, and an unidentifiable sensation blossomed deep in his chest.

"And now that the ballroom is guarded, the thievery will end," Juliet said. Though her voice was firm, she looked to Morgan for confirmation.

He nodded, for even the coxcomb would have a hard time getting all but the smallest artifact past the footman. "Indeed, this ought to put an end to the whole business: items coming up missing, mummies being blamed, and newspapers printing the tales as truth."

And yet, even as he spoke, Morgan had an uneasy feeling that, as always here in the earl's town house, things were not what they seemed.

THE surrounding rooms were quiet and dim as Juliet made her way to the ballroom, and in the stillness she could hear the thundering of her own heart, perhaps beating out a warning against her course. Indeed, she knew she ought to retire, and yet she continued onward, as if compelled by some unknown force to her fate. Or her doom.

Even as she approached the entrance, Juliet wasn't certain why she had come. Ostensibly, she could check on the artifacts, but a nod from the footman standing at the entrance told her that such inspections were no longer necessary. And as she stepped over the threshold, she was acutely aware that she hadn't been here in the evening for days, not since Morgan had come upon her, enthralling her with a brush of her cheek.

After that, she had avoided the moonlight, thinking perhaps the night did something to the room, changing it somehow into an exotic land of enticement and darkness. Now, perversely, she yearned to revisit that place, to know the sensation of entering another world of moonlight and mystery, of ancient enchantments and primal lures.

And a certain rogue adventurer.

The darkness worked its magic, for the same antiquities that were a matter of science and study during the day now seemed shadowy and strange as Juliet weaved among them. But Morgan wasn't there, and in his absence, the room that had seemed romantic now took on a more sinister cast, the objects eerie and menacing, as if a hint of threat hung heavy in the air.

Juliet glanced at the footman, knowing full well that none could harm her here, but her pulse quickened, her uneasiness increasing. She told herself she did not believe in any of Cyril's wild claims, and yet . . . she gazed at the mummy case only to find it illuminated by a shaft of moonlight just as surely as it had been by the sun. The sight was both arresting and startling, and Juliet stared, suddenly unnerved.

Shaking her head at such fancies, she turned away, trailing back toward the entrance. Without Morgan, the night was not the same and might never be, for he might not return here during the late hours. He was behaving differently when they worked together, keeping his distance, no longer nudging her and unsettling her with his nearness. Although she had decried it at the time, Juliet admitted now that she missed the closeness, and a fierce yearning rose up within her.

As she reached the heavy stela, Juliet paused, as always, to admire the message upon it, and she realized that all her life she had been driven by a fierce will to learn, to study, to decipher. She had always reached for what she wanted, so why not continue, even though the object of her desire was not a book or a consultation or a papyrus?

If she wanted to regain that closeness, why didn't she just move nearer? The simplicity of that answer astounded her. If she wanted to brush up against Morgan or lean into him, she had only to do so, using the same techniques he had used. Juliet drew in a sharp breath, for such bold actions carried a hint of danger, like a trip to Egypt itself. But what truly valuable venture did not? Still, she hesitated, feeling beyond her depth. And since she had no idea what Morgan would do in response, to make such a move would be like stepping into the unknown.

But wasn't that always what she most wanted?

MORGAN headed down to breakfast, smiling in anticipation of a sideboard laden with good English fare, one of the benefits to staying at the town house. As he kept telling Chauncey, there were advantages to civilization, namely excellent food, clean linen, a hot bath, and foremost of all, Juliet Cavendish.

Stopping in his tracks, Morgan frowned at the realization that he had just put Juliet at the top of that list, ahead of elegant meals prepared by a French chef. But he was right. Somehow, even the pleasure of the earl's bathing chamber paled in comparison to her charms.

And they weren't the charms one usually associated with a woman, at least not the women of Morgan's acquaintance. Juliet was so intelligent that it boggled his mind. She was far more learned than her father or the coxcomb. Her facility for languages, her knowledge of Egypt, and her study of the hieroglyphs roused in him an unusual sensation akin to pride. Or maybe it was simply excitement.

She definitely had that effect upon him when she whispered some bit of comment or instruction while her scent, light and clean and alluring, wafted over him. Her skin was a pale golden color, far more appealing than the usual whey-faced lady. And that hair, like spun honey, soft and wispy at the edges, but thick and full where it was caught up, as always, atop her head, made Morgan ache to set it free.

He ached in more ways than one. Her body, though straight and tall, was lusciously curved. Morgan didn't know how many times she had cut off his breath when she leaned forward over the table, her demure gown revealing a shapely bottom that made him want to grab her by the hips and pull her to him.

But it wasn't just her appearance that appealed to him. There were others probably more beautiful among the demimonde and maybe even the ton, certainly in the great wide world. But Juliet wasn't like them. She hadn't the faintest idea of her own beauty. She was too busy pushing up her spectacles and staring at mummified remains or the incomprehensible symbols of ancient peoples.

Unlike other females, Juliet was steady, calm, and reasonable . . . except when arguing with him, he thought with a grin. But he would rather she fight with him than assume the pose of acceptance she did with her father and the coxcomb. At the thought, Morgan frowned. He couldn't understand how anyone could call her flighty. Maybe she became engrossed in study to the exclusion of all else, but that was a mark of genius, not a disorderly mind.

Her peers might be feather-witted creatures, costuming themselves, perfuming themselves, and fluttering about with fans and smelling salts like so many guinea hens, but not Juliet. Juliet was in a class of her own, a new class, the class of Juliet.

A lady of distinction.

Smiling faintly, Morgan continued on to the main staircase only to halt again, arrested this time not by his own disturbing thoughts but by a sound coming from below. It took him an instant to realize that he was not mistaken, that he was indeed hearing screams, and then he raced down the steps toward the noise, which appeared to be coming from the general direction of the ballroom.

Sure enough, as Morgan approached the earl's collection, he came upon a young maid, probably intent upon lighting the hearths, who was now cowering against one wall. At the sight of Morgan, she pointed wordlessly, apparently having exhausted her voice. Morgan wasn't sure what he expected, perhaps another appearance of the mummified hand, but what he found was the footman lying on his back just inside the entrance, either dead or unconscious.

When Morgan stepped closer to investigate, the servant resumed wailing uncontrollably. And Morgan couldn't blame her. Although he could see no sign of blood on the body, there was something equally chilling. On the front of the spotless white livery that graced the man's chest was a symbol, a hieroglyph in the form of a dagger, drawn right over his heart. The stark black mark made even Morgan hesitate for a moment before kneeling to put a hand to the fellow's neck.

"What is it?"

The sound of Juliet's voice behind him made Morgan look up. Her face was pale, but, as always, she looked sensible and capable, a good woman to have in a crisis, a trusted partner to stand at your back.

"He's alive," Morgan said at the feel of the man's pulse beneath his fingers.

"Thank goodness," Juliet said. The appearance of another female, with more good sense, had reduced the servant's howling to a series of sobs and hiccups. Still, she watched in wide-eyed horror as Juliet fearlessly knelt beside the body.

Morgan inspected the man more closely, feeling around for any signs of wounds, but finding nothing outwardly visible. He began to wonder whether the footman had been drugged when he gently turned the fellow's face and found what he had been looking for: blood from a blow to the back of his head. But how had someone managed to attack him from behind?

"I've seen this before," Juliet said, drawing Morgan from his musings. She was staring in fascination at the hieroglyph, and while Morgan watched, she reached out to touch it. Lifting her hand, she rubbed the dark substance that marred the white livery between her fingers.

When Morgan lifted his brows in question, her own furrowed. "The other morning there was a footprint by the mummy case that looked like dirt but was more like this. Ash or soot," she mused.

"It's kohl," Morgan said. "It can be made from soot and is used in Egypt as a sort of paint, mainly by women to adorn their eyes."

Juliet frowned in puzzlement. "But why use it here, like this?"

"To cause a reaction like that, I assume," Morgan said, inclining his head toward the sobbing servant. "I'm sure our mummy is not making kohl with which to brand his guardians, if that's what you're thinking."

"It's a warning." The unmistakable sound of the cox-comb's voice made Morgan glance up to see the doom-sayer himself, with the butler close behind.

"A warning against what?" Morgan asked. "Guarding the ballroom?"

"Against interfering with the will of the dead," the cox-comb intoned.

"What's happening here?" the butler demanded, practically shoving Lyndhurst aside in his haste.

"He's been struck on the back of the head. Please sum-mon a physician," Morgan said. He met Cheevy's fierce glare with his own, and for a moment, he wondered whether the butler would do his bidding. But at last the man nodded stiffly and turned to go, pausing to snap at the maid.

"Stop that racket, you," he said. "Go on about your du-ties, now."

"It's all right, Cheevy," Juliet said, rising to her feet. She stepped toward the maid and so missed the dark glance the butler sent her.

But Morgan saw it, and he stiffened, uncertain what to make of it. Did the servant resent his orders being counter-manded, or was there something more sinister at work? Morgan didn't trust the butler any more than he did Lyndhurst, but surely the employee wouldn't harm his mistress. Would he?

"I was just lighting the fires, and I didn't want to come this way, but everyone said I was being silly now that someone was guarding the place," the maid wailed. "And then I saw him!"

"Yes, well, I'm sure that was alarming," Juliet said, patting her absently. "Now, why don't you run on to Cook and have a cup of tea. Tell him I sent you."

At last, the maid hurried away, leaving only Morgan, the coxcomb, and Juliet by the prone guard. Still kneeling beside him, Morgan saw the man stir and leaned over as his eyes flickered.

"Don't move. You've been hurt, and we want a doctor to tend you," Morgan said. "Can you tell me what happened?"

The guard moaned. "Someone hit me," he said, lifting a hand toward his head.

"Who?"

"Don't know," the guard mumbled, dropping his arm. "He took me from behind."

"And where were you when this happened?" Morgan asked.

"I was right inside the door, standing watch so that no one could get in. But how could anyone get behind me?" he muttered. Then he groaned, his eyes fluttering closed once more.

"That's what I want to know," Morgan murmured. Louder, he said, "Rest now, and we'll talk later."

Morgan glanced up in time to see the coxcomb draw a deep breath. "Not a word," he said, cutting the fool off with a glare.

But even if the coxcomb said nothing, Morgan knew that rumors would run rampant about the latest incident at the Carlisle town house. No doubt, the *Morning Post* would soon declare in print that an avenging mummy had attacked the footman, leaving him for dead. And even Morgan would be hard-pressed to argue.

For how else to explain how a man, alone in the ballroom, had been struck from behind?

Chapter 12

By the time the physician arrived, the footman was awake, though he could add nothing pertinent to his previous statements. Apparently, he had heard and seen nothing before his attack. As Cheevy helped the injured man to his feet, Morgan watched with a jaundiced eye. Hopefully, if the fellow remembered anything else, the news would travel through the servant's quarters to Chauncey.

The morning was well along now, and Morgan was inclined to pay a few calls on various associates to find out about other collectors, specifically the Makepeace who Juliet had mentioned, and to query whatever connections the two consuls had here in London.

But one look at Juliet, who was waiting expectantly, told Morgan he wasn't about to escape. Swearing under his breath, he strode over to the worktable, where she had already spread out his notes about a certain piece of statuary. Heaving a sigh, he looked at the papers and squinted, trying to make sense of what he had written. In fact, Morgan was concentrating so hard that at first he didn't notice anything unusual.

Then the subtle scent of Juliet drew his attention. He breathed it in, reveling in it for a long moment before catching himself. Glancing up from his writings, he saw that she must have inched closer to him, for her arm was almost brushing his. He took a step to one side, away from temptation, and studied his own words.

"It was found here," Morgan said, pointing to his rudimentary map. "Chauncey and I did a little digging around there before the local bey chased us off," he added, grinning at the memory.

Instead of a scold or a derogatory comment, his companion laughed softly. Startled, Morgan looked toward her, only to find that she was quite close once more. His brows inched upward in question, but she only smiled at him.

That smile, so full of intelligence and courage, arrested him. Morgan felt his pulse kick and his body hum in response. He practically had to shake his head to clear it, and he moved to one side, away from the allure of her scent, away from the downy softness of the wisps of blonde hair escaping its confines, away from the body he had held in his arms . . . and wanted to hold again.

Swearing under his breath, Morgan eyed his scrawls with even more difficulty than usual. Holding up the pages as sort of a makeshift shield, he put them between himself and Juliet as he read aloud. But when he had finished and tried to set them down, she was there, facing him, only a hairsbreadth away.

Maybe she was anxious, Morgan thought. After all, the grisly sight of the injured footman was enough to frighten the most sensible of women and turn even an independent female like Juliet toward a protector. But she didn't appear to be afraid. Watching her as she completed her own notes, Morgan saw that her color was high, her breathing a bit fast paced, and her famous concentration notably absent.

Morgan's eyes narrowed as he backed away. "What next?" he asked gruffly.

"Why, I think that piece right there," she said. Turning to reach in front of him, she brushed against him.

The feel of her breasts against his chest made him stiffen—all over. Morgan jerked away, suddenly suspicious. Had his naive bluestocking turned the tables on him? It certainly seemed as though the notoriously clever study was plying his own tricks to her advantage.

Unfortunately, it was working. He was just as annoyed as she used to be. "What are you doing?" he demanded, grasping her arms.

"Me?" she asked. But she was too honest, too innocent to mask her intent. A delicious pink flush rose upon her cheeks, and her eyes grew wide. Morgan could feel the heat of her beneath his palms, feel himself being sucked into her hazel eyes, and it took all of his power not to jerk her to him and continue where they had left off the other day.

One swift glance toward Cyril as well as the *two* men now guarding the entrance to the ballroom made Morgan drop his hands. "Don't tempt me," he warned her through gritted teeth.

Then he turned on his heel and stalked away, telling himself he needed some air, when he knew very well what he needed. And it didn't have anything to do with breathing.

SEIZING his chance, Morgan left the town house and made his way to the British Museum in Chelsea. Established in the last century, the museum owed its existence to Sir Hans Sloane, a wealthy intellectual, physician, and once head of the Royal Society, that great body devoted to the pursuit of sciences. Sloane had provided for the preservation of his home and collections in his will, but the place had truly come into its own with the addition of the Egyptian artifacts obtained by Salt.

After arguing with the attendant for several minutes, Morgan was ushered into the inner sanctum, where the trustees and various associates did their business. He had only a moment to wait before a weathered, wiry fellow stepped out to greet him.

"Well met, Burrows, old friend," Morgan said, rising to his feet.

"I'm surprised you have the nerve to show your face here," the man said, his expression fierce.

Morgan's eyebrows inched upward.

Burrows shook his head at Morgan's response. "Nothing ever ruffles you, does it?" he asked. Then he inclined his head toward the door. "Let us take a walk, shall we?"

Morgan nodded, silent as they made their way onto the street.

"The trustees are out for your head, you know," Burrows said.

Morgan again lifted his brows at that bald declaration. Apparently, they would have to stand in line, along with everyone else.

Burrows frowned. "What you're doing is bad for business."

"What *I'm* doing?" Morgan echoed.

Burrows waved his words away with an impatient gesture. "I imagine you thought to create a little excitement among the private collectors here, to make more of a market for your wares. But whatever you intended, it has had the opposite effect. Now you're causing problems for everyone."

Morgan halted and turned to face his companion. "Believe me, Burrows, I haven't had a thing to do with this curse business, other than to be the recipient of it. And I have no idea who is behind it. In fact, I was hoping you would be able to enlighten me."

"Me?"

"Who else has a better knowledge of the collecting

community? And, well, you can't deny that the consuls weren't too happy when I found that mummy case," Morgan noted.

Burrows's brows furrowed. "No, but . . ." He swung toward Morgan with a sputter. "You aren't accusing either of them, are you?"

"Well, let's just say it would be to their advantage to discredit me."

Burrows shook his head. "I can't see it, Morgan. They both have their hands full with new excavations and more than enough interested buyers for their finds. And their admittedly forceful tactics are limited to the field. They certainly aren't going to cause any dustups here! Bad for business! And, to be honest, I don't think either one is likely to come up with such an elaborate scheme, and if they did, I'd probably hear of it."

"That's what I was hoping," Morgan said, frankly disappointed at Burrows's lack of information. "Can you think of anyone else who has a grudge against me?"

Burrows shook his head. "Can't think of a soul who'd like to tangle with you," he said. He paused, as if in thought, then slanted Morgan a glance. "Are you sure that you are the target of this mischief?"

Morgan studied his companion with some surprise.

Burrows looked a bit uncomfortable under the scrutiny, but he continued. "While you are certainly affected by these rumors, someone could be trying to cause trouble for your patron, the earl of Carlisle."

"Go on," Morgan said.

"Well, the man is not very well thought of, even among his peers. Of course, some of that could be jealousy, but I hear hints of shadowy doings that have earned him disapproval."

"Among who? The trustees? Other collectors?"

Burrows glanced away. "Everyone, I think."

"Interesting," Morgan murmured.

"But that's just hearsay," Burrows noted.

"And what of the other collectors? Do you see anyone profiting from these rumors? What about William Makepeace?" Morgan asked.

Burrows shook his head. "Makepeace is the most nervous. Who would have thought that hard-nosed bargainer would turn out to be afraid of his own artifacts? He's been quietly putting out the word that he's willing to sell some of his prized antiquities, for a hefty fee, of course."

Morgan's eyes narrowed at that news. If Makepeace was getting rid of his collection, he could hardly be intending to buy out the earl, as Juliet had suggested.

"It's a bad business," Burrows said. "People are so afraid of this curse of yours that they are turning their acquisitions over to the museum. While that is a small boon for us, some are calling for a ban on all imports from Egypt and even the Orient. If this continues, the market for your finds and everyone else's will go soft. Or underground."

"I hope it won't come to that," Morgan said. His very livelihood depended upon a ready and willing pool of buyers. "We'll have to make sure it doesn't. So, if you learn anything else that might help, please contact me or Chauncey. We are staying at the earl's town house, at least for the time being."

Burrows's brow furrowed as he studied Morgan. "Perhaps the wise course would be a return to Egypt."

Morgan shook his head. "Not until I find out what is happening here. So I would appreciate any information you can provide."

Burrows gave him a nod, his initial expression of suspicion having given way to respect over the course of their conversation. "I will bid you good luck, then," he said and turned to go.

Morgan had only taken a few steps when his companion called him back. "Wait! I do remember hearing that someone was asking a lot of questions about you. I assumed it was in connection with the curse, but perhaps not."

"Who was it?" Morgan asked.

"A specialist on Egypt, on hieroglyphs, I believe," Burrows answered. "A scholar by the name of Brueger."

Morgan's fingers fisted at his side, though he schooled his expression to reveal nothing. With a nod of thanks, he again took his leave, but his gut was churning. Did his recent visit account for the obscure scholar's interest, or was it something else? Morgan intended to find out, but a glance at the time told him not today. It was already afternoon, and he would have to return to the town house or face Juliet's wrath. His pulse kicked up at the thought.

Frowning, Morgan realized that it wasn't so much her anger he worried about now but something else entirely.

MORGAN leaned back against the mantelpiece, his arms crossed over his chest as he looked over the expanse of his bedroom toward where Chauncey was brushing out his coat.

"He must have come through a window," Morgan muttered.

"What's that?" asked Chauncey.

"Whoever struck the footman on the head. He had to have gotten into the ballroom through one of the windows," Morgan said.

"Well, did you check them?" Chauncey asked.

"Yes," Morgan answered. "A couple of the latches are broken."

Chauncey shook his head. "Whoever it was must be either a lunatic or a brave man to break into this house. I tell you, this curse business is liable to incite a panic."

Morgan nodded grimly. "That's what Burrows said. The earl blustered his way through the first *Morning Post* story, seemingly pleased at getting publicity for his collection and himself, but when this latest bit gets out, I'll wager he won't be so happy."

Chauncey nodded. "It's one thing to be thought of as a courageous man, unfazed by ancient curses, but quite another to be blamed for unleashing some kind of havoc on the populace."

"Well, he's certainly closemouthed about it," Morgan observed. "I told him about the windows at dinner, and he said he'd have someone fix them, but he made it quite clear the topic was not up for discussion."

"Did you see the new footmen he's set to guard the ball-room?" Chauncey asked.

"Yes, why?"

Chauncey shook his head. "I'll say it again. Our host has some interesting connections."

"Really?" Morgan asked.

Chauncey nodded. "These new guards of his aren't coming off the wagon from the farm, I can tell you that."

"They certainly don't have the look of the usual servant," Morgan agreed. "Are you saying he's filling the house with more pugilists or something worse?"

"I'm saying these sorts are more likely to slit your throat first and ask questions later. Keep your eyes open and your back to the wall," Chauncey advised.

Great. Now the very guards set to protect them were a threat. Morgan shrugged his shoulders, trying to ease the tension between them as he considered Juliet working alone in the ballroom under the aegis of those two.

Chauncey cleared his throat. "I say we take our leave while we are still in one piece."

Morgan slanted his friend a glance but didn't bother to comment. He certainly was not going to abandon Juliet to a situation where she might be hurt. The very thought made him tense, and he felt a sudden urge to check on her, to make sure the locks on her windows would hold, to keep her safe. Now. Forever.

"Now where are you going?" Chauncey demanded as Morgan moved toward the door.

"To look in on a certain lady," Morgan said.

Chauncey muttered something about doom.

Morgan's brows inched upward. "Haven't you been urging me not to kick my heels here all night?"

Chauncey snorted. "That was before I knew the butler and his new footmen would happily gullet us for wandering freely about the house."

Chuckling, Morgan ignored Chauncey's snorts and slipped out the door. He told himself that he needed to talk to Juliet privately about what had happened this morning—the attack on the footman, not her own aberrant behavior. Then again, it wouldn't hurt to give her a word to the wise on that score—not to tempt him, deliberately or otherwise.

As much as it pained Morgan to admit it, there could be nothing further between them, not with Cyril and the secretary and surly guards looking over their shoulders, let alone the earl himself, who was turning out to be anything but the genial fellow he pretended. Morgan's jaw tightened. But that didn't mean he was going to leave Juliet to the fates or the curse or the manipulation of others.

Silently, Morgan found his way with confidence, even in the darkness. Possessed of an unerring sense of direction, he always made certain he knew the plan of a place when he moved in and just who stayed where. He had learned long ago that it was always good to have a quick exit nearby.

Halting before Juliet's door, Morgan listened, alert for the sound of a maid's voice, but all was quiet within. He knocked softly and waited only a moment before the door swung open and there she was, dressed in nothing except a voluminous white nightrail.

"Mr. Beauchamp!" The sound of his own name, uttered in a breathless whisper of surprise, had never arrested him before. Neither had the sight of a virgin in her nightclothes, but then, nothing about Lady Juliet Cavendish struck Morgan as it should. For a moment, he simply stood there, rendered speechless by downy hair glowing in the candlelight and a luscious figure not completely hidden by a swath of linen.

When her brow began to furrow, Morgan felt his body clench in response and remembered, finally, that he was standing outside. With a swift glance about him, he stepped in, only to see that Juliet was donning a heavy robe of some sort.

Swallowing a grunt of disappointment, he realized, once again, that she was not a typical noblewoman. Weren't they supposed to wear diaphanous creations of the finest lace and silk? But when Juliet turned to look at him, wearing a puzzled expression, Morgan decided that would never do for her. Utilitarian garments suited her far better and were far more alluring.

"What is it?" she asked. Juliet evinced no maidenly horror at his invasion of her boudoir, but she displayed her usual pragmatic curiosity. It was so unusual, so refreshing, so endearing that Morgan felt a rush of some dangerous emotion, so strong that he had to turn away, lest it overcome him. Panic beat a staccato in his blood.

"I wanted to talk to you privately about what happened this morning. With the footman," he muttered.

"Yes, that has puzzled me, as well," she said thoughtfully. With no word of reproach for his nighttime visit to her room, she stepped away from the door.

They might have been ensconced in the ballroom, for all she appeared to notice. However, Morgan was not so oblivious. Maybe this wasn't a good idea after all, he realized, as he saw the thick braid trailing down her back and gritted his teeth.

"Unlike Cyril, I do not see the dagger as a warning or even a symbol of death. What is its intended meaning? And who would make such a mark?" Juliet asked.

As usual, she was focusing on the hieroglyphs, but Morgan noticed that she said *who,* not *what.* That was a good sign. At least she wasn't swallowing Cyril's mummy theory. "Obviously, it was someone with a rudimentary knowledge of Egypt, just enough to be dangerous," he said.

Rudimentary, but not equal to Juliet's.

"Makepeace—" Juliet began, but Morgan cut her off with a gesture of dismissal.

"Makepeace is so nervous that he's trying to sell off some of his own pieces."

"I know. Father said Makepeace had offered him some statuary. Father thought it amusing, and he is considering adding the Memnon to his collection," Juliet said.

Morgan's brows inched upward at that news, and Juliet blinked at him. "Surely, you don't think Father is striking down his own men in order to buy out other collectors."

Morgan shrugged. It sounded implausible, and yet there was something in Juliet's eyes that told him it was not impossible. "What do you think?" he asked.

Shaking her head, she rubbed her arms as though cold, even in her heavy robe, and Morgan took a step forward before stopping himself. He could not warm this woman *in any way.*

"Of course, Makepeace isn't the only other person concerned with Egypt," he said, eyeing her carefully. "For instance, I have heard that someone within the community of scholars has been asking a lot of questions about me, someone with ties to you."

Juliet glanced up at him in surprise.

"Your friend Herr Brueger has suddenly become very interested in me. Why?" Morgan demanded, all of his earlier resentment of the alleged expert returning in full force.

Color climbing suspiciously in her cheeks, Juliet leapt

to the professor's defense. "He probably was curious after meeting you. You certainly asked enough questions about him!"

Morgan's body tensed at her fervid denial. "You said yourself that he claimed the rumors would scare away other legitimate scholars. Then he'll have the field all to himself."

Juliet glared up at him. "I hardly think that every other person studying hieroglyphs will stop simply because of some wild rumors about a curse!"

She was facing him again, nearly toe to toe, and upon realizing it, Morgan took a step back, wary of any further argument, which always seemed to lead to . . . something else.

"Well, the curse hasn't stopped Lyndhurst," he muttered. "I still think he is behind it all. He's the one who came up with the whole idea."

His words had the desired effect of easing the tension that had built so quickly between them, although Morgan couldn't say he felt too enthusiastic about his success.

"But the footmen found nothing in Cyril's rooms when they searched the house," Juliet said.

Morgan shrugged. "He could have sold everything to another collector by now."

"But why?"

"Because he wants to stir up trouble or keep the hieroglyphs out of your hands," Morgan said.

"But the dagger has nothing to do with hieroglyphs, and why would he stir up trouble? The only result has been the guard placed on the room, which would make it impossible for anyone to steal the artifacts. Or so I thought," Juliet mused.

"It will," Morgan said. "Once the window latches are repaired, no one will be able to remove anything, unless the coxcomb slips something into his pocket on his way out."

Juliet eyed him dubiously.

"Maybe Lyndhurst just needs the money," Morgan suggested, making a mental note. Perhaps an investigation of the baronet's finances were in order.

But Juliet appeared unconvinced. "I simply cannot believe Cyril is capable of striking that footman."

Well, there was that. Try as he might, Morgan couldn't picture the coxcomb getting up the nerve, let alone the strength, to attack the guard. He frowned.

"And why paint the hieroglyph on him?" Juliet asked.

"Let's face it, that certainly sounds like Lyndhurst's doing," Morgan said. Perhaps the coxcomb had his fiercely devoted valet conk the guard in order to keep his own lily-white hands clean. Except to add the kohl. "And it certainly will fuel rumors of his precious curse."

"Maybe someone saw the article in the *Post* and thought to use Cyril's theory for his own thievery," Juliet suggested. "He came through the window but panicked at the sight of the guard."

"So he didn't steal anything, yet paused to decorate the fallen footman on his way out?" Morgan asked, tongue firmly in cheek. *Better there than elsewhere,* he thought.

"Well, you are right. Nothing was stolen this time," Juliet said, seemingly unaffected by his sarcasm.

Morgan told himself he wasn't disappointed by her calm reply. After all, it wasn't as though he wanted to start another argument or anything. Especially not here. Leaning against the massive post of the bed, he crossed his arms over his chest and tried to keep his mind on the conversation and *not* the location.

"As someone reminded me today, these incidents may not be directed at me, for all the coxcomb keeps yammering that I'm to blame," Morgan said. "They might not even have anything to do with Egypt or the collection."

Juliet was looking befuddled again, and Morgan felt his

pulse kick in response. He ignored it. "Your father told me his heir was a nephew. George Cavendish? What do you know about him?"

Juliet blinked in surprise. "Not much. I can't say that I see him very often. Father rarely concerns himself with other family members."

Morgan refrained from commenting on that. "What I mean is, how would you judge his character? It could be that he's a bit anxious for his inheritance."

Juliet's brow furrowed, and Morgan had to restrain himself from kissing it. "I mean, what if Cousin George has cooked up these rumors in order to do away with your father in some mishap and blame it on the mummy?"

Juliet's eyes widened.

Morgan held up a hand to stave off a protest. "I'm just trying to consider all possibilities."

"Suspecting everyone," Juliet observed.

Morgan shook his head. "No, that's not true. I've decided you are innocent," he said, flashing her a grin. *Now if he could only keep her that way.*

She smiled back, a tentative truce, and a long silence stretched between them. Morgan's own lips faltered as he stared at her mouth, a certain tension gripping him. It was not the same as when they fought, but softer and gentler, yet no less compelling. And insistent.

"I'm sorry about the search, and your papyrus," Juliet said, her beautiful eyes seeming to search his own.

Morgan shrugged, trying to remain casual. "Let's make a pact," he suggested lightly, though his words came out more gruffly than intended. "I won't suspect you, and you won't suspect me."

Was she blushing? A delicate pink rose on her flawless skin as she nodded, and, for a moment, Morgan could only stare at her, unable to think of anything except that they ought to seal their pact with a kiss.

Accustomed to being in control of every situation,

whether he was surrounded by native tribesmen brandishing rifles or assailed by desert mirages, Morgan felt a prickle of unease. What was it about this woman that made him feel suddenly out of his depth, over his head, like he was sinking into the sand? Panic rose in his chest, and Morgan lifted a hand to steady it only to remember what was lodged there. Reaching inside his shirt, he pulled out his prize and thrust it forward.

"Here. Have a look at this," he said, suddenly eager for a distraction.

It worked. Immediately, Juliet's attention dropped to the papyrus, and Morgan felt a measure of relief, *certainly not disappointment,* at how quickly and irrevocably her interest transferred to the map. She hurried to a desk, where an oil lamp burned, and Morgan drew in a deep breath.

Why did he feel like he'd just escaped a tribal tribunal? Shrugging in an attempt to ease the tension in his shoulders, Morgan took his first real look around. The bed was heavy but lush and inviting, and he quickly stepped away from it. The walls were a simple blue, with white detailing the raised panels, and the furnishings were expensive but not elaborate. There was a sitting area that looked as though it never got any use, but over there where Juliet was standing . . .

The desk was tucked in beside a bookshelf and a table, and all were cluttered. It wasn't really a mess, but Juliet obviously did not keep her private quarters as neat as the ballroom. Curious, Morgan moved in for a closer look. Dictionaries and grammars of languages he'd never even heard of were stacked on the shelves, notebooks bulged with Juliet's delicate scrawls, and hieroglyphs were everywhere.

Morgan felt his body respond enthusiastically, and he could only wonder at himself. He had glanced at the bed without any extreme reaction, but now was growing hard at the sight of Juliet's scholarly endeavors. Surely, he was a man cursed, and not by a mummy.

"Look here," Juliet said, dragging him from his thoughts. He didn't want to step any nearer, but he did, trying not to notice the way her downy hair glowed in the lamplight or the way her heavy robe gaped open to reveal a glimpse of pale throat. Or the expression on her face as she studied his map, all eager passion. *Would she ever look at him that way?*

"See these enclosed pictures?" she said, pointing. "As I've said before, I think it refers to a personage of some renown, perhaps a pharaoh, since the demotic mentions a great king. The map may lead to a temple that has been hidden. Or a tomb."

"But why make a map to a tomb?" Morgan asked. "Most were emptied long ago."

Juliet shrugged, in imitation of his own gesture, and Morgan tried to ignore the thrill that shot through him. "Perhaps there were especially striking decorations on the walls, or there might be a very heavy piece, like the mummy case, that could not be removed by the old grave robbers. Or our map maker may have written down something he was told or something he read in another language, like the hieroglyphs."

"Or it could lead to nothing important. Maybe he drew a map to the cheapest public baths on an old piece of papyrus," Morgan said.

"I suppose that's a possibility," Juliet said. She straightened and turned to meet his gaze directly. "There is only one way to find out."

Morgan's brows inched upward.

"Follow the map. I'm sure between the two of us, we could find the way," she said.

She was so close Morgan could smell her subtle perfume, *essence of Juliet.* Wisps of hair escaped the thick braid down her back and clustered about her perfect features like bits of cloud, and those spectacles glinted in the lamplight, the mark of her intelligence making his body harden. As Morgan watched, she removed them, placing them carefully upon the table. Then she turned, her luscious lips parting as if she were going to speak.

Morgan remembered the feel of those lips, like a taste of heaven. And right now he felt trapped in hell, the hell of his own making. He should never have touched her, for the memory taunted him, egged him on, made him want to reach for her and regain what he had lost. And just that quickly, he was tempted beyond control.

Swearing under his breath, Morgan grasped her arms and pulled her tight against him. His mouth came down on hers, fierce and impatient, only to gentle at the first brush of lips so tender, so innocent, and yet so full of passion that they robbed him of breath. He stole hers in return, feeding off her gasps and pants, thrilling at the low sounds of pleasure she made. His own groans rose above the crackle of the fire as she returned his kisses with fevered delight.

Morgan simply could not get enough of her. He unfastened her braid and grabbed fistfuls of golden hair, so soft that it did not seem real. It clung to his fingers as he cupped her face, holding her still for his kiss, but it still wasn't enough. Tugging at her robe, he slipped his hands inside to stroke the linen of her nightrail, absurdly excited by the feel of it under his fingers . . . and the feel of Juliet beneath.

Morgan didn't even think of the bed, or perhaps he didn't trust his legs to move that far, but two steps took him in front of the hearth, where he lowered her to the thick carpet before the blazing fire. He moved on top of her, but he still wasn't close enough. He wanted to get inside her, under her skin, into her head and heart.

His frenzy must have been apparent, because Morgan felt the tender touch of her fingers against his cheek, gently staying him as they had so often before. "I'm here," she whispered. "I'm right here."

"Yes. Yes, you are," Morgan answered, looking down into her beautiful face, her prescient eyes. Could she read his mind? Did she know how frantically his heart was pounding, how hard his groin was throbbing, how desperate he was to have her? Drawing a deep breath, Morgan covered her hand with his own, turning his head to place a kiss on her palm.

She was right here, she was his for the taking, and the night stretched before them. Morgan shuddered at the knowledge. Turning onto his side, he drank in the sight of her, golden hair spread before him like a feast, her luscious body clad only in soft linen, her robe having fallen to the floor. Slowly, he lifted a hand and lay its palm upon her throat and caressed the length of her, following each curve and dip, savoring every brush of the fabric beneath his fingers.

She was his most significant find, a treasure beyond price, and Morgan touched her as he would his most prized artifacts, with reverence, with excitement, and more. His mouth followed the trail of his hand in exploration, wetting the fabric of her nightdress and plying it against her body. And when he had made his way to the end of it, he began again, tugging at the hem, exposing her skin to his touch and his taste.

The sound of her breathy sighs, the rise and fall of her breasts, and the fluttering of her hands seeking purchase told Morgan of her pleasure and need. But he moved carefully, with patience instilled in the desert, uncovering each new area to his most thorough examination.

At first, Morgan was so lost in her that he didn't hear the shouts. Indeed, he was so caught up in the heat of the moment that the vague calls of *fire* seemed only to apply to the rage in his blood, the conflagration growing here between them before the hearth. But, gradually, the noise penetrated his senses, and he jerked upward, as if waking from an erotic dream, to realize that voices were raised outside the bedroom, and someone was banging on the door in urgent summons.

Chapter 13

✠

LEAPING to his feet, Morgan dragged Juliet with him and snatched up her robe, thrusting it into her hands. She wore a dazed look, which, considering her intelligence, was gratifying. But they both needed all their wits about them now.

"Something has happened, perhaps a fire. Can you answer the summons?" he asked even as he put her arms into her robe, dressing her body when he would far prefer the alternative. *But not now,* he told himself.

Hurrying her to the door, he stepped behind it, unsure yet whether the situation warranted an escape from the window. It was a long drop, Morgan knew, and one he didn't care to investigate unless all else failed. He braced himself as Juliet swung open the painted wood, prepared for anything, including an irate father, though he could swear no one knew he was here.

Thankfully, it wasn't the earl or even the ubiquitous Cheevy on the other side, but a maid, wailing about a fire and urging her mistress to safety. From his position in the shadows, Morgan handed Juliet her glasses and gave her a nudge, whispering that he would follow. With a look of alarm, she glanced at his fierce expression, then went, but she left the door open for his own flight.

Morgan waited a moment for the sound of their footsteps to fade, then stepped outside. The wing was deserted, and at first Morgan wondered if there really was a fire, but when he headed toward his own apartments in search of Chauncey, he caught the faint scent of smoke. Rushing forward, he abruptly came upon a group of footmen in various states of undress and armed with buckets.

It appeared he had found the fire.

Unfortunately, the men were all gathered before his own room. Pushing through the crowd, Morgan breathed a sigh of relief when he saw a bedraggled-looking Chauncey standing by the side of Morgan's bed, a pool of water about his feet. With an oath, Morgan elbowed his way through the servants, calling to his friend.

At the sound of his name, Chauncey turned and stared. "Morgan, thank God! I didn't think you were here, but . . ." His words trailed off as he glanced toward the bed.

Morgan stepped forward to look for himself and stiffened at the sight. A black, charred, gaping hole lay in the middle, right about where Morgan normally would have slept.

"What happened?" he asked, his jaw tight.

"Mr. Beauchamp!"

The footmen moved out of the way as the earl's butler, fully dressed, strode into the room. The belligerent servant did not appear as excited to see Morgan as Chauncey had been.

"Where have you been?" Cheevy demanded.

When Morgan's brows inched upward, the butler's expression grew even more surly. Turning, he dismissed the other servants, except for the two maids who were trying to soak up the remaining water from the earl's expensive carpet. Then Cheevy swung round to glare at Morgan once more.

"How is it that there isn't a mark on you when your bed just went up in flames?" the butler demanded.

"I wasn't here," Morgan answered.

The butler's thick brows drew together as if in puzzlement. "But how can that be?" he muttered.

"I hadn't retired yet," Morgan said. Either the butler was more thick-headed than they thought, or he had inhaled too much smoke.

"But I saw—" Cheevy began, only to stop, his ruddy face flushing a deeper red.

"What did you see?" Morgan asked, his eyes narrowing. He and Chauncey long ago had gotten into the habit of disguising their whereabouts. Often they arranged their bedding so as to appear that they were there, fast asleep, when they were out and about elsewhere. One swift glance at Chauncey's set features told Morgan that was the case tonight.

Obviously, Chauncey had taken the precaution of putting something in Morgan's bed before he left, no doubt for an assignation with one of the maids. Later, someone had come by, thought Morgan asleep, and decided to incinerate him where he lay. Morgan didn't have to look too far to find that someone after Cheevy's little slip in speech. He glared at the butler.

"Is it your habit to enter the bedrooms of your master's guests?" Morgan asked. "Or did you make a special trip in my case . . . armed with an extra lamp perhaps?"

Cheevy's mouth twisted into a snarl, and Morgan tensed, his hands fisting at his sides in preparation for anything.

"I don't know what you're talking about," the butler declared. But he took a threatening step forward.

"Cheevy!" The earl's voice rang out, effectively leashing his man, and Morgan didn't know whether to be relieved or annoyed.

"What happened here?" the earl demanded, his usual aplomb notably absent.

"I don't know, my lord," Cheevy said, eyeing Morgan as if daring him to dispute the claim.

Nevertheless, Morgan was just about to do so when one of the maids piped up.

"Pardon me, my lord," she said, rising to her feet, and Morgan saw that her face was pale and drawn. "I, uh, came to see if Mr. Beauchamp's valet had everything he needed, uh, for the night and all, and I smelled smoke coming from the rooms."

Obviously, she was one of Chauncey's admirers, though she was trying to explain her presence in terms more acceptable to her employer. "I took the liberty of having a look, just to make sure all was well, and I saw that the bed was on fire. I called for help, and Bill and Bob fetched water from the bathing chamber to put it out."

"I see," the earl said, though he appeared dissatisfied with the explanation and spared not one word of praise for the girl, to whom Morgan, for one, was eminently grateful.

"It's a good thing you did, or the whole room might have gone up," Morgan said.

"Or the whole house," the earl said darkly.

"Or Morgan here might have been killed," Chauncey noted.

The earl gave Morgan a look that didn't evince much enthusiasm for his narrow escape. "And just where were you?"

"I thought I'd take a stroll about to check on the ballroom, but keeping out of sight," Morgan said. Since it was a lie, no one could corroborate it—or dispute it.

"And so you kept a lamp burning by your bed, or was it some kind of Turkish pipe you left lying amongst the covers?" the earl asked, his expression hard.

Morgan felt his own mouth tighten. "Are you accusing me of smoking opium?" he asked, incredulous.

The earl didn't flinch. "It is a habit that can be developed in Oriental climes."

"Well, it's not a habit of mine or my man. We left nothing burning or smoking, nor were we here when the fire started," Morgan said. He paused. "But your butler was."

The earl looked startled. "Cheevy?" he asked, swinging toward the man.

Before the butler could sputter a denial, Morgan continued. "Apparently, it is his habit to check on guests in their beds, though why he felt the need to set mine alight escapes me at present."

Cheevy opened his mouth to argue, but the earl stopped him with a gesture. With an expression of impatience, the nobleman turned on Morgan. "You are being fanciful, Beauchamp."

"Am I?" Morgan asked. "That's not the only odd thing about your man, who doesn't have the look of any butler I've ever seen." He glanced toward where Chauncey, his seeming valet, stood. "Chauncey, wasn't there a man named Cheevy who used to box, bare-fisted, before he killed a man in a fight?"

The accusation hung in the air until the earl emitted a startled laugh. "Really, Mr. Beauchamp. I think I've heard enough of your whiskers for tonight. Next you'll be blaming the mummy for your little mishap," he said, making it clear that the discussion was over.

"Well, no harm done," he said, assuming a more jovial tone. "We can find another room for you and your man. Cheevy, take care of that," he added, turning to go.

Although it appeared that the earl was dismissing the entire matter, Morgan couldn't help wondering if the nobleman had issued a similar order to his butler about them earlier, but with far more ominous intent.

"What the hell was that?" Chauncey said, staring after the departing butler, who had informed them he would send a footman for their things when a new room was readied.

With a shake of his head, Morgan hurried to the open door and watched the departing servant until he was out of sight. Then he swung toward Chauncey.

"What happened?" he asked.

"Just as she said," Chauncey replied, inclining his head toward one of the departing maids.

"Well, I don't know what other female you were fondling at the time, but we owe that one a great deal," Morgan muttered. "Make sure you give her an appreciable monetary token of my thanks, if not your own."

Chauncey grinned. Then, glancing at the bed, he sobered, his trysts forgotten. "It wasn't a lamp, as I took a look around right enough. No smell of oil, either."

Morgan stalked across the room, studying the area, kneeling to inspect the carpet and the remains of the heavy piece of furniture. "Perhaps he threw a torch that would feed upon itself, destroying the evidence, or even a stick or ember from a hearth."

"Maybe our man never even came in with the idea but saw you there asleep, looked at the fire, and decided to try his luck," Chauncey suggested.

"Counting that I would not awaken?" Morgan asked.

Chauncey nodded. "He must have thought you dead asleep since you never moved. Of course, that's a bit hard to do when you're nothing but a bunch of stuffing and blankets," he remarked wryly.

Walking round the remains of the bed, examining it once more, Chauncey shook his head grimly. "A fellow's asleep in a nobleman's town house, thinking he's safe and sound. He doesn't hear the creak of the door, nor the toss of the ember, and it's slow burning, so by the time he wakes up, he's on fire."

Morgan shuddered. He liked to think of himself as too alert to be caught in such a trap, but he could sleep heavily at times, and if Chauncey were gone or drowsing as well, he might have been burned badly . . . or worse. Anger simmering, he stalked across the room to check the windows, where rain beat a tattoo against the panes. Latched and high above the grounds, they precluded any entry. "It was someone inside," Morgan muttered.

"Yes," Chauncey said. "It could have been our friend Lyndhurst or any of the servants, acting alone or on orders, though I tend to vouch for the females. I'd put my money on one of those new guards the earl hired on. I wouldn't trust them as far as I could spit. The bloody cutthroats could be taking a second pay from anyone."

Morgan turned from the windows. "What about the butler?"

Chauncey nodded. "I know he ain't quite the thing, but I just can't see Cheevy burning up his own home. I mean, the fellow has a pretty cozy berth here and all."

"Maybe the earl told him to do it," Morgan said, eyeing his friend ominously.

Chauncey whistled low at the suggestion. "I just can't see it, and for the very same reason. I know the earl's an old bastard, and right shady, too, but he'd have to be a lunatic to burn down his own house."

Morgan shrugged. "Maybe Cheevy came back to make sure only I burned up and not anything else."

Chauncey looked dubious. "A very dicey proposition."

Morgan frowned. "But there is something strange about that butler, over and above his unusual past," he mused aloud. His eyes narrowing, he gazed at Chauncey, whose instincts he had trusted times beyond count. "You heard him. Didn't it sound as though he had looked in upon us?"

"Yes," Chauncey admitted. "But did he start the fire? Maybe he was just spying on us."

As much as Morgan didn't want to believe it at this point, that was certainly a possibility. Cheevy's little inspection, which Morgan would swear took place tonight, if not every night, might have had nothing to do with the blaze.

Abruptly struck by a thought, Morgan slanted his companion a glance. "Cheevy could have been trying to make sure one of the maids wasn't here with you. Maybe he's strict about that sort of thing—or jealous."

Chauncey grinned. "Or could be he's some kind of voyeur."

Morgan grimaced at the unpalatable thought. Unfortunately, he could easily imagine the big, burly butler peeping in on the entire household, including . . . *Juliet!* Morgan flinched at the very notion that someone else might see her in her nightrail, that other eyes might watch her at toilette or more.

"What is it?" Chauncey asked, seeing the look on his face.

"Juliet," Morgan muttered, turning toward the door. Suddenly, he wanted to check on her, to make sure she was all right, to assure himself that she had returned to her room and was well and safe and protected from prying eyes.

"It was just a jest, Morgan," Chauncey said, grabbing his arm. "She's the earl's daughter, for God's sake. No one would dare touch her."

Morgan tried to still the pounding of his blood. He told himself that Chauncey's instincts were good, that Juliet was probably back in bed and safe. But he knew a driving urge to make certain personally, to protect her himself every minute of every day and every night.

But there was only one way to do that.

Morgan sucked in a deep breath, ragged with alarm, and tried to gain control of himself, or at the very least, his wild musings. *What was he thinking?*

For the first time since seeing the shambles of his own bed, Morgan remembered what he had been doing while it was burning, and now he wondered if the fire had not actually saved his hide. After all, if it had not occurred, God knows what he would have done there in Juliet's bedroom, before the hearth, lost in his own raging heat. *Unfortunately, he had a pretty good idea.*

Morgan's jaw tightened. He shouldn't have gone to her room, and he certainly shouldn't have succumbed to temptation. He had warned her not to tempt him. Yet, even in his current mental state, Morgan had difficulty blaming Juliet for his actions. It wasn't as though she had greeted him in a seductive costume or made suggestive overtures. She had been wearing a heavy robe, her hair in a braid, spectacles perched upon her nose. Not exactly erotic, yet Morgan's body clenched at the very thought.

Oh, who was he fooling? The woman tempted him just by breathing.

"You can't sneak back there tonight," Chauncey said, reclaiming his attention. "Cheevy has turned out the whole household. We had better pack up as best we can before he returns."

Morgan nodded. He told himself that Juliet was not his responsibility. She had lived all these years in her father's household without harm and was perfectly safe now, away from him. No doubt, Chauncey was right.

So why did it feel all wrong?

IT was the first thing Juliet saw when she returned to her room. Although tempted to glance toward the thick carpet in front of the hearth that had unaccountably felt so comfortable beneath her not so long ago, her gaze had gone unerringly to her desk, where the map remained, forgotten.

He would want it back, and Juliet had nearly taken it to him, but in the confusion of the night, she had not known where to find him. Only this morning had she pried the location of his new room from her maid. Luckily, the young woman was so flighty that she thought nothing of Juliet's sudden interest in her guest, having chattered on all during the morning's toilette about the fire and its dire consequences.

"I'd stay away from Mr. Beauchamp and not go anywhere near his rooms, my lady!" Millie said, not pausing for Juliet's reply. After years of service, she probably wasn't expecting one, but for once, Juliet was listening to the girl's prattle.

"It's plain that the curse is acting on him. Why he wasn't burned up in his bed is a mystery to me. Of course, it's only a matter of time, but perhaps then the thing will be appeased," Millie said.

Juliet looked at her in the mirror. "Appeased?"

Millie's voice dropped to a whisper. "After it's killed Mr. Beauchamp, I mean."

Even Juliet, who prided herself on her clear thinking, had a moment's pause over the girl's bald statement that Morgan's imminent death was a foregone conclusion. Fear for him rose up in her throat like bile, the panic of last night returning. Of course, she had known he wasn't hurt, for he'd been with her. But what if he hadn't chosen that moment to share his papyrus with her? The possibility didn't bear contemplation.

Fires weren't an unusual occurrence. There were always sparks from the hearths and spilled lamps to blame, but how to account for Morgan's burning bed when he wasn't even there? It was yet another mystery to add to all else that had happened since the arrival of her father's latest shipment.

Juliet shivered, and the morning light seemed suddenly dimmed as if some evil will menaced the house. In her mind's eye she saw, once again, the body of the footman, with its ominous markings. Why a hieroglyph? Why the dagger? Suddenly, the symbols she had studied no longer seemed familiar or beloved, but ominous. Dangerous. *Threatening.*

Juliet cut off Millie's chatter with a gesture. "Perhaps Mr. Beauchamp left a cigar smoldering," she said, even though she doubted it.

"Oh, Mr. Beauchamp doesn't smoke. Nor his man, either," Millie replied.

Juliet frowned. "Nevertheless, there is a logical explanation for every mishap," she finally managed to say.

"Yes, my lady." Millie nodded, but Juliet knew she didn't believe a word her mistress said. And why should she? Juliet herself could not explain a floating mummified hand, a footman being attacked from behind, and now a spontaneous fire.

Taking a deep breath, Juliet smoothed her skirts and stood waiting until Millie left. Then she moved to her desk, where the map was tucked between the pages of a heavy book for safekeeping. Taking up the volume, she carefully closed her door and headed toward Mr. Beauchamp's new rooms, while trying to still the trepidation that rose in her breast.

It was not fear of impending doom that made her heart pound but the prospect of facing the man who had laid her down in front of her own hearth and awakened her body with his hands and his mouth, rousing within her something far more dangerous than any curse.

Forcing the images out of her mind, Juliet slipped through the rooms, intent on not attracting any attention, especially when she reached Mr. Beauchamp's door. The knock she gave sounded loud in the stillness, and she glanced round, glad to see no servants about this early. And then, suddenly, it struck her. It was early. What if, after last night's difficulties, Mr. Beauchamp was still abed? Her face flamed, and her hand faltered before reason asserted itself. Mr. Beauchamp was always an early riser. No doubt he . . .

Before she could finish the thought, the door swung open to reveal the object of her thoughts. Dark hair tousled, he stood before her in nothing except his breeches. Again, his feet were bare, and he must not have shaved as yet, for a shadowy growth of stubble covered his chin, sending shivers up her spine.

How would it feel beneath her fingers, rough or soft? Juliet wondered. She dragged her gaze away, only to be faced with his chest, *his wonderful, glorious, golden chest.* It was so close, she could reach out and touch it, and if she hadn't been clutching the heavy book, she might well have done so.

"Juliet!" His surprise at her appearance at his bedroom door apparently equaled her own of last night. Oh, better not think of that, Juliet told herself. Grabbing her arm, he pulled her into the room and shut the door, effectively locking them in this most private venue. *Together.*

Juliet drew a deep, unsteady breath and tried to concentrate on the business at hand. First, she thrust the book toward him, then she pulled it back and tugged out the papyrus. "I thought you might be wanting this," she said.

Something fierce and unidentifiable crossed his face at the sight of his prize. He reached for it slowly, and staring at his long fingers, Juliet realized those same fingers had cupped her breasts last night and stroked her bare skin. She nearly dropped the edge of the map.

"Thank you," Morgan said, his dark eyes intent. "I appreciate your prompt return of it. I wouldn't want it to come up missing."

"I didn't think so," Juliet said. Her voice, normally so reliable, seemed inclined to a husky whisper instead of her usual calm tones. But how could she be calm in any way when she was facing that lovely expanse of golden muscle and sinew and dark hair? Tearing her gaze away, Juliet looked round, anywhere but there, her attention coming to rest upon the tousled bed where Morgan had slept. Was it still warm from the heat of his body? Juliet blinked.

"I . . . uh, see you are settled into your new room," she

said, and the reason for his move rushed back to her, pressing upon her chest.

"I was so relieved to realize that you weren't hurt," she said, but her words came out rather ragged and hoarse, her uncooperative voice now threatening to reveal the depth of her feelings. She swallowed hard and walked somewhere, *anywhere* but toward him.

"I can't imagine how such a fire got started," Juliet said. "But you might as well know that already the servants are blaming the curse." She dared a glance at his face and saw his expression harden.

"Our mummy's been a busy boy lately," he muttered.

Startled, Juliet laughed, and the change in him, from tense anger to . . . something else made her turn away again. Drawing a deep breath, she continued to look at everything except that which she most wanted to view: his chest. And when she spied his shirt lying on a chair, she picked it up and thrust it toward him.

"There you are," Juliet said, pleased with herself for finding a solution to her most pressing dilemma. Only when he took the garment from her did she realize the enormity of her mistake, for having received his shirt, he was now forced to don it . . . in front of her.

The sight of his strong arms lifting, exposing the patches of dark hair beneath as he tugged the worn linen over his wide shoulders, was enough to make Juliet's mouth go dry. She licked her lips, but that didn't help. Her pulse raced, her skin grew warm, and her breath stopped in her throat. She turned away in dismay.

"I don't understand it," she finally said, pacing across the carpet. "I'm a reasonable, logical being. I have spent my life devoted to scholarly pursuits, to interests of the mind. I have never wanted what other women covet. So why should my heart threaten to burst whenever I see you . . . improperly clothed?"

She looked questioningly at Morgan, only to see that his lips were quirking in amusement. In fact, he appeared perilously close to laughter. She frowned at him. He was not helping at all.

"Why should I, suddenly, at my advanced years, succumb to kisses, yes, even *yearn* for them?" she asked, unable to comprehend the changes this man had wrought in her. Thrilled and pleased and horrified and frightened all at the same time, she could not decipher this most elemental mystery.

"I don't think you are quite in your dotage," Morgan said dryly. He stepped toward her, and Juliet could only admire his movements, like the easy grace of a cat. Why on earth had she given him that shirt?

"They've tried to make you into a creature of books, a walking, talking reference for their convenience, disallowing you any spark or fire, even that which springs from your work," Morgan said. Standing before her now, he placed his hand over her heart, and Juliet leaned into it, eager, *yearning.*

"But beneath your scholarly surface beats the heart of a woman, a woman full of passion—for Egypt, for hieroglyphs, and, thankfully, for *me,*" he said, his voice low and compelling.

Did he know her secret longing for adventure, as well, for travel to faraway climes, for danger and excitement beyond her books? Juliet glanced down at his hand, then up at his face, so familiar now and yet still a wonder. "Thankfully?"

At his nod, Juliet shook her head. "But I'm a bluestocking, a spinster with nothing to recommend me to a man . . . like you," she whispered. A man of adventure, a rogue, handsome, untamed, infinitely desirable.

"You're beautiful," Morgan answered.

Juliet stared, dumbfounded by his words. "But I'm too

tall, and my hair is . . . fuzzy. It won't fall into the ringlets that are so admired. In fact, I have been informed that it is totally unmanageable. My skin is not as pale as is fashionable, my eyes are a strange color, and I'm too intelligent to appeal to any man," she added in a breathless rush.

Morgan's lips quirked again. "As usual, you are thinking too much," he said, lifting his hand from her chest to tap her forehead with one finger. The loss of his touch made Juliet want to cry out. She had the most absurd desire to drag his palm to her, to feel the warmth of it all over her body, with nothing between them, to lie naked with him beneath the Egyptian sun.

Luckily, Morgan was not privy to her most fervent fantasies, for he continued speaking. "You are just the right height for me, your figure is incomparable, and your hair is glorious," he said, nuzzling the upsweep of her unruly mane. When he drew back, Juliet nearly followed him. "Your skin is golden, not the chalky white of someone like Lyndhurst, and your eyes are the color of the shifting sands."

Morgan's gaze met hers, dark, serious, intent. "And as for your brain, I find it as highly stimulating as the rest of you."

Her eyes wide, Juliet stared up at him, seeing the truth in his eyes, and yet she remained uncertain, as though one of her studies had strayed so far from her initial suppositions that she could not believe the proof before her. He lifted a hand, perhaps preparing to demonstrate, but at that moment, the door swung open.

Juliet turned abruptly to see Morgan's man march into the room. "I can't find the damn razor anywhere!" he announced. Then he saw her, closeted here with Morgan in his bedroom, and he halted abruptly.

Something crossed his face, not alarm, but suspicion or perhaps anger. "I beg your pardon, my lady," he said, yet he made no move to depart.

Obviously, Juliet was the one who should be going. "I

was just leaving. Thank you," she murmured, hurrying past the servant to the door and escape from the pressing thunder of her heart, the rising heat of her body, the confusion of her mind—and the man who was responsible for it all.

... ... - ... ...
... ...
... ...
... ...

Chapter 14

MORGAN watched Juliet leave, that familiar sensation of panic beating a tattoo in his blood. *What was he thinking?* He had meant to warn her away, not encourage her. But her honest confusion had been his undoing. And now . . .

"Playing with fire, aren't we?" Chauncey's taunt dragged Morgan from his thoughts, and he swung round to see an expression of disapproval on his friend's face. "Can't see why anyone here would like to kill you, can you? How about the earl, for one?"

Releasing an impressive array of curses he had learned in the London slums, Chauncey threw down the towel he had been carrying. "Quit thinking with your prick before you lose it—and everything else."

Morgan's brows inched upward. "You are making far too much of this," he said carefully.

"Am I?"

"Yes," Morgan answered. Taking up his stockings, he sat down to put them on. "She was just returning the map, which

I carelessly left in her room last night after I was routed by the fire. She was not here for some lurid tryst." He paused to slant a glance at his companion. "Perhaps your own experiences in this house are coloring your perceptions."

Chauncey's expression didn't alter. "I've got eyes in my head. I can see the way you two look at each other."

Morgan blinked at him, then burst into laughter. "Next you'll be writing sonnets or that rubbish of Byron's."

Chauncey scowled. "She's not for you, Morgan."

"At least we are in agreement on that," Morgan said, pulling on his boots. Juliet wasn't for him, and he knew it. Now, if he could just keep that in mind, not only in her absence, but in her presence, as well.

"What have you got your shirt on for? You haven't shaved yet," Chauncey said, suddenly giving him the eye.

"I donned it out of courtesy for the lady's delicate sensibilities," Morgan answered. Reaching down to retrieve the towel, he looped it around his neck and rose to his feet.

Chauncey snorted. "Well, I can't find your razor anywhere. You'll have to use mine for now. Must have gotten lost in the move, I guess."

Morgan watched with a jaundiced eye as Chauncey fussed over him, fluttering about like a mother hen. Finally, he gave his companion a direct look. "Taking your role a bit too seriously, are you?"

Chauncey paused, shaving implements in hand, to stare at him.

"You're not really my valet, you know, and I am not an invalid," Morgan said, taking the razor from him. "I can shave myself."

"Oh. Right," Chauncey muttered. Still, he hovered until Morgan had wiped his face clean.

"Well? What the devil is it?" Morgan asked.

Chauncey made a face. "You just might remember that someone torched your bed last night," he said.

Morgan grimaced. It was not as though he could forget.

"It might have been an accident," Morgan said, tossing aside his towel. "There are always stray sparks."

Chauncey snorted.

"Or perhaps our man acted out of the moment and has now seen the error of his ways," Morgan suggested.

Chauncey snorted even louder. "Or not."

Morgan frowned, disliking his friend's opinion. For, if not, whoever was responsible might just keep trying to kill him.

THE threat hung over Morgan, on the edge of his awareness, throughout the morning and into the afternoon. It was easy to watch his back, as Chauncey had advised, for he couldn't imagine anyone attacking him in broad daylight in the earl's town house. And since this was not his first brush with danger, Morgan felt more than capable of handling himself. What bothered him was the devious methods employed.

Had someone actually concocted the whole curse, with all its attendant little dramas, simply to do him in? And, if so, who? Lyndhurst was the likeliest candidate, since the curse was his idea, but Morgan couldn't imagine what would drive the coxcomb to kill. He had never seen the baronet before in his life until his arrival here, and though they were rarely in agreement, that was hardly cause for murder.

There was always the possibility that someone else was making use of the coxcomb's curse for his own purpose. Morgan couldn't ignore the earl or his butler or Herr Brueger or even . . . He frowned. Was it possible that someone from his old life had come after him for some unknown reason? For a moment, Morgan even contemplated contacting his family but dismissed that outlandish idea quickly enough. They were more likely to welcome his demise than prevent it.

Of course, as Chauncey had reminded him, there was one way to find out if he really was the target of attempts on his life, and that was to leave the earl's home. If he did so, would the curse die away or follow him? It was a tempting course, but one that Morgan refused to consider, for one simple reason: Juliet.

After he was gone, who would watch over her? If Morgan wasn't the only intended victim, she would be alone here with someone who was willing to do violence to servants, guests, and, yes, maybe even Lady Juliet Cavendish, mistress of the house. Morgan's mouth tightened. He didn't trust the earl's staff, especially the butler, to keep her safe. Hell, he didn't even trust the earl. And the possibility of something happening to Juliet . . . well, he was not prepared to think about it.

Although he had no intention of returning to her bedroom, Morgan had every intention of keeping her alive and unharmed. It was the only thing he could do. Unfortunately, time was working against him. Indeed, for the first time in years, Morgan was aware of it slipping away from him.

As Chauncey had often complained, he could toil in the blazing heat for hours without noticing that the sun was about to dip below the horizon, casting them all into darkness. And when he first began assisting Juliet, it had seemed as though the endless tedium of the cataloguing would go on forever.

But Morgan realized that the work they were doing, which once had seemed interminable, was approaching its conclusion with amazing rapidity. Although he had been in a rush to complete the project, now he deliberately slowed his pace, effecting even more difficulty with his notes and trying Juliet's patience. It was not as though he wanted to continue this wretched exercise forever, but when they were finished, he could hardly remain under the dubious aegis of the earl, who already appeared to want to be rid of him. Perhaps permanently. Morgan grimaced.

"Hello?"

The sound of a voice, calling from the entrance to the ballroom, made Morgan swing round, eager for any distraction. His eyes narrowed at the sight of a rather bluff, fleshy young man he had never seen before. Of course, the boy could be one of the earl's collector friends sneaking a peek at the new artifacts. *Or he might just be the perpetrator, stopped in to view the results of his latest crime.*

"Hello, Juliet!" The young man's face broke into a nervous smile at the sight of the earl's daughter, and Morgan frowned at the intimate greeting. Who was this pasty-faced fellow? Already, Morgan didn't like him.

Juliet, having turned at the hail, appeared puzzled at first sight. Then her expression cleared, though her surprise remained. "Cousin George?"

"Just so!" the young man said. "May I come in?" he asked, eyeing the two guards warily.

"Of course," Juliet answered.

Cousin George still hesitated. "Is it safe?"

Juliet's brows drew together. "Of course," she said.

George stepped over the threshold gingerly, as though he feared the parquet floor might swallow him up. Since Morgan, Juliet, and Cyril were all standing upon it without any difficulty, Morgan failed to see the reason for the man's caution.

But George's odd progress continued. He sidestepped every object in the room, putting as much space between the artifacts and himself as possible, and when he neared the mahogany table, he hung back, as if reluctant to come closer.

Morgan's eyes narrowed. This was the earl's heir?

"Cyril, may I introduce my cousin, Mr. George Cavendish?" Juliet said. Although often lost in her work, she obviously was able to recall the niceties of polite society. "George, these are my colleagues, Sir Cyril Lyndhurst and Mr. Morgan Beauchamp."

Having performed the required introductions, Juliet looked as though she didn't know what to do with her cousin, and the coxcomb was just as surly as always. "Cavendish," he said, with a nod. "What brings you here?"

"Well, now, can't a man say hello to his relatives?" the young man asked. He grinned in a display of joviality, but his gaze darted about the room in a rather frantic fashion.

Juliet was looking so perplexed that Morgan felt a rush of heat. Turning away from temptation, he eyed the visitor. "Have you an interest in Egypt, Mr. Cavendish?" he asked.

Cousin George reared back, seemingly appalled by the suggestion. "Lud, no! I just stopped in to see the earl and thought I'd pop by to take a peek at his famous collection on my way out. Nasty looking things, aren't they?" he asked, staring at the mummified hand. He shuddered. "Is that him?"

"Who?" Juliet asked, looking befuddled and annoyed and entirely irresistible to Morgan.

George lowered his voice. "The mummy, the one that, well, is . . . responsible."

Juliet flushed, but before she could comment, the coxcomb stepped in. "That is nothing but a severed hand. The mummy rests there in its case," he said in a voice laced with drama.

Morgan's brows inched upward. "Have you ever thought of taking to the stage?" he asked the coxcomb.

"What's that?"

"All that doom and gloom ought to go over well in Drury Lane," Morgan muttered.

"Now, see here, you—" the coxcomb began, but Juliet stepped between the two men.

"Did you want to see the mummy, George?" she asked.

"Lud, no!" There was no mistaking the young man's

alarm this time. "Just thought I'd see what all was here, have a look about, make sure that . . ." His words trailed off.

"Yes?" Juliet prompted, expectant.

"Well, I just wondered . . ." He glanced around, his expression anxious, then his attention fixed on the mummy case, his eyes wide. "You don't think that the, uh, curse extends to the whole family, do you? I mean, if something should happen to you and the earl, you don't think it will come after me, do you?"

Morgan couldn't help it. He burst out laughing.

"I don't think you are in any danger," Juliet assured her cousin even as she led him away from her work and toward the entrance to the ballroom. "Please give your parents my best regards and assure them that we are all well here and not the least bit concerned."

"If you say so," George said. Looking skeptical, he glanced over his shoulder at Morgan, who was still laughing, and the dour features of the coxcomb, who was not.

Morgan shook his head. Unless the earl's heir was a better actor than Lyndhurst, he could be eliminated from any list of suspects, which narrowed the possibilities down to . . . just about everybody else. The thought sobered him quickly enough. As usual, he had to wonder not only who was responsible, but why?

JULIET was glad to see her cousin depart. Accustomed to working alone, she was finding the constant stream of people in and out of the ballroom, additional guards, and interruptions most distracting. And annoying. She far preferred working alone with Morgan, despite the fact that he was far more distracting and certainly could be annoying at times. Like today.

Being the sensible sort, Juliet knew she ought to be relieved after their little talk this morning. The whole thing was out in the open now. They had discussed it calmly and logically, and she understood his reasoning. Obviously, she had many emotions that, long buried and dormant from disuse, he had effortlessly summoned to the surface. And although she still found it difficult to understand why a man such as Morgan would want to kiss her, she was infinitely glad he did.

But that left her with one question. If he was so enamored of her, why had he stopped leaning close? Again today he was distant, downright distracted even. In fact, she was beginning to suspect that he was deliberately slowing his pace, for what purpose she had no idea. Had the man simply decided it was time to irritate her again?

Finally, when he squinted at his notes so long that her foot fell asleep, Juliet turned toward him.

"What, exactly, are you doing?"

His brows inched upward. "I am trying to make sense of these. We were in a bit of a hurry at the time, and I dashed them off rather haphazardly."

"Don't pretend to misunderstand me!" Juliet whispered, not caring to draw the attention of the guards. At least Cyril was used to their arguments and kept away, for fear Morgan would snap at him as well, though he would never admit as much.

Morgan shrugged, effectively ignoring her, and lifted his papers higher for further examination. Placing her hand at the top edge, Juliet dragged them down with one hand.

"Would you do me the courtesy of paying attention to me when I am speaking?" she asked.

"Maybe if you said something new, I would," he drawled, and Juliet felt her pulse leap.

It seemed like days since their last argument, and Juliet realized that she missed their adversarial relationship just as much as his nearness. Having spent a lifetime quietly acceding to the wishes of the other males in her life, she enjoyed sparring with Morgan, who never dismissed her opinions, but who rarely agreed with her, either.

"You are deliberately impeding my progress. Why?" she demanded.

"You are the one obsessed with every minute, useless detail," he responded.

"I just want you to tell me what's in your notes!" Juliet protested. They stood toe to toe now, both of them breathing rapidly, though they kept their voices low.

"I can't read them!" he answered, his expression fierce.

"Well, maybe these will help you, then!" Juliet said. Snatching the pair of spectacles that perched upon her nose, she removed them, turned them around, and shoved them into Morgan's face.

"Damnit!" he shouted, drawing the attention of both Cyril and the guards.

Shocked at her own behavior, Juliet stared at Morgan. The sight of him blinking at her from behind the glass made her pause. Her heart was pounding, her pulse was racing, and she realized, with no little astonishment, that she was enjoying herself. She sat down hard on the nearest chair, amazed at the revelation.

She had always been the quiet one, lost in her research, trying to blend in as best she could, a woman in a man's world with a man's course of study. She had argued sometimes, especially over the meaning of hieroglyphs, but she had never felt the rush of exhilaration that came from fighting with this man.

She enjoyed it. She liked loosing the passion, raising her voice, the give and take, and the desire that flowed from it. Or sparked it. Lifting hands to her flushed cheeks, Juliet hid her face in her palms, horrified at such self-discovery.

"Juliet!" The sound of Morgan's voice, not as loud this time, made her lift her head once more. He was standing there, still wearing the spectacles, a page of notes held in front of him. Dropping the papers, he looked at her, his dark gaze of wonder piercing her heart.

"I can read them."

* * *

MORGAN had been so amazed by the power of the spectacles that he had nearly grabbed Juliet to him and kissed her, right there in front of everyone. He thought of all the years he had struggled to decipher the small print of books, when he had suffered the ridicule of his family and others for his poor reading, how at one point he had begun to question his own intelligence. Was it any wonder the hieroglyphs, carved in towering heights into stone, appealed to him far more than tiny scrawls on paper?

He had always tried to write in a larger hand, for his own sake, but his careful attempts soon degenerated into cramped lettering that later defied him. Now Morgan was glad of it, for only Juliet's exasperation had resulted in the answer to his lifelong struggle. Again, he felt the urge to kiss her, to seize her, to thank her in a more definite way than words, to give her more tangible proof of his gratitude, but it was late in the day, and he knew better than to visit her bedroom again.

Having returned her spectacles, Morgan had promised to go out on the morrow and purchase his own. Then, he had told her, they could begin again, going over all that they had already catalogued. Although she had eyed him dubiously, she had not questioned his motives, and Morgan had left it at that, hoping she would not wonder further at his delaying tactics.

Slipping in through the dressing room of his new apartments, where Chauncey slept, Morgan found it deserted. Either Chauncey was out gathering information, or he had returned to his old habits, leaving their rooms unattended. Morgan just hoped his bed wasn't on fire. Lifting the latch silently, he threw open the door, but the bedchamber was empty and, thankfully, not alight.

Breathing a sigh of relief, Morgan stepped inside and made a careful tour of the perimeter, checking windows and the hearth. Satisfied, he sank into a heavy chair, but his gaze still roamed the room, coming to rest upon the dressing table where his razor lay. Either Chauncey had found it or some maid or footman had recovered it, Morgan noted with relief. But the razor's reappearance was quickly forgotten when something else caught his eye, and he glanced upward to stare at the ornate mirror attached to the table.

It didn't take spectacles to see that something was written there. Even in the dim cast of the firelight, Morgan could make out the dark lines, and he was already on his feet, thinking it might be a message from Chauncey. But when he stepped closer, his eyes narrowed. Chauncey had not left this missive, nor could many others, for no letters graced the glass, only a picture, a very specific sort of picture.

Morgan lifted a hand to touch the surface, his finger coming away black with kohl as he glared at the hieroglyph. Resembling a dagger, it was the same one that had been drawn on the livery of the fallen footman.

With a snarl, Morgan turned on his heel and stalked from the room. The temper that had been sorely tested over the past few days snapped its tether, and he made his way swiftly through the house with a definite goal in mind: pummeling the truth from the coxcomb.

Stopping before Lyndhurst's bedroom, Morgan knocked sharply, then waited, though he was tempted to barge in without a greeting, perhaps with a glowing ember as a gift.

After several long moments that tried Morgan's patience, the door opened, finally, to reveal Lyndhurst's stiff-necked valet. "I beg your pardon?" he asked, in a haughty tone that Morgan had lost the stomach for years ago.

Pushing past the man into the room, Morgan ignored his outraged sputtering. "Where's Lyndhurst?" he asked.

"You cannot come in here! The baronet is not to be disturbed."

Paying the fellow no heed, Morgan scanned the room, noting its neatness, the fire in the hearth, and the bed, which had been turned down but was not occupied.

"See here," the valet began, but at that moment a connecting door opened, and the coxcomb himself appeared, wearing an elaborate dressing gown as though ready to retire.

"What is it, Baxter?" he asked.

"This . . . gentleman insists upon seeing you, sir," the valet said, still standing beside the open door.

"And just where have you been, Lyndhurst?" Morgan said, stalking to a halt before him.

"Why, I was having a bath, if you must know, though it is certainly no business of yours. Now, if you please, I'm sure whatever you have to say can wait until tomorrow. These are my private rooms," Lyndhurst said.

Instead of complying, Morgan reached out and grabbed one of the baronet's hands, turning it palm upwards to inspect the fingers. Although Lyndhurst snatched it away soon enough, Morgan got a good look. Unfortunately, the pads were perfectly clean. Of course, that didn't prove anything. The coxcomb could have used gloves when leaving his little calling card or scrubbed off the kohl in his bath.

"What is the meaning of this?" Lyndhurst said, his voice rising.

"Someone left a little note in my room," Morgan said.

"Well, I certainly didn't!"

"Ah, but it was someone with a knowledge of hieroglyphs," Morgan said, eyeing the coxcomb carefully.

Lyndhurst sniffed. "Although I pride myself upon my expertise, there are others with some smattering of ability."

Morgan's brows inched upward. "Are you accusing Lady Juliet of sneaking into my rooms and drawing on my mirror? Perhaps you think she knocked the footman unconscious and marked his chest, as well?"

The coxcomb sniffed again. "There are others who study hieroglyphs within this very city, but if you wish to look no further than this household, you should have an eye on the dead, not the living."

Morgan's hands fisted at his sides. "Don't try to blame the mummy. It was a human hand, and a live one, that scrawled on my mirror!"

Having had his fill of Lyndhurst's tales and scares, Morgan thought it time to put a scare into him. He stepped forward, intending to give him a good thrashing, but the valet tried to intervene, and then another voice rose above the sound of the three men arguing.

"Is there a problem, gentlemen?" The deep voice was unmistakable, and Morgan turned his head to see Cheevy's burly body filling the open doorway. Although his tone wasn't threatening, his stance definitely was one of menace.

Morgan glanced at Lyndhurst, whose mottled face bore an expression of superiority, and he hesitated, struggling against the urge to wipe the smirk away with a good poke. But then he might find himself tossed out on his ear, and who would watch over Juliet?

Morgan stepped back. "I've got my eye on you, Lyndhurst," he muttered and turned toward the door.

"You brought this on yourself," the coxcomb called from behind him. "The curse will out."

Morgan tensed, but continued on, brushing past the butler's heavy form into the dim corridor. He wondered just what had brought Cheevy here at this hour. Did the butler never sleep? And was he clever enough to draw a hieroglyph?

Morgan frowned, uncertain. But, as Lyndhurst said, there were others with that skill right here in London, most especially one that had escaped his attention of late. Perhaps tomorrow when he went out to get his spectacles,

Morgan would pay a little visit to another expert, the one who had asked so many questions about him.

And maybe Herr Brueger could provide some answers.

CHAUNCEY swore low and long as he stared at the mirror. "You aren't planning to leave it there, are you?" he asked.

Morgan scowled at the hieroglyph gracing his room, the heavily drawn symbol even more glaring in the light of day. "No. I suppose we better have someone clean it up."

"That someone better be me," Chauncey said, eyeing him askance. "One of the poor maids'll likely faint dead away at the sight of it."

Morgan nodded absently, his mind on the meeting ahead with Herr Brueger. Grabbing up a towel, he slung it around his neck and glanced at the mirror. "Hell, I can't even see to shave," he muttered, taking the edge of the material and rubbing away some of the marks.

"In a hurry, are we?" Chauncey asked, bustling around the room.

Having created a small circle where he could view his reflection, Morgan reached for the cup Chauncey set before him.

"Hold up a minute, I'll have to go get my razor for you," Chauncey said.

"No, I've got mine," Morgan said, reaching for the familiar bone handle.

"Where'd you find it?" Chauncey asked.

"It was lying right here," Morgan answered with a shrug. He lifted it to his face, but caught Chauncey's expression in the mirror and lowered it slowly. "What?"

"It wasn't lying there yesterday morning," Chauncey said. "Nor even later in the day."

"Maybe one of the footmen returned it," Morgan said,

but an eerie feeling chased up his spine, and he set the razor down.

"A bit odd, wouldn't you say, that it's lying right there beneath your little message, a hieroglyph of the dagger, supposedly a warning of death or doom or something right above it?"

The two men stared at the innocent looking utensil as though it had turned into a snake, most specifically an asp, ready to strike.

"You think there's something on the blade," Morgan said.

It wasn't a question, but Chauncey answered with one. "What about henbane? It was a favorite of the ancient Egyptians," he said, his voice a ragged whisper.

"I don't know. Do you have to ingest it or breathe it or can it slip into a . . . cut?" Morgan said, his own speech suddenly hoarse. He lifted a hand to his throat, rubbing it thoughtfully.

"Maybe it's something like those Amazon natives use on their arrows," Chauncey said.

"Darts poisoned with curare," Morgan muttered.

"If so, it wouldn't do any good unless you sliced yourself open," Chauncey noted.

Morgan swore under his breath. Although he rarely nicked himself, it was always a possibility, especially when so much else was weighing on his mind. With grim foreboding, he realized that all it would take was one single thought of Juliet in various contexts, and his hand would slip, resulting in a tiny scratch, nothing to be concerned with—unless you knew that a deadly poison had found its way into your blood.

"How can we tell?" Chauncey asked.

"I don't intend to find out," Morgan said, disinclined to touch, taste, or even sniff the blade. Those who thought to investigate poisons too often were the victims of their own experiments. Of course, there was always the possibility that the razor was devoid of any toxins.

"Maybe we're both a bit edgy, seeing shadows where there aren't any," he muttered. Glancing up, he caught Chauncey's eye and held it, but his friend's expression remained dour.

Nodding at the hieroglyph, Chauncey frowned. "Or maybe someone is determined to see you dead."

Chapter 15

NEW spectacles tucked in his pocket, Morgan made his way to Herr Brueger's apartments with grim purpose. When the servant who answered the door eyed him dubiously, Morgan's suspicion grew. Perhaps it had been the old professor all along, in league with one of the earl's staff, or even Lyndhurst himself, stealing items and concocting ghost tales for his own gain.

Unfortunately, Brueger didn't look like a madman—or even a man who would concoct such a scheme. With his own spectacles, his thick mustache, and his lined brow, he wore the mantle of a scholar. And when Morgan entered the room, the older man stood, greeting him like an old friend, a seemingly sincere smile on his face.

"Ah, Mr. Beauchamp, what a happy meeting! Please come in and sit down," he said, gesturing to nearby chairs. All were rather threadbare, indicating that the professor was not in the best financial position. Perhaps penury had forced him to act. Morgan frowned.

"I take it you are not making progress with your cataloguing?" Brueger said.

"Why do you say that?" Morgan asked, eyes narrowing.

The professor appeared surprised. "Why else would you be here, eh?"

Morgan stared at the man, hard. *Why else indeed?* "Perhaps I'm here because I got a message, a hieroglyph, directed to me personally."

Brueger looked bewildered. "And you cannot interpret its meaning? I am afraid that I do not possess any skills that Lady Cavendish does not have. Indeed, she probably has surpassed me in her progress."

"I don't need Juliet to tell me its meaning," Morgan said, his expression hardening. "Nor do I need an interpreter to guess why someone set fire to my bed and put poison on my razor."

The shocked expression that crossed Brueger's face was either genuine or very well rehearsed. "What is this?" he asked, evincing alarm.

"Someone is causing mischief at the earl's town house, stealing his artifacts, attacking the servants, and blaming it all on a body that's been dead for hundreds of years," Morgan said.

"A body? Ah, yes, the mummy! Juliet told me about this claim of a curse, but I simply cannot countenance it," Brueger said. "I have never heard of such a thing, even in the writings of the ancients, in all their known records of Egypt." He shook his head, apparently as baffled as Morgan and Juliet.

"And now you say that people are being attacked?" the professor asked. "I heard such tales were being published in the newspapers, but I could not believe them!"

"Two footmen have been injured, and there have been attempts on my life," Morgan said. He fixed Brueger with a direct gaze. "Naturally, I'm concerned about everyone in the household, and that includes Juliet."

The color left Brueger's face in a most convincing manner, and his eyes, behind the glass, met Morgan's with a sharpness that belied his age. "But why . . . why would anyone harm Juliet?"

"Why would anyone steal artifacts, strike out at footmen, or torch my bedding?"

Brueger gaped at him, then gathered himself together, his mustache twitching with the force of the effort. "Surely, you don't think *I* had anything to do with it?"

Morgan shrugged.

"But what reason would I have to perpetrate such acts upon the earl's household?" Bruger asked, looking genuinely puzzled.

"That's what I would like to know," Morgan said, his voice harsh.

Brueger shook his head, his expression not one of outrage but of sadness. "You are looking in the wrong place for your villain, Mr. Beauchamp, for I would never do anything to cause distress to Lady Juliet, who has been my colleague for many years, my colleague and my friend." He paused to stroke his mustache. "This news is most unsettling, most unsettling indeed."

"And why is that?" Morgan asked, thinking the man would launch into a discourse on collecting or researching and the ill effects on the community of Egyptian scholars. But again Brueger surprised him.

He met Morgan's gaze, his own surprisingly fierce. "Obviously, I am anxious for Lady Juliet."

The comment roused something in Morgan, and it wasn't suspicion. He felt a surge of possessiveness. "I'll take care of Juliet," he said, his voice gruff.

Brueger's brows lifted in query.

"I mean that I'll keep her safe," Morgan said.

"Indeed?" Brueger wore an expression of keen interest

that made Morgan suddenly uncomfortable. He shifted in his seat.

"After all, she is the earl's daughter," Morgan muttered.

"Ah. And he is your employer," Brueger said. "Is that the only reason for your concern?"

Again, the old man appeared to be studying Morgan too closely for his own comfort. He effected a shrug. "She's alone there, the only woman, and far too easily lost in study to pay attention to threats."

"Ah. Your concern is commendable, since your reputation is one of a rogue," Brueger said, leaning back and stroking his mustache.

Morgan didn't like the way the professor was looking at him or the way that simple sound rolled off the German's tongue just as though he had made some great discovery. And how had this interrogation been turned around upon himself? Morgan's eyes narrowed.

"If you are so blameless, just where do you suggest I look, if not here?" he asked.

Brueger frowned thoughtfully. "I can think of no one in the world of academics capable of such perfidy. Though there are always some who want to claim another's glory, I cannot envision any who would use violence to do so. Perhaps you should look to your own enemies."

Morgan swore under his breath. Brueger was no help. Meanwhile, Juliet was left unprotected. Morgan had set Chauncey to keeping an eye on her, but his position as a so-called valet allowed him only so much freedom in the household—more in some areas and less in others. Morgan rose to his feet.

"What about her father?" Brueger asked, his voice low.

Morgan stiffened and turned to fix the professor with a sharp glance. "What about him?"

"Let us just say that the earl is not what he seems," the old man murmured.

"That's true enough," Morgan said. "How do you mean?"

"I have heard that he has many enemies, though I suspect few would be daring enough to strike at the heart of his household."

Morgan's eyes narrowed. What kind of enemies was Brueger talking about? Every member of the ton had rivals, both political and social. There also might be personal feuds, relatives, and other collectors to consider, but Morgan had been through most of them. And who among them would resort to violence? "Is that why he employs a former bruiser as his butler?" Morgan asked.

"Bruiser?"

"A boxer, a former fighter."

Brueger shook his head. "I don't know, but he has a reputation for protecting his interests well."

"What interests?"

"Let us just say that he has made his fortune employing unusual methods, at odds with the moral code of others," Brueger said.

"What? How?" Morgan asked, impatient.

Brueger shook his head. "I have just heard rumors. Perhaps if you talked to someone else, you might find out more, but be careful. He has a long reach and does not like people prying into his affairs."

"And just where should I start?" Morgan asked.

"Perhaps someone at the Company," Brueger said, softly, as he, too, stood.

Morgan stared.

"I wish you luck, Mr. Beauchamp, but the earl of Carlisle is a dangerous man, and you would do well to keep that in mind," Brueger said as he nodded in farewell.

The advice was tendered in the way of a warning, and long after he left the man's apartments, Morgan wondered at his words. Just what had Brueger been warning him against—or away from?

* * *

"I told you I didn't trust the earl!" Chauncey said, whistling under his breath. "He's got his hands in something shady. I could tell from that butler of his and those cutthroat guards."

"But what and why?" Morgan asked, leaning back against the mantel. "I just can't see the point."

Chauncey snorted. "You think all these nabobs have made their money on tidy little investments? They rob their tenants, work the poor to death in their factories, run slaves . . ." He paused to fix Morgan with a sharp gaze, his question obvious. Was the earl trading in human flesh?

"I don't think so," Morgan said. "Brueger mentioned the Company."

The Company was, of course, the English East India Company. Granted a charter in 1600 that gave it a monopoly on all English trade east of the Cape of Good Hope, it had extended its reach to the entire globe, though India was the greatest of its territories and China the source of its greatest revenue. For more than a hundred years, it had imported the country's tea, while exporting to the Chinese the opium grown in India.

"We know he has shipping interests and contacts in the Orient, for it was his ship that brought us and the artifacts back here," Morgan said. "But does he have a stake in the Company?"

Chauncey shook his head. "Can't say I know much about the Company, except that it makes money without regard to much else."

Morgan nodded. There were many who didn't like the Company, including Westminster's Free Trade movement, but it had powerful allies. Was there more to Herr Brueger's insinuations than that? Morgan hated this feeling of not knowing, of chasing after shadows. He frowned.

"Or Brueger could simply be trying to throw me off his own track," he mused.

"Well, I've still got plenty of contacts here. I think I'll call in a few favors. If the earl's up to something nasty, we'll find out what," Chauncey said. "Meanwhile, I don't suppose you'd consider a bit of a move? Just to somewhere else in the city?"

Still lost in thought, Morgan simply shook his head and turned toward the door.

"And just where are you going?" Chauncey called after him.

"I'm taking a bath," Morgan said.

Chauncey groaned. "And just who's going to watch your back while you're lying stark naked in the water?"

"I guess I'll have to do it myself," Morgan muttered. Already, he had removed clean linen from his list of the pleasures of civilization, for what good was a soft mattress if it went up in flames? And now, it seemed, even his enjoyment of a hot bath was compromised.

He could hardly lean back his head and close his eyes, as had been his wont. Instead, he would have to keep a wary eye on the door, lest someone come in and drown him. It was either that or have Chauncey stand guard, and Chauncey had an aversion to hot water. But Morgan longed for a good soak. He felt itchy as he stalked through the house, impatient, needing answers, needing . . . something.

He found it in the bath.

As soon as he stepped inside, Morgan knew that someone else had been using the room recently, for steam drifted around him, a siren song calling him to the nearby marble depression. His feet already bare, he stripped off his shirt and breeches, then turned, only to discover the reason for the heat and steam.

Someone was already there, reclining in the water.

Her hair piled high, her eyes huge within her lovely face, Lady Juliet Cavendish stared at him from above the sunken tub. Her lips moved, but no sound came out, and for a long moment, Morgan simply stood rapt, while they gazed at each with a kind of mutual shock and . . . pleasure.

Gradually, the realization of his good fortune sank in, and Morgan relaxed, the restlessness that had plagued him gone, a new anticipation seizing him. Juliet was trapped, and they both knew it, unless she had the intention to flee, and from the expression on her face, she wasn't going anywhere. Indeed, the way her attention drifted from his chest to his groin, then caught and held there, made Morgan's body stir in response.

He stepped forward, his blood running hot, and moved toward the bath, pausing on the edge to take in the sight of her delicious form barely visible beneath the surface. She moved, and her shoulders rose out of the water, smooth and glistening, making Morgan eager to see the rest of her, her breasts, her thighs, the globes of her cheeks.

Without taking his gaze from her, Morgan lowered himself into the depression, moving down the stairs one step at a time until the liquid lapped at his thighs, welcoming, luring him toward another warmth, another wetness. He moved forward, luxuriating in the familiar sensations of the chamber, heightened beyond imaginings by the presence of Juliet. Stopping before her, he reached out a hand and drew her up.

She rose from the bath like Venus, a golden goddess to rival any of ancient Egypt. Her hair was a soft cloud about her face, her body tall and straight and gleaming in the soft light. Morgan took it all in—the full breasts, the slender waist, the curve of her hips, the supple, elegant lines she had hidden beneath her serviceable clothing—and he felt like a man who had stumbled across treasure unnoticed, unseen. Until now.

Lifting one dripping hand, Morgan touched her cheek in disbelief. Then he ran his palm along her throat and down her body, over her lush breast, pink-tipped and tempting, over the gentle curve of her abdomen, the sleek thighs that disappeared into the water, and in between them, to a thatch of golden curls, dewy and pale.

Like a connoisseur, Morgan explored his find, his fingers smoothing and delving over her silken skin, hot and wet and supple beneath his touch, and when he felt her own touch, tentative but eager, he shuddered. Loosing her hair, he buried his face in the softness, then pulled her into his arms. She gasped at the first brush of his wet form against her own, her breasts sliding against the hair on his chest, but her arms easily came up around his neck as he lowered his head.

He kissed her—long, slow, deep kisses that fed upon themselves—but it was not enough. The languid, sensual heat that enveloped him pressed him further, and he slid his palms down her back, flawless and straight, to the curves behind her, beneath the water.

The exquisite feel of those globes made him pull her to him, tighter, and despite her obvious innocence, she didn't flinch. Prosaic as always, she was not shocked but seemed to revel in each new sensation, and her wonder fed his own. For this was Juliet, not some jaded courtesan or flirtatious widow, and Morgan drank her in like a drug.

Indeed, he felt as if he had wandered into some opium-induced dream, a dance of pure pleasure in the heat and the steam and the liquid, the glide of her skin against his, the plunder of her mouth, the lush feel of her beneath his fingers. But still, it was not enough.

Dropping down onto one of the steps, Morgan dragged her onto his lap, and they sank into the water that pooled around her waist. The first brush of her against his groin stole Morgan's breath, robbed him of his wits, and he pulled her down for a kiss, hot and heavy. Her breasts slid against him, soft and slick and wet, and he nearly lost himself then and there. But he held on, held onto her, rocking her against him, fighting against the pull of a passion so fierce, it threatened to consume them both.

For Juliet was no passive partner. Her kisses matched his own, and her expertise grew with each heated moment. She ran her hands over his arms, his chest, and up into his hair, her fingers grasping tightly even as she rose over him. She shifted, trying to center herself over his throbbing member, and Morgan groaned.

"No. We cannot. We dare not," he muttered hoarsely. He had enough wits for that, at least. And when his eyes met hers, through the dazed desire there, he saw comprehension, perhaps even disappointment. His body jerked in response.

Morgan promptly jerked it back, but he dipped his hand into the water, finding and cupping her with his palm. The sweet surprise on her beautiful face was his reward, for in her shadowy gaze lay the rich delight of discovery.

"What are you doing?" she murmured, ever the researcher.

"Shh . . . Just feel. Just feel me," Morgan whispered, and, for once she did not argue. He watched as her lashes drifted downward and a flush rose in her cheeks. Her lips parted, and her head fell back, exposing the smooth expanse of her throat, lovely and delicate, and Morgan pressed his mouth against it, savoring the taste of heat and water and Juliet. And when he heard the change in the tenor of her breathing, the rapid increase, the hitched, ragged sounds, he lifted his head and saw the glorious change in her features as pleasure washed over her.

And just that quickly, he was lost. Grasping Juliet to him, Morgan ground against her beneath the water with a fierce, undeniable need that thundered through him and then burst forth in the longest, most potent climax he had ever known.

* * *

AND he hadn't even been inside her. Morgan was thankful
for that much, at least, but the realization stunned him, in
light of the white-hot ecstasy that had seized him. His body
stirred at the memory, and Morgan groaned, sinking back
against the sheets.

And still it wasn't enough. He had wanted more, had
longed to take his time, loving her all night within the bath
and without, on the marble floor, against the tiled walls,
then carrying her back to his bed, where he could love her
again. And again. And wake up beside her in the morning.

Morgan cursed as he realized the tenor of his thoughts
and swallowed against a hot rush of panic. He had faced
death, disease, disownment, and never had he felt the
heart-thundering, mind-numbing terror that he did right
now. He was scared, and it wasn't a moldering mummy or
any curse that frightened him. It was Juliet and her ability
to make him lose control of his body, of his mind . . . and
maybe even more.

Morgan swung his feet to the floor and ran his hands
over his eyes. What had he been thinking? Later, he had
discovered that she had let her usual watchful maid go, because the girl was fearful of being anywhere except the
servant's hall at night. If she had not, just what would he
have done when the maid returned? He ought to have
drowned himself! Morgan groaned.

At least he hadn't taken her virginity, he thought, winc-
ing. And just that quickly, the idea rose up in him, an urge,
a yearning, a want that set his blood to pounding. Good
God, what ailed him? He rubbed at his face, as if to banish
a bad dream, or an extremely good dream with bad consequences. He might be what some termed an adventurer, but
he still was aware of the dictates of society, and he had broken them.

Worse yet, what would Juliet think? What would she expect? Any woman in her position would and should antici-
pate that he do the right thing, but that was impossible. Her

father, his position, her position . . . All were untenable, even if he could banish his panic long enough to consider it. With a sigh, Morgan rose to his feet. At least he hadn't made her pregnant. But the thought, instead of comforting him, only made his pulse kick in anticipation.

Swearing long and low, Morgan splashed his face with cold water. It was nothing like a hot bath, but he didn't trust himself to return to that chamber. Ever. Another amenity of civilization gone. Morgan wiped his dripping face and groaned. Maybe there really was something to the curse, because he certainly felt like a doomed man.

THE sight of Juliet didn't help. Indeed, Morgan felt his whole body seize up and betray him at the very glimpse of her. He couldn't control the sharp stab of delight, couldn't temper the hot flow of his blood. Even across the expanse of the ballroom, her shadowy eyes met his, studying, assessing, and he realized that only he could read that gaze. Not her father, not the coxcomb, not even, he suspected, Herr Brueger. Only to him did she open and flower and give herself.

Nodding slowly, Morgan found himself reassuring her when he had intended to warn her away, and he bit back another curse. But surely she knew that this could not continue. His instincts for self-preservation were suddenly at war with instincts for *her* preservation. Why had she ceded him so much, gifted him with her innocent passion? Morgan frowned. Perhaps because he was the only one who saw that part of her, nurtured it, freed it.

Well, he had better stop doing so, Morgan reminded himself. And yet the thought of some other man taking his place made him set his teeth. He resumed his usual place with a fierce scowl, his only comfort being the absence of Lyndhurst.

"Where's the coxcomb?" he grunted.

"Cyril? Oh, I don't know," Juliet said, glancing around with a distracted air. Obviously, she wasn't concerned about Lyndhurst, which was good, but Morgan wondered what mischief the man might be making.

"Put on your spectacles," she prompted.

"What? Oh, yes," Morgan said, patting his pocket before he caught himself. Then he slanted a glance at his companion. Since when had she started looking after him?

For awhile, they worked in silence, and despite all the tension that ought to be raging between them, it was a comfortable quiet, with the ease of familiarity and habit. When he drew a haphazard sketch from memory of temple walls, she made no critique of his skill but gazed up at him with admiration shining from those beautiful eyes.

Pausing to study him as carefully as one of her precious hieroglyphs, she suddenly spoke in a whisper. "Who are you?"

Morgan stared at her, caught in that searching gaze, drowning in the shifting sands there. He jerked away and shrugged.

"Where did you come from?" she asked.

Morgan opened his mouth to deliver a blithe answer, but he realized that she deserved the truth from him—or at least as much as he was willing to give.

"I'm from England, from the north country," he said, trying to speak easily on the sore subject of his past.

"And how did you end up in Egypt?" she asked. He couldn't look at her, couldn't gaze into the dune-colored depths of her eyes for fear he would give himself away, *all of himself*, into her keeping.

"Let us just say my father had certain expectations for me that I wasn't willing to meet," Morgan said, surprised at how easily the words came after all these years. "He was very strict, utterly humorless, and devoid of imagination. So I had my choice of a religious or a military career. Although the latter was preferable to the former, I couldn't see taking orders from anyone, so I refused both. As you can imagine, there were some hideous rows, culminating in my father tossing me out upon my ear."

She watched him, her gaze gentle, her expression non-judgmental, and Morgan felt the weight of the past slip away, like sand through his fingers. "I knocked about amongst friends for awhile, then, luckily, I received a small inheritance from a distant relation. So I took my leave of my homeland and set out to explore the rest of the world. I made it as far as India and then Egypt, where I developed a taste for treasure, a fortuitous occurrence, seeing as how my limited funds were sadly depleted by then."

She smiled, as soft and welcoming as a warm breeze, and shook her head. "It is not the thought of plunder that drives you but the hunt itself and the excitement of the find."

True enough, Morgan thought. She knew him well, perhaps too well. Even now he felt the call of the hunt, the lure of the sand and the history that lay hidden beneath. But there were other treasures and other lures. What if he discovered something too rare and precious to set aside?

Chapter 16

✠

JULIET peeked into the darkened ballroom and felt a
wave of unease. Unless Morgan was standing behind one
of the heavy pieces, he was not there, and without him, her
familiar refuge took on a vaguely sinister cast. She could
almost sense a threat emanating from the shadows, a menace that made her fear, not for herself, but for Morgan.

She had heard about the hieroglyph found on his mirror,
though he hadn't spoken of it himself. Cyril had complained about the accusations tossed at his head, and
though she understood her colleague's outrage, she was
more concerned about the hieroglyph's message, especially coming so soon after the fire.

Morgan didn't believe in the curse, that much Juliet
knew, and she had difficulty imagining it herself, but
there were many things in the world not yet understood,
many processes that men of science were only beginning
to research, and knowledge once shared that had been lost
in time.

As for unbelievable occurrences, Juliet had only to look

to her own recent experience. She would never have thought she would one day find herself sharing a bath with a man who had been a stranger to her only a few weeks ago, both of them naked and wet and discovering pleasures she had never dreamed about, never even considered possible. If such a thing could happen, then might not the will of a king reach out over centuries? Juliet shivered.

She was being fanciful. A woman who had spent a lifetime with facts and words and symbols, she was allowing her newfound senses to overcome her reason. She knew that, and yet, when she glanced back over her shoulder into the ballroom, it was with distinct unease. And the feeling was not relieved by the leering looks of the guards, who did not possess the quiet and unobtrusive demeanor she had come to expect from servants. Their eyes were bright and avid, their mouths cruel and sneering.

Juliet moved away from them quickly, eager to get out of their sight. It was late, and she should retire, but she still wanted to talk to Morgan about the hieroglyph and its meaning. Privately. She had already checked the bathing chamber, only to find it empty. Where else would he be? As the answer came to her, Juliet felt her heart speed its pace and her breath catch. For, at this time of night, he most probably was in his rooms. And she knew just where they were.

Juliet hesitated only a moment before continuing on through the house, trying to avoid the eyes of others as she made her way to his door. She had stood in front of it once before, but that had been during the day, and now she was acutely aware of the night pressing around her, making her long for other things beyond conversation. Steeling her clamoring senses, she told herself that it was concern that drove her here and not some nameless yearning for what only Morgan Beauchamp could provide.

Drawing in a deep breath, she knocked softly, and the door swung open immediately. But it was not Morgan's handsome visage that greeted her. Instead, she recognized the pinched features of his valet. The man did not appear surprised to see her, but then he had come upon her here another time. Juliet felt herself blush at the memory.

She drew herself up. "May I speak with Mr. Beauchamp?"

The valet shook his head. "He isn't here, my lady," he answered in a rather surly tone.

Juliet's brow furrowed. This man did not seem like the typical body servant, though he certainly was not as menacing as the guards below. She felt an urge to step back, but concern for Morgan made her hold her ground. Did this man even know where his master was? Was Morgan safe, or menaced by some new mishap, whatever the cause? Worry made her press. "Do you know where he might be?"

The man shrugged. "It's hard to tell at this time of night, my lady. Mr. Beauchamp is rather a roamer, off on the next adventure before you can wink an eye. Not the sort to stay in one place too long, if you get my meaning."

Juliet's brow furrowed in puzzlement. Was this fellow intimating that Morgan was off dallying with some other woman? How could that be? Or did he mean that Morgan would leave her as quickly as he had charged into her life? Juliet eyed the canny fellow closely, but he refused to meet her gaze.

Unaccustomed to engaging in meaningful exchanges with servants, Juliet was inclined to make her exit, and yet, something, some point of pride or ill-fated optimism, made her speak up. "Yet he has a deep, abiding love for Egypt. I can't imagine him adventuring anywhere else," she said.

The servant nodded. "Yes, he has quite a fancy for the country and for discovery. Perhaps it's the thrill of the chase," he noted. Although spoken blithely, the words chilled Juliet, for hadn't she just told Morgan the very same thing earlier this day?

"And, my, does he love a new find!" the servant continued. "There's nothing in the world that excites him more. But then he's off to the next excavation, and all those treasures he so enjoyed discovering end up being sold to the highest bidder, such as your father, the earl."

Juliet stared, uncertain, at the man. A scholar and a dealer in facts, she was not used to searching for hidden meanings in common speech, especially in dialogue with someone such as this fellow.

He cleared his throat. "Yes, that's Morgan for you," he muttered, looking down at his feet. "He never keeps the things he loves."

Juliet blinked in disbelief at the bald statement. She was sure her shock must show, but the servant didn't even glance her way. He simply shrugged, as though they were discussing the weather or Morgan's penchant for adventure. Perhaps they were. Perhaps there was nothing more to the man's statements than a valet's attempt at conversation.

And, yet . . . Juliet felt a sudden, wrenching foreboding. She glanced about, trying to gather her composure, but her gaze fell upon the dressing table, where the hieroglyph had been. The image of the dagger leapt to mind as if to pierce her own heart with its blade. Perhaps it did, for how else to account for the sudden pain there?

Without another word, Juliet turned and fled back to her room, back to the world she knew. But how to find solace there now?

THE next morning, Juliet was decidedly subdued. It didn't matter whether Morgan's man was right or not. What was important was that he had made her think, a process she seemed to have abandoned not long after the adventurer's arrival. And when she gathered her wits about her, she realized that the cataloguing would soon be finished, the man who had come to mean so much to her would be gone, presumably without a backward glance, and she would be

forced to resume her former life. It was a truth she would
do well to remember.

But working alongside him, it was difficult not to fall
into the habits she had recently acquired, of leaning near,
of hanging on to his words, of wanting more of him. Only
now had she come to wonder: to what purpose? What
could she hope to gain except a few fleeting moments of
delight? The truth was disheartening, but better that she
face the future squarely than continue ignoring it.

What if she had met Morgan in the bath again? What if
he had not shown the restraint he so nobly did before?
Juliet was not so ignorant that she did not know what con-
stituted the ultimate intimacy between men and women.
Well, she might have been that ignorant, but *now* she knew,
having resorted to a few indelicate volumes in her father's
library.

Now she understood why one of the maids had been
banished, turned out onto the streets, for misconduct. And
now she knew just how easily a woman could succumb to
such temptations and the possible consequences. Juliet
stiffened, chilled by the thought of sharing that maid's fate.
Her father was a hard man, one with rigid rules and expectations, and an out-of-wedlock pregnancy for his daughter
would not fit into his plans.

Juliet drew a deep breath, banishing that fear as no
longer possible. She had spent a lifetime being reasonable
and logical, and as much as she had enjoyed her brief taste
of adventure, it was time to get her head out of the clouds
and back to earth.

It was a struggle, but she managed to focus her thoughts
on the artifacts and upon finishing the project that had been
assigned to her. Indeed, she was concentrating so hard on
her work that she barely heard Morgan's curt comment
from beside her. He was forced to repeated himself, louder.

"Don't be in such a hurry," he admonished, and Juliet

bristled at both the words and the tone. From her new perspective, he sounded far too much like Cyril for her comfort.

"Excuse me?" she asked, turning to face him. That was a mistake, for the spectacles perched upon his nose set her heart to tumbling in her chest. They made him look that much more intelligent, but no less dangerous. Approachable. *Beautiful.* Juliet blinked at her senses' betrayal.

"And you needn't bury your nose in your notebook. I thought you had decided not to be so rigid," he commented, his lips quirking.

But Juliet didn't want his advice or his comments. "I am not rigid," she whispered. "I am restrained. And methodical. And *dependable.*" The last word came out in a hiss, for she knew she had just listed all the things he was not.

If she had pursued discipline, it was her own choice, not a role thrust upon her, as Morgan had suggested. She had made an effort to put order into her existence in a man's world, to gain some control over her life, and if she threw herself and her passion into the artifacts and hieroglyphs, who could blame her? It was all she had.

"It's easy for you to condemn, isn't it? You waltz in here with your wild notions and your exhortations to change, and then, when you have wrought your havoc, you can leave all amiss! You'll go back to Egypt, off to some new adventure, but I have to remain here," she said. Formerly content, she now faced the future as a prisoner of her own life.

Like Dr. Frankenstein, he had created some sort of monster from the devoted scholar she had been. He'd made her want what she couldn't have: freedom, Egypt, adventure. And, most of all, *him.*

ANOTHER cold, rainy dawn, and he was no closer to discovering the truth, Morgan thought with a grimace. Yesterday had gone badly. The *Morning Post* had carried another story on the curse, citing the fire as new proof of its fulfillment. At least there had been no mention of Morgan's razor. No doubt, if he'd sliced his throat and died a lingering death, it would have been big news, the mummy having been appeased.

Morgan wasn't. Picking up Chauncey's razor, he stared into the mirror, now devoid of any message. But instead of his own visage, he saw Juliet, an accusing look on her face that had stunned him. He had made it his mission to coax her out of her hard shell, but yesterday his casual suggestion had been tossed back into his face, and not with the usual sparring he so enjoyed. It wasn't anger so much as dismissal that had been written on her delicate features.

It was as though she had suddenly put him aside. But why? *And how could she?* At the thought, every nerve in his body clamored that he go after her, to claim her as his own, to possess her in all ways possible. Shrugging his tight shoulders, Morgan tried to release some of the tension brought on by the fierce demand, but to no avail. Dragging Chauncey's razor down one cheek, he nicked himself and swore aloud.

"Here, now, I'll thank you not to bloody up my razor," Chauncey said. Morgan silenced him with a glare.

Was she right? Had he used her? His mouth tightened as he remembered his original intention, but he had never planned for things to go this far. He frowned, still not sure how he had ended up naked and wet with the earl's daughter. Even as he wondered just how it had all come about, he nicked himself again, rearing back with an oath.

Ever since his youth, he had traveled from one place to another, never staying too long, taking each day as it came, never giving a thought to anyone beyond himself, and perhaps Chauncey. Suddenly, Morgan halted, midswipe, arrested by a bleak notion. Had he cared so little for so long that he had forgotten how?

Never one to ponder the future, to spend too much time thinking about his life, Morgan now forced himself to consider that which he had ignored for so long. What would happen after he found the villain behind the alleged curse and returned to his previous existence? As the truth flooded him, he felt like someone had kicked him in the gut.

Even after he had rinsed his face and finished dressing, Morgan felt an unaccustomed sensation, a lingering sour stomach that made him skip breakfast and head toward the ballroom. As he approached the entrance, he was so tense that he nearly collided with another figure hurrying forward.

Juliet.

Despite the primal urges that suddenly swamped him, Morgan stepped back, his greeting muted, and let her precede him into the room. Glancing at the two guards, he noticed that they watched her every move, and his fingers curled into fists. They should be keeping an eye on Lyndhurst, not the lady of the household. Scowling, Morgan moved forward, only to halt abruptly as he faced Juliet's back. Why had she stopped? Slipping beside her, Morgan followed her arrested gaze and stiffened.

There was a knife sticking in the wall.

And it wasn't just any old blade. Morgan's eyes narrowed as he recognized the missing dagger. It was thrust through the papyrus that had disappeared and into the plaster beyond like some pagan sacrifice. Although he was relieved to recover the artifacts, Morgan frowned at the implicit message. It was a threat, or a warning, or, as Lyndhurst would claim, more of the curse nonsense.

One glance at Juliet's horrified expression had Morgan reaching out, and she came into his arms easily, burying her face against his chest with a gurgling sound. He knew that he tempted fate embracing her here, especially with the guards about, but it felt good to hold her like this. *Incredibly good.* Needs rose up in him, and not those he usually associated with women, but others, far deeper and stronger, more instinctive.

Glancing up at the dagger, Morgan tensed. Whoever was doing these things was growing bolder every day. What if he struck at the family next? What if he hurt Juliet? Morgan desperately wanted to protect her. But how? Just as Morgan tightened his grip around her, she pulled away, and he had to fight the urge to drag her back, forcibly, to where she belonged. Beside him. *In his arms.*

"I'm sorry. I was overset for a moment. It was such a shock, just so horrible to see someone intentionally destroy . . ." She didn't finish but glanced at the wall and flinched. Being Juliet, she wasn't frightened or worried about any curse, just her precious hieroglyphs. Morgan's lips quirked.

"Who would do such a thing?" she asked. Her expression was so bleak that it wrung at his heart. Morgan shook his head.

"You don't think . . ." She looked at him wide-eyed, leaving the words unsaid, but Morgan could easily divine her thoughts.

"There is no curse. No dead man did this, but someone alive and well. At least for now," he muttered under his breath.

"But how could anyone get past the guards, with two on watch both night and day?" she asked.

"You know as well as I do that there is a logical explanation, one not involving something that's been mummified," Morgan said. He fixed her with a sharp gaze, and to his relief, she nodded.

"Perhaps the window latches have been tampered with again," he said. *Or perhaps someone had carried in the items, someone who could stroll past the guards with ease, someone like Lyndhurst.* Morgan frowned. Where was the coxcomb? He was usually present at the unveiling of each new drama.

Morgan stalked to the wall. "Perhaps it is best if we say nothing about this latest business to anyone. Then, if an account of it appears in the newspaper, we'll know that someone flesh and blood—and talkative—is at work."

"But what about Father? He'll need to know the artifacts have been recovered," Juliet protested. Of course, she didn't believe anyone here in the house had done this. For some reason, she found it impossible to suspect the coxcomb, a continual source of annoyance to Morgan.

"Just tell him that we found the items, and leave out the circumstances," Morgan advised. Then he paused thoughtfully. "Or maybe you shouldn't say anything at all, even to the earl."

Juliet glanced at him in surprise.

"Then, we wait and see who mentions the mishap, thereby incriminating himself," Morgan said.

She frowned. "You mean Cyril."

Morgan shrugged. Why was she so loyal to her colleagues? he wondered sourly. When would he gain some of that loyalty, some of that devotion, some of that blind faith?

"But what of the guards? Surely they noticed something?" Juliet asked, glancing over her shoulder.

The only thing the guards seemed to notice was the sway of Juliet's hips, Morgan thought to himself. Aloud, he said, "Obviously, they didn't see anything amiss, or they would have sounded the alarm."

Juliet nodded slowly. She moved toward Morgan and reached up as if to retrieve the dagger, but he stopped her, his fingers circling her wrist with grim intent. "Don't touch it," he whispered. "Not without gloves or a cloth."

"What?" Her brows knitted together in puzzlement, but for once, the sight did not stir him. His heart was pounding too fiercely at the thought of what might have happened, *what might still happen.*

"There could be something on the blade," Morgan explained, capturing her gaze with his own. "Poison, curare, some ancient substance intended to cause death or illness."

Juliet slanted a telltale glance toward the mummy case, awash in morning light, its alabaster gleaming.

"Not something put there by any Egyptian, but by whomever is intent upon causing havoc in this household," Morgan said. Snatching up a cloth, he yanked the dagger from the wall and caught the edge of the papyrus before it fell to the floor.

Juliet looked around warily, as if each artifact was now suspect. "But what of . . . everything else?" she asked.

Indeed, Morgan wondered, and a chill snaked up his spine. Whoever had stuck the dagger in the wall had access to the ballroom and all its antiquities. Every last one of them might be tainted with some toxic substance. Morgan's expression hardened.

"I suggest we start wearing gloves," he said.

Juliet shook her head, as though unwilling to concede the danger, then squared her shoulders, ready to do whatever was required of her. Morgan felt a surge of admiration, along with various other emotions that made him want to reach for her again. He gritted his teeth.

"Then I am glad that the project is nearly completed," she said.

Morgan frowned. Although their time together was running short, he was determined to stop it from running out. "About that," he said, clearing his throat. "I don't think we should hurry to finish the cataloguing."

"But aren't you eager to return to . . . adventuring?" she asked.

Morgan drew in a deep breath. Yes, Egypt called to him: the climate, the exotic world of traders and natives, and even the thrill of the hunt. But Juliet held him here with gossamer bonds. He told himself it was concern for her safety that tied him, nothing more.

"Yes, but I have unfinished business here," he answered.

"What kind of business?" she asked, her dune-colored eyes probing his, searching out his secrets. Morgan could feel himself sinking in those eyes, laid bare before them . . .

His mouth tightened. "I want to see who makes a slip and mentions the dagger, and then I'll put an end to all these incidents, once and for all."

Juliet glanced away, and Morgan frowned, stifling an urge to drag her attention back to him. Now and always.

"I hardly think that is your responsibility," she said.

"Nevertheless, I'm not leaving until I make sure you are safe."

Something passed over her features, but Morgan couldn't tell what, for she refused to look at him. "Again, I hardly think that one of your assignments," she said in an odd tone of dismissal.

But Morgan would not be dismissed. He reached out to grasp her shoulders, to seize her attention and hold it. "I won't let you be hurt. I can't let you be hurt," he muttered.

She finally met his gaze then, but the shadowy depths of her eyes were distant, unreachable. "You can't control everything," she said, a finality in her words that Morgan did not like.

Swearing under his breath, he released her, but he did not back down. "You just watch me," he promised.

MORGAN was not in the best of moods when he finally cornered Chauncey with news of the latest incident. Juliet's complete and utter indifference to his desire to protect her still grated on him. In fact, he was able to concentrate on little else except his eagerness to catch the culprit in the act. Then maybe he could release some of the tension that gripped him—with his fists.

He would happily strike a blow for the papyrus, another for the dagger, and still more for the footman and the guard and the fire and the message on his mirror. Most of all, he'd like to strike one for Juliet, except she didn't care. Morgan shot to his feet.

"Did you check the windows?" Chauncey asked.

Morgan nodded. "They were secure." He strode across the earl's expensive carpet like a jungle cat pacing its cage, itchy and restless, then swung toward Chauncey. "It had to be Lyndhurst," he muttered. "He's the only one who has access to the room besides Juliet and me."

"And the earl."

Morgan lifted his brows at Chauncey's words. "Have you found out anything about his businesses?"

With an expression of regret, Chauncey shook his head. "Not yet, but, let's face it, the fellow's a strange one."

Morgan stalked back across the room. "He's going to destroy his own valuables? I don't think he's that strange."

"Well, what about that butler? He can come and go as he likes anywhere in the house, including the ballroom, and no one questions him," Chauncey noted.

"But he seems more of a bodyguard. Or a bully. The earl's personal bruiser. Why would he bite the hand that feeds him?"

Chauncey shrugged. "Past grievances? A falling out? Who knows?"

Morgan shook his head. "I still think it's Lyndhurst. He's the only one who could possibly gain anything from these tactics, and he's the one who concocted the curse in the first place." *And he's the one Juliet usually defends,* Morgan thought with a frown.

He swung toward Chauncey again. "Can you watch him, make sure that you or one of your friendly maids has an eye on him at all times? I'd like to know what he does for the entire day. And night."

"We can try," Chauncey said.

"I want to catch him in the act," Morgan muttered, his fingers flexing with the urge to pummel the coxcomb and his wild tales out of existence. "I want this bastard stopped before Juliet falls victim to his tricks."

"No one is going to hurt her," Chauncey said.

Morgan slanted his friend a hard glance. "You can't be sure of that."

Chauncey nodded. "I'm as sure as a man can be. Why would anyone harm her? She's the lady of the house and has nothing to do with the so-called curse. She didn't find the mummy case or bring it here."

Morgan's brows inched upward. "You are trying to make sense of the nonsensical. None of these incidents have any basis in logic. Otherwise, no one would have been targeted except me. And as long as I can't be certain of her safety, I'm going to stick close by Juliet," he said, turning to pace the room once more.

Chauncey snorted. "Look, Morgan, I appreciate a tasty wench as well as any man, more so, in fact, but that's all they are. One's the same as another, and you can't become obsessed by a particular female, or you'll be lost."

Morgan swung round again, his eyes narrowing.

"There's plenty of other females in the world. Remember those dancing girls in Thebes? Think, man! Use your head. This one's not for you. She's a *lady,* and not just any old one, but one with more book learning than any man. She's a *lady of distinction.*"

Morgan stared, stunned by Chauncey's vehemence.

"Why, her father and his gang of cutthroats'll have your head before you know it's gone missing. This is a man who wields nearly as much power as Ali but is far less pleasant."

Chauncey drew a deep breath. "You're a roamer, a man who likes to travel. That is your life, and God knows you aren't fit for any other. You can't stay in one place, trying to live some stiff-lipped, upright existence as a clerk or a farmer. We are what we are, Morgan," he said. "And I told her as much."

Morgan stiffened, suddenly alert. "You what?"

Chauncey must have caught the look in his eye because he threw up his hands. "Well, it's the truth! And someone's got to say it. You're like a man walking straight into the fiery pit without seeing his own doom!"

"You took too much on yourself this time, Chauncey," Morgan said, his jaw tight, his voice low.

Chauncey shrugged. "I'm just looking out for you as I always do. That's my job."

"Leave Juliet out of it, or you'll be out of that job," Morgan said. He fixed Chauncey with a hard glare, but the former ruffian met it with one of his own.

"Then maybe you need a new man," he said.

Chapter 17

MUCH to Morgan's disappointment, the coxcomb made no mention of the incident involving the dagger. And neither did anyone else. Juliet had slipped the recovered artifacts beneath a heavy swath of velvet in the cupboard, where no one was likely to come upon them, and there they had remained, untouched and unmentioned.

All through dinner, Morgan had watched and waited, and still no one exhibited the slightest bit of disappointment or fear or guilt. Between Juliet's air of dismissal and the coxcomb's black looks, it made for an unpalatable meal. Even the French food that Morgan had once so enjoyed had lost its flavor. Everything tasted sour. Either someone was poisoning him at table, or he had simply gone sour, Morgan thought with a frown.

He felt sour. And frustrated and impatient. Wandering upstairs after dinner, he stalked his rooms aimlessly. Without Chauncey, they seemed silent and empty, but he knew better than to approach Juliet, both for his good and her own. Finally, restlessness drove him downstairs to the area near the ballroom. If only he could catch Lyndhurst in the act, then they could toss the man in gaol, and he could be on his way. With no thanks from a certain lady, Morgan thought sourly.

But after several hours of standing watch in the shadows of the music room, Morgan felt even more tense. No one had approached the ballroom, and he had heard nothing except the stray conversations of the guards. Although he wondered if the surly looking fellows ever chanced to sleep at their post, they remained alert.

Of course, it was possible that someone was drugging them, then coming in and out of the ballroom at will. There was a servants' stair nearby, but Morgan was betting that the staff kept well away whenever possible, and who would be up and about at this hour? No one except him, he thought with a scowl.

Anxious to stretch his legs lest he fall asleep, Morgan finally strode forth, immediately catching the attention of the two men.

"Where do you think you're about this night?" one of them asked.

"I'm checking on the artifacts," Morgan said, giving the fellow a warning glance.

"You'd best be watching yourself, mate," the other one said. "If anything comes up missing, we'll know who to blame."

Morgan ignored their words, along with their ensuing laughter, but he felt uneasy as he walked among the shadowy antiquities. Although he had no fear of man nor mummy, he possessed a healthy desire to save his own skin. He had come here in an attempt to trap the culprit, but what if he was the one entrapped?

Chauncey had once tendered the theory that the earl was manipulating him into gaol, but it seemed too ludicrous to be true. And Morgan doubted that Lyndhurst had the cunning to plan such a trick. But now, even if neither man was scheming to such an end, Morgan was stuck here till dawn. For, if he left, who was to say the guards wouldn't help themselves to a trinket or two and fault him? They looked to be just the sort to welcome some extra recompense.

With a muttered oath, Morgan sank onto the floor, his back against the mummy case, and tried not to get too comfortable. He could ill afford to doze when he needed all his wits about him. He not only had to keep an eye out for intruders, but he had to watch his back, as well. There was no one else to do it.

Morgan frowned. He still couldn't believe Chauncey had tossed aside their long years of association simply because of Juliet. Although many a friendship had been severed by a woman, Morgan had never thought his own would reach such an end. But he had never imagined Juliet, either, or the way she made him feel.

Of course, Chauncey had been right to warn her away. Hadn't Morgan tried to himself often enough? But every instinct had screamed a denial. And still did. Yet what choice did he have? He felt like howling in frustration, for in the end he would have neither the lady nor his friend.

Leaning his head back, Morgan tried to put them both from his mind and concentrate upon his surroundings, the silence, punctuated by sudden speech among the guards, and the near total darkness that enveloped him. With the absence of the moonlight, the only glow came from the lamps outside the ballroom, where the men stood watch, and precious little of it reached into the corners of the vast ballroom. But Morgan had been in dark places before. He turned away from the entrance, letting his eyes adjust, and listened.

It wasn't much later when something roused him. Had he been asleep? Morgan blinked into the darkness, hearing something faint and vaguely familiar. Was it a rustling of wind in the trees or curtains in a breeze? Leaping to his feet, Morgan scanned the outer wall, only to find all the windows closed, and the heavy drapes stood still and un-moving. He cocked his head, listening intently, but just then one of the guards laughed, a harsh sound that obscured all others.

Morgan stood and watched and waited, but he heard nothing else. No doubt the guards had been playing a trick upon him for their own amusement. Stifling an urge to return the favor, he sank back down to welcome the dawn.

AFTER Morgan kept nodding off during the day and snoring—or so Juliet claimed—she had sent him back to bed. There he had tossed and turned, finally leaving the tangle of his blankets early the next morning. Again, he missed both Chauncey's help and his company.

But most of all, he missed the man's razor.

Glancing into the mirror, Morgan saw the dark stubble grazing his cheeks and the bleary eyes that proclaimed his lack of rest, and he groaned aloud. Wait until the coxcomb and the earl got a look at him now. But there was no help for it. He wasn't about to go knocking on Lyndhurst's door, asking to borrow a blade.

So, with a shrug, Morgan dressed and headed out the door, only to meet Juliet at the top of the stairway. His own steps faltered as he took in her figure, familiar yet always startling to him in its fineness. She was primly dressed in a plain gown, but he knew the curves that lay hidden beneath, had touched them, stroked them, tasted them.

Sucking in a breath, Morgan waited for the glance of dismissal that he had received all too often of late. No doubt she would toss it his way, then brush by him. But to his surprise, she stopped to stare at him, her eyes wide. A flush tinged her cheeks, and there could be no mistaking the admiration in her gaze.

Puzzled, Morgan lifted a hand to his face, his fingers brushing against the stubble there. "Oh. I, uh, couldn't find a razor," he muttered. His lips quirked in apology, but, hell, if this was the reaction he was going to get, he might never shave again.

Indeed, Morgan thought she was going to reach out and touch him, so rapt was her interest, and he felt his body heat in anticipation. *Yes, run your finger over my beard— and the rest of me, too,* he thought. But then the moment was shattered by the sound of a shriek coming from below. Juliet started, her eyes met his own, and they turned as one to hurry down to the ballroom.

Again, there was chaos at the entrance. A maid stood stricken, the contents of a breakfast tray scattered at her feet and her outstretched hand pointing into the room, while the guards stood by gaping, as well. Halting on the threshold, Morgan followed the direction of the woman's shaky fingers and stiffened.

The mummy case was standing open.

The lid had been moved to one side, while the mummy itself seemed to rise from its burial vault like a dark specter, wrapped in blackened linen, its face a rotting hulk. Someone somehow had managed to stand it upright, and there it remained, surely a horrific sight to the uninitiated.

Morgan barely had time to take in the situation when Juliet grasped his sleeve in urgent summons. "Oh, Morgan, help me put him back before he is hurt."

The ludicrousness of the statement brought Morgan out of his shock, and he felt like laughing out loud, even as the poor maid sobbed beside him. Leave it to Juliet to worry more about the condition of the mummy than of any living being.

They hurried forward and, using a swath of fabric, they managed to return the mummy to his rightful place without any damage. Morgan was relieved, for he had seen ancient bodies crumble into dust under far less abuse. Obviously, this fellow was hardy, having been locked away for so long, protected from the elements. The heavy lid was more difficult to handle, but between the two of them, they managed to slide it back into place.

Morgan dusted off his hands and turned, only to see the poor maid faint dead away at the sight of them handling the corpse. She crumpled to the floor with a moan while the guards, as useless as Morgan has always suspected, stood by muttering to themselves.

While Juliet went to the fallen woman, Morgan stalked toward the two men, who were not quite as cocky as they had been in the past. Instead of looking surly, they appeared to be shaken and eager to abandon their posts, which seemed to be the topic under discussion when Morgan approached.

"Did anyone come in here last night?" he asked.

Both guards, white-faced and nervous, shook their heads. "Not a soul came by us, and that's a fact," the one said. The other nodded.

"And what did you hear?" Morgan asked.

"Nothing, sir," they both said, their eyes wide.

Juliet looked up from her place beside the maid. "Well, the mummy was secure when I left the ballroom last evening. Are you saying that no one entered after I exited?"

If possible, their beady eyes grew bigger as they shook their heads, and Juliet sniffed, obviously losing all patience with them. Morgan's lips quirked.

The maid, having revived, now found herself the subject of Juliet's interrogation. "And just what did you see?" Juliet asked her.

"I . . . I . . ." She looked as though she might faint dead away again, but the expression on Juliet's face stopped her. "I was taking the baronet his breakfast, but the fellows here, they called to me," she said, pausing to flick a frightened glance at the guards. "And when I turned, I saw . . ." Her words trailing off, she shuddered and gulped. "I saw the mummy rising up to attack us all."

Her words were met by Juliet's sniff of disapproval, and

indeed, she might have received a good talking to, but for the arrival of Cheevy, who immediately demanded an explanation for the uproar. The girl was sent back to the kitchen with the remnants of her tray, while Cheevy carried on a muted but heated dialogue with the guards that continued until two others arrived to relieve them.

These fellows, who had never seen anything unusual on their watch, took their places with the usual swaggering, and Cheevy departed, leaving Morgan and Juliet alone to puzzle over this latest incident. And puzzle Juliet did, her brows furrowing so that Morgan had to turn away, lest he seize her. Glancing at the lid of the priceless alabaster case, he thought the elegantly carved surface as good a place as any to lay her down and . . .

"But how could anyone get in here past the guards?" Juliet's practical question jolted him back to reality, a reality that included a threat, perhaps to her. Morgan's mouth tightened.

"I don't know, but our mummy didn't get himself out of the grave. Nor was any curse responsible. Someone was here," he muttered, turning slowly around. He studied his surroundings with fresh eyes as a new possibility came to him.

"What is it?" Juliet whispered.

"If no one passed by the guards, and the windows are latched, then there must be another way into this room," he said, glancing around for some sign of another opening.

"No," Juliet said. "There is no other exit."

Morgan strode toward the outer wall. "It's not a regular door, but something concealed from view. Perhaps there is an old servant's entryway that is no longer used or a priest's hole, long forgotten." He glanced over his shoulder. "You keep an eye on the guards, while I have a look."

Morgan scanned the areas between the tall windows, although they were probably too visible from the threshold to hide anything. Then he stalked along the perimeter, running a hand over the carved plaster and gilt, searching for seams that might be disguised by decoration. He moved swiftly, not wanting to miss anything, but leery of the coxcomb's eminent arrival.

Once again, he rued the absence of Chauncey, who might distract Lyndhurst or track his movements. But Chauncey was gone, so Morgan watched his own back, glancing over his shoulder periodically just to make sure he and Juliet were alone.

When he reached the end of the room, where elegant tapestries flanked an elaborate, mirrored chimneypiece, Morgan felt like kicking himself. Now that he knew where to look, the answer to the mysterious comings and goings was glaringly obvious. No doubt, the heavy hangings covered an opening, either a hidey-hole or a passage, and that was the entrance the culprit had used at his will.

Standing in the far corner, Morgan was out of the line of sight of the guards, who probably rarely looked deep inside the room anyway. What's more, his movements would be obscured by several large artifacts, including a stela and some statuary. In short, it was the perfect spot to come and go undetected.

Lifting the edge of the tapestry just enough to slip behind, Morgan felt his way along the wall until his fingers slid over a crack that revealed the outline of a door. The latch was more difficult to find in the darkness, and at first Morgan pushed ineffectually at the panel. But he had been inside the temples and tombs of ancient Egypt, where he had learned both patience and the art of concealment. At last he heard a soft click, and the wood moved beneath his hand.

Tensing, Morgan paused to listen, but he heard nothing coming from the other side. He pushed on the panel slowly, inching it open just enough that he could see light beyond. Obviously, this was no hidey-hole, but whether he would find himself in a passage or another room or facing the culprit, Morgan didn't know. He slipped through the narrow opening quickly, propping the door with the heel of one boot, for he had no desire to become trapped on this side.

But the minute he stepped through the doorway, Morgan realized he was not in any tunnel or servant's passage. Indeed, he was in a full-sized room with heavily draped windows. Gazing about in surprise, he recognized the heavy, ornate furniture, the elaborate oriental rugs, and the faintly exotic perfume of the earl's personal study. For a long moment, he stood staring, as understanding dawned upon him. Then, a sound behind him had him tensing and swinging round.

It was only Juliet. She slipped through the door, letting it fall shut as she blinked in startlement. Resisting an urge to shield her from the sight of her father's perfidy, Morgan realized it was too late. She looked about her with a dazed expression, her brows drawing together in a gesture of puzzlement that this time tore at his heart.

"But we are in Father's study," she whispered.

Thankfully, Father was not in it, Morgan thought to himself. She glanced up at him, obviously realizing the significance of their discovery, and when Morgan said nothing, she shook her head, as if to deny all.

"But this is probably his private entrance, so he can view the collection whenever he wants without disturbing anyone," she said.

"Including the guards," Morgan muttered. He didn't know how devoted Juliet was to her father, but sooner or later, he suspected her innate intelligence would win out. Meanwhile, he intended to have a look around the earl's cozy little nest.

Morgan didn't know what he expected to find, perhaps the pot of kohl used to make threatening hieroglyphs, or something to explain the bizarre turn of the earl's thoughts. Here was a man who seemingly had everything, and yet who felt the need to manufacture a curse. Had his devotion to Egypt unbalanced his mind? Or was there some reasoning behind it all?

Morgan stopped to study a golden tray, crumbs littering the surface, then moved toward the carved and gilded desk, its feet apparently designed to resemble a dragon's. Shaking his head at the motif, Morgan took in the papers and ledgers stacked on the surface and wondered what they would reveal. He opened one only to squint as lines of facts and figures swam before his eyes.

The ledger slipped, knocking against a small crate, and Morgan righted it quickly, then stiffened at what he saw inside. The ledger fell to the desk with a thud, forgotten, and silence descended, broken only by the tick of the mantel clock, absurdly loud in the quiet.

"What is it?" Juliet asked from behind him.

It took Morgan a good long moment to answer, even as he stared at the brownish mass. He had not known what he expected to find, but this was definitely not it. Finally, he straightened. Drawing a deep breath, he turned to face her. "Opium," he said.

"What?" Juliet blinked in astonishment. "What do you mean?"

"I mean that your father—" Morgan began, but he never had a chance to finish the sentence, for at that moment, the heavy doors swung open. Morgan tensed, ready for anything, though they had done nothing illegal or immoral. Still, he took a protective stance near Juliet, for the earl might not appreciate their unexpected intrusion.

Indeed, the man pulled up short the moment he saw them, no show of geniality or welcome on his face. "What are you doing in my private study? It is not a public room, nor does your cataloguing bring you here," he said sharply.

"We had no intention of trespassing," Morgan said, his own voice cool. "We came in through the ballroom." He inclined his head toward the door neatly concealed in the decorative panels behind them.

The earl frowned. "That is my private entrance, for viewing my collection at my leisure."

Morgan glanced at Juliet, but there was no triumph or even relief on her face at his words. She was staring at her father as though she didn't know him.

The earl was oblivious, ~~having~~ fixed Morgan with a sharp stare. "It is not a common door, so do not use it again or speak of it," he said. "I like my privacy and do not wish the rest of the household to pry into my affairs, as you were obviously doing. Indeed, one might ask why you were touching my priceless tapestries, for they hardly fall under your purview, Mr. Beauchamp." All trace of the gracious host gone, his smile was one of thinly veiled menace.

Morgan shrugged. "Well, they came under my purview when I discovered they hid another entrance to the ballroom, allowing the man behind the mummy's curse to move about at will, despite the guards," Morgan said.

"The man behind the mummy's curse? What nonsense are you spouting now?" the earl asked, his voice steely.

If it had been just the two of them, the matter might have ended there, for Morgan could hardly turn his host in to the authorities for playing tricks with his own artifacts. But there was another person in the room, one they had both forgotten, but who made her presence known now.

"You let everyone think it was Cyril, when all along you were doing everything," Juliet said from beside him.

The earl glanced at her as though she were a disturbing gnat. "I don't know what you're talking about," he said with a dismissive gesture. But this time Juliet would not be dismissed, and Morgan didn't know whether to praise her or stop her before it was too late.

"And I suppose you don't know what that is, either," she said, pointing to the small crate on the desk.

The earl didn't even deign to look. "That is none of your concern. Nothing in this room is of concern to you. Hie yourself back to your work, or if you feel you cannot complete the cataloguing, I can hire someone else."

Morgan's fingers curled into fists, for he knew what a blow her father's words were to Juliet, and he would have liked to respond in kind. "We know what it is," he said, instead. "It's opium, unprocessed and ready for shipment, or part of a shipment received."

The earl fixed him with a contemptuous glance. "And just what would you know of it, Beauchamp? Are you looking for a sample?"

"Me? I'm no opium eater. But I know of it and what it does to those unfortunates who use it," Morgan said.

"This is for the local druggist, or haven't you heard that laudanum is a beneficial medicine? There is no crime in selling it. If so, you would fill the gaols with its peddlers," the earl said with a sneer.

"But I hardly think the local druggist has the money or the wherewithal to make use of any sizeable shipment," Morgan said. "And that's the business you are in, isn't it? Shipping? In the Orient? Perhaps this packet is just part of a larger consignment, bound not for England but for China," Morgan said, as all the pieces of the puzzle fell into place.

The earl's eyes narrowed. "So what if it is? Where do you think my money comes from? Land, yes, but there is more to be had in trade, a respectable investment as old as the honorable Company itself."

"Oh, Father, no," Juliet whispered.

"Even setting aside the moral objections, what you're doing is illegal," Morgan said. He glanced at Juliet. "Taking exception to the addiction of its populace, the Chinese forbade the sale of the drug in 1797, but still it arrives, run by smugglers eager for a share of the profits, and perhaps even the Company itself."

The earl's face twisted in fury. "And what do you know of it? Nothing. It is a trade that is fully accepted by the Chinese, except for a handful of politicians who protest while taking their bribes."

"Oh, Father. How could you?" Juliet asked in a whisper.

The earl swung toward her with an icy glare. "It is a business, a business that has kept you in expensive trinkets to study."

Juliet reeled as though he had struck her. "You bought those antiquities for yourself, not for me. And at what price?"

"Did I?" the earl asked. His expression stony, he turned back to Morgan. "You have outlived your usefulness. I suggest you provide my daughter with what information she might need today, for I expect you to take your leave tomorrow."

He stalked away without another glance at either of them, and Morgan had to fight the urge to tackle him from behind and pummel some sense into him. But some men, especially those reared in the rarified air of the peerage, had no sense, not when it came to family or anything of real import.

Instead, Morgan turned to Juliet, who was standing there staring after her father, white-faced and shaken. He longed to take her in his arms, but the heavy doors stood open following the earl's exit, and the man might just turn back and take exception to Morgan embracing his daughter.

"Are you all right?" Morgan asked.

"No," she whispered. Shivering, she rubbed her arms as though cold, despite the warmth of the room. No doubt, it was her heart that was chilled. Morgan's wrenched in sympathy.

"I feel as though my whole life has been a pretense, and now . . . to be responsible for ill-gotten gains," she murmured.

"You are not responsible," Morgan said.

"It just makes me shudder," she said. Then she gazed up at him, her lovely eyes dull with shock. "Did you know?"

Morgan shook his head. "I was told he had his hand in something that ran afoul of accepted morals, but opium . . . It's a bad business, Juliet. I've seen the natives take it."

He had watched others, too, men with promise, who fell into the dens and were lost to life, drifting in a netherworld of bare existence. Was the earl one of them? He seemed too alert to have succumbed to the drug, and yet perhaps that would explain the bizarre turns of his mind.

As if reading his thoughts, Juliet reared back in horror. "He's the one who has been playing all the vile tricks, hiding the artifacts, attacking the servants, terrifying everyone," she whispered. "But why?"

"I don't know," Morgan answered honestly. "Perhaps he thought to frighten other collectors away from the market or to draw attention to his own purchases, to make the Carlisle collection famous above all others. Who knows?"

Juliet shook her head. "I thought his sudden attraction to Egypt was simply a passing interest of his, but I must have been mistaken. Perhaps it's an obsession."

Morgan had seen men driven mad by less, and if the earl truly were mad, he might believe his own delusions, of a curse and a vengeful mummy, and act them out. The thought struck Morgan with no little alarm. Was Juliet even safe here in his household? Would the man harm his own daughter?

Suddenly, she reached out to grasp his arm, and Morgan felt his heart leap. Had she the same concern? She glanced up at him wildly. "He's already talking about mounting an expedition, of sending his own people to find more and better treasures in Egypt."

Although Morgan didn't greet the news eagerly, he saw no reason for Juliet's panic. His brows inched upward.

Her fingers tightened on his arm. "He's seen your map," she whispered.

Morgan's eyes narrowed. "You don't think he'll actually try to follow it?" he asked. But, even as he spoke, Morgan knew the answer. A man who would flout both laws and morals to fund his ever-expanding collection would not hesitate to steal someone else's property. Morgan felt an eerie sensation chase up his spine. The map might already be stolen or copied and replaced. Perhaps the fire had been set to destroy all evidence . . . or any complaints. He sucked in a harsh breath.

"We must stop him," Juliet said. She lifted her chin, and Morgan saw that her color had returned, along with her fierce determination. She looked him in the eyes, her own brooking no resistance. "You must get there first."

Morgan felt a hot surge of excitement at the lure of the chase, ratcheted up a notch by the higher stakes involved, the promise of a race against the earl's minions. He nearly leapt forward, but the warmth of Juliet's fingers resting on his sleeve stopped him.

"I can't leave you here," Morgan said. The map, and any treasure it might lead to, was as nothing compared to Juliet's safety. The last few weeks had been harrowing enough with danger coming from some unknown quarter. Now that he knew her father was dangerous, if not mad, Morgan couldn't abandon her to the man's machinations.

"He won't hurt me. He needs me for his exhibition," Juliet said. But Morgan knew her too well. She wouldn't meet his gaze, couldn't do so because she wasn't as sure of her words as she pretended. Now that she knew his secret, would her father turn on her? He certainly had seemed to today. He had even threatened to hire another expert. How could Morgan trust his most precious find to a man who would do such things, a man whose mind might be unbalanced?

And just that quickly, he knew the answer. "Come with me," he said.

The look on Juliet's face was priceless, a mixture of

startlement, hope, and a yearning so profound that it tore at his heart.

"Dare I?" she asked.

It was dangerous, to be sure, as Morgan well knew. Egypt had only been open to foreigners for a few years and inflicted upon them all sorts of hazards from heat and disease to murderous tribesmen. However, Juliet might just be safer there than in her own house. She was capable and strong and passionate about the love of her life: hieroglyphs and Egypt.

But a lady traveling alone with a rogue such as himself? Morgan grimaced. He didn't want to risk the ruination of her reputation, as a woman or as a scholar. And what of her father? To say he would not approve was laughable. Morgan's mouth tightened. Indeed, he might very well send his cutthroats after them both. Morgan drew a deep breath. There was only one way to legally escape him. He turned to Juliet.

"We'll marry," he said. Something crossed her face, Morgan wasn't sure what, but before she could refuse, he spat out his reasoning. "That's the only way to keep your father from interfering."

Whatever had brightened her features abruptly dimmed, and she glanced away, ducking her head. "If you think it's necessary," she said in a low voice.

Hell, yes, it was necessary, necessary to life, breath, heartbeat . . . but Morgan voiced none of those wild notions. "I think we'd better," he said simply. Lifting his hands, he squeezed her shoulders. "Meet me at the side entrance, the one to the west that is little used, at midnight."

"Very well," she answered, her eyes downcast.

It was only after Juliet left the room that Morgan realized she was far more excited about going to Egypt than marrying him.

Chapter 18

JULIET wandered out of her father's study, aimless and unsure. Her first inclination was to retire to her room, but that might raise questions, as well as tempting her to take to her bed. And that she refused to do. But neither could she endure another afternoon in the presence of Cyril and the guards while working beside the man she might marry.

Might. Although she had agreed to Morgan's proposition, Juliet was not certain she could go through with it. She felt numb, dead inside, at the prospect of the loveless union. Oh, it would not be completely devoid of emotion, of that she was assured. For Juliet was already hopelessly, helplessly in love with Morgan.

That love simply wasn't returned.

Swallowing hard, Juliet walked through the house but found no comfort within. The once-familiar walls seemed garish and threatening, her father, never warm, now strange and perhaps unbalanced. Her refuge had always been her books and artifacts, but even those seemed

tainted, purchased with ill-gotten gains. The whole building seemed to close in upon her until, at last, she donned
her cloak and hurried away from it, seeking the only other
place that had ever been her sanctuary.

Juliet made her escape to Herr Brueger's out of desper-
ation, as a last effort to gain some semblance of order in
her careening world. But when she saw the professor rise
from his chair by the fireplace to greet her, all the pent-up
feelings of the day burst forth. Although she had never
been demonstrative or emotional, Juliet rushed forward,
threw her arms around her stunned colleague, and burst
into tears.

Thankfully, Herr Brueger did not pull away in horror
but patted her awkwardly. "There, there, *Liebchen*. What is
it? What has happened to upset you?" he asked.

His steady presence was a balm that invited her to remain, but Juliet knew she could not hide here forever. No
longer could she bury herself in her books, away from life.
So she pulled from his arms, letting the professor lead her
to a chair beside his own, where he turned his gentle gaze
upon her. He didn't press or pry but waited expectantly,
while Juliet tried to form an explanation for her outburst.

"I . . . I came to say good-bye," she finally said, for want
of anything else. And, it was true enough. She could hardly
leave without a word to the man who had been more father
to her than her own.

"What is this? Are you going away?" Herr Brueger
asked, looking confused.

"I'm leaving England, and I wanted you to know,"
Juliet said.

"What?" His heavy brows rose in surprise.

"Considering what has been happening at the town
house . . . I'm not sure how safe it is to remain there," she
said.

"But what is this? Have there been more attacks?" he
asked, his expression fraught with concern.

"Yes, and . . . well, I've discovered that Father is engaged in some rather unsavory activities. I'm not certain he's . . . thinking clearly."

Herr Brueger's brows furrowed. For a moment, Juliet feared he would ask about the curse and her father's hand in it, a subject she was loath to discuss. But he only nodded slowly. "Where will you go?"

She lifted her chin. "I am going to Egypt," she said. And even through her dismals, the words she had never thought to utter had the power to thrill her. She produced a rather triumphant smile.

But the professor did not seem to share her enthusiasm, for his eyes widened in alarm. "Surely, not alone?" he asked.

Juliet shook her head. "I'm going with Morgan, that is, Mr. Beauchamp. We're to be married."

The professor's worried look was replaced by one of delight. "Congratulations, then, are in order."

Again, Juliet shook her head, for how could she accept his good wishes under false pretenses? "It is a marriage of convenience. Mr. Beauchamp insisted upon it so that we may travel together without questions or interference."

"I'm sure he did," the professor said, a small smile playing about his lips. "And there is nothing of romance in this union, eh?"

Juliet flushed and shook her head once more. There was romance on her part, though she didn't know how or even when it had happened. Indeed, she wondered why the sensation was called *falling in love,* when she could recollect no pivotal plunge. She only knew that when Morgan had asked her to marry him, she had held her breath, hopeful and eager and suddenly aware of all that he meant to her. Then he had dashed all those hopes with his next words, so cold and calculated that she thought her heart would break. She had been unable to think or even draw air, simply forcing herself to give her assent, for what else could she do?

Herr Brueger leaned back and stroked his mustache thoughtfully. "Are you so certain? Mr. Beauchamp made his concern for you quite clear when he was here not long ago."

Juliet blinked at him. "He was here?"

"He stopped by one day to question me about the strange occurrences at your father's town house," Herr Brueger said.

"What?" Juliet straightened.

The professor waved away her distress. "He was only doing his best to find out who was behind these bad things. He is very protective of you."

Juliet frowned. That was no excuse to bother the professor, who obviously was too frail to wander about setting fire to beds and attacking footmen.

The sound of Herr Brueger clearing his throat brought her out of her thoughts. He eyed her benignly. "And, is this not the same man who was spying on you here? Who cannot bear to have you leave his sight, eh?"

"Yes. I mean, no," Juliet said. She knew better than to impute motives or imagine emotions where Morgan was concerned. "He feels a responsibility toward me."

To Juliet's dismay, Herr Brueger started chuckling. She glanced at him quizzically, but the professor simply shook his head, a knowing smile beneath his thick mustache.

"That is not all he feels."

MORGAN slipped through the darkened house with a stealth honed from long practice, but never before had so much rested on his abilities. Removing a heavy mummy case from its centuries-old berth or slipping beyond the watchful eyes of the local bey was nothing compared to this: escaping with his most precious find, a living, breathing treasure.

He dared not go to her room for fear the earl had set someone, most probably Cheevy, to keep an eye upon him.

He had gone out today to obtain a special license and make arrangements, all the while wondering if she would be safe or even *here* when he returned. Thankfully, no one seemed to have made a connection between them, beyond their prickly working relationship.

Morgan was counting on that lack of awareness to work in their favor, that the earl would have no reason to lock his daughter away or send her elsewhere, that he would not suspect Morgan of doing anything except packing to leave on the morrow, a disgruntled but highly paid employee. However, Morgan knew there was always the possibility that the earl might decide on a more permanent punishment than banishment for his former associate, either out of madness or arrogance. And so he made his way carefully, ruing once more the absence of Chauncey.

His missing partner was on Morgan's mind now more than ever, and it wasn't just because he wanted Chauncey's help. His upcoming exit from the town house, the city, and the country made him frantic to find his friend, no matter what disagreements had separated them. In truth, Morgan couldn't imagine leaving for Egypt without him. Morgan had tried to get messages to him today through old contacts in the streets, but no one was talking about his whereabouts. Perhaps he was already bound for Egypt, striking out on his own, their long history together just that: history.

A faint sound up ahead made Morgan halt in his tracks. There was normally little activity here by the state rooms, especially at night. Was Juliet already there, waiting for him? Creeping to the end of the gallery, Morgan peered around the corner and reared back with a curse. A shadowy figure loomed near the doors, but it was not Juliet. What the devil was Cheevy doing there?

Had the omnipresent butler found Juliet here earlier? If so, what could the butler do to the lady of the house? Nothing, in a normal household, but the earl's domain was far from usual. Even now Juliet could be spirited away or locked up. Morgan's mouth tightened. He was going to have to chance her bedroom, just to make sure. Swinging on his heel, he turned, only to slip back into the shadows of a heavily pedimented doorway.

Someone was coming.

Morgan palmed his knife. He had no intention of being caught between Cheevy and one of his minions, should his plans have been uncovered. Plastered against the carved panel, he waited until he heard the swish of skirts. A maid? Then he caught a whiff of scent. *Juliet.* Stepping from the shadows, he covered her mouth with his hand and pulled her back against him before she could turn the corner and run into Cheevy.

Morgan felt her stiffen and then relax when she realized who held her. And he hadn't even spoken. Smiling into the darkness, he let his fingers fall from her lips.

"Cheevy's watching the exit. We're going to have to use another one," he whispered into her ear.

She nodded and inclined her head toward the door behind him, so Morgan lifted the latch silently and swung it open, pulling her with him into the dark room beyond.

One glance told him the place was unused, a bedroom fit only for the very highest of personages, with massive furniture and gilt everywhere, glittering in the moonlight from the tall windows. Beside him Juliet lowered a small reticule to the floor, the only evidence of her expected departure, and Morgan realized that until this very moment, he hadn't been sure she would come. But despite all, she was here with him, ready to marry him. A sudden, overwhelming sense of relief was tempered by the knowledge that they had yet to make their escape.

Juliet echoed his thoughts when she spoke. "I think all the entrances are being watched," she whispered.

Morgan's mouth tightened. Had someone discovered their scheme, or was the earl only making sure Morgan didn't slink off in the night with his best silver? He swallowed a curse. What were they to do now, wait till morning? Presumably, Morgan could leave then unfettered, and Juliet could meet him later, at Herr Brueger's or some arranged point. But all his instincts screamed that tomorrow might be too late. Once Morgan was out of the house, she would be out of his reach, out from under his protection.

He swore softly, then turned, his finger to his lips, at the sound of a sudden noise, loud in the silence. Searching the dim room for the source, Morgan stiffened in surprise when he realized that one of the tall windows was inching upward. Pulling Juliet with him, he stepped back against the door, ready for a hasty exit, even as he wondered wildly if they were surrounded. All they could do now was wait, hoping that the shadows hid their presence as the window lifted and a head slowly became visible, poking above the ledge.

"There you are! Well, what are you waiting for, man? Hurry up, will you? They've got someone at all the exits."

"Chauncey!" Morgan said, unable to believe his eyes. "What are you doing here?"

White teeth flashed in the darkness. "Watching your back, of course."

JULIET let them hurry her from the only home she had ever known, placing her fate firmly into the hands of the two men. Once they were ensconced in a hired coach, the servant named Chauncey explained that he had found out that her father was selling opium to China illegally.

"The man's a criminal, but the kind that no one can touch," he muttered, his outrage plain. "Why, a pickpocket gets strung up, while the likes of him runs loose, gaining more money and more power . . ."

At a subtle gesture from Morgan, Chauncey trailed off with a muttered apology. "Well, be that as it may, once I found out, I returned to the town house, only to hear of your ouster. I thought you'd be making a break tonight with the lady," the fellow said, flashing her a grin, and Juliet felt a sudden kinship with the man who had once so put her off.

They rattled on through the night to a small inn in the countryside, where Morgan had planned that they be married. The wedding itself was a swift and practical thing, appropriate to Morgan's sentiments, if not Juliet's. He had secured a special license, and Chauncey and the innkeepers served as witnesses.

Bleary-eyed, Juliet remembered little beyond, "Do you, Morgan Adrian Randolph Grenville Beauchamp, take this woman to be your wife?" The adventurer's lengthy list of names made her pause, and Morgan had to nudge her when it came time for her own response.

Then, without even staying for a rest, let alone a wedding night, they left again for the coast. Morgan was in search of a ship to Egypt that was leaving soon from a port other than London, lest her father guess their route or use his own shipping contacts to stop them.

Even in the blur of her own weariness, Juliet realized that Morgan and Chauncey thought her father was a very powerful man, and she was not about to argue. Although she had little experience with the world beyond her books, she had a very real fear that the earl might try to stop the wedding or annul the marriage. Whether he was capable of even worse than that, she didn't know, but she didn't want to find out.

Fast on the heels of her worry came a heavy dose of guilt for putting Morgan and his man in possible danger. They wouldn't be fleeing now, if not for her. And she couldn't help thinking that they should have left without her, off to their lives of adventure, while she returned to her own stifling existence. Despite the earl's aberrant behavior, Juliet did not think he would have harmed her. He needed her to research and catalogue and care for his collection.

But now? Juliet shuddered. Her father was not a man to

cross, and Morgan might soon rue the day he gave up his careless, carefree existence for the responsibility of a wife he didn't love. She swallowed hard. When he had insisted she accompany him, when he had asked her to marry him, she should have refused.

Yet knowing all that could not change her fate. And even now, rattling around in the ill-sprung coach with only a small case to call her own, her books, her artifacts, her clothes and personal belongings all behind her, Juliet's heart leapt when she stole a glance at her husband.

How would she ever have found the strength to resist him?

BY the time they reached the quay, Juliet was so tired she could barely stand, and even the cramped quarters on board the merchant ship were a welcome respite from the road travel. Juliet sank down upon her bunk, fully clothed, while Morgan went to confer with his man, who was awfully resourceful for a valet. And there she stayed, falling into a troubled sleep, without a thought to her lack of a wedding night.

In the days ahead, however, Juliet was not so blissfully oblivious. When the ship set sail, she and Morgan fell into a routine of waking and sleeping and walking on deck when possible, of eating unpleasant food—and of staying out of each other's way.

In Juliet's case, it was a form of deference. After all, Morgan was the one putting himself in danger to marry her, a marriage he insisted was one of convenience. But considering the sort of intimacy they had shared on other occasions, Juliet was left yearning and puzzled by his behavior. He seemed to avoid her deliberately, a reality even more depressing than the stark coldness of their wedding.

Juliet began to wonder if she had imagined those stolen moments in her father's house or even the easy closeness of their working relationship. But there was no denying Morgan's distance now, and in the face of his dismissal, she formed a most unlikely alliance with Morgan's man, Chauncey, the one who originally had tried to warn her away from him.

That fateful conversation, which had affronted her at the time, now seemed a kindness. And when Juliet saw Chauncey tucked into a corner on deck, whittling, she approached him, intending at last to broach the subject.

Chauncey greeted her with a flash of white teeth and a gesture to join him. When she did so, Juliet looked down at his hands, flying over the wood, and took a deep breath.

"I wanted to thank you for . . ." she trailed off, unsure of what to say. That he had been right? She smiled ruefully.

"That's all right, my lady," he said with a knowing smile. "I'm glad you've come along to help us find the tomb."

There was that. Whenever she decried her marriage, Juliet had only to remember that she was on her way to Egypt and a new life of, if not adventure, then far closer to it than she had ever imagined possible. Would she really rather be back home, buried in her books, with the threat of a marriage to Cyril hanging over her head? She shook her head and smiled at Chauncey. Far better to be here and alive and free, no matter what Morgan's mood.

"He's just getting his sea legs," Chauncey said. Apparently, he was offering an excuse for her dismal marital state, but one that Juliet could only regard with skepticism. She lifted her brows in perfect imitation of her husband, and his man laughed.

Heartened, Juliet gave Chauncey a speculative glance. "He seems to have an awfully long name for an adventurer," she said. When she had asked Morgan about his elaborate moniker, he had brushed her off, but perhaps Chauncey might prove more enlightening.

He looked down at his carving and shrugged. "All I

know is that he's related to some lord somewhere. He told me that if any of his relatives ever come looking for him, not to punch them right off, but wait until they said something to deserve it, which ought to be fairly quickly," he said, flashing a grin.

Juliet smiled, then furrowed her brow thoughtfully. Beauchamp was the earl of Bellemere's family name. Could it be possible that Morgan was related to them? Juliet shook her head, amused by the very notion. But there were rogues in the best of families, black sheep and cast-off relations, which is what she now was, she thought, with a sharp pang. She shrugged it away, knowing she far preferred her current status. If only her husband preferred it as well.

"Here, now, my lady," Chauncey said, obviously guessing the tenor of her thoughts.

Juliet laughed. "I am no longer a lady, but Mrs. Beauchamp. And, besides, you must call me Juliet, for we are partners, are we not?"

Chauncey slanted her an assessing glance and then smiled. "And we have an adventure ahead. Let me tell you about where we're going. But, first . . ." He paused to study the utensil in his hand, then gave her an inquiring look. "Do you happen to know your way around a knife?"

Juliet blinked. "Just the daggers among the artifacts."

Chauncey shook his head. "No. That won't do. It's a lawless place we're going to, my lady. I mean, Juliet. And you had best know how to protect yourself. Now see here," he began, extending his hand to display his own blade, and Juliet leaned over, rapt with attention.

SHE had won him over, there was no doubt about it, Chauncey thought with a rueful grin as he watched Juliet toss his knife fifty paces into a bit of planking. It was easy to see why Morgan had fallen for her. She was a clever girl, full of book learning and expertise that made his head swim, but without the airs of most others of the peerage. She didn't waste time in the mindless chatter of females, either. Eager to learn and eager for life, she was, and Chauncey couldn't help but admire that.

Yet no matter how endearing he found her, it appeared he had been right to warn Morgan against her, for the man walked on deck, took one look at his wife, and headed in the other direction. Watching with a frown, this time Chauncey followed.

"What the devil are you doing?" he demanded, catching Morgan aft.

"Just getting a breath of air," he muttered.

Chauncey snorted. "With your wife, man! You're acting as though she has leprosy. Why aren't you cozied up in your berth with her, passing the time in a more pleasurable fashion?"

"It's a marriage of convenience," Morgan said, his face grim. "I married her to protect her."

Chauncey took one look at the hard set of his friend's jaw and burst into laugher. "And I'm the King of England! You might be able to fill her head with such nonsense, but I have eyes. I can see the way you look at her, like she's some rich desert, and you've been starving your whole life."

It was an apt description, but one which Morgan shunned. With a shrug, he turned away to stare out over the sea as though deep in contemplation of his own misery. *Self-induced misery,* Chauncey noted. Then, just when he thought Morgan would say no more, his friend turned to eye Chauncey bleakly. "We are heading for Egypt, a harsh land with a harsh climate. I have to think of her health."

At Chauncey's puzzled look, Morgan's mouth tightened. "I don't want to make her pregnant," he muttered.

Chauncey gaped at that explanation. "There are ways to

prevent that, as you well know," he said, sending his friend a speculative glance.

But Morgan said no more, and Chauncey could only shake his head at the foibles of fate. At last, the man had what he'd been wanting all along. And now he wouldn't take it!

BY the time they reached Egypt, Juliet was feeling no more a wife than when she left England. Despite of, or perhaps because of the close quarters on board, Morgan had become more distant, and Juliet could only blame herself for thinking that her marriage of convenience might include something else. And yet, she couldn't help harboring a bit of resentment for the man who now seemed to deliberately avoid her.

But when they finally stepped off the ship, Juliet looked up at the endless sky, the very same that had sheltered the ancients, and any lingering bitterness faded away. At last, she was gazing upon the land she had yearned for all her life. How could she regret anything that had brought her here?

They landed at Alexandria, and Juliet breathed in the sights of the city: Arabs peacefully fishing, a pair of camels led by their driver, then more natives and more camels, veiled women, ostriches, and a Babel of tongues. She blinked at the bright colors, the flashes of white teeth, the flowing robes, the dusty feet, the shouts and laughter and cries of the camels.

The narrow streets, the red and white stripes of marble, the latticed balconies, the dark, noisy bazaars, and the air heavy with the fragrance of perfume sellers all beckoned to her, while the heat seeped into her very bones. Juliet felt suffused with warmth and light and life, a world away from her former stifling existence. She reached out to touch the stone buildings, wondering about the age and history of each. And in the evening, the world turned golden, the muddy Nile, the houses, the desert, and the setting sun joining together in orange and browns of every possible hue.

Any lingering awkwardness between Juliet and her adventurer was forgotten in the sheer joy of discovering the palms, the mists, the plains, and in the distance, the desert extending on forever. This was her dream, and Morgan had fulfilled it. How could she not be grateful?

His own joy was obvious. He wanted to show her everything, and she wanted to see it all—remnants of colossal statuary, bazaars, temples, empty tombs, and the pyramids—but they both felt an urgency to seek out the site on the map. And first, Morgan had to obtain the proper permits. There was also the small matter of his previous hasty exit from the country. So they continued on by boat, watching the country drift by, its sandy hillocks, sometimes dotted with palms, disappearing into limitless dunes.

At Cairo, Juliet was soon just as spellbound by the narrow alleyways, the exotic edifices with their grilled windows and shadowy places of mystery, and the dark-skinned natives, descended from kings. They ate dates and lamb and cakes unlike anything Juliet had ever tasted, and high above the city, they looked out upon the desert on one side, and on the opposite, beyond the plains and the Nile, upon the pyramids.

The sky was vast and absolutely blue, and at twilight, it turned gray, blue, and purple in a palette unequaled anywhere else. And at night, Juliet fell into a dreamless sleep, exhausted and content to be living her adventure.

Chapter 19

AFTER weeks of waiting and negotiating, the permits were obtained, and the party was on its way up the Nile once more. When the wind blew, the enormous triangular sails were unfurled, and when it was calm, the boatmen used long poles to move the ship forward. Juliet sat watching the water pass by, smooth and yellow.

On one side lay the reddish gray desert, on the other an immense green plain, with squares of rich, black soil denoting the recently plowed fields, left fecund by the receding waters of the Nile. And dotted along the route, they saw mud houses and palm groves, waterwheels turned by a camel or an ox, and even some buffaloes grazing by a muddy creek.

They disembarked at Thebes, where Morgan hoped to hire many of the locals who had worked with them before. The men were eager to greet Morgan's new wife and marveled at how well she spoke their language. When there had been congratulations all around, Arif, who served as the head of the group, stepped forward.

"We thought you had forgotten about us, that you abandoned your old friends," he said.

Morgan smiled. "Why would you think that? Because I was gone so long?"

A stately man resembling the ancient kings, Arif shook his head. "We heard you were hiring upriver. An Englishman, a traveler, returning from journeys there, said he had met you and that you were mounting a caravan and hiring men from the neighboring village."

Juliet glanced at Morgan in surprise. "He must have been mistaken," her husband said.

"He said that he had met another Englishman, the famous Morgan Beauchamp, and that you planned new excavations and a great find," Arif said.

Chauncey frowned. "What did this man look like?"

"I don't know. I never saw him. I only heard of him. But if you are just arriving here, then it could not have been you," Arif answered.

Chauncey's eyes narrowed as he glanced at Morgan. "I don't like the sound of this. Is someone impersonating you?"

Morgan shrugged, apparently unconcerned, but Juliet felt a chill chase up her spine, despite the day's heat. It had been a long time since she had thought about Cyril's claims of a curse and the events that had led her to flee her homeland. Now the eerie sensation she had known when plagued by those mishaps returned.

Juliet glanced at her husband and Chauncey, but they were now deep in conversation with their guide, having dismissed tales of an imposter. Although she tried to do the same, long afterwards she remembered. And she shivered.

JULIET watched the world turn to twilight as they walked back to their tents, erected on the outskirts of the town, and she felt the peace of the Egyptian night settle over her.

They had enjoyed an impromptu feast with Arif and his family on this, their last evening here. The supplies were all in order, and tomorrow, Morgan promised, the small caravan would set out into the desert toward the Theban Hills to the valley of Beban el Malook, with permission to dig.

Juliet felt a hum of anticipation and not only for the adventure that lay before them. Lately, her husband had not been quite so distant. At times, she had even caught his gaze upon her, hot and intent, only to see him turn away, and hope had flared again in her heart.

Ahead, Juliet saw the little white cloth lanterns hanging from the tent poles that denoted their makeshift homes. But when they neared, Morgan stretched out an arm to hold her back. Blinking in the dim light, Juliet soon realized just what had made him pause.

Their tent, the one she would share with Morgan, had been slashed, the remnants of one side flapping loosely in the breeze as if torn apart by a violent gale. But there had been no windstorm, and Chauncey's tent stood fast, untouched.

A jackal howled, and Juliet shivered. She rubbed her arms as Chauncey moved ahead of them, rifle in hand, muttering a stream of curses. He returned shortly, a scowl upon his pinched features.

"Well, that tent's ruined, there's no doubt about it. You'll have to move in with me or set up the spare," he said.

"Who would do such a thing?" Juliet asked.

Chauncey shook his head.

"Probably raiders, upset they couldn't find anything of worth to steal," Morgan said.

But Chauncey appeared skeptical. "Then why didn't they take any of the supplies?"

Morgan shrugged. "What did the guard say?"

Chauncey scowled. "I think the man fell asleep. He said he heard something, but when he got up to look, all he saw was a shadowy figure disappearing into the desert."

"On foot?" Morgan asked, his tone scornful.

"Yes, well, perhaps we ought to replace him with someone a bit more reliable," Chauncey said.

Morgan nodded. "I'll have a talk with Arif tomorrow."

As Juliet watched and listened to their practical solutions, never once did the men offer a less prosaic theory, one that had come to her mind immediately. Loath to mention it for fear she'd be dismissed as easily as the guard, nevertheless Juliet felt a shiver of fear for herself and especially for Morgan. Reports of an imposter, this senseless attack upon their tent . . . Both incidents fell in well with the pattern that had been set back in England, and Juliet couldn't help but wonder.

What if the curse had followed them to Egypt?

THE hunt for the tomb was a painstaking one. Even with the map, they were not sure of the exact location. Landmarks shifted and disappeared over time, and they could not be certain of the accuracy of the directions in demotic or Juliet's interpretation of the hieroglyphs.

To Juliet's eyes, the rocky valley floor they were searching yielded no clues, but Morgan said piles of rubbish and stones might very well hide an entrance. After several false starts that took days to eliminate, he settled on one spot he claimed was especially promising. It was hard for Juliet to see that promise, but she was unaccustomed to excavation and so tried to train her eyes to see what he did, wondering if she ever would. Morgan had a gift for discovery, they said, and those natives who had been with him before were well convinced of his expertise.

Still determined to help, Juliet quickly lent a hand, but after moving rocks in the heat with her long skirts, she decided that a more practical costume was in order. Although she studied Morgan's spartan attire with new appreciation, at more than six feet in height, he could hardly be expected to share his wardrobe with her. Indeed, the very thought of wearing her husband's clothes, preferably warm from the heat of his body and heavy with his personal scent, made Juliet shake her head. She would never be able to concentrate in such attire.

And so it was Chauncey's trunks that she raided. The shorter, wiry fellow's pantaloons were still big and baggy but would perform far more admirably than even her most utilitarian gowns. Thankfully, she had purchased some boots that served her well, and she returned to the site just as a great shout of excitement went up from the workmen.

Morgan's insistence that they keep digging had come to fruition, for they had found that part of the rock was cut, forming an entrance. Juliet hurried to the edge to peer down at the opening, at least fifteen feet below. Although Morgan had come to rely on her translation skills, they were not needed now. Anyone could tell that the workmen were excited by this find. Obviously, it led to a tomb, and a large one, not one of the mummy pits or lesser burial places that had already been uncovered in the area.

However, they soon were thwarted when the natives claimed they could go no farther, the passage being blocked by a wall of stones. Indeed, when Juliet went down to take a look, even she could see the interior of the entrance was choked by rubble. But in his inimitable way, Morgan seemed to know just where to dig, and before long, they had created a passage just below the ceiling.

They had agreed earlier on the manner of entry, should they reach their goal. Of course, Morgan would go in first, followed by Juliet, while Chauncey, as always, would watch his friend's back, in this case, the opening to the tomb. As Morgan stood poised on the threshold, the three of them, thrown together by circumstance but held there by friendship, shared a look of triumph, of hope, of anticipation, and well wishes. Then Morgan carefully climbed the rubble and disappeared into the darkness.

Juliet made her way up the pile, as well, only to pause, struck dumb by the beautiful paintings on the ceiling and the deeply carved hieroglyphs that had been uncovered, perhaps for the first time in centuries. She would have been content to linger there, in awestruck study, if Morgan had not called to her.

There were more wonders waiting.

Blinking at the sights that flashed by her in the torchlight, the brightness of the colors and the majesty of the depictions, Juliet passed them by as if in a dream, following Morgan along a corridor that ended in a staircase. The shadowy stone steps took them down into darkness, deep into the recesses of the mountain on a journey few had taken before them.

Breathless, Juliet followed Morgan to the bottom, where they faced an enormous door, beautifully carved and decorated. Once through, they traveled along another corridor, its walls covered with hieroglyphs so magnificent that Juliet was wont to dally, so Morgan hurried her on with whispered promises of the burial chamber itself, surely to be found ahead.

But this corridor led to no door or stairway. Indeed, Juliet had good cause to be glad that Morgan was in front of her, for while she gawked, her gaze traveling everywhere except to her feet, he took more care of their route. And when he stopped, he held out an arm to bar her way.

"What is it?" Juliet whispered, unable to see anything except the glint of stone surrounding them.

"We have reached an impasse," Morgan said. He held up the torch, and to Juliet's shock, the floor dropped away into sudden darkness. It stretched forward and left and right, a vast pit that looked to be at least twelve feet wide and across, with depths beyond their vision. Worse yet, Juliet could see no sign of a path on the other side, only a sheer rock face.

"It's a dead end," she whispered, stricken.

Motioning her away from the ledge, Morgan paced the area, studying the crevice from all angles. Finally, he uncoiled the rope looped at his belt and dropped it into the great hole. There was a dull flapping sound as it hit the side on the way down, then nothing. Morgan was left hunched at the edge, dangling the rope in his hand. Frowning, he straightened.

"It's at least a thirty-foot drop," he muttered.

Juliet couldn't see lowering herself or anyone else into that endless void. "Perhaps this is a false passage, and there is another way," she suggested. If so, it might take days or weeks to find another entrance. She sighed as a far more dismal possibility struck her. "Or this might even be an unfinished tomb that ends here. Nowhere."

But Morgan was having none of that. "Oh, there's a burial chamber somewhere in this mountain. We just have to figure out how to reach it," he muttered, pacing the area once more.

His dark head tilted back, he glanced up and down and took measurements of all that he could, while Juliet looked on in admiration of his skill. How had she ever thought him naught but a witless plunderer? His mind was so quick, so sharp, working constantly to see all the possibilities that she could not. Perhaps he had not her education, but he was just as intelligent, his methods merely different from her own.

Standing there watching him, Juliet felt need rise up in her, a need she had suppressed for too long, a need she had locked away as fiercely as she once had her youthful dreams. But now it rose up, urging her to reach out and touch the lock of Morgan's dark hair that had fallen forward, to run her hands over those wide shoulders and the firm muscles of his chest that she remembered so well.

Flushing, Juliet drew in a sharp breath. Here she was at last in Egypt, living those lost dreams, having seemingly achieved her heart's desire, surrounded by works of beauty beyond price and yet the most beautiful and beloved was not a painted figure, but flesh and blood: her husband.

The realization was stunning, shaking Juliet to the core with a force far more powerful than the euphoria of deciphering any grammar or hieroglyph. Had she found the secret to the ancient symbols right here and now, she realized it could mean no more to her than this man. Her life's triumph lay not in language or study or even in finding this tomb, but was right here, standing before her.

How foolish she had been to set him aside, to let him set *her* aside, to allow this sham marriage when she wanted so much more. She had reverted to her old ways, accepting the order of things when she just might have the power to change that order, if not to make him love her then at least to try, to give him her love.

And in the very moment that Juliet had decided what was truly important at last, it seemed fate would deprive her of the chance to act upon that knowledge. For even as she stood gaping at her husband, a commotion erupted in the corridor behind them.

Alarmed by shouts from the workers, Juliet turned, fearful of some sort of cave-in, only to see the natives that had followed them were being pushed aside by several strangers. She glanced at Morgan, who swore softly at the sight.

"Who—?" she began, but he cut her off with a gesture, pulling her behind him.

"They could be strongmen from the local bey, wanting a share of the treasure. If so, don't say anything, as the politics in these situations can be tricky," he said. Under his breath, he added, "Let's hope that's who they are."

"We want them to take our treasure?" Juliet asked as the strangers strode toward them.

Morgan shrugged. "At least we might get to keep some of it," he whispered. "The alternative is that they're a lawless group, a raiding party that will try to take it all."

The attendant possibility that they might die here, murdered by thieves, went unsaid, and Juliet let her hand drift to her belt and the knife she had tucked there, a hard resolve settling over her. From her position behind Morgan, she watched the new arrivals step aside, presumably to make room for their leader, the bey perhaps, and she tensed, prepared for anything.

But Juliet could never have prepared herself for the sight that met her eyes. She felt Morgan stiffen, and she leaned forward, curious, only to fall back with a gasp as she recognized the figure that strode forward.

He was dressed like Morgan, and Juliet's first thought was that here was the imposter, come to face them, to do them in and assume Morgan's identity. But beyond his similar clothing, the man looked nothing at all like her husband. He was shorter and more slender. His hair, though dusty, was pale, his skin blotched a frightful red from the sun, and his eyes a washed-out blue that roved over them with such insolence that she almost didn't realize their familiarity.

"Lyndhurst," Morgan said before she could speak, before she could even find her voice. Juliet was in such shock that her mouth worked, but nothing came out, and then her husband's staying hand in front of her kept her silent.

"A bit out of your depth, aren't you, baronet?" Morgan asked. "Or are you here as the earl's lackey?"

"The earl?" Cyril laughed, a cold, odd sound that echoed within the confines of the tomb. "That fat old bastard has no control over me. I am my own man."

Juliet stifled a gasp at his arrogant dismissal of her father, who had allowed Cyril access to priceless artifacts and given him free rein for his studies. In return, Cyril had rendered nothing except fawning flattery that obviously was as false as his own theories.

"If you are your own man, then why aren't you manning your own excavation?" Morgan asked evenly. "Why follow us here, with those fellows in tow?" he added, nodding toward the menacing natives who stood behind Cyril.

"Oh, but this *is* my excavation. I'm taking it over," Cyril said blithely. "It will be *my* discovery, *my* triumph, *my* retribution for all that you stole from me."

Her mouth gaping open at his shocking admission, Juliet realized that Cyril *was* the imposter, having come to Egypt for that sole purpose. Belatedly, she realized that he had seen Morgan's map, and she rued her thoughtlessness. She and Morgan had been so concerned about her father's glimpse of it that they had not considered that Cyril had taken a good look at it, as well.

But who could blame her for seeing no threat in her mannered, scholarly colleague? Who would ever have imagined that fastidious Cyril, who fussed over the slightest interruption of his work, might brave the heat and cold, the sand and flies and mosquitoes of Egypt, that a man who claimed to believe in ancient warnings would willingly delve into the dark abode of the dead?

As if reading her thoughts, Cyril smiled evilly at Morgan. "It looks like the curse has finally caught up with you."

Juliet gasped aloud, but Morgan covered the sound with his own snarl of outrage. "Just as I thought. You concocted the whole story. But why?"

Cyril's face twisted. "To get rid of you, for one thing, though you proved to be a bit difficult to dispatch."

This time Juliet swallowed her horror in silence, but she could not so easily slow the pounding of her blood or the racing of her breath at the implication of Cyril's words.

He was the one who had done all those terrible things: stolen artifacts, attacked footmen, and set Morgan's bed alight. The realization made her lift a hand to Morgan's back in a gesture of both warning and assurance. His solid frame, alive beneath her fingers, reminded her that Cyril had not succeeded, *would not succeed.*

Morgan obviously had reached the same conclusion.

"So you did everything, all the thieving and the violence, and then attributed it to your curse. And just how did you get past the guards?" Morgan asked, his voice surprisingly cool for someone who had been threatened. Juliet had to steel herself against her own fluttering pulse and weak knees, holding as firm as her husband.

Cyril looked so smug and contemptuous that Juliet wondered how she could have ever defended him, dismissing Morgan's earlier suspicions of the man as impossible. In truth, she had not thought the dilettante capable of such dire deeds, but, obviously, he was not only capable but reveling in them.

"The earl's not as omnipotent as he thinks," Cyril said. "He has his own private door to the ballroom, hidden behind one of his moldy old tapestries. I had my pick of artifacts and could have looted the entire collection," he bragged.

"Bringing you a pretty profit, no doubt," Morgan commented.

"You think I would sell them?" Cyril scoffed. "I'm a collector, and now I will have my very own collection with the riches to be found in this tomb, the first to be discovered intact. Now, where is Juliet?" he asked, glancing around.

Obviously, he had not noticed her standing behind Morgan. No doubt, he would never imagine her here, uncaring of the conditions or confines. Nor would he think to find her wearing men's garb, dusty and dirty, her long hair plaited into a serviceable braid down her back.

"She's dead," Morgan said, and Juliet flinched at his words, her hand on his back jerking before she forced it to stillness.

"What?" Cyril asked. He did not appear grief stricken, merely skeptical.

"She died of dysentery on the way from Cairo," Morgan answered, his voice grim.

Cyril's face twisted. "What do you mean, she's dead? Your workers said she was in here."

"I thought you were after the tomb," Morgan said.

Cyril sneered. "I'll have both."

Morgan shrugged. "As I said before, Juliet's gone. The natives probably feared punishment, should they tell you the truth."

For the first time, Juliet saw Cyril's arrogance slip.

"And as for the tomb . . ." Morgan lifted an arm toward the solid wall behind them. "I'm afraid we've reached the end."

"What?" Cyril asked, his voice rising.

"This is it. There's nothing but a sheer rock face ahead," Morgan said.

An expression of both disbelief and horror crossing his features, Cyril stepped forward, but his men remained where they were, effectively guarding the only exit. Turning, Morgan drew Juliet aside, keeping her at his back, while Cyril snatched away his torch and marched ahead.

Juliet drew in a sharp breath. Her natural instinct was to warn Cyril about the pit, but she was wary of this stranger, so little like the colleague she had known. What did he want with her? Indeed, what did he plan to do with both Morgan and her after he stole their find? The answer that came to mind was not comforting, especially since the man had admitted to trying to kill Morgan. What would stop him from trying again?

And so Juliet remained silent and tense as she watched him, but Cyril did not rush headlong into the abyss. Despite his anger, he moved carefully, stopping to stare into the blackness below.

"It's more than thirty feet deep and impassable," Morgan said.

And those seemingly simple words had a startling effect upon Cyril. Rather than study the problem as Morgan had done, he swung round in a rage. Unable to reason on his own, to do anything except steal from others, he was like a child whose expectations had been thwarted.

"You bastard. You led me here, into this godforsaken desert, and for nothing," Cyril said, his expression ghastly in the glow of the torch he held. So horrified was Juliet by the look on his face that she stepped back, away from the sight, yet unable to turn aside. For a long moment he stood there, his agitation growing, his eyes wide and wild, his chest heaving.

"You've taken everything from me!" He screamed the words so abruptly that Juliet flinched.

"I've taken nothing from you," Morgan said, preternaturally calm in the face of what surely must be lunatic behavior.

"I would have had it all: Juliet, the collection, and the earl's money. It was all to be mine!" Cyril shouted.

"No, Lyndhurst. The earl had no intention of allowing you to marry Juliet. He was holding out for a duke or an earl, if he would have let her marry at all. He told me himself," Morgan said. But he was trying to reason with a man who was beyond all reason.

"I was biding my time," Cyril argued. "When she— when *I* deciphered the hieroglyphs—he would have changed his mind. Then I would have had it all: the fame, the glory, the admiration of men like Thomas Young and the earl himself."

"You mean, when *Juliet* deciphered the hieroglyphs, don't you?" Morgan asked, his contempt obvious. "You were waiting for her to discover the key, then you were going to present her findings as your own, taking credit for something you did not do."

"Together! We were going to do it together!" Lyndhurst screamed. Then he quieted, a quiet more frightening than his frenzy. "But you ruined everything. And now you must pay. The wrath of the gods will out."

"There are no gods, Lyndhurst, only—" Morgan began,

but his words had no effect. Tossing aside the torch, Cyril pulled a gun from his belt and aimed it right at Morgan.

"Are you mad? You can't set that thing off in here. You're liable to bring the whole mountain down around us," Morgan said.

"A fitting end to be buried with kings!" Cyril said. He cocked the gun.

"No!" Juliet shouted. Without even thinking, she drew her knife and threw it as Chauncey had taught her. Although the pistol went off, Cyril's aim was skewed, his arm jerking with the force of the dagger that pierced his shoulder. The bullet struck the stone above them, echoing throughout the tomb harmlessly.

Cyril screamed, clutching his wound and shouting to his native attendants, but the sight of their leader falling to his knees, wailing, gave them pause. What good was the promise of gold when there was no treasure to loot and the man who had promised it to them was prone? With Morgan's workmen closing in on them, the interlopers turned and fled.

Without the threat of Cyril's natives and their weapons, Morgan could move, and he lunged forward to snatch Cyril's gun, but the wounded man was not ready to release it. Although Morgan fell upon him, Cyril suddenly exhibited renewed strength, perhaps fed by his madness. The two men grappled, lurching to their feet, their struggles taking them perilously close to the edge of the crevice, while Juliet stood by, helpless and uncertain.

They dropped to the floor once more, and Cyril rose above Morgan, his throat in a stranglehold. Panicked, Juliet glanced about wildly for another weapon, but the fallen torch was burning haphazardly, casting fantastic shadows over the stones, and the workmen and the others hung back, fearful. Frantically searching the area, Juliet finally spied her knife just as Morgan threw Cyril over.

She glanced up in time to see Cyril's head hit the edge

of the pit with a sickening thud, and then he went slack, his body slipping over the ledge. With a cry, Juliet flung herself forward, intent on keeping Morgan from following his foe downward. Catching at his legs, she blinked as he grasped at Cyril in vain, and the man pitched soundlessly into the crevice.

Everything happened so fast that it took Juliet a moment to realize that she wasn't falling, that she and Morgan were both lying on the floor of the tomb, together and safe. Swift on the heels of that discovery came the knowledge that she still had hold of her husband.

And she was never going to let him go.

Chapter 20

MORGAN lay on the cold stone, listening for the sound of Lyndhurst's body hitting bottom, a faint thud that made him wince. Despite all, he wouldn't have wished for such an ending for the man, who obviously had gone mad. But perhaps Lyndhurst was better off dead, his crimes unknown to all except themselves, rather than facing foreign authorities.

Morgan grunted, trying to move, but a weight had settled over his legs, and he realized that Juliet was clinging to him with startling strength. Keeping him grounded. Trying to save him. *Surely, it wasn't too late for her to succeed?*

Reaching down, he pulled her up his body and wrapped his arms around her, anxious to hear the sound of her breath and feel the beat of her heart, telling him she was alive and safe. *And his.* Coming so soon after the mind-numbing terror of nearly losing her, it felt like heaven, as if he had gotten something right at last. And he wasn't talking about finding any tomb. Indeed, Morgan might have remained there, embracing his wife indefinitely, but for the sudden, loud appearance of Chauncey, rushing to the rescue.

"Where is he?" Chauncey demanded, brandishing both a heavy cudgel and a deadly blade. "What the devil does he mean by tying me up?"

"He's dead," Morgan said, inclining his head toward the crevice.

"Well, that's good news. Now I don't have to kill him!" Chauncey said. "I had the devil of a time getting loose, all the while wondering what sort of foul deeds he was up to in here."

He paused to draw a breath, and with his own agitation coming under control, Chauncey seemed to focus on Morgan, crouched on the floor with Juliet. Apparently, he realized that he might not be the only one suffering from the coxcomb's treatment.

"Yes, well, you're all right now, are you?" Chauncey asked a bit belatedly.

Morgan nodded. "But it is growing late. Let's halt for the day and look at things anew in the morning." He rose to his feet but did not release Juliet, holding her easily in his arms. *Where she belonged.*

"I'm not hurt. You can let me down," she said.

"No," Morgan muttered. "I can't." He didn't know whether he'd ever be able to let her down.

Carrying her along corridors and up steps, Morgan kept her close until he was forced to put her down in order to get through the remaining tunnel to the outside. Once back upon solid ground, he swung a startled Juliet into his arms again, and he did not stop until they reached the privacy of the tomb where they slept, open to the sky.

Morgan had barely stepped inside, out of sight of any prying eyes, when he lowered his mouth to hers for the kind of hot, drugging kisses that he had wanted for so long but hadn't allowed himself. All these weeks he had been held back by the knowledge that whatever he did to her, with her, it would never be enough, followed by the frightening thought: What would ever be enough?

Now he didn't care. Nothing mattered except that Juliet was alive and well and here with him. *His wife.* In all ways. Without breaking the kiss, he set her down upon the bedding atop a rocky outcropping, his fingers tugging at the shirt she had tucked into her baggy breeches. But he stopped when they brushed against the waistband and makeshift belt. There was something about the pants . . .

Drawing in a harsh breath, Morgan stepped back to take a good, long look. He had not been so occupied with the find that he had not noticed her attire, but now he could give free rein to the impulses it roused. No longer were her long limbs hidden beneath voluminous skirts; they were plainly visible and incredibly inviting.

"I wish you wouldn't wear these," Morgan said.

"Why?" she said, breathless but indignant, as she watched him wide-eyed.

"Too revealing. Too arousing," he muttered. Tugging off her boots and his own, Morgan whispered his pleasure at the view and all it enticed him to do. Freed at last of his own restraints, Morgan ran his hands over her calves, her knees encased in the thin material, and her thighs. Spreading them wide, he moved over top of her, settling himself in the cradle there.

He loosed her hair, damp with sweat, and pulled off her dusty shirt and his own. His chest, cooling from the heat of the day, grew hot again at the touch of her breasts, and he rubbed against them, unable to get close enough. She was a feast for the senses for a man long starved, and he stroked her supple flesh, tasted her salty skin, reveled in the unfettered release of his passion—and her own.

For her hands roamed his chest and his back, tangling in his hair, and her lips followed. She whispered her love for him, and Morgan answered in kind, rough, half-formed words that didn't begin to explain what he felt, even as his blood pounded with a fierce urgency to show her.

Slipping off her makeshift belt, Morgan slid his hand inside the breeches, his body jerking as his fingers met the slick heat between her thighs. He groaned, nearly undone by the sensation, by the throaty sounds she made, by the frantic clutching of her hands.

Keeping his own thundering needs in check, Morgan stroked her, pressing and probing until she arched upward with a cry. Then he stripped off both pairs of breeches in record time and moved over her once more. Glancing down at her, into the shadowy depths of her eyes, Morgan felt a primal instinct to claim her as his own.

"My wife," he whispered, and he sank into her, slick and hot. She gasped, and he waited, gritting his teeth against the sheer ecstasy, until she moved beneath him, joining him in a rhythm more ancient than their berth, shifting as the sands, and elemental as life itself.

JULIET stepped into the hot sun and took a deep breath, her whole being flooded with contentment. Not only was she in Egypt, living her dream, but she was now well and truly married. Against all odds, her husband, the tall, handsome adventurer who had stolen her heart, *loved* her.

Juliet felt a flush climb her cheeks at the memory. After that first, heady experience, she had drifted to sleep in Morgan's embrace, only to waken later in the night to feel his hands stroking her breasts, his body seeking entrance, and she had welcomed him with her own fevered whispers.

Later, at dawn, they had attempted to wash as best they could with their pouch of water, but the sight of her husband, tall and strong and naked, stroking his own body with a wet cloth, had roused Juliet beyond bearing, and one thing had led to another. . . .

Now she stretched, achy but feeling better than she had in her entire lifetime, and blinked at the workmen below. With a sudden start, she realized that the tomb she and Morgan had so coveted had been momentarily forgotten, a heretofore unimaginable possibility.

Glancing up at him, she saw his lips quirk. Was he thinking the same thing? With a rush of euphoria, she smiled as he led her down to the entrance, toward another adventure, and this time, there would be no one to ruin their discovery.

Or so she thought.

At the tomb opening, Chauncey greeted them with unusual enthusiasm. Perhaps he was just happy to see them alive after Cyril's murderous attempts—or to see them at all. Retiring to their berth early, they had remained closeted there until now.

"I need some extra things today," Morgan said, ignoring his friend's effusive welcome.

Chauncey nodded, then cleared his throat. "What about his nibs? Are you going to try to retrieve the . . . body?"

Morgan shook his head. "I don't see why we should endanger more lives, especially when we don't know how deep the pit is—or what lies at the bottom."

Chauncey nodded, apparently satisfied, and Juliet soon forgot yesterday's horrors as she once again viewed the tomb's ancient paintings and carvings, at least until she stood before the crevice again.

"So we don't have to go . . . down?" she asked.

Morgan shook his head. "I'm guessing the abyss was put here to prevent anyone from gaining access to the recesses of the tomb, which must lie across it," he said, pointing to the sheer rock face on the other side.

"But how?" Juliet asked. She could see no sign of a door or point of egress, but while she stood back and watched, Morgan took a long pole that reached across the pit and prodded the far wall with it. Although seemingly impenetrable to her eyes, a portion of the area gave way, and Morgan continued his efforts until he had made a hole large enough to crawl through.

Once he had created an opening, Morgan hauled wooden planks to the spot to span the crevice. Then, tying Juliet to him, he crawled across the boards, while she followed close behind. When she made it through the ragged gap, Juliet knew Morgan had guessed correctly, for they found themselves in a vast, pillared hall, breathtaking in its decoration. It led into another, larger hall, even more beautiful than the last, and Juliet gaped, wide-eyed, as ancient Egypt came to life around her.

She found most startling the brightness of the colors of the enormous figures that marched upon the walls. Hidden away from human eyes for centuries, they looked newly painted in the light of the torches, and Juliet marveled, awestruck at the sights, even as Morgan led her onward into a smaller chamber, then another large, pillared hall. Finally, she followed him into the very heart of the tomb, where an arched roof resembled the sky, complete with zodiac figures above.

Alas, the occupant of this elaborate burial chamber was gone. Indeed, nothing remained of the original contents except a few scattered shards of broken pots. There was no mummy case this time to be removed in triumph, no treasure, and no gold or statuary to be carted back for collection or display. Yet they were both as excited about the empty tomb as any discovery.

"I could spend my life studying these walls," Juliet whispered. And if Morgan rued the lack of saleable items, he did not appear upset. Juliet suspected he had received quite a bit from her father for his last collection, surely enough to fund more expeditions, if not to remain here indefinitely copying hieroglyphs. Indeed, when she glanced at her adventurer, he smiled, seemingly content.

"Not a lifetime perhaps, but some time," he said.

* * *

AFTER several days spent drawing the most spectacular scenes she had found inside the tomb, Juliet let Morgan drag her away on a trip for more supplies and to the nearest baths. Indeed, a liberal supply of hot water seemed to be the only thing her husband missed in their dusty domain, and they returned clean and well stocked. But as they were nearing the site, Juliet noticed what looked like additional men and donkeys, denoting the presence of another caravan.

Hurrying forward, they had just reached a grim-faced Chauncey, positioned at the entrance to the tomb, when a figure emerged, and Juliet reeled in astonishment. She clutched at Morgan, knowing that she would not escape detection this time, for she had forgone her breeches for the trip, and there was no disguising herself from her father.

Indeed, the earl saw them at once, though he gave no sign of welcome or greeting. He climbed up over the rubble, watching his footing until he reached level ground. Then his eyes flicked over them emotionlessly, his face a hard mask of disgust. "This is an empty tomb. It is utterly worthless, a waste of time and money." He spewed out the words as if in challenge, one that Juliet took up.

"How can you say that? Did you see the ceilings, the walls, the floors, nearly every surface covered with such beauty, such history, such amazing decoration?" she asked. How could the man claim to be interested in Egypt and turn a blind eye to such an important find?

"Bah. Scrawls for the gawkers, useless to anyone but the pedestrian few who might traipse through here," he said, his voice harsh, his expression cold.

"That is where we differ, Father," Juliet said, shaking her head sadly. "For I could spend a lifetime here, just studying the hieroglyphs."

"But you won't. Did you think I came all the way here to

stare at your precious drawings?" he asked. "I have my pick of the best artifacts in the country from men like Salt and Drovetti, men far more skilled in finding treasure than Morgan Beauchamp. I came here for you, daughter, to fetch you home."

Juliet's fingers tightened on Morgan's sleeve as real fear gripped her. If mad Cyril had been frightening in his wild way, so was her father, certain of his own power and just as willing to abuse it.

"Our marriage is legal and binding," Morgan said.

"And will be annulled," her father said. "I didn't save her all these years for a worthless adventurer like you, Beauchamp. I told you once before, an earl or above, nothing less for my girl."

"But Father—" Juliet began, only to halt in surprise as another man stumbled out of the tomb. Although he looked to be a gentleman, she did not recognize him as a member of her father's usual entourage. Overly dressed for the climate, he mopped his sweating brow.

"Chauncey," Morgan said, with a nod of his head, and Chauncey stepped forward to help the man, though he kept one hand on the dagger at his waist and a wary eye on the earl.

Juliet blinked as she realized the dangerous position they were all in. Chauncey had once called her father a criminal who flaunted the laws and morals of other men when it suited him. Just how far would he go to get his way?

As Juliet watched and waited, the stranger made his way up the slope, huffing and puffing. Stopping before them, he gave Chauncey a nod of thanks.

"Very interesting. Can't say that I've ever seen the like," he said.

Obviously, he did not share the earl's contempt of the tomb. Indeed, he did not even spare a glance to her father but stared openly at her husband.

"Are you Morgan Beauchamp?" he asked.

At Morgan's nod, the man slumped as if in relief and mopped his brow once more. "I admit I am glad to hear that. Can't say I have the stomach for any more traveling in this heat."

Juliet's brow furrowed in puzzlement. "Aren't you a part of my father's caravan?" she asked.

"Your father?" the man asked. He glanced about in confusion before his gaze settled on the earl. "Oh, his lordship. Yes, indeed. We met aboard ship, and he was kind enough to allow me to join his party. Otherwise, I'm not sure how I would ever have found you," he said, turning back to Morgan.

The stranger smiled. "I beg your pardon. My name is Wilberson, Mr. Clarence Wilberson of Wilberson and Bartley, solicitors," he said. Fumbling in his coat, he then proffered a card.

When Morgan took it, the man frowned. "I am afraid I have some ill news for you, my lord," he said.

Juliet blinked in confusion. Was he talking to her father or Morgan?

"There has been an accident. Both your father and your brother have been killed," the man said. He mopped his brow. "Thus, you are now the rightful earl of Bellemere."

Juliet gaped, glancing from the man to her husband in astonishment. But she could be no more startled by this news than her father, who wore a look of both amazement and annoyance, now that his plans had been thwarted. And thwarted they were. For how could he protest her marriage when she was a countess? Juliet's lips curved upward at the irony of fate.

As for Morgan, he threw back his head and laughed.

Epilogue

✦

LADY Juliet Beauchamp, countess of Bellemere, sat at her desk glancing over her correspondence. Along with a curt message from her father, there were letters from around the world, requesting either her expertise or that of her husband in connection with all things Egyptian. Between the two of them, they were accounted authorities on nearly every aspect of the country's history, its treasures, and its languages.

Leafing through a few pages from a man who wanted to establish a new museum, Juliet set the missive aside for further reading. Others she stacked into particular piles, until at last she thought she had finished, only to find something else tucked below all that had littered the surface of the desk: a single, small communication of the most peculiar nature.

Juliet drew in a breath at the sight of hieroglyphs drawn upon a scrap, perhaps a stray piece of papyrus, but the markings were recent. She felt the old jolt of excitement, along with an eerie recollection of events past, when the symbols had not always been used with good intent.

Here, however, the sign for man followed several others that, when put together, meant husband. Another grouping she quickly recognized as denoting love, and lastly, she saw herself as "mistress of the house." Juliet felt a swell of heady emotion.

Who else but Morgan would leave her a love note written in the language of the ancient Egyptians? And who, except Juliet, would be able to read it? To anyone else in the household, it would be "that gibberish," she thought with a smile.

But to her, and to many other scholars, it was no longer gibberish. On September 27, 1822, a Frenchman named Jean-François Champollion had revealed to the Academy of Sciences in Paris his breakthrough discovery that some of the Egyptian symbols were based upon the sounds of speech. Later, he established that the hieroglyphs consisted of three different types of signs: picture signs that corresponded directly to their subject; idea signs that denoted a thing or idea, but not a particular word or phrase for it; and signs that represented the sounds of speech.

The intricacy of the system had foiled all those who had looked for a single word or concept in each drawing. For, in hieroglyphs, a picture of a duck might mean a duck, or it could stand for "son of" or it could be used as the sound "sa," while other symbols represented ideas that applied to the text preceding them. Only Champollion, who devoted his life to the effort, had divined the complex truth.

Unlike some of her colleagues, Juliet did not covet the Frenchman's work, but had rejoiced in his findings. Her own studies had fallen off during her trip to Egypt, for she had been too busy viewing the ancient sites and symbols to pore over the meaning behind them.

Juliet smiled anew as she remembered that glorious year spent tramping through the sands, eyeing breathtaking vistas and monuments, and opening up the tomb they had found to others. Although she had not tried to decipher the hieroglyphs then, she had copied down as much as she could for later study.

When they finally wrested themselves away from Egypt, they brought home a few choice finds with them, as well, although Morgan insisted he was not a collector. Since he claimed all collectors were prigs and dilettantes, Juliet had assured him he was neither, but was entitled to keep some of his favorite treasures from their travels.

Even after returning to England, Juliet had not found time to devote to her old passion. Although the hieroglyphs had still excited her, she had found other things that excited her more, such as her husband, and later, her son. While Juliet reveled in the arrival of the latest Beauchamp, a living and breathing subject far more interesting than even the stone found at Rosetta, Morgan had taken the reins of his family fortune, as well as his own, and they had settled into the Bellemere seat in a state of eccentric bliss.

But recently, Juliet had taken up her studies again, trying to keep abreast of all the new developments that had come upon the heels of Champollion's revelations and to make her way through her copious copies of hieroglyphs. She had even made time to join Morgan in a shared project, an illustrated edition of their observations and discoveries in Egypt. They were hoping to have at least part of the work completed soon, for the publisher was anxious to print it—and the new baby would be arriving in the spring.

Juliet sighed contently, for her days and nights were well occupied beyond her wildest dreams. No longer did she yearn for adventure, for she had found it—and more. And, of course, there was always the possibility of another voyage up the Nile.

After all, they had titled their book *Travels in Egypt: Volume One.*

BERKLEY SENSATION
COMING IN JUNE 2004

Hot Pink
by Susan Johnson

Chloe Chisolm was sure she was done with serious
relationships, but flings with strangers in elevators
were getting tiresome. It isn't until she meets Rocco
Vinelli that her hardened heart begins to melt.

0-425-19682-8

Beauty in Black
by Nicole Byrd

Louisa Crookshanks is having her coming-out in
London and the one man she's set her sites on is in
love with another woman—Louisa's chaperone.

0-425-19683-6

Jane's Warlord
by Angela Knight

The next target of a time travelling killer, Jane Colby is
in the hands of a warlord from the future who has
been sent to protect her. And in his hand is just where
she wants to be...

0-425-19684-4

Dangerous Curves
by Jacey Ford

When three female former FBI agents begin their own
PI business, the sparks—and bullets—fly.

0-425-19685-2